TYPE

AND

CROSS

TYPE
AND
CROSS

CATHEDRAL LAKE

BOOK ONE

STACI
TROILO

FOYLE
PRESS

an imprint of

THE OGHMA PRESS

OGHMA

C R E A T I V E   M E D I A

Bentonville, Arkansas • Los Angeles, California
www.oghmacreative.com

Library of Congress Cataloging-in-Publication Data

Names: Troilo, Staci author.
Title: Type and Cross/Staci Troilo | Cathedral Lake #1
Description: Second Edition | Bentonville: Foyle, 2020
Identifiers: LCCN: 2020931184 | ISBN: 978-1-63373-568-2 (hardcover) |
ISBN: 978-1-63373-569-9 (trade paperback) | ISBN: 978-1-63373-032-8 (eBook)
BISAC: FICTION/ Family Life/Marriage & Divorce | FICTION/Medical |
FICTION/Romance/Medical
LC record available at: https://lccn.loc.gov/2020931184

Foyle Press trade paperback edition September, 2020

Cover & Interior Design by Casey W. Cowan
Editing by Patty Stith

Published by Foyle Press, an imprint of The Oghma Press, a subsidiary of The Oghma Book Group.

For Him Who Strengthens Me

ACKNOWLEDGEMENTS

A BOOK TAKES A LONG time to write, a longer time to edit, and a lot longer to get into print than a writer would expect. I am grateful to the staff at Oghma Creative Media for all their hard work preparing and marketing my novel and getting it into print. Special thanks to my editor, Patty, and designer extraordinaire, Casey. Your time and efforts made a difficult process easy.

To my medical experts, Dr. Aaron Lane and his assistant Liz, whose medical terminology and knowledge helped me to create an authentic ER scene. And to Joan and Christi, your feedback really helped shape and fine-tune those medical sections. Many thanks, all of you.

To my beta readers, Brad, Missy, and Michele. Your input was invaluable and your insights helped make this a stronger book. I'm so grateful for your time and feedback.

To my parents-in-law, Edward and Barbara. You were there at the inception of this story; you know where the idea came from. As grateful as I am for the inspiration, I'm even more grateful to you for raising such a wonderful son and for welcoming me into your family. Thank you.

To my parents, Robert and Carmella—When I was little and making up stories, you always stopped and listened. When I changed my college major (for the third time) to writing, you supported the decision. When I was home caring for my babies, you suggested I write a novel. And when I started this book, you were encouraging and excited for me. Thank you.

And most importantly, to my children, Seth and Samantha. You brighten my world every day. You help me as a person by lifting me when I'm down, and you help me as a writer by taking interest in my work (prompting me to work smarter and better). Thanks for all you do, for who you are, and for all your love.

TYPE

AND

CROSS

CHAPTER 1

THE ON-DUTY TRIAGE NURSE interrupted Royce as he sat reviewing the day's patient charts.

"We've got a motor vehicle accident coming in," she said. "Should be here in two minutes. EMT's on the line."

He hated Carnival Weekend for this reason. Always at least one major accident. Royce ran to the phone and took the EMT's call. "What do you have?"

"Two level one traumas, two level two. Motor vehicle versus motorcycle. Driver of motorcycle no vitals on scene. Down for five minutes before CPR started. Passenger of motorcycle unresponsive at scene. CPR started with spontaneous return of circulation. Two doses of epinephrine given en route, coded twice. Vitals—heart rate fifty, BP sixty over palp, respirations ten per minute, satting eighty-two percent, temp ninety-seven point two. No breath sounds on left side. Pupils 5 millimeters bilaterally and non-reactive."

Damn it. The cycle vic was in severe shock. Head trauma, probably tension pneumothorax. They'd need to do a needle decompression if the EMTs didn't. "Did you treat the pneumo?"

"Done."

He moved carts around and called orders to his staff. They prepared the bays and stood ready for the first ambulance's arrival. When the EMTs burst in, Royce rushed to them. He looked his patient over, running alongside the first gurney through the door, and listened to the EMT recite her condition again. He'd seen girls like her before. What a freak show. What wasn't covered in blood or embedded gravel was an equal mess of dyed hair and a facial homage to Alice Cooper. Maybe if her parents had done a better job with her, she wouldn't be in his ER.

No time to dwell on that, though. He had work to do. He started running through the checklist. Ellie and Savvi had already transferred her to the table and begun hooking up the monitors. Royce checked the EMT's work on the decompression to make sure the girl was getting oxygen. When he was satisfied, he checked her neuro function. She didn't open her eyes, didn't speak, didn't move at all when jostled or touched. Three out of fifteen. He called out her score. "GCS three. E-one, V-one, M-one at," he glanced at the clock, "ten oh-seven a.m."

Ellie glanced up, but Royce had to move on. He ran scissors up the center of her already-in-rags-anyway bustier. What kind of people let their daughter buy a getup like that, let alone wear it in public? Shaking his head, he tore the material aside, and started examining her for injuries. "Damn it." Her abdominal cavity was swelling. Had to be bleeding internally. "Savvi, we need blood."

"We're empty up here."

"We've got to have some. Go find some o-neg, now! Wade!" He called out the bay to another ER doctor. "Bay one! Get in here, I need you!"

He had no intention of losing this girl, and he'd be damned if he missed something that would cost her life. "Ellie, help me tip her over." The nurse helped him roll her onto her damaged side. Had she been responsive, it would have caused her pain, but she didn't move.

"Damn," Wade said when he entered.

"What?" Royce asked.

Wade nodded toward the top of the bed. Blood soaked the cot where the girl's head had been. Another fucking injury. Obviously she hadn't worn a helmet. A quick examination of her head and Royce knew things were severe.

"X-rays," he barked.

He had to find all the bleeders and get them under control. And he needed that blood.

The machines sounded shrill warning tones as numbers started plummeting.

"She's bleeding out." Royce started dressing the girl's head wound. "Where's the damn O-neg?"

"Savvi had to go downstairs for some," Ellie said. "She should be back any minute."

Just this morning, he and Vanessa had discussed her organizing a blood drive. His wife worked fast, but not this fast. This girl was fading on him for lack of blood. Savvi would start the massive transfusion protocol, and the blood bank would keep sending units up to them, but it could be too late.

"We don't have a minute," Royce said. "Type and cross her. *Now!*"

Ellie reached for the girl's hand and gasped. "Royce."

"Now, Ellie."

Ellie shook her head.

"Do it, or get the hell out of the way."

"It's Hope."

"Hope? Hope for what?"

"No. *Your* Hope."

Royce looked up from the head wound and saw Ellie staring at the girl's face. A face she recognized before he did. His daughter's face.

And he didn't even realize it.

What kind of father didn't even recognize his own blood?

The sounds of the room faded behind the thundering of his pulse. He could do nothing but stare at the damaged body on his table who barely resembled his baby girl.

"Royce? *Royce!*" Wade brought him back to reality.

"Forget about the blood," he said to Ellie. "Wade, take over here."

"What are you going to do?" he asked, switching places with Royce.

"Transfuse her."

"*What?*" everyone in the room asked at once.

"She's my daughter. I'm a match." He worked quickly, getting the tubing and the needles he needed. "Ellie, can you help me tie this around my arm?"

"You should wait for Savvi," Wade said.

"You should step out," Ellie said. "Royce, you can't work on family. You're compromised. You *know* that."

"There's no time. Besides, it's okay. I know what I'm doing."

"No, you don't. Parents aren't always matches for their kids."

"I know I am. It's fine."

"But protocol says—"

"I know what I'm doing." He attached a needle and tubing to Hope's arm. "Now are you going to help me?"

She stood there, eyes wide.

He shook his head, irritated at her hesitation, and used his teeth to tie a tube around his bicep. Then he inserted the needle into his arm and watched as the blood began to flow from him into his daughter. Once it started moving, he released the band around his bicep and flexed his hand, helping the transfusion along.

"Wade, how's it going back there?"

"Dressing's done."

Royce looked at the monitors. Her blood pressure had risen to fifty-five over thirty-five and kept climbing. Her pulse had increased to forty-five and grew stronger with each beat. "Good. Good. Let's get her prepped for surgery, huh?"

While he watched Wade move over his little girl, he took her hand with his free one.

And noticed her skin felt warm. Too warm.

Royce looked up, his gaze meeting Wade's. "Does she feel hot to you?"

The cardiac machine began its countdown again.

"Doctor," Ellie said, looking at Wade. "Her pressure's dropping."

"No. No." Icy desperation clawed at Royce. "That doesn't make sense."

"Her pulse rate's rising," Wade said.

"She's in tachycardia," Ellie said. "Stop the transfusion! Now!"

Savvi ran into the room. "I've got the O-neg. Oh, my God, is that Hope? What are you doing?"

Royce looked down at his daughter as he clamped off the tubes and pulled the needles out of their arms. Her skin yellowed in front of his eyes. Hyperbilirubinemia.

"Jaundice," Ellie said. "You know what this means."

"This wound's bleeding again," Wade said, reaching for her head.

"So's her arm where the transfusion needle was," Ellie said. "And look at all the abrasion sites where she has road rash."

Hope leaked everywhere. It wasn't possible. What were the odds she'd have a reaction to a transfusion from him?

Royce broke out in a cold sweat. It seemed everywhere his daughter poured blood, he dripped sweat in terror and desperation. How had this happened?

"Ellie." Wade started barking orders. "Get fluids going. Savvi, get that bag hooked up. We need to get a catheter in her…."

The machine mocked Royce with sputtering, rapid flutters.

"She's in v-fib," Wade said. "Starting compressions. Ellie, get the cart. Charge to one-fifty."

"Charging to one-fifty."

Royce watched, detached, as his friend worked on his daughter, pumping on her chest. He wanted to remind him of her fractured rib and punctured lung, but no words formed. Wade probably remembered. Wade seemed to know a lot more than he did right at that moment.

"CPR's not working. Paddles," Wade said.

Ellie handed Wade the paddles of the defibrillator. *"Clear!"*

Hope's body twitched, then lay still. Wade resumed CPR. With each compression of his hands on her chest, Royce heard a mantra in his head. *You. Did.*

This. To. Her. You. Did. This. To. Her. He heard the sentence six times, so he knew thirty seconds had passed. No change. Time to try defib again.

"Charge to two hundred."

"Two hundred," Ellie said.

"Clear!"

Again Hope twitched, then fell back on the table, still. The machine continued to hum its taunting tone at Royce, sounding more to him like a mourner's dirge than a physiological monitor. Wade pushed harder on Hope's chest, sweat beading on his forehead. His daughter was damaged, broken, and despite their heroic attempts to save her, they were just making it worse, prolonging the inevitable.

The machine wailed a steady tone.

His synapses fired at lightning speed, telling him to crack her chest cavity open and massage her heart muscle with his bare hands until it took over beating on its own.

But his own heart knew her abused body had had enough. Bruised and bloody, she had abrasions, broken bones. Internal injuries he hadn't begun to diagnose. Fatal ones he had.

The work they were doing should be causing her agonizing pain.

But she couldn't feel anything.

She was gone.

He couldn't watch it anymore. Royce walked to his friend and put his hands over his, stilling his movements. Then he turned off the machine. "I'm calling it."

"Royce," Wade said. Then softer, "Royce…."

"Time of death," Royce said, "ten twenty-two."

"Royce," Wade said again, the only word he could apparently manage.

Ellie took her mask off and left the room.

Savvi put her hand on his arm. "I'm sorry." She followed Ellie out.

"Royce…."

"Wade, really, it's… okay." Royce put his hand on his friend's shoulder.

"I'm going to need a minute alone in here. And the rest of the day. And I guess the next few days."

"I'll take care of it. Whatever you need, buddy. Take all the time you need. Do you want me to call Vanessa?"

"She should probably hear it from me. I'll just need some time first."

"Sure, man. No problem."

"Thanks."

Wade threw his gloves, mask, and gown in the bin and met Royce's gaze. "I'm really sorry, Royce. I tried. I mean, I did everything I could. I never wanted this...."

Royce nodded and turned back to Hope.

Only after everyone left did he let the tears fall. He stroked her hair back from her face and pulled a sheet up to cover her nearly naked and totally abused body.

How could he not have recognized his own daughter?

He'd like to think he'd focused so intently on his work that he just didn't care who was on his table, but he knew that wasn't the case. He remembered judging the girl on his table. He thought she was a nutcase and her parents were unfit.

Right on one count.

When had she turned her hair into a Dr. Seuss wig?

When had she started wearing more makeup than the whole Kardashian family—combined?

When had she decided lingerie made an acceptable fashion statement? In public, no less?

When had she met the biker she had been with? Who was he? How long had they... known each other?

When had he become the unfit parent he accused her of having?

When? When? *When?*

He allowed the tears to fall freely for a while as he reminisced. She was once, so long ago, his beautiful little girl. He'd held her on his lap and read to her. He'd received butterfly kisses as he carried her to bed. They'd shared ice cream cones and sticky hugs before catching lightning bugs and watching fireworks. He'd kissed boo-boos away before doctoring real ones, and he looked for monsters in her closet and under her bed... until she was too old for any of those things.

When was the last time he'd done any of it?

What had it been? Ten years? More? As she got older, she went to school and learned to read and put herself to bed. She didn't care about lightning bugs anymore, and God help her if he found a boy in her bedroom at night. God help the boy, too. No, they didn't share ice cream—or any snacks—any longer. In fact, he could hardly remember the last time they ate together. Well, the last time they'd shared conversation with a meal, anyway.

And he wouldn't have the chance to offer to buy her a cone. Or a hotdog. Or even talk with her at one of her mother's stuffy charity events.

Somehow he had managed to miss the last damn decade of her life.

And now she would miss the rest of his.

He walked over to the sink and filled two pans with warm water, added soap to one of them. It wouldn't be right to let Vanessa see Hope all bloody and mangled.

He took rags and the two pans over to his daughter and gently dabbed her body with a soapy cloth, then rinsed her off. In mere minutes, the water in both pans turned a violent red and needed replacing. After refilling the pans, he laboriously cleaned cinders out of Hope's flesh, taking special care with her face, her side, and her arm and hand. When he tried to get the cinders and blood out of her hair, he noticed that not only did the cotton-candy color wash out, but the wave came back. By the time he finished, she looked more like the innocent, fresh-faced, curly-haired beauty he remembered. He went and got a small pair of scrubs to dress her in, and threw away the trashy, ruined clothes she had been wearing. He covered her to her waist with a sheet, crossed her arms over her chest, and sat beside her, his ministrations a pitiful reminder of his attempts to right the wrongs of the past ten years.

"Royce?" The curtain slid back and Stanford Hammond stepped inside. A rumpled white coat, 'Chief-of-Staff' embroidered on the pocket, covered crisply pressed shirt and slacks. He held a medical bag in one hand and fumbled with his tie with the other. Frustrated, he finally pulled it off shoved it in his pocket.

"Stanford. What are you doing here?"

"Ellie called me. I rushed right over." He gestured to his pocket. "I wasn't even dressed when the phone rang. I'm so sorry to hear about Hope."

Royce nodded and turned his back to his friend and mentor. "I don't suppose you could call Vanessa for me?"

"What? You haven't called her yet?"

"I planned on it, but I don't really know what to say."

"The truth, boy. It's always best to tell the truth."

"I really don't want to have that conversation on the phone. And I don't want to leave Hope right now. And then there's the matter of the kids…"

"I'll send a car for Vanessa. But you owe her an explanation."

Royce turned and looked at Stanford. "I'm sorry? An explanation for what, exactly?"

"For what you did knowing what you knew."

"Stanford, you've known Vanessa and me for years. You know we don't keep secrets."

"What are you talking about?"

"What are *you* talking about?"

"Hope."

"Stanford, I'm not really in the mood for this right now. If you have something to say to me, just get on with it."

"You really don't know what I'm saying to you right now, do you?"

Royce just looked at him.

Stanford put a hand on each of his shoulders and met his gaze squarely. "Royce, remember, I'm always here for you as a friend. But right now I need to talk to you as your boss. Let's go sit down a minute." He let go with one hand and guided Royce toward the curtain.

"What? Wait. Where are you taking me?"

"We need to go have a talk."

"I don't want to leave Hope."

"I'm not asking."

Royce glanced back at Hope's lifeless body as Stanford led him out of Trauma Bay One and through his ER. It didn't escape his attention that most of his staff stared at them as they walked toward the elevator bank. With each step away from his daughter, away from his people and his unit, he left more and more of himself behind. As he stepped onto the elevator, the confident Royce he'd been that morning had been left behind. He turned forward as the elevator doors closed on the ER, Ellie's disapproving look the last thing he saw.

"What's going on, Stanford?"

"In my office."

Each *'bing'* indicating the passing of another floor sounded like the tenuous threads of sanity popping in his head. By the time they reached the tenth floor, Royce was certain he'd gone mad. He trudged along behind Stanford to his office, but what he really wanted to do was run in the other direction.

Stanford waved him into his office and stopped to speak to his assistant for a moment. Then he stepped inside and closed the door. Gesturing to a leather chair in front of his desk, he put his doctor's bag on his desk.

"What are you doing with a medical bag?"

Stanford sighed, opened the bag, and retrieved a bottle of scotch and a glass. He poured a double and offered it to Royce.

"Liquor? At the hospital?"

"These are special circumstances."

"I'd rather have coffee." Actually, he'd rather have his housekeeper's coffee. He didn't know what she did to it, but she brewed a better cup than Starbucks.

Why the hell was he even thinking about coffee?

"Isn't it a little early in the morning for the hard stuff, Stanford?"

"Not for this conversation."

"I'm still on duty."

"No, Royce. You aren't."

"I don't drink." He almost never had a drink—Stanford knew that—and certainly never at the hospital. He prided himself on always being in control of his faculties should he be called to work.

"You do today."

Royce considered his mentor for a moment. He still held the scotch out to him. Apparently his bereavement leave had begun, so drinking a glass didn't break any rules. And if ever he could use a stiff drink, it was at that moment.

"Fine." He took the glass and Stanford continued to stare at him. Only after he brought the glass to his lips did Stanford seem satisfied. The burn of the liquid barely registered as he waited for his friend to continue.

Stanford paced the room, then joined him in front of the desk instead of behind it.

"I've had a rough day," Royce said. "Just get to the point."

"Before I came to see you, my phone wouldn't stop ringing. Several people grabbed me in the hallway. It's a damn mess."

"And?"

"And? And you don't care?

"I have more important things on my plate right now."

"Don't you get it? Don't you understand why everyone's been calling?"

"To tell you Hope died, I guess."

"No. I learned that when Ellie called."

"Then what?"

Stanford sighed and rested his elbows on his knees. After a moment, he looked up and met Royce's gaze. "To tell me *you* killed her."

CHAPTER 2

VANESSA WAS IN HER ELEMENT—planning a blood drive and hospital fundraiser—when the doorbell rang. She kept working, but when it rang a second time, Vanessa sighed and took her reading glasses off. "Lydia!" she called. No answer, other than a third ring of the bell. Apparently Lydia had no intention of answering the door.

Or doing anything Vanessa wanted her to do.

She saved her document and walked to the door. "May I help—Oh. It's you. What do you want?"

Ben Lyndon stood there, eyes hidden behind mirrored shades, dark curly hair wind-mussed from the ride over. "Is that any way to greet an old friend?"

"I'll give you the 'old' part, especially if you think mirrored lenses are in fashion. 'Friend' is a bit of a stretch."

"Ouch." He placed a hand on his heart like she'd wounded him, took off his sunglasses, and stepped inside.

"I didn't invite you in."

"I'm not staying."

"Shouldn't you be at work?"

"I *was* at work. Stanford's assistant called. Said he wants me to come get you."

"For what?"

"Do I look like Fox News? She said to bring you straight to his office. He and Royce are in a meeting."

"Is this about Royce's promotion? Why didn't she just call me herself?"

"Look, Ness." He pinned her against the wall, his hands close to her head. "I had to cancel a full docket of patients to do this. I'm sorry if the timing isn't good for you, but I'm here now, so clear your schedule."

Lydia walked into the foyer and cleared her throat. She stood there, bucket in one hand and rags in the other.

Ben turned to look at her, but didn't move his arms. "You need something, sweetheart?"

"Not from you. I just need to see Dr. Keller this evening." She hurried away, a smile on her lips. Her brown hair, pulled into a loop, bounced as she retreated, and her hips swayed dangerously hard with each step. And Vanessa thought she only worked it around Royce. Apparently any warm male would suffice.

"Lydia." Vanessa scrambled to get out from between Ben's arms. *"Lydia!"*

But Lydia kept going, humming on her way up the stairs.

"Damn it, Ben. I have enough problems with her without you adding to them."

"Trouble in paradise?"

"Just fix this."

"I didn't do anything."

"You're always doing something."

He shot her a wolfish grin and looked her up and down. "Are you ready?"

"For what?"

"Get your damn purse or whatever it is you need, Ness. Because in five seconds, if you haven't walked out that door willingly, I'm carrying you out."

Vanessa crossed her arms over her chest. She had no interest whatsoever in going anywhere with Ben, particularly if Lydia reported it to Royce.

"One."

Of course, Ben was taking her to see Royce, so it wasn't like Royce wouldn't know about it. Still, it was Ben.

"Two."

And she'd have to be alone with him in his car—his way too small convertible—for the entire ride to the hospital.

"Three."

She looked at Ben's face. He wasn't joking. He'd really pick her up and carry her to the car. She'd be in his arms, cradled against his chest. Or over his shoulder, his hand on her thighs. Or higher....

"Four."

"All right!" She grabbed her purse out of the closet, checked to make sure she had a suitable amount of cash in her wallet and keys to the house, and walked out the front door. Skirting the hood of the Corvette, she crossed to the passenger side and climbed in.

"Too bad," Ben said.

"What?"

"I was hoping I'd have to carry you."

Choosing not to dignify that remark, she said, "Do you have to leave the top down?"

"It's a gorgeous day. Why wouldn't I?"

"It rained last night and we're going under a lot of trees. Not only am I going to get windblown, I'm going to end up wet."

He snorted. "You've never looked bad a day in your life. And a ride with me will only put a flush on your cheeks. You know that."

Hating herself, hating him, she felt the heat rise in her cheeks. Instead of giving him the satisfaction of a response, she fumbled in her purse and came up with a hair tie, then arranged her hair to the side in a loose, messy braid, pulling a few tendrils free to frame her face.

"Anything else before we leave?"

"Oh, yes, actually. Hope left her phone behind today. Let me just run inside and grab it. We can drop it off on the way."

"Cathedral Lake Prep is hardly on the way to the hospital."

"It won't take us too long."

"I got the sense I wasn't supposed to dawdle. Get in the car."

She huffed, but climbed in. "Why'd you offer if you didn't mean it?"

He ignored her question and said, "Buckle up." Then he roared out of the driveway and headed toward the hospital. They weren't two miles on their way when he had to slow for the remains of a traffic accident. Only one lane of the road was passable. A road crew worked on clearing debris from the other lane.

"Looks like something nasty happened here," Ben said.

"I heard sirens earlier. Must have been for this. I hope everyone's all right."

"When you see wreckage like that," he gestured to a mangled pile of metal on the side of the road as they made their way back to two-lane traffic, "all you can do is hope for the best. But it doesn't look too good."

"I wonder if Royce got this accident?"

"Probably. He's the closest ER."

"It's no wonder he never wants to talk about his work. I guess I never really saw this end of it before. I always think of it as ear aches and flu patients."

"That's my world. Not his. Not always."

"It's just what I think of when I think of emergency room visits."

Ben looked at her. "What kind of world do you live in?"

"Excuse me?"

"You always make it sound like he's off neglecting you. Where do you think people go when they're stabbed? Or shot? Or lose a finger? Or are in a wreck? You've been playing the martyr for too long, Vanessa. There are two sides to every story."

"Where do you get off—"

"There are two sides to ours."

"We don't have a story."

"Like hell we don't."

"I'm not discussing this with you." She fumbled with the radio and found an eighties station which she blared, then she turned away from him and stared out the window. Eighteen years of water churned under their particular bridge, and she didn't feel like swimming against that current. It had a nasty undertow. She ignored him the rest of the all-too-short drive.

He whipped the Vette into the lot, parked in the physicians' section, and turned off the engine. "You know, Ness? I've already lost more than I should have. More than I deserved to. And for what? Your warped sense of what's proper. I've kept quiet all these years thinking I was doing the right thing for you, for Royce, for the kids. And for what? You're as screwed up now as you ever were."

"Ben, please, listen to me...." Panic churned in her gut, a swirling vortex of dread and desperation.

"No, *you* listen. After Stanford and Royce have their meeting with you, I think Royce and I are going to have a little talk of our own." He got out of the car and strode across the parking lot.

She scrambled out of the car and chased after him.

She couldn't broach the subject in the hospital, it bustled with activity. Staff and volunteers rushed around while patients and visitors meandered up and down the halls. A couple huddled in a corner, clutching each other, tears streaming down their faces. A man argued with one of Royce's staff about his wife and her care. Security hurried toward them. No, their private conversation could be overheard by any number of people, so she decided not to have it there at all. They and two others rode the elevator in silence. She glanced at Ben, noticed the set of his jaw. She knew that expression. He wouldn't listen to reason. And she was out of time. Her mind reeled. The only option was to occupy Royce after the meeting so he and Ben couldn't talk. She needed time to convince Ben to stay silent.

Vanessa led the way down the hall. She wasn't going to give Ben a chance to even greet Royce first, just in case he planned on leading with the request of a discussion after their meeting.

She needn't have worried. When Stanford's assistant opened the door for them, Stanford actually stepped out. He kissed Vanessa on the cheek and shook Ben's hand. "Vanessa, Ben and I are going to get some coffee in the staff lounge. You and Royce have some things to discuss, and I told him he could use my office. Take all the time you need. Emma will notify me when you're done." He nodded at his assistant and walked away.

Vanessa walked into Stanford's office and closed the door. She'd never seen Royce look so terrible. She crossed to him immediately and reached for him.

He held her off.

She felt like she'd been struck. "Royce? What is it? What's going on?"

He poured himself a scotch and downed it in one gulp. His eyes were red-rimmed with dark shadows underneath. His scrubs weren't fresh. There were a few spots of blood on them.

"Royce?" Backing away, she took a seat in front of Stanford's desk. Then she lowered her voice like she was talking to a small child or a skittish animal. "You're scaring me. Talk to me."

"An accident came into the ER today." His voice shook as much as his hand as he poured another scotch and picked it up. "A bad one. There was an injured couple. The wife ended up dying of a heart attack."

"That's too bad."

"And a younger couple. The boy was DOA."

"I'm sorry to hear that." She wondered what he was getting at, but decided not to rush him. If he didn't get to the point soon, she'd hurry him along. Curiosity warred with annoyance, but she kept quiet.

"The girl coded a few times on the way here, but she was still alive when I got her. With a little luck and a lot of skill, we could've saved her. At least, I think we could have saved her. If we had had blood in the bank."

"Is this about the blood drive? You just asked me to organize one today."

He pointed his glass at her, the amber liquid sloshing over the rim. "You'd think that, wouldn't you? Your first thought would be about you and your charities."

"Then what's this about?"

"I gave my own blood to save her."

"That was… generous of you."

"It wasn't a match. She died."

Vanessa sat still for a moment and watched her husband finish his drink. Something was way off. Even she knew that wasn't protocol, and her husband was Mr. Protocol himself. "Don't you usually screen blood before you transfuse a patient?"

"Yes. Always."

"Then… why didn't you this time? Surely that violates ethics or something, right?"

"I thought she was a type A. But I was wrong. She was a type B."

He was scaring her. He rambled, jumping from one thought to another and making him hard to follow. She worried he'd had too much to drink. Whatever happened must really have affected him. Mr. SOP never drank at work. She tried to hold him on topic, to understand why he had thrown his career away. "Why would you just think that? Was she a former patient?"

He tried to pour another glass, but missed the tumbler and the liquid sloshed on the desk. He pointed the bottle at her. "Remember when Ben, Wade, and I were interns? Wade was dating that phlebotomy student? Carley? He made the three of us hang out with her all the time?"

Vanessa shook her head. "That was a long time ago. Is that who was in your ER?"

He shook his head, blowing off the question, and continued. "One night, before her finals, she used each of us for practice. She drew our blood and ran a full DNA analysis. What do you know about alleles and antigens?"

"Nothing. What are they?"

He waved his glass again. "Not that important. What you need to know is, my blood type isn't just A. It's really AA. One A antigen from my mom, one A from my dad. So all of my kids have to have at least one A antigen. Definitely one A antigen from me, and then whatever antigen you give them. Giving any of my kids my blood should be safe. You get that? Because they should have one A antigen from me."

"O-kay." Was the girl in the ER an illegitimate child of his? Maybe Saint Royce wasn't as perfect as he'd pretended to be throughout their whole marriage.

"This girl got an O antigen from her mother and a B from her father."

"How could you possibly know that?" she asked. "Were her parents here? Did they donate?"

He scoffed. "I know her mother is type O. She could only pass an O antigen. Nothing else. And the girl was typed after my donation as type B. Which means she could only have gotten the B antigen from her father."

"So knowing all that is good, right?"

"No. I learned it all too late. You know, I keep going over it in my head again and again. Would she have died if she had the right blood? Would we have saved her? She had so many injuries…" He was quiet for a moment.

She almost reached out to him again, he looked tortured. Tears welled in his eyes, and he scrubbed them away with the back of his hand.

"The back of her head was caved in," he whispered.

"She wasn't wearing a helmet?"

He shook his head.

"That's a shame. They could save so many lives."

"She didn't have protective gear, either." His voice broke. "Her clothes, what little there were, were ripped to rags. Her rib punctured her lung, and the whole side of her body was cinder-scraped."

"It sounds awful."

"You still haven't figured out the worst part." He glared at her through bloodshot eyes.

Red-faced, he trembled. His anger and pain vibrated through his body and dwarfed everything else in the room, but she still couldn't figure out what it all had to do with her. Apprehensive, she confronted him.

"Tell me." She didn't want to hear the words, but she had to know. Was the girl his? Had he been unfaithful? She'd always had her suspicions, given the hours he worked and the sick co-dependent relationship he had with Lydia, but to have proof he'd had an affair? She hadn't wanted it like this.

He shook his head and tried again, without success, to pour more into his glass. His hands trembled. She didn't know if it was from the liquor or from his grief.

Was he having a breakdown? Was she here to help him over this devastating loss? Why else would he have given the girl his safe-for-his-child blood? Why else would he risk his career?

He dropped the bottle and bent over so his nose nearly bumped hers. "She died, Vanessa. I don't know if I could have saved her or not, but they're saying she died because of my blood. She's O negative, not A positive."

"Okay. You made a mistake. Or two. We can get past this. That's what malpractice insurance is for. We'll talk to the attorney, and explain—"

He stood and paced the room. "God, you really don't get it. Do I have to paint you a picture? She died because of me. Because I didn't know." He stopped midstride and looked at her. "And because of you."

How could he possibly rationalize his infidelity as being her fault? "Royce. I'm sorry. I just don't understand what you're saying."

"It wasn't all my fault. It was you."

"How did your patient die because of me?"

"Because you never told me! Because I never knew!" He shouted so loud his face reddened. "If you had just been honest from the beginning, I never would have done it!"

She rose to her feet and met him decibel for decibel. "What the hell are you talking about? What didn't I tell you?"

He grabbed the scotch bottle and threw it against the wall.

Vanessa jumped as the glass shattered. She watched the liquid trace shiny patterns on the plaster as it dripped to the floor. Only then did she go to him. He panted, clutched his hair, and rocked in place... trying to regain control. She reached her hand slowly toward him, and again he cringed from her. "Royce, I think you'd better calm down. You've got to talk to me. Why is that patient special to you? And why do you think her death is my fault? I still don't understand."

He took a deep breath, hunched his shoulders, and flung himself into a chair in front of Stanford's desk.

"That 'patient' isn't just special to me, Vanessa. She's special to you, too. She's our—or I guess I should say *your*—daughter."

That moral high ground—that false sense of superiority—she'd been clinging to, dropped out from under her like a lodestone. "What?" She barely whispered the word.

"It's *Hope,* Vanessa. They brought in Hope."

She hadn't had a drink, but she felt drunk. The room lurched, and the next thing she knew, Royce held her on the sofa. He rubbed her arms, but she was cold. So cold. Her teeth chattered, her bones ached.

"Drink this," he said, shoving the remainder of his glass of scotch at her.

She tried to lift her hand and take it, but she couldn't move her limbs. He held it to her lips, but she didn't know how to swallow. She sputtered and coughed, and he took the glass away.

"Are you all right?"

She blinked.

"Damn it. You're in shock." He wrapped a spare doctor's jacket around her and rubbed her arms, trying to warm her. He rubbed her cheeks, her hands, her feet. She knew he said more, but she couldn't process what.

Finally, something he said got through to her.

"At some point, I'm assuming you're going to want to see her. I can take you to her."

"Hope?"

"Yes. To Hope."

"Take me to Hope."

"You have to prove to me you're okay first, or you stay here."

Be okay.

For Hope.

She snapped out of it. For her baby girl.

He made her answer some absurd questions, like her name and location, the time and what had happened. After she had choked out her answers, he proclaimed she was "A and O by Four."

"What?" she asked.

"Alert and oriented to person, place, time and event," he said, all the while continuing to monitor her pulse and temperature. He was the Royce she remembered dating all those years ago—calm, authoritative, in control. And as he assumed the doctor's mantle, she felt herself slipping back into the fog. She fought to stay lucid, though, so he'd take her to Hope. She kept focused on him, watching his efficient and professional movements.

Once he proclaimed her fit, he was the angry and devastated Royce again. And she was the destroyed but determined Vanessa again.

He led her downstairs to his ER. The grieving couple was gone. Security had apparently dealt with the angry man. She noticed Royce's staff didn't look at them with the pity she expected but with that soap-opera-gossip look she despised. She hated it when her volunteers had that look instead of working. She hated it in church when she saw that look on women who were supposed to be praying but clearly weren't. Not that she went to church these days. But she definitely hated it as she walked past the nurses' station and into Trauma Bay One.

Hope's body lay still and pale under the harsh ER lights. A new wave of grief and anguish flooded Vanessa's system, rooting her where she stood. She gripped Royce's arm and moaned.

She didn't notice the man with the clipboard until he walked away from the soiled linen bin and blocked her view as he moved toward them.

"Who are you?" she asked.

"Who are you?" the person asked back.

"We're the parents of Hope Keller," Royce answered.

"Well, I'm afraid you can't be in here," the man said.

"And why not?" Royce asked.

"Her death is under investigation. No one is allowed access to the body or the trauma bay until it's been cleared by the administrator. You'll have to leave now." He pointed to the curtain."

"But—" Vanessa said, looking past the investigator at her daughter's still form. He quickly covered Hope fully with the sheet that moments ago stopped at her waist. Seeing her covered, shrouded, was almost more than she could bear, and she whimpered and clutched Royce's arm harder.

"Do I smell liquor?" the man asked.

"Let's go," Royce said.

"Wait," the man said.

Royce turned and left, pulling Vanessa out with him.

CHAPTER 3

IF ROYCE HAD BEEN FEELING a buzz, it had completely gone after seeing the investigator with Hope, leaving him with nausea in his gut, pounding in his head, and hollowness in his chest. But his heart hurt most of all. By far. It felt like it had been torn out of him.

He strode away from Trauma Bay One, ignoring the stares of his coworkers. His subordinates. Not more than a few hours earlier, if someone there had dared look at him that way, he could have called them on it, embarrassed them because of it, written them up for it if he felt like it. Instead, he was the one being humiliated, written up, investigated.

His daughter was dead and he was on unpaid leave.

But Hope wasn't really his daughter. Not biologically.

He couldn't dwell on that at the moment. So he did what he always did... he focused on work.

And the fact that he was likely permanently out of a job.

He intentionally avoided all eye contact with everyone as he made his way down the hall. He stopped in front of the door labeled 'Chief of Emergency Medicine' and looked at his name printed in block letters under it. Just briefly, he wondered how long it would be before administration had those letters removed and someone else's put up in their place. Shaking his head, he stepped inside. He had to get out of there. It took him just a moment to grab his keys out of his desk drawer and turn around.

And bump into Vanessa.

"What are you doing?"

"Following you."

"Yeah, I figured that out. Why?"

"What do you mean, why?"

He looked at her, stunned anyone could be so dense. Maybe she was still in shock.

"What happened to her, Royce?"

"I already told you."

"But, why? Why was she on the motorcycle? Who was she with? What the hell *happened?*"

He shook his head. "I don't have all the answers, Ness. Apparently I never did. Now, I have to get out of here." He stepped around her and headed for the door.

"But—we have a lot to do. We have to tell the kids. Once Administration clears... us, we have to make arrangements to move... Hope. Franklin's Funeral Home does the best work. We'll have to call them. We need to call the church—"

"Stop. Just stop." He squeezed his head, then advanced on her, taking a step with each sentence he spoke. "How am I supposed to pay for all that? I'm on suspension. I'm going to lose my job. I'm probably going to lose my license. Because of your lies!"

She retreated from him, finally backing into a chair and sinking into it as her shaking legs gave way. "What?"

He sighed and turned away from her. "Do you have any idea what is going on here?"

"Our daughter just died. I'm trying to discuss arrangements with you."

"No, Vanessa. *Your* daughter just died."

She shook her head and reached for her necklace, twisting the St. Luke medal in her fingers. *"Our* daughter."

He glared at her. "I guess it doesn't really matter now."

"Of course it matters."

"I'm being accused of killing her. A girl I raised as my own flesh and blood."

She raised the medal to her mouth with trembling fingers.

"But she wasn't my flesh and blood, was she? I was betrayed—by my own blood!" He leaned into her, his face no more than an inch from hers.

She cringed from him, leaning back in the chair, but she had nowhere to go.

The door flew open and Wade and Ellie stood there.

"What's going on in here?" Wade asked. "We heard yelling all the way down in the ER."

"I'll get security," Ellie said, turning and leaving.

"No, it's okay," Vanessa said. But Ellie had already gone.

"Royce, man," Wade said.

"I know."

"No, you don't know. Ellie's campaigning for your removal. She's already gone to administration, and now this?"

"Stanford said someone told HA. I figured it was her. She never liked me, anyway, and she freaked when… Well, you were there."

"You should go. Before she has you escorted out."

"I was just leaving."

"Royce, I'm really sorry."

Royce shook his hand.

"If you need anything, let me know."

Royce walked out of his office and heard the click-clack of heels behind him. "For the love of God, Vanessa. What do you want?"

"I don't have a car here."

Royce closed his eyes and dropped his head to his chest. Was there no limit to how bad his day could get?

They walked to the parking structure in silence. Royce didn't know what to do with himself. Where would he take her? Where would he go himself? What about the kids? Were they even his? God, he loved them, he wanted to be with them, but did he have any rights to them? Well, to Jensen, as clearly Faith wasn't his. And if he did, could he stand to be around them knowing they'd remind him of his wife's betrayal?

Even if he had the kids, how would he support them long-term? He'd just thrown his career away. Their savings would only go so far.

Left with no other option, he resigned himself to talking with Vanessa for answers to all his questions.

That meant more face-time with the woman who'd cost him everything.

When they'd reached his car, Stanford stood there, leaning on it.

"Where—where's Ben? Isn't he with you?" Vanessa asked.

"No. He said he had some things to take care of. Why? Did you need him for something?"

"No. No… I just—" She looked around then rooted in her purse and grabbed her phone. "I may have left something in his car. I'll just send him a text. Do you need something?"

Royce looked at her. She was the biggest damn puzzle in his life. One minute she was a basket case, the next she was a socialite. It gave him a headache. Well, a bigger one than he already had. He turned his attention to his mentor. "What's going on, Stanford? It's not like you to play Deep Throat."

"That's kind of how I feel, hanging out in the parking garage. Can we go somewhere and talk? The three of us? I know you want to get the kids, and you probably don't want to wait too long, in case word gets out somehow, but there are matters we need to discuss."

"Why don't we get the kids out of school, take them home, and then you can meet us there?" Royce said, dreading the rest of the day.

Stanford shook his head.

"No. I don't want to have that discussion where we might be overheard."

"Overheard?" Royce asked. "By whom?"

"Do what you need to do, then come by my house. As soon as you can."

"Once we have the kids, I don't want to leave the house," Vanessa said.

"You're right. You shouldn't." Stanford sighed. "We do need to talk, though. It's important. Come to the house tomorrow morning."

"Can't you just tell us now?"

"No. Not here. It's private, and it'll take too long. Plan on breakfast at my place. You can even bring the kids. They can stay in the kitchen while we talk."

Royce sighed. "But I don't know where I'm going to be in the morning."

Vanessa gasped. Her eyes widened. Royce pretended not to notice.

"I do," Stanford said. "In your house. That's one of the things we're going to talk about. No one can know something's rotten in the state of Denmark. No one. Not the mailman, not the paperboy. Not even the maid. Especially not the maid. You stay in your house, in your bedroom. We'll discuss the particulars tomorrow." He kissed Vanessa and squeezed Royce's shoulder.

"But—"

"No buts! Just do what I say. Now, before I forget." He reached into his pocket and pulled out two medicine bottles. "These are mild sedatives. You should both take one tonight. You need to try to get some rest before this all hits the fan." He handed a bottle to each of them and walked away without a backward glance.

Royce shook his head as Stanford left, then he got in his car. Vanessa still stood by the bumper. After turning the key in the ignition, he rolled down the window. "Are you getting in?"

She seemed to be texting. What the hell was wrong with her? He sighed and rolled his eyes.

Glancing up, she said, "Hmm? Oh, yeah." She typed a few more things into her phone, then threw it in her purse and got in the car. "So, where to?"

"How do you do that?"

"Do what?"

He backed out of his space and sped through the garage, heading for the school. "Compartmentalize everything. You're only half aware of everything going on around you because you're so focused on… on you."

"I'm aware of the things that go on around me. And I'm not focused on me. I'm just trying to put out fires all the time."

"So what blaze were you so busy dousing this time that you couldn't focus on what was going on just now?"

She looked out the window. "Just get the kids, Royce."

"You only know we're getting the kids because you recognize the road."

"I know we're getting the kids because I know we need to get the kids."

"Your kids."

"Our kids."

He sighed and tightened his grip on the wheel. "I'll be wanting proof of that. Jensen, anyway. Obviously Faith isn't mine."

"You're wrong."

He snorted. "Please. Don't even bother trying that one."

"I think I know who fathered my children."

He whipped his vehicle into the school lot, tires squealing as he took the turn. When he put the car in park, he turned to face her, not trusting himself to let go of the wheel. "I don't know what kind of head games you're playing, but cut the act. I can't take much more today. We need to act civil when we go in there, and keep it together until we get Jensen and Faith home. Past that, I'm not making any promises. I suggest you keep your damn mouth shut and let me handle this. Can you do that?"

"Fine. Handle it. But you better not imply anything I disagree with, or I will say something."

He got out of the car and, without waiting to see if she followed, headed toward the school. The click-clack of heels on the asphalt told him she followed close behind him. Knowing his way around well, he turned left inside and headed for the principal's office, not bothering to stop at the secretary's desk. He tapped at the door before the secretary could catch up with them.

"Dr. Keller, Mrs. Keller," Mrs. Prindle called. "You have to be announced!"

He couldn't stand that old biddy.

Principal Pendleton opened the door and leaned into the hall to talk to his battleaxe of a secretary. "It's fine. The Kellers are always welcome here." Gesturing into his office, he said, "Please. Come in. Take a seat."

When they were seated, the principal leaned back in his chair. "It's not often you're both here together. What can I do for you? Have you lined up a big whale for Carnival?"

"No, Mr. Pendleton. Nothing like that. Could you please have Jensen and Faith summoned to your office? We need to speak with them. And please make arrangements to have them removed from school for the rest of the year. They won't be returning. Faith will be back in the fall."

"I see." He put his elbows on his desk and steepled his fingers together. "And what about graduation? Jensen was to be told this afternoon... He's been selected valedictorian. Will he be attending graduating ceremonies?"

"Oh, Royce," Vanessa grabbed Royce's arm. Royce looked at her hand, then at her, and she let him go.

"And when is commencement?" Royce asked. He scrolled through his calendar on his phone.

"Two weeks from tomorrow."

There it was in his calendar. Was it really in two weeks? It seemed like it should be in two months. And that morning seemed like a lifetime ago. Time was all relative.

He sighed. "When do we need to let you know?"

"Is there a problem?"

"Can you please summon Jensen and Faith?"

"And what about Miss Hope? Are you aware she, uh, missed school again?" Vanessa choked back a sob.

"I'm actually glad the two of you are here. Hope has been a matter of concern among the faculty and staff for some time now. Not much like her brother." Royce clenched his jaw.

"Certainly nothing like her twin. I mean, I know they aren't identical twins, but you'd think there'd be some similarity between them. Night and day, those two."

Royce worried he was going to crack a molar.

"I noticed you didn't mention Hope returning next fall," the principal continued. "Maybe we should just get the particulars out of the way now. Before we get the other two down here, if we could just take a few moments—"

"You know, I wanted to give my children the courtesy of being the first to know, but you just won't drop it." Royce stood and put his hands on the desk, leaning down to look at the principal. "Hope's dead, Jeffrey. She died in an accident today. I had to pronounce her dead in my own goddamned ER. So do you think you could get up off your pretentious ass for one minute, lift a fucking finger, and page my kids to this shithole you call your office so I can tell them there's been a tragedy in our family?"

He didn't use vulgar language often in public. There were usually better ways of expressing anger. Better ways of getting things done.

But sometimes people just left him no other choice.

And sometimes they just pissed him off.

By the look on Pendleton's face, his outburst had the desired effect.

"I'm… I'm so sorry, Dr. Keller. Mrs. Keller. I had no idea. Hope was a lovely girl. She had so much untapped potential." He fumbled for the phone and whispered into it. "Get me Jensen and Faith Keller, now… No, she isn't in today… Just the other two. Yes. Yes. Immediately." He put the phone down. "You both have my deepest sympathies. The school and all its resources are at your disposal. Whatever we can do to ease your suffering at this time…."

Royce held up his hand. Hope had gone from lost-cause delinquent to gone-too-soon rising-star in the blink of an eye. He couldn't take much more of the emotional one-eighties going around.

Jensen walked in. "Mr. Pendleton. You wanted to see—Dad? Mom? What's going on?

"Sit down, Jensen," Royce said.

He sat. "What's this about?"

Faith knocked and opened the door. "Mr. Pendleton? Dad? Mom? What are you doing here?" She looked at Jensen. He just shrugged. She sat beside him on the sofa.

"I'll give you some privacy," Mr. Pendleton said. "Take all the time you need." He left the room, closing the door behind him.

Royce rubbed his chin and looked at the two teenagers sitting across from him. A man wasn't supposed to lose a child, wasn't supposed to ruin his children's lives.

A man certainly wasn't supposed to ruin some other man's children's lives.

He didn't even know who the hell he was any more, let alone who these people were.

What was he supposed to say?

His whole adult life, he fixed things. He was a doctor. He made things better. That's what he did.

As he looked at these people, knowing he was about to rip their lives apart, he didn't have the words, the tools, the skills.

It was like performing surgery blindfolded.

And it scared the shit out of him.

"Dad?" Jensen said. "What is it?"

"You're scaring us," Faith said.

Vanessa stooped down in front of them and grabbed each of their hands with one of her own. "We need to talk to you about something."

"We figured," Jensen said.

"That's why they called us here," Faith said.

"Where's Hope?" Jensen asked.

Vanessa took a deep breath. "There's been an accident."

Royce saw her squeeze their hands and wanted to be the one to offer comfort, but he couldn't go to them.

Faith pulled hers away. "Mom. Dad. Where's Hope?"

"Dad?" Jensen said. He pulled away, too.

Vanessa stood up and looked at him. "Royce?"

It always fell to him.

Jensen stood. "Dad? Where's Hope?"

Faith started to cry. "Daddy?"

"She came into the ER today," Royce said. The words cracked painfully past the rawness in his throat. He shook his head. "I'm so, so sorry."

Faith launched herself into his arms, sobbing. He held her, rocking and stroking her back. He whispered nonsensical syllables and crooned a soft melody in her ear. Jensen stood stoic for a moment, then he went to the window and looked out at the trees blowing in the late May breeze. The afternoon sun cast a dappled shadow on his tear-streaked face. He looked so much like a man, standing there, facing his grief alone. Vanessa reached for him, but he shrugged her off. Then he joined Faith, apparently seeking solace in his father's embrace. Well, the embrace of the only father he'd ever known. Royce didn't know what the following days would bring, but he would offer comfort to those poor children for as long as they wanted it—no matter whose children they were.

Royce watched Vanessa stand alone in the strange room, tears flowing freely down her face. She didn't bother wiping them off, but rather let them fall, unhampered. Like wearing their trails was penance enough for her sins. He was no priest, but he couldn't conceive of a penance harsh enough for what she'd done, what she'd put him through. Them through. She twisted her St. Luke medal around her finger and then glanced down at it. St. Luke—patron saint of physicians. She'd bought that medal when Royce graduated med school, prayed for him over it for years, not that he'd ever needed it, until she stopped praying. Around the time the twins were born, she tucked her rosary away and stopped saying it. She quit going to church and saying morning and bedtime prayers. Even stopped saying grace before meals. But even after her faith wavered, she still wore the medal. He couldn't remember ever seeing her go a day without it. Why the hell couldn't she have worn a St. Aloysius medal instead? Why wasn't she praying for their troubled teenage girl?

Because she wasn't praying at all. The necklace was just there to give her comfort. Always about *her.*

For a moment, she met his gaze, and he thought she might join them, because she started walking toward them. He knew, because the kids were there, he wouldn't turn her away. But instead, she walked past them and over to where she had left her purse. Looking inside, she took out her phone. He didn't know who she texted or what was so damn important, but he hoped to God it was worth it. Because before he was done with her, whoever was on the other end was all she was going to have left.

CHAPTER 4

JENSEN STAYED SILENT THE WHOLE way home. Faith sobbed uncontrollably. Vanessa didn't know what to do for either of them. She occasionally turned around and offered her daughter tissues, but that was all she had to offer. She didn't have any advice, any words of comfort, any miracle that would take the pain away. And if she did, the kids would probably refuse it from her anyway.

They always seemed to prefer Royce to her, so unless he offered the solace, they wouldn't accept it.

And Royce didn't offer them anything. He drove... silent, stoic.

Vanessa recognized his expression. The kids, if they cared to pay attention, would think he was grieving, but she knew there was more to it. Yes, he was in pain. More than she'd ever seen him in. But he was also scared. And mad. She'd never seen him so angry before. By the time they pulled into their garage, his knuckles were so white as he gripped the steering wheel, she would have sworn his bones had popped through his skin.

Faith bolted out of the car before Royce even had it in park, but Jensen sat there when Royce turned off the ignition. Eventually he said, "Aren't you coming in, Dad?"

"I wanted to talk to your mother in private for a moment."

"Can't you come in first? At least for a little bit? I don't want to... Never mind." He reached for the door handle.

"He doesn't want to be alone when he sees the house without her," Vanessa whispered to Royce.

Royce got out of the car. "I should probably tell Lydia what's going on, anyway. We'll go in now for a bit."

"Of course you have to run to Lydia," Vanessa mumbled.

Royce shot her a dirty look, but stayed silent.

"So, you're coming in now?" Jensen asked.

Royce nodded and headed toward the door.

Vanessa noted the relief wash across Jensen's face and wished she had been the one to put it there. She followed them into the house. Jensen stood just inside the door, looking around. She wondered if he'd be able to walk any further than the mudroom. Trying to get his mind on something other than his sister's absence, she said, "Jensen, do you want a snack?"

He turned and looked at her. "I'm not really worried about eating right now, Mom."

"It's not a bad idea, Jensen," Royce said. "You probably haven't eaten since breakfast. Your mom doesn't have to make it. Lydia will fix you something."

Jensen walked toward the kitchen, grabbed an apple out of the bowl, and held it up so his father could see. "I'm going up to my room." Without a look back, he bolted for the stairs.

"Dr. Keller!" Lydia came down the hall, dust cloth in hand. When she saw Royce, she took her hair down and shook it out, fluffing it with her fingers. "You're home early. What a nice surprise! You know, I was hoping you'd have some time for me this evening. Or perhaps now is better?" She shot a look at Vanessa. "There are some important matters I'd like to discuss with you."

"Now is probably best, Lydia. I have something to tell you, as well. Why don't you come into my study?" He gestured toward the study and followed her in, closing the doors behind them.

Vanessa didn't miss the small smile Lydia directed at her before she turned and walked away with Royce. She could hardly care at that point. Royce knew about Ben's visit. What damage could Lydia do?… Oh, my God. *Ben!* She'd almost forgotten.

She grabbed her phone and went into the sunroom where she had a clear view of anyone walking down the hall to her. Ben hadn't returned any of her texts. Losing Hope caused a pain in her chest… palpable, raw agony. The thought of losing the rest of her family was too much to even consider. She wouldn't survive it. She had to stop Ben from calling Royce and destroying her life. So she called him.

"Vanessa? Why are you calling me? What could you possibly want?"

"I want to make sure you aren't going to say anything to Royce."

He was silent for so long, she looked at her phone to be certain the line wasn't dead. Finally he spoke. "You've got to be kidding me."

"What?"

"I've kept this secret for years. Through my divorce, through your loveless marriage—"

"My marriage is not loveless." Her heart pounded so hard her chest hurt. He didn't understand. How could she make him understand?

"Through all the problems you had raising those kids."

"What problems? Jensen and Faith may be a little distant, and Hope might have been a little independent, but—"

"Who are you kidding?" he said. "Royce only has time for, plans for, Jensen and Faith. He barely knows Hope exists, unless he has a complaint to throw her way."

"That's not true."

"Bullshit. And now—now, after I gave up the one thing I wanted the most, you cost me the chance to ever have it. And you never even appreciated it! Now you come to me to ask me not to say anything to Royce?"

"The damage is done, Ben. What's the point in making things worse?"

"The damage? Nice way to talk about Hope."

"He's your best friend. He's *my* husband."

"And she was *my* daughter! And she never knew. Because of the two of you! How do I get those years back, Ness?"

Fear was an icy floe in her veins. "You don't, Ben. You can't. But confronting Royce isn't going to change any of that. It will cost you a best friend, though. Why lose a daughter and a friend today?"

"Don't call me again, Vanessa. If I have anything to say, I'll call you." He hung up before she could say anything else.

That was it. She lost Hope, and she would end up losing Royce, too. And with him, Jensen and Faith. She was losing everything. She could blame Hope for her decisions that morning. Or the kid driving the bike. Or Royce for breaking protocol. Or Ben for deciding to confront Royce. But deep down, she knew.

She might not have the courage to say it out loud, but…

It was all her fault.

Oh my God, please… let this not be happening. It can't be happening. It isn't real.

She took a few deep breaths to try to settle her pounding heart, the spinning room.

The sunroom had always been Hope's favorite room of the house, next to her bedroom. When she was ten, she said the color of the walls reminded her of cake batter. As she got older, the frosty shades of blues and greens in the pillows and curtains appealed to her. She said it was like being at the beach without getting sand in uncomfortable places. Remembering that made Vanessa smile for a moment, and she allowed the room to soothe her. She picked up Hope's favorite pillow—a misty blue with green piping—and hugged it. It smelled like Hope.

She choked out a sob.

She sat there, rocking with the pillow and crying silently for all she had lost.

When Royce came down the hallway, Lydia tight on his heels of course, she hurried to put herself back together.

"Are you all right?" he asked.

She wiped her tears away, then carefully placed the pillow on the sofa. She smoothed it until she was satisfied it was perfect, like its position was somehow imperative to the well-being of her family. When she had it the way she wanted it, she turned to Royce. "Are you ready?"

Lydia stepped around her and crossed to the sofa. She gathered all the pillows and started to leave the room with them.

Vanessa blocked her path. "What do you think you're doing?"

"These pillows haven't been laundered in a while. They all need refreshing. Especially this one." She tried to wiggle the one Vanessa had been holding. "It has tears and who knows what else on it. I'm going to wash them."

"Put. Them. All. Back."

Lydia just stood there.

"Now."

Lydia looked around her at Royce.

Royce touched Vanessa's shoulder, but she didn't turn around, not wanting to take her eyes off Lydia for even a moment.

"Ness, what does it hurt if she washes a few pillows?"

"I said no."

He sighed. "Put them back for now, Lydia. It's not worth the aggravation. There's plenty more that needs doing. Maybe you can clean Hope's room before we pack it."

"Absolutely not," Vanessa said.

"Vanessa," Royce began.

"If you want to do laundry, I'm sure Jensen and Faith have some. For now, do not touch *anything* in this room or Hope's. I'll be giving you your instructions regarding her things, should I require your assistance in those matters."

Lydia looked at Royce, who shrugged his shoulders.

"And let me make one more thing clear, Lydia. You work for us, not just Dr. Keller. If I tell you to do something, you don't need to look over my head at him for his approval. Do you understand? Think long and hard before breaking eye contact with me."

Vanessa could see Lydia struggling not to look at Royce. But she finally said, "Yes, ma'am," and walked away.

"You were a little hard on her, don't you think?" Royce asked.

"You've been a little too easy with her since you hired her, don't you think? She's our maid, not yours."

He sighed. "I'm not discussing this. Lydia didn't have any plans for dinner yet, so I thought we could order in Chinese."

"That's fine."

"Until then, I'll be in my study."

"Great. I'll be upstairs."

"Fine."

When did conversations with Royce become so forced? She'd like to say since Hope's accident that morning, but honestly, she'd have to admit it had happened much longer ago.

As she climbed the stairs, her body felt fatigued, like she had run a marathon, climbed a mountain, been hit by a car... God, what was she thinking? She had thought that so many times before, but she'd never meant it like that. Hope died from her accident. She didn't just feel bone weary, she felt actual pain, and probably heart-racing terror.

Did Hope recognize her father as she lay in the hospital? Did that give her any relief, or did it bring on shame? Was she even conscious to know what was happening to her?

Would Royce ever tell her what happened in the ER? Would he lie to make her feel better? Lie to make her feel worse?

At the top of the stairs, she peeked in on Jensen. He gazed out his window, the apple sitting on his dresser, untouched. "How are you, honey? Do you need anything?"

He shook his head. "I called her a name this morning."

"What?" she asked.

"Her and Faith. I called them Thing One and Thing Two. Those are my last words to my sister."

She crossed to him and hugged him from behind. At first he didn't move, but then he turned and hugged her, finally breaking down and sobbing into her hair.

"She knew you were joking, Jensen. That's how the two of you were together. But never doubt she loved you. And she knew you loved her." She held him until he was cried out, then she led him to his bed. "Get some rest, baby." She covered him with his blanket and closed his door.

She crossed the hall to Faith's room. Her daughter sat on her bed holding a stuffed bear wearing a t-shirt that read *TUFF GUY*, tears falling silently down her cheeks. When Vanessa walked in, Faith held up the bear. It was one of a hundred stuffed animals the girls had.

"Remember this?"

Vanessa shook her head.

"It was Grandpa Gene's. We always liked to play with it at his house, and one time when we were there he told us to take it home. We both wanted it, and fought about who would keep it. Finally Hope told me she was tough enough without it, so I should have it." She sobbed. "But she wasn't. She wasn't tough. She died, and now I have the bear but no sister."

Vanessa sat beside her and held her while she cried, rocking her and stroking her hair until she was soothed. She didn't have any words to make things better. She wasn't tough, either.

When Faith had cried herself out, she collapsed on her bed. Vanessa kissed her, covered her with a blanket, and left her to rest.

She had every intention of going to her room for a nap, but Hope's room beckoned her.

CHAPTER 5

ROYCE PACED IN FRONT OF his desk. Why did Stanford insist he stay in his house? In his bedroom? As if everything that happened wasn't bad enough, confining him to that room at night was the icing on the cake. If cake was prison and icing was his cell. And Vanessa was the cellmate everyone dreaded. He'd rather be in solitary confinement.

He looked at the stack of bills on his desk.

Unpaid leave. That meant no income.

They'd have to dip into their savings to pay their mortgage, utilities, car payments, insurance… They. He said *they*. How long before they became simply *Royce* and *Vanessa?* And how would he pay for her lifestyle with no job? All the unnecessary updates to the house? All the shoes and outfits, most of which he didn't think she wore more than once. Some of which still had tags on them in her closet. All the trips to the salons and the spas? And the jewelry! And the way she basically paid for all her fundraisers herself? He'd have to talk to her about making some changes. What would he do if he lost his license to practice? Their savings would last for a year, maybe two, but the way Vanessa burned through money… And *tuition!* What would he do about Jensen's college? He'd have to check and see if he'd set enough aside for the kids to go to school. Of course, he could split Hope's college fund between Jensen and Faith.

He choked back a sob, disgusted he was already considering what to do with her money.

But he was in a bind.

Although, it was possible he'd get his job back and they wouldn't have to worry. He snorted in derision and rubbed his eyes. Who was he kidding? His career was toast. He should probably contact his attorney.

But what would he say?

He sat down and looked at the pictures on his desk, ignoring the piles of bills he'd yet to pay. They could wait. His family, what was left of it, could not.

Vanessa's photo was in a shiny silver frame. She stood outside somewhere and smiled at the person who took the picture. It wasn't him. In fact, he didn't even recognize the event. One of her volunteers probably took it at one of the seven thousand charities she organized. She looked good that day. The smile was obviously genuine—it graced her whole face with a light of pure happiness. Was it her lover behind the camera? Was that why her smile was so radiant?

He flipped the picture face down on his desk.

He looked at a family photo, but it had been taken years ago, when the kids were little and Cornelius, their lazy but loveable sheepdog, had still been alive. God, those kids loved that dog, especially the girls. Especially Faith. Losing Cornelius began her fascination with all things animal. She turned vegan after he died, and started supporting animal rights causes. He couldn't imagine what she'd do after losing a sister.

He looked at the three children in the photo. Jensen had a huge gap where his front baby teeth had been and the girls wore their hair in pigtails. They all had huge smiles on their faces. Were they biologically siblings? Did it matter?

He gazed at Hope's innocent smile. That was the Hope he remembered, the Hope he mourned.

Unfortunately, he didn't know the Hope who died on his table.

He could never rectify that failure.

There were more pictures, individuals of the kids from the current school year. Jensen in his lacrosse uniform. Faith in her dance team outfit. Hope at what he was told was a poetry slam, whatever that was. She was on a stage, behind a mic, wearing all black. He picked up Hope's picture and ran his finger over her face. Where had the little girl with the pigtails gone? And why hadn't he noticed she was missing?

He leaned back in his seat, held her picture to his chest, and let the tears fall.

ROYCE DIDN'T KNOW HOW LONG he hid in his study. He either dozed off for a while or just completely got lost in his thoughts. But when he looked out the window, the sun had drifted in the sky. A quick glance at his watch revealed the late hour. He knew they had to eat dinner, whether they felt like eating or not. He booted up his laptop, found Chin's website in his bookmarked pages, and in a few minutes had an order placed for his family. By the time he drove there, the order would be ready.

He walked to the foyer and yelled up the stairs. "Hey guys? I'm going to pick up dinner. Can you have the table set for when I come back?"

Jensen came to the top of the stairs. "I'll come with you." He ran down the stairs and past him, straight out the mudroom door.

Royce shrugged and followed him out. When he got in the car, he asked him, "So, how are you doing?"

"I'm fine. Mom talked to me."

He pulled out and looked at his son. "Really? What'd she say?"

"Why? What was she supposed to say?"

"Nothing. I'm just worried about you."

"I said I'm fine."

"Okay."

They drove in silence for a while.

"Is something going on?" Jensen asked.

"Why would you ask that?"

"You just seem… off."

Royce took a deep breath. "It's just been a hard day. Nothing for you to worry about."

"You'd tell us, though, right?"

"When we have something to tell you kids, we'll tell you together. Just like we did today."

"That's not much of an answer, Dad."

"We're here." Royce pulled to a stop in front of a little Chinese restaurant. "You coming in?"

"You need help?"

"No. I've got it."

"Then I don't really feel like it. I just needed to get out of the house. But I don't really want to see anyone right now. I'm not even answering my phone."

Their phones! Royce had forgotten about that. He really didn't want Jensen and Faith hearing any gossip from their friends before he could talk to them. "Okay. Be right back."

He hurried in, got the food, and rushed back out. "All set. You ready?"

"Dad? For real, are you okay?"

"I'm fine. Let's go."

The whole drive back to the house, Royce worried over the kids hearing something they shouldn't on their phones. He grew so obsessed, he forgot Jensen was even in the car with him. Until his son sighed.

Royce looked at him, but he stared out the side window.

"What's wrong, Jensen?"

"That's what I'd like to know. I've been talking to you for five minutes and you haven't heard a word I've said."

"I'm listening now."

"Never mind. We're home."

They walked inside and saw the dining room table had been set for four. Royce looked at Vanessa and raised an eyebrow.

"I thought maybe something different tonight. Instead of the usual…" She tipped her head toward the kitchen table where they took most of their meals.

As much as Royce hated to admit it, she'd had a good idea. It would be difficult to see Hope's empty chair. He didn't know if he was ready at the moment. It was a good bet Faith and Jensen weren't.

Vanessa helped him put the food on the table and they all sat down. Usually Faith and Hope sat beside each other on one side of the table across from Jensen, but Vanessa had the table arranged so there were only four chairs, Faith seated directly across from her brother. As Royce took his seat at the head of the table across from his wife, he glanced at one of the side chairs in the corner of the room. Empty.

How was he going to swallow anything past the lump in his throat?

"Would someone like to say grace?" Vanessa asked.

"We only do that on holidays and when Grandma Rose is here," Faith said.

"It never hurts to say grace, honey," she said. "Besides, we have a lot to be thankful for."

Jensen snorted. "Are you kidding me?"

Royce had to agree, but he didn't say anything.

Vanessa reached across the table and grabbed Jensen's hand with one hand and Faith's with the other. "We suffered a terrible tragedy today. And the next few days will seem unbearable. But we have each other. I'm grateful for everyone here at this table."

Royce grabbed his water and swallowed with noisy gulps. Then he grabbed his kids' hands.

Vanessa glared at him, but continued. "Lord, I ask You to bless the bounty at this table. We know without Your mercy and Your love we would not have it. I ask You to bless the people at this table. We rely on You to keep us safe. In Jesus's name, amen."

"Amen," Faith said and let go of her parents' hands. She looked around the table, and finally settled on looking at her plate.

Jensen didn't say anything. He pulled his hands away and sat back in his seat.

Royce sighed and reached again for his glass.

"Sorry," Vanessa looked at Royce. "Was there something you wanted to add?"

He had plenty to say, but not with the audience they had. He stared at his plate, trying to remain calm. "No. Nothing to add to the blessing. We could talk about something else, if you'd like." He looked up and met her gaze, then picked up a container and tipped it toward her. "Chicken?" he asked, the word laced with double meaning.

He watched with satisfaction while the color drained from her face. Then she smiled that phony smile he recognized from her charity events. "No, thank you. I don't care for it."

"Since when? That's what you've always ordered."

"No. That's what you first ordered for me when you took me to Jimmy Tsang's in college. I told you it was fine. Which it was. It was fine. But it's not what I like. I like food with a little more heat." She picked up an egg roll and dipped it in mustard. Then she took an enormous bite.

He knew her mouth must be on fire, but she chewed and swallowed and never reached for her water. Her face turned red and her eyes watered, but she didn't flinch.

"My apologies." Royce flung a heaping spoonful of the bland chicken onto his plate. "I didn't realize this," he ladled another portion of food onto his dish with a thud, "has been so unappealing to you for all these years. That won't happen again."

"I didn't say it's unappealing. I said I prefer something else. If you'd ever taken the time to ask, you'd have known that. But you didn't. You just did what you thought was best. As usual."

"And what's that supposed to mean?"

"Just that you seem to like taking charge of situations." She kept nibbling on her egg roll, but she stopped dipping it in the mustard, opting instead to use the duck sauce.

"You didn't mind me taking charge today, though, did you? I can always take charge of the difficult situations. What do you want to take charge of?"

"Anything might be nice."

"Have at it."

"Thanks for getting some vegetarian dishes," Faith interrupted. She grabbed a spring roll and nibbled on it.

"I'm sorry, honey," Vanessa said.

"Won't happen again," Royce said.

Jensen shrugged. "Can I have the beef?" Faith passed him the container. He put some on his dish, but then pushed the plate aside and stood up. "Forget it. I'm not hungry. May I please be excused?"

"Me too?" Faith asked, standing too.

"We're supposed to be having a nice family dinner," Vanessa said.

Jensen scoffed. "You guys aren't even talking to us!"

"Sit down and eat," Royce said.

Jensen and Faith sat back down. Royce put more beef in Jensen's dish and passed a tofu dish to Faith. She dutifully put some in her plate and began picking at it.

They ate without speaking for a long time, the only sounds the clattering of flatware against the plates. Royce spent most of his time glaring at Vanessa, who returned his glower with a heated one of her own. When Faith sniffled, Royce glanced her way. She had cleared her plate and mindlessly munched on the fried chow mein noodles that accompanied their meals. Jensen had eaten one, maybe two pieces of beef. His rice and broccoli appeared to be untouched.

He sighed. If he couldn't be the support his kids needed, they were going to turn to their friends. And he couldn't have that. Not until he'd told them more about what was going on. And he wasn't ready to do that.

"I was wondering whether either of you planned on contacting your friends regarding today's... events," Royce said.

Vanessa shot him a panicked look, but he didn't concern himself about allaying her fears. She could hear his plan as it unfolded.

"I don't know when I'll be ready to talk to anyone," Faith said.

"I tried to talk to you about that in the car," Jensen said. "Simone has called me several times, but I haven't answered. I don't feel like talking. I don't know what to say. And a lot of the guys keep texting."

"I'm glad your friends are concerned about you," Royce said, "but I'd like to keep this a family matter for now. At least for another day. I want you to give me your phones."

"What?" Jensen asked. "Why?"

"I just told you why. You need time to process this on your own before you start talking to other people. We need time as a family before we let the outside in."

"But why do we have to give you our phones?" Faith asked. "We told you we haven't even talked to anyone."

"Because I want to be sure you don't." He held out his hand until they both surrendered their phones.

"I thought you said nothing was going on," Jensen said.

"There isn't."

"You said when you and Mom were together, you'd tell us what was going on."

"When I know something, you will."

"If you're taking my phone, you know something. Did Hope do something bad, Dad?"

It was Royce's turn to lean forward and take Jensen's and Faith's hands. "Hope was in a bad accident and she died. That's all the information we have right now." He squeezed their hands.

"Are we going to the funeral home to, you know, make the arrangements?" Jensen asked.

"Not yet, baby." Vanessa said. "They haven't released her yet. And we won't make you do that."

Faith sighed, relief evident on her face.

"If they haven't released her, it's because there's something wrong."

"Jensen—" Royce began.

"What aren't you telling us?"

"—calm down."

Jensen turned to Vanessa. "He's protecting us. He's always trying to make things seem better than they are. What's going on?"

"You're making a big production out of nothing, honey."

"I should have known you wouldn't tell us. You wouldn't want to make Hope look bad."

"Jensen!" Faith said.

"What? You know it's true. She always took Hope's side when we argued. Dad always tried to put a shine on everything in public. Image is everything. I want to know what's going on!"

Faith broke into tears.

Royce looked at Vanessa. "Are you happy?"

"I didn't do this."

"I suppose you think I'm responsible?"

"You're the one requisitioning phones."

"And why do you think I have to do that, exactly?"

"So you're putting this all on me?" Her voice squeaked at the end.

"What's going on?" Jensen yelled.

"Go to bed!" Vanessa and Royce said together.

Royce closed his eyes and looked down, taking a deep breath as he tried to calm himself. Then he said in a softer voice, "Jensen, Faith. Go to bed. We have to be at Stanford's tomorrow for breakfast."

"You've got to be kidding me," Jensen said. "You aren't telling us anything? But you expect us to go out? At a time like this?"

"It'll be fine, Jensen," Vanessa said. "We'll go and have a nice breakfast. Then afterward, we'll stop at the school and get your car and you and Faith can clean out your lockers—"

Royce cleared his throat and glared at her.

"I don't want to go to the Hammonds'! I don't want to go to school!" Faith said. "I don't want to see anyone!"

"And you don't have to," Royce said. "Mom and I can go ourselves. There's a matter of some urgency we need to discuss with Stanford. It can't be postponed."

"But we can't know about it."

"Jensen, when the time is right, you'll know. I promise. Right now, just please go upstairs."

"Whatever."

"So, are you two coming with us tomorrow?" Vanessa asked.

Faith shook her head.

Jensen said, "Can I be part of the conversation?"

Royce just looked at him and raised an eyebrow.

"Then no."

"Leave your keys," Royce said. "We'll bring your car home when we come back."

"Like I care about that right now."

"You have no idea what's going to happen over the next few days. You might need it."

Jensen reached into his pocket, grabbed his keys, and tossed them on the table. Faith ran out of the room and Jensen followed her at a slower, angrier pace.

"Well, that was a raging success." Royce threw his napkin on his plate and stood.

"Maybe we should tell them what we know."

"I want to know what Stanford has to say first. Maybe his perception of this mess isn't as bleak as mine."

"Royce?"

"What?"

"I'm sorry about tonight. Arguing about the chicken was silly."

"It doesn't change the fact that I've been wrong for all these years. Apparently about a lot of things."

A few tears rolled down her cheeks, but she didn't wipe them away. "I'm going to put this food away. Are you going upstairs?"

He headed for the door. "I'm going out."

"Will you be home tonight?"

He didn't look back. "I don't know."

He heard her sobbing, but he kept going.

CHAPTER 6

VANESSA COULDN'T SETTLE HER NERVES. She put the food away, paced the halls, cleaned up her workstation. Finally she had no choice but to go upstairs. She checked on Faith, but all she did was cry and blubber. She didn't make any sense, and after she cried herself into exhaustion, Vanessa tucked her into bed.

She hadn't been that lucky with Jensen.

She'd found him looking out the window again, but he hadn't been receptive to her hugs and comforting. When she had reached for him, he shrugged her off.

"Go away."

"I'm just trying to help."

"What? Am I your new favorite now that Hope's gone?"

That stung. It took her breath for a moment. "How could you say that?" she managed.

"You've been in my room more in the last twelve hours than you were in the last twelve months. You've asked me how I was more today than you have in the last year. You've never shown this kind of interest in me. Not since Hope was born. You never wanted to be bothered before. Don't bother now."

"Jensen. That's simply not true."

"Okay. If you want to bond so badly, tell me what the big secret is."

"It's not that simple."

"Just get out."

"Jensen."

"I mean it, Mom. I want to be alone."

She hesitated, and he screamed, "Get out!"

So she fled and pulled the door closed behind her. The rest of the night she spent in her room, waiting for her husband to return.

But he never did.

She thought she'd heard the garage door open, but Royce had never come to bed.

By the time the sun broke on the horizon, she had bloodshot and shadowed eyes, a desperate need for coffee, and a sick feeling in her soul telling her she'd ruined everything beyond reparation.

Staying in bed seemed pointless. She showered, did her hair and makeup, dressed, accessorized, and trudged downstairs. She looked a hell of a lot better than she felt, and her cosmetic wonders only hid so many flaws.

It was too early for Lydia to be there, but she was surprised to be greeted by the aroma of fresh coffee. "At last, something's gone right."

"It's not as good as Lydia's," Royce said. "She told me her secret is chicory, but I don't know where she keeps it."

She had jumped when he spoke, and she clutched her chest. "You startled me. I didn't see you."

"Sorry."

"Why are you sitting in the dark?"

"I didn't want to wake anyone."

She turned on the overhead light. "There's no one in the kitchen. Who would you wake?"

He sighed. "I don't know, Vanessa. I came in, turned on the lights, made the coffee, and turned them out again so I wouldn't bother anyone. Does it have to be a federal case?"

She pulled down a cup and poured herself some coffee. "No." She took a sip and closed her eyes. "You're right. It's not as good as Lydia's."

"Then don't drink the damn thing."

She took another sip and allowed the warmth to seep through her. "Still, it's better than mine. It's just what I needed."

"I couldn't find the chicory."

"That's what you said. She probably hides it so we have to rely on her."

"She does make good coffee."

"She's not perfect, Royce."

He sighed. "I'm going to go grab a shower, then we can go to Stanford's. I thought we'd get Jensen's car on the way back."

"Fine." She took another sip and watched him walk through the kitchen. Just before he left the room, she asked, "Where were you last night?"

"I told you I was going out."

"I know. I just wondered where you went."

"Why?"

"Where were you? Hotels have showers. So do friends' houses. Besides, Stanford told you to stay here."

"If you must know, I did stay here. I got back around two-thirty."

She breathed a sigh of relief to herself and hoped he didn't hear it. "I thought I heard you come in. But you didn't come to bed."

"With you? No. I stayed in the guest room."

"But Stanford said—"

"I don't really care, Ness. I really hoped I'd wake up in my own bed and it would all have been a horrible nightmare, but I didn't. I woke up after a restless sleep in the guest bed in my own home. So don't tell me what Stanford said I'm supposed to do. Stanford isn't me. Stanford didn't go through what I went through. If he thinks it's so damn important, he can come stay with you. I can't bear it right now. I'm only going to be here as long as I think one of the kids might need me. Or until I can make suitable alternative arrangements. Now, if you don't mind, I'm going to go get a shower."

"What do you mean by that? Suitable alternative arrangements?" He was leaving. He was going to divorce her and take the kids and leave her and she'd have nothing and no one. Ben didn't have to ruin her marriage. It happened without him.

"You're a smart girl, Ness. You can figure it out." He turned to leave the kitchen, then turned back around. "While I'm gone, contact the school. Make sure they have the kids' things packed and ready for us. I don't want to have to wait for them today." Then he walked upstairs to get ready, leaving Vanessa alone in the kitchen. It didn't matter that she was drinking coffee. She was chilled to her core.

He was a mere facsimile of the man she'd married. A harsh veneer, a brusque copy. If he could be all business and no emotions, then she could, too. She squared her shoulders and took out her phone, busying herself by composing a message to the school. By the time she was done with the task Royce had assigned her, she had steeled herself for the car ride with him and resolved not to start any discussions or arguments.

Fifteen minutes later, Royce came into the kitchen, freshly shaved and dressed for the day. "Let's go," he said. "Stanford's waiting."

She followed him out of the house and into the garage, where she got into the car and stared out the window. Neither of them said a word during the drive to the Hammonds'. She was determined not to give him the satisfaction of breaking down or cracking under the pressure. So she let her mind wander. She only briefly thought about where he had been until two-thirty the night before. She even managed to put the destruction of her marriage out of her mind for the time being. Her thoughts took a decidedly darker turn, and began to spiral out of control.

She needed to grieve for her daughter, but she didn't know when the hospital would release the body so they could have the funeral.

She needed to reach her other children and repair their relationships before she told them her secret and lost them for good.

She needed to figure out how to salvage Royce's career.

My God! If she needed to do one more thing, she might explode.

She was so absorbed in her thoughts, she didn't hear Royce talking to her right away. "Hmm… what?"

"I said, 'Snap out of it. We're here.' Are you sure you're up to this?"

"Given the situation, it must be important, or he wouldn't have called us out here. Let's go see what he wants."

Royce pressed some buttons at the entry, and the gate opened to a long, private drive.

Vanessa had always loved Stanford's house. Her home was beautiful, but his was quite grand. An estate, really. They drove along a tree-lined path until they came upon a large brick colonial with columns flanking the front porch and a ram's head pediment over the door. She often felt like Cinderella when entering their home, too plain for it in her usual attire and magically enhanced if she was there for a party. But that day she barely noticed where she was, let alone the splendor of place. She just wanted to hear what Stanford had to say and get back home.

Carlton, Stanford's butler, greeted them at the door. They had a housekeeper. Stanford and Joan had a butler. And that's why she usually felt like the cinder part of Cinderella at the Hammond residence.

"Dr. Keller. Mrs. Keller. My condolences on your loss."

"Thank you, Carlton," Royce said.

Vanessa could only sniffle and nod.

"Dr. Hammond is waiting for you in the study, sir." He gestured to the study. "And the children?"

"They decided to stay home today," Royce said. "Sorry. I should have called."

"It's not a problem, sir. I'm sure this is difficult on them, too." They stepped into the hallway. "Ma'am? Mrs. Hammond asked that I take you to the conservatory before you join the gentlemen."

Vanessa nodded. "Okay." She raised her eyebrows and shoulders at Royce before they parted ways and she followed Carlton down the hall. He opened the door to the conservatory and led her inside where Joan stood to hug her.

"Oh, Vanessa. I'm so sorry."

"Thanks, Joan."

"Can I get anything else, ma'am?"

"No, thank you. That will be all, Carlton."

The elderly man nodded and made a discreet exit.

Joan showed Vanessa to some comfortable seats near a large ficus plant. She held a plate out to her. "Biscotti? Tea?"

Vanessa shook her head. "So, what's this all about?"

"Stanford is talking to Royce right now about the seriousness of his situation. And you need to hear that. We'll join them soon. But we need to know if Royce knows how bad things are."

"I'm not sure I know what you mean."

"You know Stanford has always been more than just a boss to Royce. He's been a mentor. A friend. A confidant."

"Yes. Of course." Vanessa didn't know where Joan was going with her line of questioning, but she didn't like it. She poured a cup of tea so she had something to do with her hands and waited for Joan to continue.

"Royce isn't the only one, though. Ben and Wade went through at the same time. Stanford was close with all of them."

"I see." Vanessa took a sip of tea and studied Joan over the rim of her cup. Joan looked as nervous as she felt, which only gave her the slightest bit of relief.

"Ben came to Stanford years ago. Almost eighteen years ago. Told him about a terrible thing he had done. His marriage was already in ruins. He was afraid his relationship with his best friend was going to follow suit."

Vanessa took another sip of tea, but didn't say anything.

"Stanford told him to wait it out. Maybe no one had to know. But then… well. It became obvious something had happened."

"Obvious to whom?"

"Come on, Vanessa. He had an affair. I'm assuming he took Stanford's advice. He obviously didn't tell his wife who the woman was. Or his friends.

The aftermath would have been catastrophic on so many levels if he had. His silence salvaged all the important relationships, save one. His own marriage, which, by his own account, was over anyway."

Vanessa put her tea down on the serving cart with a little more force than she intended. "What do you want from me, Joan?"

"Fine. I'll stop beating around the bush. It's obvious Ben stayed quiet all these years because of you. But it's time you break the silence, Ness. Royce is going to need to mount a defense, and he can't do that if he doesn't have all the facts. He'll be going to battle without his guns fully loaded."

"That's not something that ever has to come out."

"You don't know what will come out during the investigation."

"I don't see why that information would."

"Better to be prepared than blindsided."

"I'll take my chances, thanks."

"Do you really think that's wise? You're playing with a man's life here."

"And how do you know any of this?"

Joan's face was blank for a moment. She blinked, and she took a long time before finally answering. Vanessa didn't think she was going to say anything at all, but finally she said, "He's my husband, Ness. We tell each other everything."

That baffled Vanessa. She couldn't remember the last time she and Royce had shared any meaningful details about their days with each other. That was, before Hope's death.

"Joan, how long have you known about Ben?"

"What do you mean?"

"Did Stanford just tell you today so you could talk to me?"

"We talked about it today and decided I should talk to you."

"But was today the first you'd heard of it?"

"No. I've known since it happened."

"And you never treated me…."

"How? How should I have treated you?"

Vanessa didn't know.

"I'm ready to see what Stanford has to say." She rose and headed toward the study, effectively cutting off anything further Joan had to say.

CHAPTER 7

"I JUST DON'T BELIEVE IT," Royce said. "It doesn't make any sense."

"What's going on?" Vanessa asked as she stepped into the room.

Royce looked at his watch, but he couldn't focus on the dial. Of course, it felt like he had lived three lifetimes in the last twenty-four hours, so who the hell cared what time it really was? Logic told him it was only morning, but he couldn't wait for that day to be over so he could crawl into bed.

Bed. Where the hell was he going to sleep? The guest room again? Exiled in his own home? The alternative, though... . The thought of lying next to Vanessa after her betrayal made him sick to his stomach. He sat down and held his head in his hands.

"Briefly bringing you up to speed," Stanford said, "Hope's death is under investigation because the symptoms of her death indicate she died from receiving the wrong blood, not from the seriousness of her injuries. Although it's likely she wouldn't have survived anyway, so Royce has that in his favor. The burden is on the two of you to prove Royce had no idea his blood wasn't a match."

"Of course I didn't know," Royce snapped.

"No, he didn't," Vanessa said quietly.

"Well, Wade is implying otherwise."

"Wade? He's one of Royce's best friends. He wouldn't do that."

"It's got to be Ellie. She hates me."

"Ellie doesn't hate you," Stanford said. "And I'm telling you, Wade's the one who called HA and the police."

"Wait, what?" Vanessa said. "The police?"

"I'm telling you, this is more serious than you think," Stanford said. "At first, I thought Wade just wanted your job, maybe your promotion."

"It's not Wade," Royce said.

"It is Wade. And it's more than just your job. He called the cops. He told them he believes you knew Hope wasn't yours and you did the transfusion anyway, hoping it looked like an accident so you could… well, you know. Your history with her isn't exactly a secret."

"What are you talking about?"

"No one who has seen the two of you together would nominate you for Father of the Year where she's concerned."

Royce winced. "So?"

"Sorry, son, but now's not the time to pull my punches. Point is, what happened in the ER doesn't look good. Ellie said you didn't even know it was Hope when she came in."

"But shouldn't that be in my favor? How could I try to kill someone I didn't recognize?"

"It was a crime of opportunity. When you realized you had a chance to eliminate a problem, you seized your chance."

"That's ridiculous," Vanessa said. "Hope isn't… Hope *wasn't* a problem. Not only did Royce not know about Hope's parentage, he would never hurt her if he did."

"So you're finally admitting it?" Royce turned on her.

"That point is moot. What we should be focusing on now is what to do from here."

"Who was it, Ness?"

"What?"

He stood up and looked at her. Her eyes were wide. Deer-in-headlights, kid-with-hand-in-cookie-jar wide. She glanced all around the room, her gaze finally landing on Stanford, a silent plea for help.

And the other shoe dropped. Royce followed her gaze and looked in disbelief at his mentor. "Do you know?"

"What I know is immaterial."

"How could you keep this from me? You've been like—"

"I know, son." Stanford walked toward him.

"Don't call me son!" Royce spun away, closed his eyes, and rocked. Nothing soothed the roiling tide of pressure and emotions in his head.

"Royce. I'm sorry. But I wasn't keeping it from you. It wasn't my secret to tell. Besides, who knows doesn't matter. It's where you go from here that matters."

Royce spun to face his mentor. "No. I think who knows what does matter. And I think who the father is matters." He stalked to Vanessa and grabbed her by the arms. "Why'd you tell Stanford and not me?"

She swallowed and shook her head.

"*Why!*"

"*Royce!*" Stanford crossed to them and pulled them apart.

Royce breathed heavily and strode away from them so as not to reach for either of them again. "Why the hell am I the last one to know everything? You've both kept this secret from me and it ruined my life!"

"I'm sorry, Royce," Vanessa said. "I really am."

"That's not going to bring Hope back."

Vanessa grabbed a crystal tumbler off the bar and hurled it at him, striking him in the head with it. "I lost her, too, damn it! You aren't the only one hurting here!"

Royce reached up and touched his temple with two fingers. He had a gash on his hairline and blood trickled down the side of his face. "Are you serious? Did you just throw a glass at me?"

She covered her mouth with her hand. "I didn't mean to. I don't know what came over me. You were shaking me and blaming me and I—"

"Stop it," Stanford said. He walked over to Royce and gave him a handkerchief. "Both of you. Right now. The horror you've gone through in just the last twenty-four hours was more than most people face in one lifetime."

"Most people don't have that horror brought on them by their own wives."

"I said I'm sorry!"

"That's not going to fix it!"

"Enough!" Stanford said.

Royce went to the bar and got some ice for his head. Even though Vanessa sat there on a bar stool, he sat beside her, too exhausted to walk away. He couldn't believe just yesterday morning he was discussing toasters with his son and looking forward to Spring Carnival. He didn't even feel like the same person.

"Now, no one could have predicted Hope would end up in your ER," Stanford said to Royce. "You should have recognized her. You shouldn't have worked on her. You shouldn't have transfused her. You made mistakes."

"I only—"

"All that aside, though," Stanford continued as though he hadn't been interrupted, "you thought you were saving her life. There will be a police investigation. Because of Wade." He held up his hand to ward off more interruptions. "The Dean of Hospital Administration told me himself. It was Wade who reported it. Not Ellie. She told me. No one else. Wade is the one who turned you in. And the hospital is conducting its own investigation. I'm certain the police will clear you. But I don't know what their investigation will turn up. You need to be prepared for the dirtiest of laundry to be aired. The dirtiest."

He turned to Vanessa. "And my dear, that applies to you as well. These investigations will not stop at just Royce. They will affect your life. And very likely Jensen's and Faith's. You and Royce need to have some frank discussions with each other and with the kids, before all this becomes public knowledge. Everyone needs to hear from you before they hear from the rumor mills."

"I don't think it's going to get to that point."

"I know it is going to get to that point. And even if the truth didn't get out there, the lies that would spread would be far worse for your family to hear than what the truth actually is. You need to tell them. Before they get hurt."

Royce snorted. "I think that ship has sailed."

"I said I'm sorry about a million times. What more do you want?"

"What do I want? Uh, let's see. What I want is for you to tell me the truth so I'm prepared. What I really want is for you to not be a whore in the first place so none of this even becomes an issue."

She spun toward him and slapped him across the face.

"That's two," he said and put the ice down to rub the sting off his cheek. "Don't think about going for three."

"Don't call me names. I'm not a whore."

Stanford reached in between them a slapped a business card on the bar. "I'm a medical doctor. I thought maybe I could help you two see reason, but I'm definitely not trained for this."

"What are you talking about?" Royce asked.

"Call him. I know him well. I've already spoken with him and he's agreed to squeeze you in. Which is unheard of. People wait months to get on his calendar. He's doing this as a favor to me."

Royce read the card. "Tod Jeffers. Family Therapist. Tod with one D. Come on, Stanford. I'm not going to a therapist."

"He's actually a psychiatrist. But he finds people are more receptive if he leaves his titles off his card."

"I'd be more comfortable with it the other way," Royce said, "but I'm still not going."

"Actually, you are. This is another one of those hospital-mandated, not-a-request things."

"I thought I didn't work there anymore."

"You're suspended, not fired. And as part of the terms of your possible return, I'm telling you—you need to see someone for bereavement counseling, family therapy, and anger management issues."

"I don't need to manage my anger."

"Ellie told me she sent Security to your office yesterday because she thought you were attacking your wife."

"And didn't you witness my wife attack me twice in this very room today? If anyone needs counseling, it's her."

"You're going as a couple."

"I really don't think—" Vanessa started.

"I really don't care," Stanford said. "This might be the only way to save Royce's job. There needs to be some tangible proof your marriage is solid, or that you're working on it. That means you live in the same house—"

Royce didn't mean to react, but he gasped.

"That's right. I figured you planned on cutting out. Not going to happen. You're growing roots. You stay in that house, you go to social functions together, you stop causing public scenes. You go to counseling and address these issues. Get it together, at least as long as these investigations go on, or you're just throwing fuel on the fire. Got it?"

Royce and Vanessa both nodded.

"And when I say stay in that house, I mean in the same damn room. I told you yesterday and I meant it. You've got a housekeeper just itching to tell the world your lives are a mess."

"Lydia wouldn't do that," Royce said.

"Stop interrupting me. And she would do exactly that. I don't know how you've missed it all these years, but that woman has been doing her damnedest to weasel her way into your life. She hates Vanessa and will stop at nothing to get rid of her so she can have you to herself. She's a schemer, a manipulator, and at this point, one of your worst enemies."

"What are you talking about? Lydia's great. She'd never do anything to hurt me."

Stanford shook his head. "You're blind to the situation. Do not give her any ammunition. She will use it against you. So that means no sleeping on the couch. No staying at a friend's. You both sleep in the master. If you refuse to share a bed, clean up after yourselves before she finds signs one of you was in a chair or on the floor. The whole world needs to see a united front from you until this is over—and that goes double for Lydia."

Royce sighed. "And what if this is over now?"

Vanessa's head whipped up and spun toward him. He knew she wanted to meet his gaze, try to see if he was just being mean or if he meant what he said. But he wouldn't give her the satisfaction of turning her way. She hadn't given him any satisfaction in years. Why should he help her out?

"Don't say or do anything now that you'll regret later," Stanford said. He nudged the card toward Royce. "Call and make the appointment."

Royce glanced at his watch. "He's probably with someone now. I'll call tomorrow morning before appointments start."

"That's his personal number on that card. And he's waiting for your call. He'll answer."

Royce dialed the number.

A man answered on the second ring. *"Tod Jeffers."*

"Hello… Tod. This is… Dr. Royce Keller. Stan—"

"Royce! Yes. Glad to hear from you. I was expecting your call."

"I see. Well…."

"So, Stanford tells me you and Vanessa would like to come in for a chat or two."

"Uh, well…."

"How's tomorrow sound? Ten-thirty?"

"Tomorrow? Ten-thirty?" Royce looked at Vanessa.

She shrugged.

"Sure. I guess that will be fine."

"Splendid. You have my card?"

"Yes. Stanford gave it to me."

"Wonderful. The address is on there. I'll see you both tomorrow." Dr. Jeffers ended the call before Royce could say another word.

He felt like fresh asphalt. Hot and steamrolled. "Damn it, Stanford."

"I don't want to hear it." Stanford put his hand up and walked behind the bar. He poured himself a drink and downed it in one gulp. "He's the best I know, and I expect you to make use of his services. Both of you. Don't just go through the motions but actually participate in the program."

"There's a program?"

"How the hell do I know?" Stanford asked. "My marriage and career are fine. I never needed counseling."

Royce glared at him.

"Make this work, Royce. Because, honestly, I don't know what I can do to save you on this one. It was bad enough when we were dealing with office politics and missing meds trying to get your promotion to go through."

"I didn't steal the meds."

"I know you didn't. But someone did. And now, with your character impugned, you become suspect number one, whether they have proof or not. We've got a whole shit storm to deal with on top of the pharmaceutical thefts just trying to save your job. So I'll say it again. Make this work. Now go home."

Royce led Vanessa to the car and they left the Hammond estate in silence. After they were on the road for a while, Vanessa said, "I really am sorry."

"For what, Ness? Slapping me? Hitting me with a glass? Lying to me for all these years? Cheating on me?"

She was silent for a while, then she finally said, "Yes."

"Yes, what?"

"Yes. I'm sorry for all of it."

He sighed. "Are you going to tell me who? Why? How long? How the hell it happened?"

"It's a complicated story, Royce. And we're at the school. I don't think, when we look back at the moment we had this conversation, we're going to want to remember having it in the front seat of your car in the parking lot of the kids' school."

Seeing Jensen's car, he pulled up beside it and put his car in park. "I don't think we're ever going to look back on that story fondly, Ness. Do you think it really matters where we are when you tell me?"

She turned toward him and rested her head against the headrest. "Do you think we'll be together long enough to ever look back?"

He searched her face for a while, then he turned and looked at the horizon. It didn't matter where he looked, he didn't find answers anywhere. "I don't know, Ness. At the moment, it's not looking likely."

He heard her trying to stifle her sobs. On reflex, he reached for her, but he pulled his hand back and let her go. It wasn't his responsibility to comfort her anymore. She apparently had someone else in her life she could turn to for comfort. Someone she loved enough to share her body with, so why not her grief as well?

That's probably who she had been frantically texting since Hope had died.

He needed to get a look at her phone.

In that respect, staying in the master suite was a good thing. It gave him the access he needed to get the answers no one was willing to give him. Maybe his bad luck could be put to good use soon.

He reached in his pocket and took out Jensen's keys. "Pull yourself together and take Jensen's car home. I'll go get the kids' things and follow along shortly."

As soon as Vanessa took the keys, Royce got out of the car. He didn't wait to see if she composed herself or left the parking lot. He just walked into the school without a backward glance. Seeing Vanessa in pain was always hard for him. If he couldn't be around her when she cried without instinctively trying to comfort her, he just wouldn't be around her.

Inside, Mrs. Prindle met him by the door. She stood in the hallway to the principal's office like a good little sentinel, making certain he didn't get past her. "Mr. Pendleton is busy and can't be disturbed."

She didn't even greet him.

Apparently the good will and sympathy from Hope's untimely death had run its course. The rumor mill must have made its way to Cathedral Lake Prep.

"I'm not here to see him, Charlotte." She gasped when he used her first name. "I'm here to pick up my kids' things. Vanessa sent a message this morning telling you one of us would be by."

She pursed her lips. "Yes, we got her message. But what makes you think we have all the free time in the world that we can just drop everything and do what you command?"

"Excuse me?"

"You heard me. A druggie for a daughter. A harlot for a wife! You, a doctor fired for malpractice. You don't belong here. We don't have to jump when you bellow anymore, doctor."

Royce's vision began to cloud with a haze of red, and he clenched his fists and took a few deep breaths before answering the old crone. "Are you telling me you're holding my children's possessions hostage, Charlotte? My dead daughter's? My valedictorian son's?"

"Valedictorian? We'll see about that! You've marched through my doors looking down on me one time too many. Now the truth is out. And you're getting everything you deserve."

"Your doors?" The woman was mad. He'd always disliked her, but he never thought she was unstable. Certainly not as spiteful and hateful as she'd proven herself to be. Why was she so jealous? Didn't she have anything better to do than harbor such resentment? He'd never treated her badly, had he? Then he realized he didn't care. "I want my kids' things. Now."

She reached behind the desk and hauled out a large box labeled TRASH. "As it turns out, I made some time to box up their things. I wanted all traces of your family gone as soon as possible. Don't let the door hit you, and all that. Or do, I really couldn't care less."

"You know, Charlotte, I could have you fired for speaking to me this way."

"Maybe if your family still had any clout here. But you don't. You're done, Royce. Your family violated the morality clause and you're out of here. You're everything that's wrong with society today, and this school is just too good for you. Now get out."

Royce took the box and left without another word. She wasn't worth responding to. There were probably plenty more Mrs. Prindles out there just waiting to dish out more of the same, or worse. He shook his head as he carried the box to the car. Mrs. Prindle was a little crazy, and prone to overreacting. But she already had heard rumors, and ones that weren't even true. If the grapevine had reached the school, how much of the town was talking about his family already? What were they saying? And how were they reacting?

CHAPTER 8

DESPITE VANESSA'S DESIRE FOR THE day to just end, it was going to be a long time before she could shrug off the horrors of the day and bury her head under the covers. Once Royce got home, the next order of business would be facing their children.

Their children—even though Royce kept saying otherwise.

When Royce pulled into the driveway, she went to meet him in the garage. "How do you want to handle this?" she asked as he got out of the car.

He sighed. "Might as well do it like you pull off a bandage. Fast. The more we drag it out, the worse it's going to be. Of course…."

"What?"

"Nothing."

"What? You *want* to see me suffer?"

He sighed. "I wouldn't put your kids through that."

"Our kids, Royce. *Our* kids."

He turned toward her. "You keep saying that, but come on, Ness. I'm not an idiot. I'm testing Jensen, and we'll go from there."

"You can test them both. They're yours. And what does it matter, anyway? You raised them. Could you really walk away from them at this point?"

That she couldn't read the look on his face scared her. They'd grown apart over the last, well, several years, really, but she'd always been able to tell what he was thinking. Even when she didn't like what it was.

"Let's get this over with." He headed toward the door.

She chased after him and stopped him with a hand on his arm, a hand he looked at with disgust. At least she could read that expression. She dropped her hand and said, "But we still need a game plan."

"I don't want to go over this any more than I need to."

"Well, I want to be prepared. We should at least figure out where we're going to talk to them. And who's going to do the talking."

"We can talk in the sunroom. And you can do the talking," he said. "It's your story, after all."

Again he reached for the door, and again she stopped him.

"Vanessa." He looked at her hand on his arm and then into her eyes. "I'm on the edge right now. You're really pushing it."

She dropped her hand. "Not the sunroom."

He raised an eyebrow, but didn't respond.

"Hope loved that room."

Royce still said nothing, but he didn't walk away, either.

"Besides, we need somewhere private. Stanford said we have to show the world a united front. That means we can't risk Lydia overhearing this story. Or did you plan on sharing it with her?"

"Who I choose to trust is my business, Ness. Apparently you have someone you share everything with. You have no right questioning me about my confidants."

"But Stanford said—"

"I know what Stanford said. But it's me on the line. *My* career. *My* life. Let me handle things my way."

Tears welled in her eyes.

He sighed. "We can talk to the kids in my study. We'll close the doors. That should afford you the privacy you're looking for."

She sniffled. "Fine. But I'm still sending Lydia home for the rest of the day."

"Then what difference does it make where the hell we talk to the kids?"

"Just not the sunroom."

He shook his head and opened the door. "Kids!"

Lydia came running before either Jensen or Faith appeared. "Dr. Keller. How are you doing? Can I get you anything?"

"You know what, Lydia?" Vanessa said before Royce could answer. "We really just need some time alone with our family. You may go home now."

"Dr. Keller," she turned toward Royce.

"Really, Lydia," he said, giving Vanessa the support she'd been waiting nearly two decades for. "We just need some time to grieve as a family. We'll be back to business as usual tomorrow."

Vanessa cleared her throat, but he ignored her.

"Go on home now, and we'll see you at your usual time tomorrow."

"Actually, tomorrow—" Vanessa started.

"If you're certain you don't need anything else today," Lydia said.

"I'm sure," Royce said.

"I thought you might want some comfort food, so I have a pan of lasagna in the oven. It's baked off already. It's just in there to stay warm. And I made Faith a pan of eggplant, spinach, and Portobello mushrooms. There's also a tossed salad in the fridge, garlic bread in the freezer, and a pineapple upside down cake on the counter. I left the nuts off and put extra cherries in all the holes."

"Just the way I like it. Thank you, Lydia."

"No nuts on any of it? Half? A corner?" Vanessa asked.

"I forgot you like it that way. There are no nuts on it. Anywhere."

"Forgot," Vanessa muttered, and sniffed.

"Call if you need me, Dr. Keller." She walked out.

"Might as well eat this for lunch and just talk to the kids while we eat," Royce said.

"She probably put carrots in the sauce," Vanessa said.

"What?"

"Never mind. I don't think we should talk to the kids until they've eaten something. Jensen might eat, but Faith won't eat a bite if she gets upset."

"She's already upset. Besides, you're thinking of Hope. She's the one who doesn't eat when she's upset. Faith is a nervous eater. She's probably been nibbling on fruit or something since she woke up. It wouldn't surprise me if she's too full to eat."

"Let's get them in here and find out."

They called the kids again, and this time they came into the kitchen. Both of them had red-rimmed eyes, and Faith had a carrot in her hand.

"See what I mean?" Royce said.

"We're going to eat our big meal for lunch," Vanessa said, and took the salad out of the refrigerator. "Later we can munch on sandwiches or leftovers for dinner."

"I don't know if I'm really hungry," Jensen said.

"Lydia made lasagna," Royce said.

"You know I don't eat dairy." Faith said.

"Lydia made you some kind of layered vegetable thing," Vanessa said.

Royce got the food out of the oven while Vanessa set the table. Faith stifled a sob when Vanessa realized her mistake and had to put the fifth place setting back.

"Look, this is going to take some getting used to, but we're going to have to do it, so we might as well start doing it now," Royce said.

They sat at the kitchen table, the only sounds the scraping of forks and the occasional sniffle. Hope's empty seat became a glaring beacon during the meal, until Vanessa couldn't take it any longer. "Maybe this isn't a good idea. We shouldn't be eating here. We shouldn't be doing this. I can't do this!"

She pushed back from the table, knocking her chair over, and ran from the room. When she ran, she had no plan. She didn't know where she was going. Her feet carried her straight to the sunroom, to Hope's favorite pillow. She dropped to her knees and grabbed it, holding it to her face and breathing in deeply to take in her daughter's scent.

Fabric softener.

Lydia.

Vanessa distantly heard a grief-stricken wail, a howl so deep and mournful that she only recognized on a cellular, maternal level the kind of pain the woman who uttered it must be feeling. Only after she felt arms on her, pulling her up into a strong embrace, stroking her hair and rocking her with a soft, soothing rhythm, did she realize that far-off keening bawl was her. For the first time since Hope's death, she allowed herself to breakdown and cry. Not the tears she had let escape earlier, but the gut-wrenching, energy-sapping sobs the death of a daughter deserved.

She didn't know how long she devolved into the mess only remotely resembling Hope's mother, but she finally pulled herself together. She'd soaked the blue pillow with green piping with her tears. If it had smelled like Hope, it wouldn't any longer, so it was a good thing the smell had already been ruined. At least she didn't have to blame herself for losing that tenuous hold on her baby girl.

Sitting back, she realized she was in Royce's arms. Jensen and Faith were nowhere in sight. "Are you done?" he asked.

She nodded.

He dropped his arms and stepped away. "In the future, it would probably be best if you could contain your outbursts for when your children aren't around."

"I didn't see that one coming. Lydia washed the pillows."

"What?"

"We told her not to, but she did it anyway."

"So what? They probably needed it."

Vanessa picked up the tear-stained pillow and thrust it at Royce. "This was Hope's favorite. She always used this one. It still smelled like her! Now even that's gone! Lydia had no right! I specifically told her not to touch them!"

Royce sat down and rubbed his head with both hands before resting his elbows on his knees and staring at her. "I had no idea what that meant to you, Ness, or I would have been more insistent with Lydia."

She looked at the pillow and rubbed the surface. "She should have listened to *me.*"

He sighed.

"I can't live like this anymore, Royce."

"It won't be for much longer," he said. "There will be a lot of changes in our lives soon."

She looked at him. "Like what?"

"We'll deal with them as they come. They're already starting. Like lunch today. For now, we have to have a talk with the kids. Let's go. They're waiting in my study."

Vanessa carried Hope's pillow in front of her like a shield. She needed some kind of protection from that pending conversation, and apparently that pillow was the only buffer she'd be getting.

In the study, Jensen and Faith sat beside each other on a leather loveseat tucked into a bay window. Instead of taking one of the two club chairs facing them, Royce went behind his desk, leaving Vanessa alone in the "hot seat." She sat in the club chair closest to the kids and looked at Royce. He merely gestured for her to begin.

Like she had any clue where to start.

She'd told him at dinner she wanted more control. Now she had it.

"So, you know about Hope's accident and how she ended up in the ER."

"Are we really going to go into all the details?" Jensen asked. "Because I really don't think I want them."

"Yeah," Faith said.

"No. No details," Vanessa said. "But there are some things you need to know. Some things people are going to be talking about, gossiping about. And you deserve the truth. So you know how to respond. Or, even better, can choose not to respond at all, and can do so with dignity."

Royce snickered.

"What'd Hope do?" Jensen asked.

"No. It's nothing like that." Vanessa looked at Royce.

He merely lifted an eyebrow and left her to feel her way through the conversation on her own.

"Okay, well, you see, when Hope ended up in Daddy's ER, he shouldn't have worked on her. But he did, which breaks protocol. And he broke regulations again by giving her his blood without testing it first for a match. So he's in some serious trouble for that."

"Dad, why?" Faith asked.

"Seriously, Vanessa? This is the story you're telling? What about your part?"

"I'm getting to it." She clutched and re-clutched the pillow, hoping to receive some relief. But none came.

"And there's the alcohol."

"Vanessa...."

"Okay. On top of those infractions, someone accused him of doing the bad transfusion on purpose, so in addition to the hospital investigation, there's going to be a criminal investigation."

"Why would he want to... kill Hope?" Faith asked.

"Why would his blood kill Hope?" Jensen asked. "Dad?"

"Vanessa?"

"Well," Vanessa said, massaging the pillow, "that's where my part comes in. You see, since Hope was born, I knew she wasn't your father's. Biologically, that is. But I never told him. He thought she was, so he thought he could save her. Not everyone believes that story, so they think he used her accident as a convenient way of eliminating a problem."

Everyone was silent for a moment, then the kids jumped to their feet and the yelling began, beginning with Faith and alternating between her and Jensen.

"Wait! Hope wasn't Dad's?"

"You *cheated* on Dad?"

"So *I'm* not Dad's?"

"Am I even his?"

"Who's my father?"

"Would Hope be alive if you'd known, Dad?"

When Jensen turned his attention from Vanessa to Royce and asked that last question, the room fell silent again. Vanessa looked at him, too.

"I don't know, Jensen. I just don't know. Her injuries were… severe. Even if she had received the right blood… There was just so much wrong with her. My ego wants to say I could have brought her back, but pragmatically, I have to say her chances weren't good."

"Are you just saying that so we won't be as mad at"—Jensen looked at Vanessa—*"her?"*

"Jensen, she is your mother and you will treat her with respect."

"That's not an answer." The boy stood with his fists clenched while Faith wiped tears from her eyes.

"Being angry isn't going to solve anything," Royce said. "We need to circle the wagons right now."

"And that's going to solve our problems?" Jensen said. "Hope's gone. You're in trouble. We don't even know who our fathers are." He used his thumb to gesture to him and his sister.

"Yes, you do," Vanessa said. "Nothing's changed."

"Everything's changed!" Faith yelled and ran from the room.

"Way to go, Mom. You know, if we had to pick a parent who wasn't ours biologically—"

"Don't finish that sentence, Jensen," Vanessa interrupted.

"It doesn't matter. You know the answer." He turned to Royce. "Just for clarity, I'd like a paternity test."

"I figured you would."

"It doesn't change anything. I'd just like to know."

"I'll take care of it in the morning."

"I'm going to my room. I won't be back down today. 'Night. Dad."

"Good… good night, I guess, Jensen."

Vanessa reached for him, but he walked around her and out of the room. She sighed, nestled into the club chair she'd been sitting on, and clutched the pillow to her chest. "Well, that could have gone better."

"The worst is over. By tomorrow, they'll realize they should be angry with me, too."

St. Royce? Never. "Doubtful."

"I guess we'll see. I, for one, have had enough for the moment. The kids already put the food away while you were having your meltdown in the sunroom, and I have no qualms about leaving the dishes for Lydia, so I'm going for a ride, and then I'll probably come home and take a nap. I didn't get much sleep last night, and I'm kind of tired."

"Yeah, I'm pretty tired, too."

"So you're going upstairs now?"

"Yes, Royce. I'm going up to the bedroom we share. Now. I waited for you to come to bed all night last night. I'm exhausted. Do you have a problem with that?"

"I suppose it doesn't really matter, does it?"

"No. No, it doesn't." His lack of argument answered her question. He didn't want to share their room any longer, but he was going to anyway. She didn't know when, but at some point that evening, he'd be joining her in their room.

He stood, grabbed the newspaper, and walked out.

Vanessa walked upstairs and paused at Hope's door just long enough to open it and look inside. It was just as she had left it. She reached around the door, locked it, and pulled it closed behind her. That should be enough of a deterrent to keep Lydia out of it, at least until Royce had a chance to speak to her about boundaries.

She tried to check on Faith and Jensen, but both of them had their doors locked as well. She didn't force the issue. Instead, she continued down the hall and walked into the master suite. That had always been something of a retreat to her, the dark woods set off against the pale linens and walls reminding her of some of the luxurious hotels Royce had taken her to over the years. Even when she felt she had been sharing her retreat with a stranger, she felt relaxed in her oasis. But for the first time in her life, it began to feel like a prison. The furniture looked harsh against industrially light walls and textiles, and her husband had become nothing more than a hostile cellmate.

She sat at her vanity to remove her jewelry and makeup. The earrings Royce bought her in Florence. The bracelet he gave her for their fifteenth anniversary with the locket charm on it that had his photo on one side and the kids' on the other. The watch she just had to have from that little boutique downtown. Her St. Luke medal, which she always wore as a constant prayer for her physician husband. Her family ring: two emerald stones for the girls' birthdays in May, one diamond for her in April, and two rubies for the guys in July. They always teased her and called it her Italian flag ring. They could call it whatever they wanted. She loved it. Then she took off her engagement ring, a gorgeous solitaire well over a carat, topping the charts on all the other Cs. Her husband really knew how to pick out jewelry. She left her wedding band on. She hadn't taken it off since he'd put it on her finger in the church twenty-three years ago and promised to love her forever. She wondered how long that promise would hold.

The makeup-removing wipes sat next to a family portrait, and she turned the picture toward the wall before opening the container. No need to add more tears to the mix. She scrubbed her face until it turned rosy from cleanser and friction. That was the only color her skin was going to see for a while. She looked pasty, drained. There were shadows under her red-rimmed, bloodshot eyes. For the foreseeable grief-stricken future, it would be pointless to bother with cosmetics. Max Factor himself couldn't help her. It was what it was.

Unwinding her hair, she let her fingers run through it and rub her scalp. Royce used to love to play with her hair. That was the only reason she kept it long. He liked it that way. It had been years since he'd so much as wrapped a tress around a finger, though. She massaged her head, hoping to alleviate some of the tension collecting in her temples and neck, but to no avail.

Miserable and exhausted, she didn't care that it was only mid-afternoon. She craved the comfort of her bed. It would be so easy to just bury herself under the covers and sleep for weeks.

She turned when Royce walked in. Before she could say anything, he started arranging blankets and pillows on the floor at the foot of the bed.

"I thought you were going for a ride."

"I'm too tired. And I didn't really have anywhere to go."

"Oh."

"Listen, Ness?" But he didn't say anything more.

"Yes?"

"People are starting to talk."

"How do you know?"

"The paper."

"Of course, the newspaper." All the latest technology at their disposal, and Royce insisted on reading a paper copy of the news. Of all things.

She shook her head, disgusted.

He continued, ignoring her irritation. "Yesterday's news focused on the missing meds from the hospital and the local dog fighting ring they can't find. Today was all about… us."

"Okay."

"It's not pretty."

"I didn't think it would be."

"I just wanted you to be prepared."

She rubbed her temples again. How could she prepare for any of this? She watched him fluff his pillow and wiggle as he tried to get comfortable on the floor. "What are you doing?"

"Getting ready for a nap."

"On the floor?"

"I don't see a better alternative."

She bit back the scathing retort on the tip of her tongue. Instead, she said, "If you won't sleep in the bed, why don't you use a chair?" She glanced over to the two overstuffed chairs near their television.

"Because I can't stretch out on a chair." He rolled over, presenting her with his back.

"Royce, are you sure you don't want to—"

"Just leave me alone. Maybe we'll trade off on who gets the bed each night."

She sighed. "I think I'm going to take a shower." She walked into the bathroom. The man was insufferable. Sleeping on the floor. Like that was necessary. They'd shared a bed for decades, and if the last few years were any indication, they could easily lie beside each other and not touch. But he had to make a statement of his disapproval. If he'd only listen, give her a chance to explain… Who was she kidding? That would never happen. She might as well buy a damn cot for him. He'd made up his mind. He was going to freeze her out, make her miserable, try to get her to crack. And he was succeeding. She was miserable.

And it was only the beginning.

CHAPTER 9

ROYCE LISTENED FOR THE SOUND of running water. While Vanessa showered, he would take the opportunity to go through her things. He had to get a look at her phone.

Nothing like playing secret-agent in his own home. Who would have thought he'd ever spy on his wife? Things sure had changed in such a short time.

When he was certain she was in the shower, he grabbed her phone off the charger and went to type in the numerical password. She'd used the same four-digits for everything since college. It was her alarm code, her ATM code... Hell, he wouldn't be surprised if her computer passwords were that number repeated twice with an ampersand in between.

Anger surged through him when he realized she'd changed her phone password from the four-digit numerical code to an indeterminate alphanumeric one.

Like he had suggested to her for years. And she had ignored for, oh, ever.

Why had she gone and listened at the most inopportune time?

He could try and guess the new password, but if he guessed wrong too many times, her phone would lock. And if she tried to use it before it unlocked, he'd be busted.

If she was smart enough to realize what had happened.

Which, to be honest, she was.

While he sat there considering his options, her phone rang.

It startled him so much, he nearly dropped it. The water still ran, so he knew she hadn't heard it. Maybe the person on the other end was the person with the answers. But would he have the courage to answer it? He looked at caller ID.

Ben Lyndon.

Why the *hell* was his best friend calling his wife and not him?

Four rings. Another and it would go to voice mail. The decision would be made for him. Curiosity and anger far outweighed any fear or sense of propriety he felt. He swiped his finger across the screen.

"Ben?"

There was just the slightest hesitation before Ben answered. *"Royce? I thought I called Vanessa."*

"You did. Why?"

"I was returning her call."

"What did she want?"

"I don't know, man. That's what I was calling to find out."

Royce let go of the breath he didn't even realize he'd been holding. "Sorry, Ben. It's been a rough couple of days."

"I know. I'm sorry. About everything."

"Thanks."

"How're you holding up?"

"I'm barely keeping it together. The kids need a rock, though, so…"

"You need anything, you just let me know."

Royce was quiet for a moment. "You know, Stanford said something."

"He did?"

"Yeah. Wait. Why? What do you know?"

"Huh? About what?"

"What?"

"What are you talking about, Royce? What did Stanford say?"

None of that made any sense, but Royce didn't have time to dwell on it. "He said Wade reported me. He said he's been jealous and resentful of me for years. Did you know that?"

"Well, I don't work with the two of you, and we don't hang out like we used to, but it was kind of obvious. Even to me."

"Really? I never saw it."

"People only see what they want to see."

"And I didn't want to see one of my best friends making an ass of me?"

Ben sighed. *"No. You didn't want to see someone you cared for being petty and vindictive."*

"But other people could see it?"

"Yeah, buddy. Other people could see it. The signs were there."

"Why didn't you tell me?"

"Then I'd look petty and vindictive."

Royce sighed for what felt like the hundredth time that day. He really just wanted a nap. He heard the shower water turn off. "Listen, Vanessa was in the shower, but I just heard the water turn off. You want me to tell her you're on the phone?"

"Sure."

Royce knocked on the bathroom door.

"I'll be out in a minute. Geez."

"Ben's on the phone, returning your call," he called through the door.

The door flew open. Vanessa had a towel wrapped around her and was wrapping another around her hair. She reached her hand out and said, "Gimme that." Then, snatching the phone from him, she closed the door on him before he even had a chance to say goodbye.

It wasn't long before he heard her blow dryer running.

When she came out twenty minutes later, her hair was dry and she was in her pajamas. She plugged her phone back into the charger, turned out the lights, and climbed into bed. Despite the blinds being drawn, the room was only semi-dark. He could make out her face in the shadows.

Royce couldn't stand not knowing. "So, what was that about?"

"I'm missing a credit card. I was hoping it fell out of my purse and was in his car. I left him several messages about it. He was finally getting back to me about it."

"Everything that's happened and you were worried about a credit card? How did you even realize it was missing?"

"Well, money may be an issue now, right? I'm trying to be more careful. And not only do I want to prevent identity theft, that's the card I plan on using at the funeral home. But as it turns out, I didn't lose the card. It was tucked behind another one in my wallet. So it was all for nothing."

"And you know that from the bathroom?"

"No. I know that from earlier today."

"Then why didn't you just leave Ben another message telling him not to worry about it?"

"Well, I kind of had a lot on my mind, didn't I?"

"Whatever."

"Have a nice nap, Royce."

He didn't answer her. Her story didn't quite make sense. His wife was a marketing genius, always quick with answers, but that didn't mean her answers—her lies—were bulletproof, and that story sure sounded like a lie to him. Although, she had managed to lie to him for the better part of the last eighteen years and he'd never noticed. What had Ben said? He only saw what he wanted to see. Well, his eyes were wide open from that minute forward. And he planned on seeing everything.

He tried to relax, but his mind reeled. Then Vanessa turned on her bedside lamp and started rummaging through her nightstand drawer.

"What are you doing?"

"I can't get settled. I'm looking for—here they are—for the sedative Stanford gave me."

He heard her fumble with the pills and then she turned off the light.

As much as he hated to admit it, she had a good idea. He got up and went into the bathroom where he had stored his bottle of pills. After taking one, he returned to the bedroom.

He made himself as comfortable as possible on his makeshift bed—the floor—and fell asleep. Despite the early hour, exhaustion claimed him. He managed to sleep straight through to the middle of the night, when he woke groggy and miserable. He was never taking one of those pills again. Knowing he was well past dinner but too early for breakfast, he crept downstairs, made coffee to clear his head, and sat outside with his thoughts to keep him company. They weren't good companions. He watched the sunrise with a scowl on his face.

Lydia came in early—ridiculously early, in fact—cleaned up from their lunch the day before, and started to make a Caprese frittata and fruit salad. While she worked and Vanessa still slept, Royce woke the kids and asked them to join him in his study. He closed the door behind them, making sure they had their privacy. He took swabs from his medical bag, swiped the inside of their mouths and put the tests back in his bag to take to the lab later. He didn't believe what Vanessa said, but he tested Faith anyway, if for no other reason than to end the argument once and for all.

By the time he finished, breakfast was ready. They ate their meal nearly as quietly as lunch the day before. When the chime of the doorbell sliced through the silence, Royce jumped. He glanced at his watch. Quarter to seven. "Who could be calling at this hour?"

"I'll get it, Dr. Keller."

"That's all right, Lydia." He got up from the table. "I'll get it."

Royce opened the door to a muscular man in jeans and a v-neck t-shirt standing on his porch. He tucked his sunglasses into his collar and squinted at Royce. "Dr. Keller?"

"Detective."

The corner of the man's mouth lifted. "Detective Tony Cooper. What gave it away?"

How snobby would it be if he said the clothes and shoes screamed cop? "What can I do for you, Detective?"

"I'd like to ask you a few questions, if I could. May I come in?" He started to step inside.

Royce held out his hand to block his way. "Regarding?"

"You know what it's regarding, sir. The death of Hope Keller."

"I'd like my attorney present before I answer any questions."

"Very well. I'd hoped to wrap all this up quickly, but that's your right. We can do this at the station in a more formal manner." He handed Royce his card. "When can you be there?"

"I'll give him a call now."

"Let me know when you're coming in. I expect to hear from you today." He put his sunglasses back on and grinned. "Or I'll be back. In a more *formal* manner."

"Understood. Detective."

Detective Cooper had already turned his back and was walking away, but gestured with two raised fingers to acknowledge he'd heard Royce's reply.

Royce shut the door and took his phone out of his pocket to call his attorney.

Vanessa descended the stairs, rubbing her temples, as the detective strode to his car. "I think Stanford messed up my dosage. I can't believe I slept all—" She stopped mid-step and looked at the door he had just closed. "Was that who and what I think that was?"

Royce just kept dialing. "Spencer Bradley, please... Dr. Royce Keller... Yes, I know how early it is. It's an emergency... He'll take my call... No, I'll hold... Very well. Your name?... Thank you."

"I take it he isn't in," Vanessa said.

"He's in. His assistant wouldn't put me through. But I expect to hear from him soon."

"But isn't Spencer's specialty contract law? He did our will."

"He also handles malpractice cases. That's why he's our attorney and not any of his partners."

"Does he have a partner who handles criminal law?"

"For God's sake, Ness. I'm not a criminal." His phone rang before he finished the sentence. "Spencer. Thanks for getting back to me. I need you. This morning, if possible. I'm being… Oh. You've heard already."

"We have our session with Tod this morning," Vanessa whispered.

He turned his back on her. Like the two even compared in importance.

"Now would be fine. I'll see you at the station. Let me call the detective and tell him we're on our way, then I'll call you back from the car… Great. Thanks." He hung up and looked at Vanessa. "I don't know how long I'll be. Make my excuses to Tod if I'm not there."

"I should come with you. For appearances. And moral support."

"That's not necessary."

"I insist."

They were wasting time. "Fine. But keep your mouth shut. And take your own car. Just in case you need to leave and go to Tod's without me."

She ran upstairs to get ready while he called Detective Cooper to make the arrangements. Then he left for the police station, not waiting for Vanessa to come back down. He didn't really care if she came or not, and he assumed she could find her own way. The drive, though long, went by far too quickly. He spent most of it on the phone with Spencer, apprising him of the situation and trying to prepare for the—what was it? An interview? An interrogation? But no amount of prep work could cut through his nerves. He was rattled.

Royce arrived first, so he waited in the parking lot. Vanessa got there before Spencer, and she charged out of the car.

"Are you telling me you couldn't even wait for me?"

"I needed to get here, Ness. And I had to call Spencer."

She huffed. "You just didn't want me to come. You hoped I wouldn't follow."

"No, I didn't want you to come. Not only do I not want to do this, I don't want you to witness it."

"Because you love me or because you hate me?"

He recoiled like he'd been slapped. After thinking about it, he said, "To be perfectly honest, a little bit of both."

She sighed and turned away from him. After a few minutes, she faced him and said, "Well, deal with it. For better or worse, I'm your wife, and we need to look like we're together. I'm here to support you."

"Fine."

They leaned against his car and waited for Spencer. After a few moments of silence, he gasped and said, "Ness. In the stress of everything, we completely forgot to call anyone."

"What do you mean?"

"Our parents. Our siblings. We haven't told anyone yet. While I'm in with Spencer and the detective, can you call our folks? It will give you something to do while you wait."

"But I wanted to be with you."

"You're showing your support. That's enough. Besides, I don't even know if they'll let you in. And we can't put those calls off any longer. Our families are going to be upset we've waited so long as it is."

"But what am I supposed to tell them?"

"Whatever you have to. Oh, here's Spencer. I have to go. Give me a hug in case someone's watching." He squeezed her and walked over to his attorney, not giving her a second thought. Better her making the calls than him.

Spencer Bradley climbed out of his Bentley, adjusted the silk tie inside the jacket of his designer suit, and shook Royce's hand. "Ready to do this?"

"No, but let's get it over with."

"Answer everything as honestly as you can, with as few details as possible. If I don't want you saying something, I'll let you know."

"Got it."

"Let's go," Spencer said.

Spencer stopped at Vanessa, who was staring at her phone like it was going to explode in her hand, and said, "Vanessa. Good to see you. Why don't you come inside with us?"

"Oh. Okay. Do you think they'll want to talk with me?"

"I don't think so. But it will be good for them to see the two of you walk in together. Put your arms around each other."

Royce draped his arm around her, trying desperately not to flinch or cringe.

"And try not to look so… terrified," Spencer said. "It makes you look like you have something to hide."

That one was even more difficult for him. He wasn't hiding anything, but the fear was palpable.

They walked into the station and asked the desk sergeant for Detective Cooper. He told them to take a seat, which none of them did, and soon the detective came out for them.

"Dr. Keller. Thanks for coming down so quickly. This shouldn't take long."

"This is Spencer Bradley, my attorney." Spencer nudged him. "And my wife, Vanessa."

"Pleasure. Ma'am, if you wouldn't mind waiting out here?"

"Ness? Make those calls, please."

Royce recognized her forced smile and watched her perch on a hard plastic seat. Then he and his attorney followed the detective to an interrogation room. He and Spencer took seats beside each other across the table from Cooper.

"Can I get you anything?" the detective asked.

"Actually, we both have appointments after this, so if we can just get on with it?" Spencer said.

"I see." The detective sat down, opened a file, and flipped through his notes. "Well, I won't beat around the bush, then, doc. Did you intentionally kill Hope Keller?"

"What? No!" Royce said, ignoring Spencer's hand on his arm.

"It's my understanding that you and Hope have had a strained relationship for years."

"That's not a question," Spencer said.

"Did you and Hope argue a lot?"

"She's a teenager."

"So that's a yes."

Royce looked at Spencer, who inclined his head.

"We may have had some differences of opinion regarding certain things."

"Is it true that you didn't get along because you knew she wasn't your biological child?"

"No, that's *not* true." Royce started to sweat. He knew the guy was trying to get to him, but he made it seem much worse than it really was.

"It's not true that you didn't get along, or it's not true that she wasn't yours biologically?"

"I thought we already established Hope and I didn't always see eye to eye."

"I'm not sure we've established anything yet. So you and Hope argued?"

"Sometimes. I'm her dad." He cleared his throat. "Was her dad."

"Were you? Biologically, that is?"

Royce glanced at Spencer, who nodded. "As far as I knew, yes. I was her father. In all senses of the word."

"As far as you knew? And what do you know now?"

"I don't know anything more than I knew before. But certain events indicate I might not be privy to all the pertinent information."

"Dr. Keller. Are you trying to say you aren't biologically Hope's father? Yes or no, please."

"I believe I'm trying damned hard not to say it."

"Royce," Spencer warned.

The corners of Cooper's eyes crinkled as he smiled for the first time. He sat back in his seat and shuffled through some papers. "Did you ever break protocol in the ER before?"

"No."

"In fact, you would write up anyone who tried to."

"Yes."

"And yet, you broke not one rule but two when Hope was there. You worked on a family member and you gave blood to an un-typed patient."

"I didn't know who she was when she came in."

"You didn't recognize your own daughter?"

Royce looked down at the table. There were scuffs all over it, presumably where handcuffs had scraped the surface. Would he be in a similar situation before the whole Hope-ordeal ended? He shook his head and his voice cracked. "No."

"Then why did you give her your blood?"

"Ellie—Nurse Vernor—noticed and pointed it out. That's how I knew it was safe. My blood should be compatible for my biological children."

"That doesn't seem like it's necessarily true," Cooper said.

"It has to do with alleles and antigens. I can get you information explaining how."

"But Miss Vernor didn't think it was safe?"

"She didn't know what I knew about my blood."

"Dr. Unger said you didn't react when you saw Hope's adverse reaction on the table."

"Wade would say that."

"Why?"

Spencer cleared his throat. Royce continued without addressing Wade's role in the inquisition. "I couldn't react. I was stunned. In shock. That shouldn't have been happening. Combined with the fact that she was my daughter… I was rendered immobile."

"So your statement is an unknown female came into your ER. When you realized who she was, you treated her with your own blood, knowing it to be a match. When it wasn't, shock prohibited you from performing further life-saving measures. You at no time knew the girl was not a blood relative of yours."

He was being awfully helpful for a detective. It felt like walking into a trap, but Royce had no choice but to agree. "That's correct."

"Would you take a lie detector test confirming that statement?"

"Yes."

"No, my client will not," Spencer said. "The burden of proof is on you, not him."

"I want to prove my innocence."

"No." Spencer remained firm on the matter.

"Very well," Detective Cooper said. "What can you tell me about the missing medication from your ER?"

"What does that have to do with Hope Keller's death?" Spencer asked.

"That's not really your concern, counselor."

"Don't answer that," Spencer said to Royce.

The detective stopped smiling and sat back in his seat, studying Royce.

And there was the trap Royce was waiting for. It felt pretty darn close to snapping shut on him.

Detective Cooper closed his folder. "That's all I need for now. I have a witness to talk to. I'll be in touch."

"What witness?" Spencer and Royce asked together.

"There was a witness to the accident. I need to get his statement. Make sure I have all the facts. Then I'll know how the state will want to proceed."

"What do all these things have to do with each other?" Spencer asked.

"Just tying up loose ends." He clapped the lawyer on the shoulder. "Like I said, I'll be in touch."

"I'll need the name of that witness," Spencer said.

"If this matter goes to trial, it'll be provided to you."

"I'm free to go?" Royce said.

"Do you have anything else to add?"

"No."

"Do you want to stay?"

"No."

"Then yes, you're free to go." He opened the door and ushered them back to the waiting area, where Vanessa sat, talking on the phone and crying.

Royce couldn't help but feel an enormous, if temporary, sense of relief.

He was relieved he didn't have to take the lie detector test, which he didn't know if he could pass. He sweated profusely and his pulse jack-hammered in his veins. And he was being honest! How could he pull that test off?

He was also relieved Vanessa was dealing with the family calls. She looked wrecked, sitting on that sad plastic chair, surrounded by a motley assortment of down-on-their-luck folks waiting for their turn in the rooms or their loved ones who were in the back somewhere. She clutched her phone like it was her only tether to her sanity. Or like she was trying to crush it between her fingers. His heart broke a little for her in that moment. No one should ever have to make those kinds of calls. Especially to their parents, who could be… trying. To have those painful conversations from a police station waiting room? He couldn't fathom it.

He started to go to her, when Spencer grabbed his arm. He assured him the interview went well, then he said goodbye as Vanessa disconnected her call and wiped her eyes.

"We need to get going," she said. "We don't want to be late for our meeting with Tod."

And just like that, his heart hardened and the pity was gone. Clenching his teeth, he strode out the door and through the parking lot to his car. He took mild satisfaction on slamming the door closed, shutting off the running Vanessa commentary. And he gunned it out of the lot. He didn't care if she kept up or not. He didn't want to go there, anyway, and he definitely didn't want to go there with her.

CHAPTER 10

VANESSA HAD TO HURRY TO catch up with Royce, but she managed to pull behind him about two blocks from the police station. She followed him the rest of the way to a gorgeous community of five-story brownstones reminiscent of Bostonian architecture. She tried to tamp down her anger. They were supposed to be going to their appointment with Tod Jeffers, not be… well, she didn't know what they were doing, but they didn't have time for a detour. Especially one that took them to a community of multi-million dollar Victorian terrace homes. Vanessa got out of her car and stormed over to Royce's vehicle. "What are we doing here? We're going to miss our appointment."

"According to my GPS, this is where our appointment is." He pointed to one of the more elaborate homes, one with a sidewalk-to-roofline bay extension and a triangular pediment above the door.

"But that's just someone's home."

He shrugged and got out of the car. "Let's go see."

She led him to the door. Mounted above the doorbell, a small, tasteful black plaque with brass letters announced the name of the occupant. "It says, '*Tod Jeffers, Therapist.*' I guess we're in the right place."

"Just ring the damn bell. Let's get this over with."

"Fine."

Before she could ring the bell, the door opened.

Vanessa heard Royce groan, and she barely suppressed a chuckle. One of the most attractive men she'd ever seen stood before them wearing only sweat shorts. He had a towel hung around his neck, and his dark hair dripped onto it. His eyes, an arresting shade of hazel, seemed to twinkle with amusement at their unfortunate timing, and they crinkled in the corners when he smiled.

"Hi," she said, a little more breathlessly than she intended. But then, she was exerting herself trying not to stare at his abs. And she definitely preferred this welcome distraction to the situation at hand. She swallowed and smiled. "We're looking for Dr. Jeffers."

He swung the door open. "You're in the right place. Come on in."

"And are you his... partner?" Royce asked, stepping over the threshold.

"No." He laughed. "You caught me a little behind schedule. I'm Tod Jeffers." He held out his hand.

Vanessa shook it right away. He had a firm, reassuring grip. So very, very warm. She might have held on just a tad too long.

Royce didn't bother acknowledging the offer of a handshake. "If you're too busy, we don't need to do this."

"Nonsense. I just stayed in the shower a bit too long after my run. Please, follow me." He led them to a comfortable parlor where he directed them to an overstuffed sofa. "I'll be right back with refreshments."

Vanessa turned to Royce, who looked more than a little ill-at-ease. She decided to break the ice. "So, what happened at the police station?"

"We should discuss that in private, don't you think?" he whispered.

"If we can't talk about it at our therapist's office, where *can* we discuss it?"

"I'm not convinced he's the right therapist for us. In fact, I'm not convinced we need a therapist at all."

"Stanford said it's mandatory. And Dr. Jeffers is the one he recommended."

"And if he recommended a Victoria's Secret model, I suppose you wouldn't have a problem with that?"

"I don't know, Royce. Does the supermodel have a degree in psychiatry and several published books?" She pointed to the bookshelves, where in addition to textbooks and other experts' books on therapeutic techniques, Dr. Jeffers had several of his own works.

"What's your point, Ness?"

"Just give this a chance. Let's try to make this work."

He sat back and crossed one leg over the other as Dr. Jeffers came in.

He wore jeans and a polo shirt, but still no shoes. His hair had been combed, and he had a tray with glasses, a pitcher of water, a pitcher of iced tea, and lemon wedges which he placed on the coffee table in front of them beside a box of tissues. "Please, help yourselves." Then he went to his desk over by the window, grabbed a notebook and a pen, and took a seat in a wingback chair across from them.

"Anyone want anything?" Vanessa held the pitcher of water and looked around. When Royce and Dr. Jeffers shook their heads, she poured herself a glass of water and squirted some lemon in it, then sat back in her seat.

"Do you always do that?" Dr. Jeffers asked.

"What?"

"Play hostess. Even when it isn't your home."

"I… I don't know. I was just being polite."

"Do you feel that's your role? That you have to wait on people to be polite?"

"Now just hold on a minute," Royce said. "She offered us a drink when she was already pouring herself one. It's a common courtesy. Anyone with manners would do the same thing."

"Would you have offered me a drink? Me, who answered the door barely dressed and am currently sitting here with no shoes?"

"Is this some kind of test?"

"Just answer honestly, Royce," Dr. Jeffers said.

Vanessa knew the answer already. She wondered if Royce would answer honestly, though.

"Of course I would."

Dr. Jeffers closed his notebook and stood. "We're done here. I can't help you. There will be no charge for this session. Please give my apologies to Stanford."

"Wait, what?" Royce asked.

"You're smart enough to recognize a test when it's presented to you, Royce, and yet you still aren't smart enough to pass it. I can't help you if you aren't going to be honest here. If you won't be open about meaningless things regarding total strangers, how can I expect you to be forthcoming about your deepest feelings concerning personal matters and loved ones?"

"Fine. You're right. I didn't want to hurt your feelings."

The doctor just cocked his head to the side.

"Okay!" Royce threw his hands in the air. "I didn't want to look petty. Like a snob. But come on. Look at how you came to the door. Your house probably costs more than ours and you had on ratty sweat shorts and nothing else. That's hardly professional. You can understand my skepticism."

"Don't question my methods until after you see them at work. *Doctor.*"

Royce studied the man for a moment. "Fair enough."

"Now, let's talk about your situation." He settled in his chair and turned to look at Vanessa. "It's my understanding you are here for a number of reasons. You need marriage counseling, grief counseling, anger management tools—"

"Who said I need anger management tools? I don't have a temper issue."

Royce snorted.

"*I'm* not the one who had Security called on him at work."

"And *I'm* not the one who threw a glass in Stanford's study." He turned his head and pointed to a faint bruise and small cut on his temple.

"Time out, folks," Dr. Jeffers said.

Vanessa took a long drink from her water. The cool liquid, while refreshing, did little to bank the heat of her temper.

"I want to start at the beginning. Due to the special circumstances of your case, Stanford has filled me in on some of the particulars of your relationship. I'd like to go back to Hope's paternity, Vanessa."

She sighed. It was all being heaped on her.

"Can you tell us the details of her conception, please?"

Royce spun toward her and crossed his arms over his chest.

Finding her throat dry, she picked up her glass and drained it, refilled it. Not knowing how to begin, she got up and began pacing the room. Twisting her St. Luke medal around her fingers, she lost herself in the memory of the day the twins were born....

"BEN, WHAT ARE YOU DOING in here?"

Ben had come into her room not five minutes after Royce had stepped out. "Don't worry. Royce is crashing in the doctor's lounge. He'll be gone for hours."

"You don't know that. What if he comes back? What if someone else sees you in here?"

"Then I'll tell them I'm a family friend checking on you. Or your pediatrician checking on the babies. I am your pediatrician, right?"

"I don't know, Ben. That might not be a good idea."

"And what are you going to tell Royce? You chose a new doctor for the babies because you were suddenly unhappy with my services? Postpartum depression made you do it?"

"I don't know. What do you want, Ben?"

"I wanted to tell you, as their pediatrician, I took blood samples from each of them."

"What? Why? Is something wrong with them?"

"No. Don't worry. They're perfectly healthy. But I have to know."

"Know what?"

"If they're mine."

She narrowed her eyes. "They aren't. They're Royce's."

"They might not be."

"No matter what, they're his."

"And what if they aren't?"

"Oh, my God!" She struggled to sit up in bed, clutching at her incision as pain ripped through her abdomen.

Ben raced to her side. "Are you okay? You shouldn't be moving like that."

"Whose name did you put on those blood tests?"

"Don't worry. A friend in the blood lab is running the tests for me personally. And I didn't put any names on them. She's doing me a favor."

"It's a pretty big coincidence, don't you think? Royce has twins and you ask for paternity tests on the same day?"

"What are you going to do if they're mine?"

"Nothing, Ben. And neither are you. I don't care what your tests say. The girls are Royce's."

REMEMBERING BEN'S VISIT TO HER hospital room left a sour taste in Vanessa's mouth, and she drained her glass of lemon water. Again.

"Vanessa," Dr. Jeffers said. "I realize this is difficult for you, but you really need to share this information. I need to hear it to coach you through your feelings about it. You've carried the burden alone for too long. Royce needs to hear it so he can process the information. The first step to healing is admission."

"Fine. Like a bandage, right?" She looked at Royce for encouragement, but his expression was blank.

Dr. Jeffers poured her more water and slid her glass toward her.

"When the girls were born, the man in question had a paternity test done."

"Who is he?" Royce asked.

"You're getting ahead of yourself," she said. "He wanted to know if he was the father or if you were." She crossed the room to a window and stared out at the street below. It struck her she'd parked her car right behind Royce's: two Infinitis, a sedan and an SUV. Both from the same family, both manufactured the same year, both bought at the same time. Twins, but so different. She wiped at the tears that had begun to fall and turned away from the window.

"And we know he was," Royce said. "So who is he?"

She crossed to the table and took a tissue from the box. Dabbing at her eyes, she continued. "Three days later, when you weren't in the room, he came back to me with the results. I still wasn't quite recovered from my c-section, but I was being discharged the following day. The girls weren't named yet and the nurses were nagging us to fill out the birth certificates. Honestly, I don't know how he found the time to get into the room without being seen."

"His name?" Royce insisted.

"He gave me some shocking news."

"We know the damn news, Ness." He jumped to his feet. "What's his *name?*"

"No, you don't know!" She once again began twisting her medal and pacing the room. "Did you ever hear of superfecundation?"

Royce's eyes grew wide and he dropped back down in his seat.

"Superfecundation?" Dr. Jeffers said. "What's that?"

"It has to do with paternity and ovulation."

"No," Royce whispered, shaking his head. "No way."

She found talking to Dr. Jeffers easier, so she focused on him. "Basically, Hope and Faith, while twins, are half sisters. They have two different fathers."

"Amazing!" Dr. Jeffers said.

Royce stared at her for a moment, then he rubbed his hand over his face. "No. No. I don't buy it. I remember reading about that in med school. Double ovulation, right? The odds of that are next to impossible."

"Yes. I would have had to have had a fertilized egg to one father, then ovulated again and had the second egg fertilized by the other father. In a... very short time span." Vanessa's finger was numb. She looked down and noticed she'd wrapped her necklace so tightly around her finger that it was turning purple. She released the medal and let it drop back against her chest, the metal cool against her flushed skin.

"No. No. I don't believe it. No. The odds...." Royce got up and paced in the opposite direction from where Vanessa had been walking.

"He showed me the results himself. I saw them with my own eyes."

"Do you know the chances of that happening?"

"I did some research, but the numbers are all over the place. It's hard to pin down, because there are a lot of cases where people don't know they had heteropaternal superfecundation births."

"Heteropaternal superfecundation. The odds—Oh, God."

"What's wrong?" Tod asked.

"For that to have happened, she had to have slept with each of us within a day of each other. Possibly *hours!*" He turned toward Vanessa. "So what was it? Booty call by day and squeeze me in that night? Or was I first and just not enough for you?"

"It wasn't like that!"

"I can't believe this!"

"I didn't mean for it to happen. And I was just sick afterward. I showered for hours, trying to wash the betrayal away, but I couldn't! I cleaned my body, scrubbed all traces of him away, but the sin wasn't on me. It was *in* me. How could I remove my mistake when it had tainted my vows to you? Corrupted my very soul? One mistake, and I was ruined. And then when you came to me... It had been so long, and I wanted you so much. You looked at me with such desire... I needed you. I needed us, together. I thought making love with you could erase what I'd done. But it only got worse! I didn't know what to do!"

"So of course you kept it from me. Acted like it never happened. Just shared your body with me and... whoever he was. You brought his whole love life into our bed, and I never knew any of it!"

"If I could take it back, I would!"

"Even if it meant never having Hope?"

She recoiled like he'd slapped her. She always regretted her decision, always carried the shame and anguish with her. But would she give up her daughter to be freed from her misery? She couldn't bear to consider it.

"Let's get back on topic," Dr. Jeffers said. "You had tests done."

So much for that brief reprieve. "Look. The tests were anonymous, so no one knew. Just me and the father. And I told him I didn't care. In my mind, the babies were yours. Both of them. So I called the nurses in and filled out the birth certificates. Faith became Faith because I always had faith you were the father. And Hope I named Hope because—"

"Because you hoped I would never find out she wasn't."

"Because I had hope she would grow to be yours, regardless of her blood."

"But it was her blood that doomed her, Vanessa. Or mine. If you had just been honest, this never would have happened."

"You said yourself, Royce, you don't know you could have saved her."

"I know I wouldn't have *killed* her! I have to live with that! Not you! *Me!*"

"You think I'm not living with that? You can drop the fake martyr act, because we all know you blame me. And so do I. The hospital might say it was your actions in that room that caused Hope's death, but we know it was my actions eighteen years ago that caused it! It's been my decision to keep the secret all these years that caused it! You may have witnessed her death first hand, but I'm just as culpable, maybe more so. And you know it, or we wouldn't be here!"

She was out of breath after her rant, but the thought of sitting just made her more antsy, so she walked back to the window and stared out at the 'twin' vehicles. The only twins left in her life, cold and mechanical mockeries of the warm and lovely twins she'd created. And destroyed.

"Okay, folks. We made significant progress today. But that's all we have time for. I want you to do some homework before we meet the next time."

"Homework?" Vanessa said.

"Next time?" Royce asked. "Wasn't this enough?"

"Oh, we're just getting started."

Royce sighed.

"I want the two of you to keep journals. Before bed at night, take a few moments to write down your feelings."

"I'm not really much of a journaler," Royce said. "Or a feelings-sharer."

"You only have to share your feelings if you want to. But this is a good way to get used to expressing them. You'll never be able to acknowledge your feelings to your partner if you can't acknowledge them to yourself."

"What do we have to write about?" Vanessa asked.

"Whatever you want. Yourselves. Each other. Hope. Faith. Jensen."

"We never told you Jensen's name," Royce said.

"I told you I have a complete dossier on you already, due to your extenuating circumstances."

"Stanford," Royce muttered.

"Write about work."

"I'm on leave."

"Home. Anything or anyone you have strong feelings about."

"And we don't have to share them?" Vanessa said.

"Not if you don't want to," Dr. Jeffers said.

"Why?" Royce asked. "Are you planning on writing Hope's father's name it in?"

Vanessa turned her back on him and headed for the door. "Thank you, Dr. Jeffers."

"I want to see you in three days. Same time work for you?"

"Works for me. Maybe we should ask Hope's father if he's free. That's probably the only way I'm going to get his identity."

"You aren't helping matters, Royce." Vanessa walked to her car and left without waiting for Royce to follow her.

CHAPTER 11

ROYCE DIDN'T KNOW WHERE VANESSA had gone, and he didn't care. He drove straight to the hospital and walked in the front door rather than into the ER entrance. Hoping not to bump into anyone he knew, he kept his head down and headed for the blood lab.

Even though Wade's relationship with Carley had only lasted a few months, Royce had managed to stay good friends with her. Over the years, she had done him a favor or two, and he'd reciprocated in kind. He hoped she was on duty and willing to do a big one for him, even though technically he wasn't really employed there at the moment.

He flashed his hospital ID and walked back into the lab area. Looking around, he saw the slender woman in Winnie-the-Pooh scrubs and shook his head, smiling. "Planning on working the pediatric unit today?"

She turned and offered him a big smile. "Nope. I just love Eeyore."

"But you aren't wearing Eeyore. You're wearing Pooh."

"Same franchise. I couldn't find my Eeyore scrubs today. I think they're in the wash."

He laughed. "Sounds like your reasoning."

"Are you saying I'm not logical?" She crossed her arms over her chest.

"Of course not. You're the definition of logic. Your picture is in the dictionary next to the word."

"Hmm. Flattery will get you nowhere."

He grinned at her.

"Who am I kidding? It'll get you whatever you want. What can I do for you?"

"I need you to run a couple of paternity tests for me."

"Aren't you suspended?" She leaned against the counter.

"I thought flattery would get me anything?"

She cracked her gum and kept looking at him.

"Come on, Carley. It's just a couple of routine tests."

"Yeah, routine. Because our lab has nothing else going on."

"Please? It's important."

She held out her hand. He put three swabs in it. "Test C to see if he fathered S and D."

"C? Why not R? Your name is Royce."

"What?" His stomach flipped over when she mentioned his name.

"Come on, Royce. I'm not an idiot. I heard what happened yesterday. I'm sorry, by the way."

"Thanks."

"Then you come in here with S and D. Son and Daughter, obviously. A bit more obscure than J and F, but not a stretch. But what's the C all about?"

He felt his face flush and looked down at the floor. "Cuckold, okay. It stands for 'cuckold,' which apparently I've been for almost two decades."

She sighed and placed her hand on his. "Yeah, I'll run these. But if I'm not mistaken, I already know the answer."

"Why do you think you know the answer?"

"Well, for starters, they both look just like you. But also—never mind."

"What?"

"I promised I wouldn't say."

"Come on, Carley. Don't toy with me. My job's on the line here, you know that. Maybe more."

She cracked her gum again, then she leaned in and whispered, "Okay. I'll tell you this much. No more. When the twins were born, I did a similar favor for someone else. Someone brought in unlabeled blood asking for a paternity test. Only one of the two samples was a match to the paternal source. I thought the timing was interesting, but who am I to judge? Plus, do you know the odds of two twins having different fathers? So I just minded my own business."

He pinned her against the counter. "*You* did the favor? Who brought in the blood?"

"If you expect me to do this favor for you, or any future favors, I suggest you back off. Now."

Royce stepped back and straightened his clothes. "I'm sorry. I really am. But don't you understand? If you had told me about this back then, Hope might be alive right now!"

"We don't know that. All we know is I probably would have destroyed your marriage, and more. But Hope could still have ended up on that motorcycle that day."

"What do you mean by, 'and more?'"

"I've already said too much. Do you want the tests run, or not?"

He sighed. "Yes. I'm desperate. I need to know."

"Fine. I'll do it. And I'm sorry, Royce. I really am. But you need to realize, I can get in a lot of trouble for the favors I do for my friends. That includes the one I did seventeen years ago and the one I'm doing for you now. So I'm sure you'll understand when I tell you keeping everyone's secrets is crucial. You're lucky I told you this much."

He sighed and ran his hand over his face. "Yeah. I get it."

"Okay. And we're good?"

No. "Yes. We're good."

"Good." She smiled at him. "Now get out of here before someone sees you. I'll call you when I have the results."

"Thanks." He turned to leave.

"And Royce?"

He looked back.

"I really am sorry."

FURIOUS WITH THE WORLD, ROYCE had no desire to drive home. Secrets! Everyone knew the answers except him. And he couldn't bear to see Vanessa after she'd admitted her culpability in Hope's death.

He also didn't want to face all the things that reminded him of Hope.

Usually when something bothered him, he buried himself in work. But for the first time in his life, that wasn't an option. He felt completely, utterly lost, with nowhere to go and nothing to do.

He drove to a strip mall near the outskirts of town, praying the people he knew would be at work or, if they were out and about, were closer to the heart of the city. Stopping at a large office supply store, he went inside and chose a leather-bound journal with a combination lock. Then he had to track down an attendant to retrieve an executive Montblanc fountain pen from behind the case. No point in keeping a journal if he couldn't do it in style. He'd worry about the money another time.

Three hundred and some odd dollars later, Royce left the store and drove to the lake. Getting out of the car, he made his way across the uneven ground on the far bank and sat, looking across the water at the large, flat clearing where preparations for the Spring Carnival were well underway. Most of the rides looked to be assembled and many of the tents appeared to be erected already. His family should be attending the event, schmoozing with donors, trying to raise funds for the school and hospital. Jensen should be learning he made valedictorian. Faith and Hope should be deciding where they wanted to intern over the summer, rounding-out their college applications for the fall.

Instead, his family suffocated under a black cloud of suspicion and grief.

Given everything Vanessa and Carley had said, it was almost certain they were his family. In both spirit and blood.

If he was honest with himself, he'd realize that never mattered to him. He loved those kids, regardless of their paternity.

And if he was brutally honest, he had to admit he was closer with Jensen and Faith than he was with Hope.

He opened his journal. Took out and uncapped his pen. Leaned forward, book in his lap.

Did he take risks with Hope's life he wouldn't have with Jensen's or Faith's because he didn't think her life was worth as much as theirs? Was she more expendable and therefore easier to gamble with?

He began to write.

I've always prided myself on being the go-to man to solve problems. I like being the man of the house. I like being Chief of Emergency Medicine. I like that I'm calm, in control, decisive. Maybe Vanessa's right and I do control too much. But people have come to expect that of me. And I've always delivered.

There's a time for emotion and a time for reason. I've always been able to separate the two.

Now I have doubts. When Hope was in my ER, I don't know if I acted with my head or my heart.

And what scares me the most is, as her father, I don't know which way I should have acted.

And I am her father. There's no doubt in my mind, in my heart—I loved that girl. I loved her from the day she was born, and I'll love her until the day I die. It doesn't matter that it's not my blood in her veins. Wasn't my blood.

I am her father.

I just don't know if I liked her very much. Not the girl she had become.

I don't even know if I knew the girl she had become.

And I wonder if my feelings impacted my judgment. If even for a nanosecond. If even on a subconscious level.

And if they did, did that make a difference?

He closed and locked his journal. Capped his pen and tucked it in his pocket. Leaned back on his elbows and looked across the lake at the Spring Carnival.

His family should be over there enjoying themselves and planning for their futures. All five of them.

TIRED OF CARNIVAL MUSIC AND the smell of fried dough and hotdogs, Royce drove home. Barely in the door, Jensen and Faith accosted him.

"Well?" Jensen asked.

"Did you get the results?" Faith asked. "How are we going to find out who I belong to? Not that I don't feel like I belong to you, but—"

Royce held up his hand and cut her off. "Whoa! Slow down." He looked around, relieved not to see Lydia anywhere. But that didn't mean she hadn't overheard anything.

"Let's go into the study, okay?" He ushered them into the study and closed the door behind them. This time, when they sat in the loveseat, he sat in the nearest club chair facing them.

"So?" Jensen asked. "What'd you find out?"

"First, where's your mom and Lydia?"

"Who cares?" Faith said. "We want answers."

"I care, because walls can have ears."

"Lydia went to the store," Jensen said. "Mom hasn't been home since you guys left this morning. I thought you two were together."

"Well, we had... an emotional day. I'm sure she'll be along soon."

"God, Dad, I can't take it anymore!" Faith said.

"Okay!" He held up his hands. "First, I did drop off the DNA samples. My friend is putting a rush on them. But it's still going to be a few days."

"Aaah!" Faith threw her body back in the loveseat.

"Geez, relax. Dad will tell us when he knows something. Right, Dad?"

"It's not the same for you, Jensen. You're probably really his."

"We don't know that."

"Stop, you two," Royce said. "Listen to me. You're both mine, regardless of what some stupid test says."

Faith blinked back tears.

"But I have more news."

Faith sat up, and she and Jensen gave him their full attention.

"There is a very good chance both of you are biologically mine."

Faith flung herself back against the loveseat again.

"Come on, Dad," Jensen said. "Hope was, well, someone else's."

"There is a medical phenomenon called heteropaternal superfecundation in which a woman can have twins to two fathers."

"Come on," Jensen said.

"Hetero what?" Faith asked.

"Heteropaternal superfecundation. *Hetero* means different and *paternal* means father. So, different father. *Super* means power and *fecundation* means ability to have children. So, powerful ability to have children. It's rare, but it is a documented condition."

"She still cheated on you," Faith said.

"That's between me and your mother, not you. What you need to focus on is the fact that your family unit is very likely the same family unit you grew up thinking it was. And soon we'll have DNA proof of it."

"Who was Hope's father?"

"We aren't there yet, Faith. One step at a time, okay? Right now, we need to get through this testing, get through Hope's funeral, and get through these investigations. Then we'll deal with the rest of it."

"Okay."

"Jensen?"

He looked at Royce for a moment, then said, "Okay."

"Good. Now, I need to do some work in here. Go... do something."

"Like what?" Jensen asked.

"I don't know. What do you usually do?"

"Hang out with my friends," Jensen said. "But I really don't want to see anyone who knows what's going on."

"I get that," Royce said. "What about you, Faith? What do you do for fun?"

"Pick on Hope," Faith said, and broke into tears. Jensen pulled her into his arms while tears welled in his own eyes.

"Why don't you guys go a town or two over, where you aren't going to bump into anyone you know, and watch a movie? My treat." He pulled a couple of twenties out of his wallet. "Find the silliest comedy playing and just take a break from all this."

"I don't feel right about that," Jensen said.

Faith shook her head.

"There's nothing you can do here right now. And you need a break. Go."

The kids looked at each other and shrugged.

On their way out, a momentary bout of fear gripped Royce's heart in its icy claws. He called after them, "And drive safely!" but he knew his warning wouldn't protect them from reckless drivers.

Once they were out of sight, he let the tears fall.

He had just pulled himself back together when Vanessa walked in the door. "Are you okay?" she asked.

"Fine." His voice sounded scratchy. Before she could pursue her line of questioning, he countered, "Where have you been all day?"

"Our session was brutal. I needed some time before coming back here. I went to the lake for a while to think, then I went shopping for journals for the both of us." She reached into a bag and held one up. "I thought you might like one with a lock."

It startled him to see she'd chosen one identical to the one he'd purchased for himself, but he didn't react. Because he just sat there, she put it back in the bag and laid it on his desk. He finally had the presence of mind to respond to her. "That was thoughtful of you. Thanks."

"Well, if we're going to make any progress with Dr. Jeffers, we need to do all the steps."

"You're probably right." He couldn't believe she'd gone the same places he had, and made the same purchases. They'd probably passed each other once, maybe even twice. Funny he hadn't even noticed. Of course, neither had she.

"Are you going to do the steps, Royce?"

His phone rang, saving him from answering. "Hello?"

She stayed in his study, watching him.

"Yes… I see… That's good news… And the hospital?… Very well. We'll make the arrangements. Thank you." He disconnected the call.

"What was that about?"

"Hold on. I want to call that detective and confirm. I don't need any more problems." He scrolled through his recent calls list and hit the send button.

"Detective? Royce Keller. I just received a call from the hospital saying you've released my daughter's body. I wanted to confirm that before I made any arrangements that might upset you, should that not be the case… Uh-huh. I see. No, that's all. Thank you." He disconnected the call.

"Well?" Vanessa said.

"The police and the hospital have released Hope's body to us. We can make our arrangements."

"That's good news, right? The police wouldn't release her if the investigation was still going on, would they?"

"I wouldn't think so, but he didn't say I was officially cleared, either, so I don't know."

She walked to him and flung her arms around him. "I don't care. That's a good sign."

He patted her back awkwardly, then pulled away. "We should call the funeral home and let them know we're ready to make arrangements for Hope."

Vanessa wiped tears off her cheeks and turned away from him. "I'll call. Are you ready to go soon? I think the sooner we take care of this, the better."

"Sure, fine. Whatever. If they can see us tonight, let's go tonight."

"I'll see when they're free." She grabbed her phone and dialed from her contact list.

"Are you kidding me? You have the funeral home in your contacts?" Who did that? Was she sick?

"After Hope died, I wanted to be prepared."

She was sick. Totally certifiable.

The doorbell rang as Vanessa started talking into the phone. She gestured to him to get the door.

"Don't get up. I'll get it." He walked to the foyer and opened the door. And his day got worse.

"Royce, baby!" His mother threw her arms around him. "We're here for you, honey."

"I'm so sorry, son." His father embraced them both. "So, do you have any scotch around here?"

CHAPTER 12

WHEN VANESSA WENT IN SEARCH of Royce to tell him they could go right over to Franklin's, the last thing she expected to see was him enveloped in his parents' embraces. She briefly considered turning around, but Gene spotted her before she could get away.

"Hey there, sweetheart. Where are you running off to? Come here." He snatched her hand and pulled her into a smothering hug, his left hand a little too low on her back to be considered appropriate. "I'm so sorry about Hope, honey."

She glanced at Royce, but he didn't seem to be paying attention, so she patted his back and wiggled her way out of his arms. He looked like he enjoyed the wiggle a bit too much.

Liz patted her hair, not bothering to offer Vanessa her condolences, and looked around. "Where are the children?"

"I sent them to the movies, Mother," Royce said. "They needed to blow off some steam."

"Do you think that sends the right message, darling? People shouldn't see them out enjoying themselves. They should think they're home, grieving."

"I don't think people's impressions are what matters, Mother. Besides, they went out of town. They didn't want to deal with anyone, either."

"Very well. Take our bags to the guest room. We'd prefer the one upstairs. It faces the garden, and the lilacs are in bloom."

"Hurry, Royce," Vanessa said. "We're running late."

"And just where are you gallivanting off to? Does no one in this family see the need to observe the rules of propriety and stay in this house? First no one calls us," she shot Vanessa a dirty look, "then no one even stays home! You obviously need your mother's help, dear." She turned back to Royce and patted his cheek.

"We're meeting the funeral director to go over arrangements," Vanessa said.

"Oh. Very well. Leave the bags. We can get them when we get back. We'll go with you."

Vanessa looked at Royce and pleaded with him through wide eyes and a subtle tilt of her head to stop his parents from accompanying them. When he stayed silent, she assumed he either didn't understand her signal or didn't care what she thought. "I don't know if that's a good idea, Liz. I only told the funeral director to expect two of us."

"Nonsense. What's two more people?"

"This is probably hard enough for them," Gene said. "They don't need an audience watching them fall apart. We'll stay here and wait for the kids."

"But I want to be sure they choose the best. Money's no object."

"It's not for them, either. The boy's Chief of Emergency Medicine, he's not some poor schlub working two jobs just to scrape by. Let's get you settled. I'll carry the bags up," he said. "You two go on, now." Gene winked at Vanessa and bent to grab their luggage.

She swore he flexed his biceps intentionally as he picked up their bags.

"Goodbye, Mother." Royce gave her a peck on the cheek and walked out the door.

Liz smiled at him, scowled at Vanessa, and followed Gene up the stairs.

Vanessa seethed as she walked out to the car. She tried to hold her tongue and her temper, but lost control of both by the time they were on the road. She turned to face Royce as he drove away. "Are you kidding me?"

"What?"

"Are you telling me you couldn't back me up in there?"

"I wouldn't have minded them coming along."

"You don't have a problem with how they treat me?"

"Are we really going to have this conversation again? Now?"

"Your dad grabbed my ass!"

"He did not."

"Your mother hates me."

"Your seatbelt isn't on. Buckle up."

"Stop changing the subject."

He pulled the car over on the side of the road and put it in park. "I'm not moving this car another inch until you fasten your belt."

"Since when is this an issue? You're just trying to avoid another fight."

"It's an issue since *Hope!* God, Vanessa. How can you be so self-centered? I don't know if my dad groped you. I don't know if Mother hates you. And guess what. I don't care. I'm on my way to arrange my daughter's funeral. She died because of me in my ER because of a motor vehicle accident. So, yeah, I care about that goddamned seatbelt. You might not, but I do. You'll wear it when I drive you because I can't have another death on my hands." He rested his head against the headrest and closed his eyes, his breathing labored.

Vanessa didn't say anything. She reached back for the seatbelt and fastened it.

Royce must have heard the *click,* because he opened his eyes and started driving again. His breathing didn't return to normal for a few miles.

They drove the rest of the way to the funeral home in silence.

Franklin's Funeral Home was a pristine white Victorian sitting on the corner of a broad, tree-lined street in the middle of town, just a block from their church and less than a mile from the cemetery. Across the street was a large parking lot for mourners, and because the street was so wide, when the cars lined up on the day of the funeral, traffic would be able to pass safely until the procession actually started.

Vanessa appreciated the practicality of the venue as much as its beauty.

And she dreaded going inside with each beat of her heart, with each breath she drew, with each step she took.

She reached for Royce's hand, and to her surprise, he let her take it. She clung to him, the only warmth her body felt in an otherwise cold reality.

Mr. Franklin met them at the door. He escorted them through the reception area she was all too familiar with and down the stairs into a comfortable but dark office. They took seats across from him and he offered them water and candy from the dish on his desk.

"I'm so sorry for your loss." His voice soft, soothing. It must be a prerequisite for morticians to speak with that tone of voice. "I'm going to try to make this as easy for you as possible, but I know it's a difficult and painful process."

"Thank you, Sid." Vanessa accepted his hand and squeezed it before dabbing her eyes with a tissue from his desk.

"First," he said, "we have some decisions to make."

They had to give him the information for transportation of the body, death certificate, and permits for burial. He promised to coordinate with the church and cemetery as well as reserve the hearse for the appropriate day and time. He also contacted the newspaper on a conference call and made sure the obituary placement had all the appropriate details and would make the morning edition.

"And now, the plot. Will you be wanting a mausoleum or one of our lovely garden sites?"

"I don't know." Vanessa looked at Royce. "I hate to think of burying her in the ground, but I don't want her in an ugly box where we can't put flowers, either."

"You've got to stop thinking that way."

"Excuse me," Sid said. "I realize how difficult this is, and I don't mean to be indelicate, but have you given any thought to purchasing your own plots now? So you can be put to rest beside her?"

Vanessa couldn't swallow. The room started to close in on her. She knew he expected an answer, but the only words running through her head were, This isn't happening. This isn't happening.

Finally, Royce said, "Could you please give us a minute?"

Sid excused himself, and Vanessa felt Royce's hand on the back of her head, pushing it down between her knees.

"Breathe, Ness."

She focused on her breathing, staring at the oriental-print rug under her feet. She blinked rapidly several times until her eyes could focus on every color—brown, rust, black, cream—in the well-worn textile. Only then did she realize her breathing had returned to normal and Royce's hand rubbed small circles on her back. She sat up and looked at him.

"You don't want to be buried next to me, do you? Just like you won't sleep next to me."

"I didn't say that."

"But you're thinking it."

"I don't know what I'm thinking."

"I don't want Hope to be alone. For eternity." She grabbed his shirt and fisted it in her hands, pulling him closer. "Eternity, Royce. That's too long to be alone. We have to be near her."

"We'll buy two plots beside her. You can definitely have them. I'll decide later if I'll use one of them or buy one somewhere else."

Vanessa let him go and started sobbing. She already lost her daughter, she couldn't lose her husband, too. Dwelling on the possibility right then was too painful to bear, so she focused on Hope. "If we only had more time. Just another day, just to hold her, just to tell her…"

He rocked her and held her close. "Vanessa, stop. You can't do this."

"But the last things I said to her… I was trying to change her."

"She knew you loved her."

She sniffled against his chest until she calmed down. She'd trade anything for this not to be happening. She'd trade anything to be the one being buried, give anything for another minute with her daughter. But there were no magic lamps, no genies granting wishes. God certainly wasn't answering her prayers. She straightened her shoulders and wiped her eyes. Then she smoothed Royce's shirt, determined to finish making the arrangements. "Where do you want to be? Garden or mausoleum?"

"What do you think Hope would like?" She sniffled.

"You do understand she's gone, right?"

"Royce! What would she like?"

He shook his head. "Garden, I think. She seemed to like nature. At least she did when she was young."

"Fine. Garden it is." She walked to the door and poked her head out. "Sid!"

The mortician reappeared and took his seat. They discussed their choices and found three plots together in the cemetery under an old oak. Sid told them there was a bench under the tree and a water pump nearby for landscaping needs. Vanessa thought it looked perfect.

"Now it's time for the hardest part," he said. "Follow me."

She thought they'd already done the hardest part, but she got up and followed him down the hall. He guided them to a giant room she'd never been to before and flipped on the lights. Rows and rows of caskets filled the room… white ones, black ones, and brown and charcoal. There were a few metallic colors, and all different shades of wooden ones. There were even small pink and blue ones. Some of the caskets had brushed nickel adornments, some gold, some brass, some black. Some matched the color of the caskets they were on, others contrasted, a macabre decoration to an otherwise depressing item. She saw the very fancy and the severely understated. A few had nothing on them at all. All the insides were almost exclusively white or cream satin or velvet, tufted or pleated. One or two displayed pastel linen instead. In the far corner sat a plain pine box with no handles or adornments whatsoever.

It was the most depressing room she'd ever been in. Her resolve shattered. She broke into tears and flung herself into Royce's arms.

Sid said, "I'll give you some time to look things over. The price tags are inside the caskets, but basically the room is arranged from least expensive," he gestured toward the pine box, "to the most luxurious." He pointed to a mahogany casket with a gold crest and cream velvet tufted interior with gold embroidery inside.

Vanessa couldn't contain herself. She just sobbed harder.

"Press this button if you need anything," Sid said, indicating an intercom system by the door. He closed the door as he left.

Vanessa clung to Royce, and he held her, stroking her hair and rubbing her back. Soon she noticed that not only was she soaking his shirt, her own shoulder was getting wet. She pulled back to look at him.

He turned away and wiped his eyes.

"Royce," she said, and reached for his arm.

But he shrugged away.

"Royce," she insisted. "This is hard for both of us. I'm glad you're trying to be strong for me, but I hope you know you don't have to hide your feelings from me."

"I'm fine, Vanessa."

"If you can't let go in front of me, who can you let go in front of?"

"Who says I need to let go at all?"

"You're not a machine, Royce. You're a man. A flesh-and-blood man."

"And there it is."

"What?"

"Blood. It's always going to come back to that."

Vanessa didn't know what to say. Even the most innocuous comments were going to set him off. She didn't mean to hurt him. They were sharing a raw, private moment, something only the two of them could share, and instead of bringing them closer together, it was forcing them apart.

"Do you want to ask Hope's father to do this with you?"

It felt like a knife in her heart to hear the catch in his voice as he asked the question. It hurt even more to see the determined set of his jaw when she realized he'd leave with his head held high if she said yes.

"Hope's father is here with me. Now please help me get through this." She reached her hand out to him. After what seemed like an eternity, he took it. And they began the morbid task of walking up and down the aisles to choose their daughter's final resting place.

After half an hour of deliberation, she said, "Hope wouldn't want anything light or pastel. Certainly not shiny satin."

"I wouldn't know," he said. "You knew her better than I did."

"You knew her."

He scoffed. "The girl I knew loved black. You want to bury her in that?" He flung his hand toward a black coffin with a pewter crest on the top, reminiscent of a gothic crest.

"She wasn't a vampire, Royce."

"Just pick something."

"We have to do it *together*. We have to agree. Don't you understand that?" She sniffled into a soaked tissue.

He sighed and walked down another aisle.

She followed and stopped in front of a copper-colored casket. "What about this one?"

"It's beautiful."

"She always loved the fall. This reminds me of autumn. And it's not too masculine, not too feminine. She'd hate something frilly."

"You're right," Royce agreed. "This is perfect for her."

"It's a warm color. It will be good for her complexion."

"You chose well, Ness."

"We chose well."

"We chose well."

"Do you think she'll be cramped? Or cold?" Vanessa started crying again. "She going to be all alone…"

"Vanessa. Don't." Royce took her in his arms and wrapped her hair around his finger as he rocked her. That time, he sobbed aloud, and he didn't hide it from her.

When they were both done, he wiped the tears from her eyes before wiping his own face. "Are you ready to call Sid?" She nodded, and he pressed the button.

They placed their order, and Sid helped them make floral selections to complement the color of the casket. He also suggested a color for her clothing and asked for the outfit to be dropped off the next day.

"I'll have Mandy get to work as soon as Hope is prepared. She's my very best cosmetologist."

"Thanks," Vanessa said. "We'll get you the outfit tomorrow."

He saw them out, and the first thing Vanessa did when she got in the car was fasten her seatbelt. She looked at Royce, who acknowledged her action with a nod.

They drove back to the house in silence. She felt they had made a small step forward at Franklin's. He'd held her, grieved with her. Accepted his role as Hope's father. Maybe he hadn't given up after all.

There were two cars in her driveway when they pulled in. One was her in-laws'. She assumed the other belonged to a friend of the kids, so she didn't think anything of it.

She was wrong.

They opened the door of their home to chaos.

Her father stood in the foyer, almost nose-to-nose with Royce's father. They looked ready to exchange blows. Her mother and Royce's mother stood on the stairs, wrestling with a suitcase. Other suitcases were knocked over on the floor.

"What's going on here?" Royce bellowed.

"Vanessa!" her father said, and wrapped her in a big bear hug.

Her mother dropped her suitcase on Liz's foot and rushed down the stairs to embrace her daughter. "We came right away, honey. We're so, so sorry. What can we do for you?" She pulled Royce into her hug, too.

"For starters, you can tell me what's going on."

"Oh, this? This is just a little nonsense between in-laws. We can work it out ourselves. Nothing you need to worry yourselves over. Can I get you some hot tea?"

"A little nonsense, Rose?" Liz said. "This is more than a little nonsense. You're trying to evict us. From my son's home!"

"What?" Royce asked, looking from one woman to the other.

"I'd say that's a bit extreme," Linc said, keeping one arm around his daughter and draping the other over his wife. "We weren't trying to kick you out of our daughter's house. Just out of our bedroom."

"Your bedroom?" Gene said. "What on earth makes you think that guest bedroom is yours?"

"Why, my little Rosy decorated it. She handmade the quilt on that bed. We always stay in that room. It's *our* room."

"That explains the tasteless décor," Liz said.

"Mother."

Liz turned her nose up as she looked away.

"Look, I can't deal with this right now. Mom, Dad, Royce's parents are already up there. How about I get the quilt out of that room and settle you in the guest room downstairs. That way, you still have your quilt, but they don't have to move. It's the easiest solution right now."

"One gives freely, yet grows all the richer; another withholds what he should give, and only suffers want. Proverbs, chapter eleven, verse twenty-four," Rose said, arms folded across her chest.

"What?" Royce said.

"She said that's fine," Linc said.

"I think she said we should give the room up," Liz said. "Fine. We'll give the room up."

"No. We'll go downstairs," Rose said. "We're happy to."

"Really, we'll go," Liz said. "We insist."

Linc picked up their bags. "Already on our way."

"Gene, stop them!" Liz said. "I'll go pack up." She dashed upstairs.

"What's happening?" Royce asked Vanessa.

"Everybody stop right where you are!" Vanessa bellowed. "Now!"

She didn't think they would, but they actually stopped and faced her.

"We just came back from making funeral arrangements for our daughter. *Your* granddaughter. This is an incredibly difficult time. Now, we appreciate you coming to help us, but if you really want to help, this has to stop. Dad, take your bags downstairs. Mom, go upstairs with Liz and get your quilt. Gene, go downstairs with my dad and get the comforter off their bed. From now on, if there are any disagreements, work them out like adults and leave us out of them."

Everyone stood there, looking at her. She waved her arms in a circle. *"Go."*

The women went upstairs and the men down, talking quietly as they went.

"I'm pretty sure my mother is going to be pissed at you," Royce said.

"Why? She got her way."

"She doesn't like to be talked to like that."

"Eh." Vanessa shrugged. "She doesn't like me anyway."

Royce chuckled and sat down on the bench in the foyer.

"Besides, my mom will be doing extra praying for my soul after that outburst. So I'm sure it will all even out." She sat beside him and sighed, resting her head against the wall and closing her eyes.

"It's going to get pretty ugly around here over the next few days."

"Yep."

"Are you going to tell them?" he asked.

"Nope."

He leaned forward and turned to face her. "Don't you think, with the investigation and the scandal, they're going to find out?"

She opened her eyes. "Those are four of the most self-centered people I've ever met. If we have a chance of getting through this without any four people finding out, those are the four."

"I don't know," he said. "They might be pretty self-absorbed, but they're also pretty shrewd."

"I'll jump off that bridge when I have to. Right now, I don't have to."

"Death jokes? Really?"

"I found it appropriate, given you're trying to make me confess to the executioner. I mean, your mother."

"This is going to blow up in our faces."

"And who's talking explosions, now?"

CHAPTER 13

THE ARRIVAL OF THE HOUSEGUESTS made things extremely difficult for Royce. He immediately launched into survival-mode, shutting his emotions down as best he could and preemptively arranging things so their secret wasn't exposed.

First on his list was contacting the kids before they got home from the movies. He needed to prepare them for the houseguests, to remind them to act like nothing had changed between them and Vanessa. Fire number one. The compromise? They planned on hiding in their rooms a lot and if questioned about it, claiming they were sad. He took the deal. He knew they were sad, and he needed a win where he could get it.

Next was keeping the local news out of the house. He put a temporary hold on the daily paper and tried to keep the televisions off during the news hours. He didn't know if he'd make the news or not, but there was no reason to tempt fate. He couldn't do anything about his parents and in-laws having phones, however. Hopefully they'd only use them for business and family communication. Hopefully.

His parents had finally heard from his brother. Miles and his family couldn't make it back in time. They were on a trip to Europe and by the time he got the flights arranged, they would be too late, so they sent their condolences. Royce didn't want to deal with them, anyway.

Linc and Rose still hadn't reached Grace and her family. That wasn't unusual, though. They often went on camping excursions for weeks at a time, and they didn't have phone reception in the mountains. That was just another family Royce didn't have to try to deceive, so it didn't bother him, even though Vanessa seemed to want her sister there.

Vanessa insisted he help choose Hope's attire, despite the fact she already had what she wanted in mind and he didn't have a clue what any of it was. When he accompanied her into Hope's bedroom, he steeled himself for the barrage of memories and Vanessa's meltdown. What he wasn't ready for was his own struggle with the sights and smells in the room. She had posters of bands and boys he didn't recognize along with photographs of friends from school tacked on her wall. Clothes dotted every surface of the room—bed, chair, dresser, floor—where she had flung or dropped them. When had she become a slob? Bottles and tubes, brushes and clips littered every available surface, and the room smelled like her perfume, which she seemed to think smelled exotic but always reminded him of apple pie.

One well-loved tiny stuffed bunny lay between her bed pillows. He picked it up and held it to his face.

Apple pie.

Vanessa sobbed violently while she rooted through the closet for a Creamsicle-colored wraparound dress and gold sling backs. Royce was less than useless trying to help. He didn't know a sling back from a sneaker. So he sat there, clutching the bunny and looking around for clues about who Hope had become. He knew nothing of her likes, dreams, and aspirations. He only knew he'd given Hope that bunny when she was a baby and it was the only thing in the room he recognized. That and the spicy scent fading from his memory.

Vanessa emerged from the closet and he pocketed the stuffed bunny. He hugged her until she calmed, then he closed the door on Hope's room and on his grief. Another fire dealt with.

The thing that kept him busiest was his parents and in-laws. Rose constantly irritated his mother by quoting scripture implying things she did or said were morally reprehensible. Liz retaliated with condescending remarks about her sedate—and therefore unstylish—attire. Which only prompted more scripture verses about material possessions. Linc and his father almost came to blows over whose car had to be parked under the tree out front. Like his driveway wasn't big enough so neither car would suffer from bird droppings. They couldn't agree on what brand of scotch was better, although neither of them cared for what he had on hand. All four of them still groused about the sleeping arrangements. And they all had an opinion on the funeral plans—the music, the viewing, the reception. He thought the ladies might actually get physically violent when they ordered the flower arrangements. Like the flowers really mattered. Ridiculous. He exhausted himself trying to referee all those battles and arrive at compromises that satisfied everyone.

The hottest fire, though? Lydia. She questioned everything he said. He bumped into her every time he turned around. It would probably have been easier to give her some time off, but with four extra people in the house, they needed her help. Especially around mealtimes. If only he could get her to keep her mouth shut. She picked the absolute worst time to stop listening to him. Maybe Vanessa was right. Lydia was too brazen. And apparently shrewd and nosy. She'd put together enough details of what was going on that she could make his life miserable if she wanted to. And, at the moment, she did. Every time family visited, Lydia's attitude worsened. Vanessa claimed Lydia felt threatened by their family unit, and bringing the extended family into their home only made her feel worse. He didn't see why that would be. Lydia knew she wasn't officially part of his family. He just assumed the extra work made her grumpy, so she took it out on him. To try to circumvent the hassle, he sent her on pointless errands to keep her away from the houseguests. But the day of the funeral, she was in rare form at breakfast. Vanessa and her parents had eaten early, leaving him alone with his parents and the kids.

"So, Dr. Keller," Lydia said, placing a large plate of sausages down on the table beside an even larger bowl of scrambled eggs. "Are you concerned members of the administration will be there today?"

"Well, I would think everyone who works with Royce would make an appearance in some manner," his mother said, scraping a light layer of apple jelly on her toast. "Either yesterday at the viewing or today at the funeral."

"I just thought it might be awkward for him," Lydia said.

"You know, Lydia," Royce said, "this whole situation is one awkward ordeal after another. Could you go see that my black suit is pressed? I'll be getting dressed soon, and I'd like to be sure it's ready."

"I'm sure it is. I don't hang clothes in your closet un-pressed."

"I guess you keep her around for something other than her cheery disposition, huh, son?" his father said, and elbowed him.

Lydia spun toward Gene and opened her mouth.

Royce recognized a tirade in the making and cut it off as best he could. "It could have gotten wrinkled in the closet. And check on the shirt too, please. I just want to be certain everything is ready."

She harrumphed and walked off, obviously miffed, and Royce looked at Jensen and Faith, hoping they'd take his the hint and start talking before either of his parents could take up the conversation again.

They didn't.

"So Royce, why would it be awkward for the administration to attend the service today?" his mother asked, still scraping the toast with her knife. She didn't make eye contact with him, not then. She just stared at the swirls of jelly as she slowly dragged the knife over the bread.

That woman couldn't let anything go. She reminded him of the people in his ER who were told not to pick at their injuries, but they just couldn't help it, and even though the cuts had scabbed over, they ended up bleeding again. Just like those people, she picked at wounds until they gushed.

He didn't want to gush.

"Come on, kids. Better go get ready."

The kids got up from the table, their breakfasts barely touched.

"Royce," his mother said and looked up, fixing him with a piercing stare. "They haven't finished eating."

"We need to get dressed, Mother." He couldn't take the pressure. He pushed away from the table and followed his kids up the stairs.

Too many fires.

THE VIEWING HAD BEEN DIFFICULT. Friends, colleagues, even Detective Cooper had been by to pay their respects, as well as countless schoolmates of the kids and many faculty members. Seeing Hope inside the casket he and Vanessa had chosen, lying so still and lifeless, her hair and make-up expertly done and yet so unlike her… he wasn't prepared for that. He was used to death, just in the more immediate sense. The dead bodies he dealt with were still warm, still had an element of soul in them.

And they weren't family.

As hard as the viewing was, the funeral was infinitely worse. He didn't think there could have been more flowers in the room than there were the day before, but Sid kept carrying arrangements in and tucking them into corners and putting them behind chairs on the floor. The pungent aroma of roses and lilies, carnations and gladioli, chrysanthemums and alstroemeria, and assorted filler flowers masked the cloying scent of the air freshener that had filled the funeral home the day they'd made Hope's arrangements. He'd only known three of those blooms the day before, but standing in that room, he understood why his mother and mother-in-law obsessed over their choices. It mattered. Every detail mattered. He made Vanessa teach him what they all were as they'd looked around the room. He listened and repeated until he had learned each blossom, each exact shade… it became imperative to him to commit it all to memory. Somehow it mattered to him how people chose to say they were sorry, to say goodbye.

He found it peculiar that such beauty was used to represent such pain, but despite the strangeness, he desperately absorbed every detail.

The spray they'd purchased for the coffin consisted of white lilies, apricot gladioli, and forget-me-nots. Vanessa insisted on those flowers so Hope would know she'd never be forgotten. Beside it sat the bouquet from the kids, a display of peach roses, white carnations, and burgundy alstroemeria. Despite all Royce's pleading and negotiating, the grandmothers wouldn't pitch in for one shared arrangement, finding it more important to out-do the other than to show solidarity in the face of tragedy. They'd sent lavish displays of chrysanthemums, roses, and gladioli in shades of orange, pink, and white. Thankfully, they'd ordered from the same florist, and she managed to make the arrangements coordinate in size, color, and style. Just those four sprays took up the whole casket area, severely hampering Sid's ability to place all the other arrangements in the room. The offerings from loved ones, friends, and colleagues lined the walls, sat on tables and windowsills, and even trickled out into the hallway.

For the viewing, there had been a few comfortable arm chairs scattered about the room, but for the funeral, rows and rows of folding chairs had been set up for the priest to conduct a service in the parlor before the casket was closed for the last time and the mourners moved on to Mass at the church. Royce ran his finger under his collar. His tie strangled him. He couldn't breathe.

The day before, he had avoided the casket after the initial family viewing. It made it easier, not seeing Hope. He'd shaken hands with people, accepted condolences. He'd kept everything distant, clinical. He knew distant and clinical. He did that for a living. Distant and clinical comforted him.

He wasn't prepared for the crushing reality of the funeral day.

The unemotional detachment, the indifferent disconnect... gone. Completely failed him, forcing him to experience it all, in the moment, on an emotional level.

He abhorred every second of it.

He and his family sat in the first row of seats. Vanessa clasped his hand, her grip icy, her fingers trembling. He held onto her as much to support himself as to support her.

The priest spoke, but Royce had no idea what he said. He stood when everyone else stood and sat when they sat, their voices an annoying drone in his ears. His vision clouded, blurred with tears no longer unshed. Pride and strength be damned. He was saying goodbye to his daughter. He didn't care about the blood. None of that mattered. Hope had been his daughter.

People marched past him. Some gripped his shoulder, some bent and whispered in his ear. He sat, back straight, clutching Vanessa's hand.

At some point, he didn't know how long it had been, Sid shook him gently to get his attention. "It's time, Dr. Keller."

Royce turned his head and looked at him. "Time? For what?"

"Time, sir. To pay your last respects."

Royce looked around him. All the non-family members had vacated the room, leaving him alone with Vanessa, the kids, and Hope's grandparents. Sid held his palm out, gesturing for them to approach Hope's casket.

Royce wiped his eyes and leaned over toward his parents. "Mother, Dad. Linc, Rose. Go ahead."

Thank God, they didn't argue. The four of them walked to the front of the room and said their goodbyes. Royce barely paid attention to them, other than to note that even the men needed tissues on their way out of the room.

Royce didn't need Sid to direct him. He knew what they needed to do. He helped Vanessa up and escorted the kids toward the casket. He let Jensen and Faith approach first. Jensen's shoulders shook, and Royce laid a hand on his back for support. Faith broke down, sobbing uncontrollably, and put the Tuff Guy bear in the coffin. Then she ran out of the room. Jensen squeezed Hope's hand, shivered, then ran after his sister.

That left Royce alone with Vanessa.

"Remember when she was learning how to walk?" Vanessa asked.

"She clung so tightly to my fingers."

"She'd only walk with you. No one else."

Tears rolled down Royce's face. "But she'd only walk to you. No one else."

Vanessa sniffled. "She was stubborn." She wiped away tears, only to have new ones replace them. "Remember when you taught her how to ride a bike? Again, she'd only let you hold her. Not me."

"She said, 'Daddy, don't let go.'"

"And you didn't. Not until she was ready."

"But I did let go." Royce choked on a sob and reached into the casket, brushing at a curl by Hope's shoulder. "I let go, and she fell, and I wasn't there to pick her up."

"No. Don't do this, Royce. You were a good father. You are a good father."

He shook his head and dropped to his knees. "Hope. Oh, Hope. I'm so sorry. Can you ever forgive me?"

"Not like this, Royce. Our goodbye can't be like this."

Sid came into the room then. "Dr. and Mrs. Keller. Are you ready?"

"Hope…" Royce, still on his knees, sobbed at the casket.

Vanessa, also in tears, pulled him to his feet. Sid led them toward the exit, offering them tissues.

Royce heard the lid of the casket close as he walked out the door toward his car.

THE ONLY PART OF THE Mass Royce remembered was the pallbearers bringing in Hope's casket. And the only part of the cemetery service he remembered was placing a rose on her casket before leaving.

Everyone headed for the reception. And it was a damn good thing. Because he needed a drink.

He was done playing referee. Vanessa could do it. She'd been hiding long enough. It was his turn to let go a little.

When they got home, Vanessa lapsed immediately into hostess-mode, putting the mothers to work with Lydia. They set out food and arranged beverage stations. Royce went straight to his study and opened a bottle of scotch. He hadn't even taken a sip when someone knocked at his door.

"Carley. Didn't expect to see you today. Come on in. Want a drink?" He held up an empty glass.

"I thought you didn't drink."

"I usually don't. Today's an exception."

"Sure. Why not?" She held her hand out for the glass and took what he offered. "To Hope."

Royce raised his in salute and downed it in one swallow while she sipped hers. He poured himself another. "Thanks for coming today."

"That's what friends are for."

"Is that what we are?"

"Isn't it?"

"Then why won't you tell me what I want to know?" He tossed another drink back and poured himself a third.

"As your friend, I'm going to tell you three things. One, I already answered that question. Two, I'm not going to sit here and let you get wasted, so either slow down or I'm out of here. And three, I have something in my purse you might be interested in."

He got ready to down his third, but looked at her instead. "What is it?"

"Put the glass down."

He put the drink on his desk. "What is it?"

She sighed and took an envelope out of her purse. "You should have trusted me. It would have saved me a lot of work. But it's like I told you. They're yours."

He ripped the envelope open and squinted at the printout. Then he looked up at her, relief warming him as much as the liquor. "It's true, then? I really am their father? Even Faith?"

"Even Faith. Now stop acting like a tool and start acting like a dad."

"I made such a mess of things, Car."

"So what are you going to do about it?" Stanford asked from the doorway.

Carley cleared her throat. "If you'll excuse me."

"You don't have to leave on my account," he said.

"Oh, I'm not, sir," she said. "I was just stepping out anyway. I'm just going to go see if Vanessa needs any help in the kitchen." She scooted around him and walked down the hall.

"Has she ever even met Vanessa?" Stanford asked.

Royce sipped at his scotch. "No."

Stanford sighed and sat in a club chair. "Pour me one of those."

Ben stepped in and closed the door behind him. "Me, too."

Royce poured them each a glass and sat back down behind his desk. "I'm glad you guys are here. I really need my friends right now."

"We all loved Hope," Stanford said. "Of course we're here for you."

"You were always so close with my kids, Ben," Royce said. "Not having any of your own, you've been like part of the family."

Ben tossed his scotch back and put his glass down, hard, on the desk. "Don't mention it, Royce. Really."

"No, man, I'm serious. I mean, I know you're here for me, but I know this is probably hard for you too. I just want you to know I appreciate you coming out here like this. It's been tough." He put the bottle of scotch in Ben's reach.

Ben poured himself another drink. "Why don't we just talk about something else, huh?"

"First, a toast," Royce said. "To my mentor, who, despite harboring a secret I desperately want to know, is going out of his way to help guide me through this ridiculous mess I've made of my life."

"Here, here," Ben said and lifted his glass.

"Wait," Royce said. "And to my best friend, who turned out to be an even better friend than Wade, who betrayed me."

"Okay," Ben said. "Cheers."

"Wait." Royce held up his glass. "And to Hope. Who deserved a better father than the one she was stuck with all these years."

"Royce, really," Stanford said.

"I'm done," Royce said. "Let's drink."

"That's the best thing you've said yet," Ben said. "I'll drink to that."

Royce sipped his scotch and studied the two men who sat there, supporting him through the toughest time of his life. He had survived the worst life had to offer and come out the other side with a support system intact.

The cops had released Hope's body, so obviously the investigation was going in his favor. His parents and in-laws hadn't figured out what was going on, and with the funeral over, there was no reason for them to stay. The odds of them not finding out were pretty good. He'd lost Wade, but he still had Stanford and Ben to rely on. Maybe things were looking up.

CHAPTER **14**

BECAUSE OF THE FUNERAL, TOD had moved their appointment
to Monday. Vanessa was not in a morning mood. Definitely not in a Monday mood. When she looked in the mirror and saw the bloodshot eyes and
dark circles, she decided to not even bother with cosmetics. The appointment
would probably be spent in tears, anyway. Why add raccoon to the list?

She donned black capris and a black draped cowl neck tank. The funeral
might be over, but she still mourned. She bypassed her favorite silver sandals
for a pair of sedate black Mary Janes and twisted her hair up into a clip. Other
than pairing her engagement ring with her wedding band, the only jewelry
she put on was her St. Luke medal. She threw her phone and her journal in
her bag, checked to be sure she had sunglasses, and went downstairs to meet
Royce. Instead, she met her mother-in-law.

"Where are you off to looking so… well, like you, I suppose?" Liz said.

"Royce and I have some errands to run."

"Isn't Royce going to work?"

"He's on leave."

"How long do they give him for bereavement leave? I mean, he's been
off for a week."

Thinking quickly, she said, "He's an important man, Liz. They'll give him all the time he needs so when he does go back, he's refreshed and ready."

Royce entered the room and looked back and forth between the two of them, stopping to meet Vanessa's gaze with wide eyes.

"Royce," Liz said, "do you think it's a good idea to take so much time off? You're not setting a very good example for your underlings."

"Mother, my daughter just died. No one expects me back to work so soon."

"And what kind of example does that set? Taking more time than the standard leave offers?"

He sighed and shook his head. "I have plenty of time at my disposal to do with as I see fit. It's fine."

"And you 'see fit' to use your leave to go gallivanting around instead of staying in with your family and mourning appropriately?"

"We do not 'gallivant.' Stop saying that. And we have to go." He kissed her on her cheek. "Come on, Ness."

Vanessa walked out, listening to Liz continue to rant. She'd probably still be yammering when they got back.

In the car, Royce turned to her. "Why were you discussing my leave with my mother?"

"I wasn't. She was discussing it with me. And she disapproves."

"I gathered that." He pulled out and headed toward town. "I'd appreciate it if you wouldn't engage with her. They should be leaving soon, and we've avoided telling them anything. I'd like to keep it that way."

She turned and faced him. "What do you think I've been doing? I've been hiding in the basement with my parents. I get up early every morning to make them breakfast and bring it down to them so I don't have to sit at the table with your folks, and my father hasn't liked my eggs or my pancakes."

"Are you surprised?"

"Really, Royce, how bad could they be? They come from a box."

"The eggs or the pancakes?"

She huffed and crossed her arms. "I've played so much eight-ball, I could probably beat you now. My poker skills have improved to the point that I'm ready for a run at Vegas. Do you think I want to be doing those things when my daughter's just died? But I need a reason to stay downstairs with them, and what other reason do I have?"

She noticed him re-grip the wheel when she said 'my daughter,' but she couldn't take the words back. She started to continue, to try to take his mind off it, but he spoke up instead.

"Let's just get through this session, okay? Maybe when we get back, everyone will be packed up and we can get back to normal. Or what amounts to normal for us."

Normal for them. Normal lately consisted of Royce sleeping on the floor and the two of them passing each other like jets in the sky. They needed the assistance of someone in a control tower—someone like Tod—to help them navigate around each other, to make sure they maintained an appropriate distance. To the casual observer, it looked like they occupied the same space. But to a person in the know? They were miles apart.

She thought they had made progress. They'd had a breakthrough when they planned Hope's funeral and shared some tender moments the day they buried her. But she felt like she was playing Mother-May-I with him, taking steps forward and back with no real logic to the progress other than his whims.

Apparently his whim dictated it was a 'two-steps-back' kind of day.

They drove the rest of the way to Tod's in silence and still hadn't spoken a word to each other when Tod opened the door to them and escorted them inside. Vanessa noted he was dressed more like a therapist, wearing chinos, an oxford, and loafers. She wondered if Royce would approve or if he'd just find something else to complain about.

"So," Dr. Jeffers began, "how did the two of you do through the funeral?"

"Before we start, I just wanted to thank you again for coming," Vanessa said.

Royce's head snapped up. "What?"

Vanessa looked at him. "For coming. To the funeral. I was thanking him."

"I don't remember him coming."

"You spoke to him. We both did."

Royce shook his head. "I'm sorry. It was a stressful time, and there were so many people…."

"I noticed that," Dr. Jeffers said. "That's a testament to the two of you. Who you are. Who Hope was. I thought maybe we could talk about that today for a little bit."

"No," Royce said.

"No?" Dr. Jeffers said.

"No. I'm sorry, but this is just eating at me." He turned to face Vanessa. "I know you want to move past this and get on with our lives, but I can't. I can't until we've cleared the air. You have this huge secret, and I need to know."

Vanessa was glad she skipped breakfast that morning, because her stomach roiled. She started shaking her head, but Royce stopped her.

"Don't say 'no.' You don't understand. Every man I see, I wonder if he's the one. Every time you mention someone's name, I wonder. I'll always wonder." He clenched his fist and held it to his chest. "It's eating at me. I can't sleep at night. I can't function all day. You might think you're sparing my feelings by keeping this a secret, but whoever it is, I can take it. It's the not-knowing that I can't take."

"And what if knowing makes it worse?"

"It can't possibly."

Dr. Jeffers looked at her.

She clutched her medal and slid it back and forth on its chain. "You don't know what you're asking."

"Yes, I do."

She stood up and walked to the window. It seemed easier to her to tell her stories if she had a physical distance from Royce, and the window gave her the largest buffer. She ran her hand over the sill. It was smooth and cool despite the sun pouring through the glass. She'd need to touch the pane soon. She'd need the warmth.

"Do you remember when Jensen was born?" she asked. "What a good baby he was?"

"Of course."

She remembered, too....

JENSEN WAS JUST THREE MONTHS old. He was the best baby. He only cried if he was hungry, about every three hours. Other than that, he was an angel. She couldn't be luckier.

He was such a good baby, she was able to take him with her to her post-partum checkup. And like she expected, he slept in his carrier the entire time. Even when the nurses fawned all over him. When she got home, she called Royce with the good news. "We're good to go tonight. I got the all-clear."

"Oh, thank God. It's been too long."

"Champagne and lingerie?" she asked.

"Don't need any of that. Just be naked and in bed when I get home. Hell, I don't even need the bed!"

She laughed. That was the longest conversation she'd had with him since the baby had been born. She wondered what more she could say to keep him talking.

"I get off at eleven," he said. "Don't fall asleep."

But that was it. He hung up.

She spent the afternoon the usual way, playing with Jensen, feeding him, changing him. At seven o'clock, she gave him a bath and put on his pajamas. Then he started fussing. He never fussed. And he kept on fussing. She rocked him. Changed him. Burped him. Tried feeding him, but to no avail. His fussing just got worse.

In fact, he wasn't fussing. He was crying.

So she called Royce.

"Hey, Ness. Can't talk." She heard a woman's voice in the background and Royce telling someone to be quiet. "Actually, I was just about to call you. I have to pull a double tonight. Someone called off. So I have to take a rain check on our plans. Sorry." He disconnected the call before she could even tell him what she wanted.

Surely he heard his son crying.

But he didn't care.

Then she did what every desperate new mother would do. She called her pediatrician.

Luckily, he also happened to be a close friend.

"Ben. Thank God. Can you come over?"

"Ness? What's wrong?"

Jensen picked that time to let out an ear-piercing wail.

"I think Jensen's sick. I took him to the OB-GYN with me today, and people were touching him, and now he won't stop crying, and I can't reach Royce, and—"

"Okay, relax. I'm coming right now."

Ben made it there in record time. Vanessa had Jensen clutched tightly to her chest and hated to surrender Jensen to him, but the enormous wails coming from his tiny body made her decision easier.

Ben took the baby, unfastened his pajamas, and checked his vitals. The wails turned to softer sobs, and Ben smiled.

"Why are you smiling?" Vanessa asked. She hovered at Jensen's side, watching Ben's every move.

Ben stripped Jensen down to his diaper, and his sobs turned immediately to coos. He stretched his arms and legs, then fell to sleep, a peaceful look on his face.

"What's going on?" Vanessa asked, still frantic, but calming. "What just happened?"

Ben chuckled. "He was just hot, Ness. He got hotter when you hugged him. He's fine."

She sighed, deep and long, and threw her arms around him. "Then I'll smother you instead. Thank you so much. I was so scared."

"Why is he in thermal PJs in the summer?"

"October isn't summer, Ben."

"It's not winter."

"Our furnace is on."

"Exactly. Your furnace is on, and he's in thermals and under a blanket."

"Okay. I'll go lighter on the layers until the snow falls. Thanks." She hugged him again. "Do you want something to drink?"

They headed toward the kitchen.

She saw the bucket of ice with champagne in it and thought about trying to hide it, but Ben saw it before she could.

"Big night tonight?"

"No. Royce canceled."

"Been there," he mumbled.

"What?"

"Nothing. Sorry about that."

"Don't worry about it. Look, no point in this going to waste. Let's drink it." She pulled it out of the bucket and handed it to him.

He looked at the label. "You sure? This is a good bottle."

"I was saving it for something special."

"So save it." He handed it back.

She pushed it back to him. "This is special. You saved Jensen."

"Hardly."

"Come on, Ben. This was supposed to be a big night for me. Royce already ruined it. Let's salvage what's left."

Ben sighed. "Fine." He opened the bottle and filled their glasses. "To salvaging what's left."

She clinked her glass against his. "I can drink to that."

Ben downed his and sighed.

"What's wrong?" Vanessa asked.

"Mia's leaving me."

"What? Are you sure? She never even told me she was unhappy."

"I'm sure."

"Why?"

"She's decided she doesn't want kids. And that's a deal-breaker for me. That's the one thing I always wanted."

"That doesn't mean she's leaving."

"We've talked it to death. Neither of us is budging. It's not that we don't love each other. It's just that we want different things. She's home packing right now, actually."

They drank the champagne, and two bottles of wine, and commiserated with each other about their spouses. Ben, because his wife changed her mind about their future, and Vanessa, because her husband put everyone else's lives before hers.

And somewhere between a robust cabernet and a full-bodied merlot, they sought solace in the comfort of each other's arms.

VANESSA WAS CHILLED TO THE bone remembering and retelling the events of that night. She rested her head against the window pane, trying to soak up the heat of the sun streaming through the glass. It was warm on her skin, but the heat was superficial. It couldn't warm her soul. She felt dead inside.

"Are you fucking kidding me?" Royce didn't yell. He didn't even speak out loud. His voice barely registered above a whisper. "All this time, and it was my best friend?"

"I'm sorry, Royce. I never meant for it to happen. We were drunk, and we were both hurting, and I swear, it was just the one time…"

"I think I'd rather it have been an affair. At least if it had meant something to you…."

She turned to face him. "Royce, please. We're both so sorry. We both love you so much, and—"

He held up his hand. "No. No more. Not now. You're going to need to find your own way home." He left without a backward glance.

"Why don't we discuss your feelings about this, Vanessa?" Dr. Jeffers said.

"My feelings about it?" Vanessa assumed her snort of derision said all she needed to say. She reached into her purse and pulled out her phone. A quick web search and she had the number she needed. "City Cab Co.? Hi, I need a pick-up, please." Once she'd given Dr. Jeffers's address to the dispatcher, she disconnected the call and looked at her therapist. "If you think Royce isn't ready to process any of this, you can imagine how I'm feeling. Now, if you don't mind, I'm going to wait outside for my ride."

"Vanessa, we need to meet Wednesday. Same time."

"Yeah. I'm sure Royce will be up to that." She walked out and stood on the sidewalk until her taxi came.

Vanessa had always hated riding in cabs because they seemed germy and a bit dangerous. The nice thing about them? The drivers never insisted on small talk. She rode in the grime-mobile in total silence until she got home. Unfortunately, all her houseguests were lingering when she appeared, and they all wanted to know why she needed a cab to get home, sans-Royce.

Jensen saved her from thinking up a lie. "You and Dad have a fight at the therapist's? Or did he have to go in for more questions about his responsibility in Hope's death?"

"What?" Liz asked, and the four of them turned toward Vanessa.

And with his back to his grandparents, he sneered at his mother and walked away, leaving Vanessa to deal with the fallout.

CHAPTER 15

ROYCE DROVE BACK TO THE lake, seeking solace. But even the
calm waters of that serene setting couldn't settle the churning tide of emotions swelling inside him. He looked across the lake. The Spring Carnival had
packed and departed. All that remained were the frameworks of a few booths,
empty cartons and used napkins blowing across the campgrounds, a few rusty
old dumpsters ready to clear the gathered and the as-yet-uncollected trash, and
two sad port-a-potties he swore he could smell from where he sat. How could
something that brought joy to so many be reduced to such a barren, reeking
waste in such a short time?

He rolled up his windows and drove away, the memories of happy times
as long gone as the scent of hotdogs and the sounds of the merry-go-round.

He gave no conscious thought to where he drove, but several minutes later
he found himself in the doctors' lot at the hospital. He might be suspended,
but his parking pass was still valid.

Instead of entering the hospital, he crossed the street and entered a suite
of professional buildings. Walking through a series of unlabeled doors instead of into the main lobby, he found himself behind the reception desk of
a doctor's office.

"Hi, Sheila. He busy?"

"Hi, Royce. How are you?" Sheila turned from her computer.

"Uh, there's someone at your window."

"There's *always* someone at my window. They can wait a minute."

"Go ahead and take them. I'm going to go back to Ben's office."

"I think he's with a patient right now."

"I'll wait. Is his door open?"

"Should be. If not, let me know. I'll dig up a key."

"Thanks." He turned toward the hallway.

"I'll make sure he knows you're back there." Sheila sighed and slid her window open. "How can I help you?"

Royce marveled at the derision in her tone. It was no wonder people hated to go to the doctor. Not only did they have to fear a negative outcome, they had to deal with long waits, grumpy office staff, sick patients spreading germs making them even sicker, and insurance headaches. If he had to seek treatments the way regular people did, he'd hate it, too.

But he didn't.

He circumvented the system on a good day. But this wasn't a good day, and he wasn't there to see the doctor for a medical visit.

Royce let himself into Ben's office. It had been a few years since he'd been in there. When they got together during the day, which seemed to happen less and less often lately, Ben usually went to the hospital or they met somewhere else. When Royce did go to Ben's practice, he didn't end up in Ben's actual office. He usually stayed in reception talking to Sheila. What he found in Ben's office shocked him.

Besides the ubiquitous diplomas on the wall and medical reference tomes on the bookcases, the shelves and walls were covered with photos. There was one of him, Ben, and Wade on graduation day. One of Ben and Stanford together. One of Mia and Ben on their wedding day. Royce figured that one would have been burned a long time ago. Every family photo Vanessa had ever insisted they pose for was in there, along with every class picture Hope had ever given him. There was even a very nice candid shot at a picnic of Ben, Hope, and Vanessa playing with sparklers. They looked like a family.

Bastard.

Royce studied the collection closer and found artwork from Hope's younger days. A sketch of a butterfly… or it might have been a flower. And one of a house with her whole family inside, including "Uncle Benny."

Uncle Benny was taller than Daddy and standing beside Mommy, holding Mommy's hand.

Royce took the picture off the wall and stared at it. He backed up and fell into a chair, still transfixed with the picture. Vanessa said it wasn't an affair, right? She said it was only once?

Didn't she?

Then why did Ben look so close to Vanessa in that drawing? Kids draw what they know. Their perspective on paper is skewed based on their perception of reality. Maybe Ben was there more than Royce realized. He was busy building his career when the kids were young. Ben could have moved in and he wouldn't have noticed. Besides, when Ben and Mia got divorced, Royce suggested Vanessa should spend time with him.

He rubbed his hand over his face. Hell, he actually encouraged it. He thought being around kids would remind Ben of what he wanted in life and it would inspire him to start dating again so he could start a family with someone new.

But he never did.

Why would he? Royce had already given him a family. Handed him his own on a silver fucking platter.

When Royce felt a hand on his shoulder, he jumped. He had been so completely absorbed in his thoughts about the artwork family that he didn't hear Ben enter the room.

"Hey. Sheila told me you were back here." He glanced around, but didn't meet Royce's gaze. "You want to go somewhere and talk? I can take the rest of the day off."

"How many times, Ben?"

Ben tipped his head. "How many times, what? Can I take the afternoon off? Well, I guess that depends...."

Royce thrust the picture at him. "How many times? You and Vanessa."

Ben lifted his hands. "I don't know what you're talking about."

"It's over, Ben. She told me." Royce stood. "My wife and my best friend. My wife, and my best friend." He took a couple of steps toward him." My wife. And my best friend."

"Look, Royce, buddy." Ben shut and locked his door.

"Don't call me 'buddy.' Buddies don't sleep with their friend's woman." He took a few more steps, and Ben retreated behind his desk. "Buddies don't have a child with their friend's wife. Buddies don't hide the paternity of said child from their buddy, ultimately causing that child's death and the destruction of that man's career!"

Ben stopped backing up and stood toe-to-toe with Royce, his breathing as labored as his friend's. "That's enough! I'm sorry you lost Hope. I lost her, too. But while you got to raise her for the last seventeen years, I've had to stand on the sidelines. And you never even acted like you wanted her. She's all I ever wanted and you didn't even care! And then you go and pull a bone-headed stunt in the ER and break protocol? What were you thinking?"

"She was *dying!*"

"And now she's dead! If you had followed procedure, she might have lived!"

"She didn't have time!"

"We'll never know!"

Royce slammed his fist into Ben's face, the sting of his knuckle slamming into Ben's nose as satisfying as the sound of cracking bone. He watched with detached fulfillment as Ben's head whipped to the side. "Bastard."

He started to turn and leave, but Ben grabbed his shoulder and spun him back around. His cheekbone connected with a fist that left him seeing stars for a second.

Then he saw red.

The next few moments he didn't really see anything at all. He was all primal instinct and raw adrenaline. It was no Ivy League boxing match. It wasn't even an uptown gym sparring round. It was a street fight. Punches landed from the tops of heads to the kidneys when backs were turned. When fists were out of position? Thrown elbows or butted heads. Royce took a kick to the ribs that left him breathless. He delivered a knee to Ben's chin when he was bent over, sending him crashing back into the wall. Royce didn't know how, but they were on the floor at one point, grappling and reaching for objects off the desk to use as weapons. Ben came up with a glass paperweight. Royce grabbed the framed picture Hope had drawn and swung it downward toward Ben's knee.

"Wait!" Ben said.

Royce paused, inches from having glass shards and wooden sticks to choose from. Only then did he hear pounding on the door.

"Doctor! Doctor!"

Ben called out, "Don't worry, Sheila. Just two old college mates rough-housing."

"Are you sure?"

"We're fine. Go back to work."

Royce stared at Ben, and the two of them waited until they heard Sheila walk down the hall.

"Good thing I locked the door."

Royce sighed.

Ben put the paperweight down and raised his hand in surrender. "Are we done? You win. I quit."

"I win?" Royce said. "What the hell do I win?"

"The fight."

"Big deal. I was winning that, anyway."

Ben snorted.

Royce raised the picture, intent to destroy it.

Ben pleaded with him. "Please, don't. You win… whatever you want."

"I can't have what I want."

Ben sat down on the floor. "I've lived my whole adult life without what I wanted."

"You're kidding, right? What did you want? My wife? My family? You could have had your own, but you didn't. You had Mia, but you let her get away. For what? To blame me for your sad, lonely life? Forget it. You made your choices, whatever they were. It's not my fault you don't like where you are now."

"You don't know anything about my choices."

"Whose fault is that? I've always been here for you. You can't say the same."

"I've always been a friend to you. That's part of my problem. That's why I never got what I wanted. Why I'll never have what I want." He spread his arms and gestured to the wreckage in his office. "So welcome to my world."

Royce put the picture on Ben's desk and walked to the door. "I don't want to be in your world, Ben. And I don't want you in mine."

Royce didn't want to take the long way around, so he decided to leave straight through the waiting room.

As he passed Sheila, she gasped. "You're bleeding!"

"Yeah?" He swiped at his mouth. Blood dripped from his fingers. "You should see the other guy."

"Let me get some bandages." She got up, but he kept walking. He was through the lobby and out the door before she could reach him. She could play nurse to Ben. If the nurses weren't already.

Out at his car, he pulled down the visor mirror. He had a split lip and the beginnings of a shiner. His ribs were sore, but he didn't think they were cracked or broken. Probably bruised, though. Explaining his appearance to his parents would be difficult. Maybe he could rent a car and say he'd had an accident. But he didn't want them to worry. Perhaps a mugging…

As he drove home, he thought of different scenarios, and finally decided just to say he was sparring with a friend at the gym and things got out of hand. That was close enough to the truth and should cause the least amount of worry.

When he walked in the house, he was prepared for questions about his condition. Perhaps shock, and a lecture from his mother.

He didn't expect to hear five people yelling around the dining room table.

"What's going on in here?" he yelled over the din.

"Royce Emerson Keller," his mother said. "What happened to your face?"

"What, this? It's nothing," he said, trying to put his plan into action. "I was at the gym, and—"

"Is this another one of your lies?"

"What?" He looked between his mother and his wife. Vanessa's eyes were wide and she was shaking her head almost imperceptibly.

"Stop looking at that tramp and answer me."

"You need to stop calling my daughter a tramp," Linc said. "If your boy was getting things done right, she never would have strayed and this whole situation wouldn't have happened."

"Don't you *dare* blame this on my son!"

"Who else should we blame?" Rose said. "He was the one not following the rules at work. It is the hard-working farmer who ought to have the first share of the crops. Second Timothy, chapter two, verse six."

"Now, what the hell does that mean?" Gene asked.

"He didn't do the work, so his crops are suffering," Rose said.

"Are you comparing my daughter to wheat, Mom?" Vanessa asked.

"Truly, truly, I say to you, unless a grain of wheat falls into the earth and dies, it remains alone; but if it dies, it bears much fruit. John, chapter twelve, verse twenty-four."

"Mom, for the love of God…."

"Don't take the Lord's name in vain, dear."

"Getting back to the matter at hand," Liz said, "I want to know what you plan to do to get my son's career back on track."

"By all means, Liz. Let's forget my daughter's dead. Let's not worry that my marriage is in shambles. Let's not even care that your son is standing there, swollen, bruised, and bleeding. Let's worry about his career. Because at the end of the day, if you can't tell your friends Royce is Chief of Emergency Medicine and next in line for Chief of Staff, then you'll have to hang your head in shame at the next ladies' tea. And that's really what's important, right?"

"Why, I never," Liz began, hand to her chest. "Are you going to stand there and let her talk to me that way?" she asked Royce.

Vanessa pushed her chair back and looked at Royce. "If you want help with your injuries, I'll be upstairs." Then she walked out of the room.

"If she was my wife, I'd turn her over my knee for talking to her elders like that," Gene said.

Royce shook his head. "Dad, not now."

"I'm sorry. You want to do what to my daughter?" Linc asked.

Royce left the room and headed for the stairs. He didn't really feel like being with Vanessa at the moment, but given the choice between her or his houseguests, she was definitely the least objectionable option of the two.

When he opened the door, she was sitting on the bed, looking at his journal.

CHAPTER 16

"DR. JEFFERS TOLD US PART of moving on was to get our feelings out. You won't talk to him. You won't talk to me. I bought this damn journal for you, and you haven't even opened it."

"What are you doing going through my things?"

"You said you were going to try, Royce. Is this you trying? Leaving the journal in the shrink wrap?"

"I asked you what gave you the right to go through my things."

"And I asked you when you were going to start participating in our therapy. We're never going to move past our history, past Hope's death, and into our future if you don't take this seriously."

"Take this seriously? That's rich." He walked into the bathroom and came out dabbing a wet washcloth on his lip. "Bruises and blood aren't serious enough for you?"

"That's not taking anything seriously. That's losing your temper like a child and blowing off steam. Why don't you try settling an argument with your head and heart for once instead of your smart mouth and quick fists."

"I've never hit you."

"Hit me? No, you haven't. But you haven't settled any arguments with me, either. You just walk away at the beginnings of any disagreements. Before all this, I don't think we've had more than a tiff in fifteen years."

"Most people would call that a successful marriage."

"Most people wouldn't call this a marriage at all! You're never home, and when you are, you're nicer to the maid than you are to me. Or is there a reason for that?"

Royce didn't answer. He walked calmly out the door and closed it softly behind him.

Vanessa threw the journal after him. It hit the wall with a loud *smack* and landed on the carpet with a soft *thud*. She'd been suspicious of Lydia for years. It seemed the only time Royce ever made it home for lunch was when Vanessa had obligations across town. And the way Lydia looked at him, the things she did for him....

She sat on the edge of the bed and looked at her engagement ring. She remembered when Royce had given it to her. He had promised to make her every dream come true.

She just didn't think he meant her nightmares, too.

Sighing, she removed her ring and her necklace and put them in her jewelry box. What she really needed was a good soak, so she stepped into the bathroom, stripped, and filled the tub with steaming water and some of the verbena bubble bath Hope had given her for Mother's Day. It wasn't her usual scent, but it reminded her of her daughter, so she used it instead. Sinking into the water, she lay back, closed her eyes, and tried to relax.

Steam billowed in the bathroom. She immersed herself in the hot and foamy water, inhaled the scent in the perfumed air. Soon Vanessa drifted off. She didn't know how long she was out, but when she woke up, the air was clear, the water was cool, the bubbles deflated. As she started to rise, the handle of the door turned. "Royce, I'm in here. Just give me a minute."

The door opened, but she was in no mood to share any intimacies with her husband. She sank into the water and prepared to launch into a lecture about boundaries. To her shock and dismay, it wasn't Royce.

It was Gene.

Vanessa scurried to scoop the few remaining bubbles into strategic locations. "Gene! What are you doing in here?"

"I saw Royce downstairs in his study. It looked like he was settling in there for the night."

"And what does that have to do with you being in here?" Her voice squeaked as it rose. She pulled her knees up and together, and still fought a losing battle to gather the bubbles around her.

"I thought you might want someone to talk to. You know," he sat on the edge of the tub and trailed his finger through the scant foam, "a sympathetic ear."

She batted at his finger. "Thank you, but I think you need to go. This is quite inappropriate."

"Inappropriate!" He threw back his head and guffawed. "Darling, that ship sailed long ago. About eighteen years ago, wouldn't you say?"

"Gene, please." Her teeth chattered as much from the cold water as from fear of her father-in-law. Royce never believed her that he was too... affectionate... with her. He said it was all in fun and she misinterpreted it. He said it so often, she'd begun to doubt her instincts about him. To the point she'd let her guard down. Royce would never forgive her if this happened. He'd never forgive her if she accused Gene of it, either.

"Come on, Ness. You played the good girl for all these years. And I went along with it. I believed you. But now I know better. Let's have a little fun. No one has to know."

The tears fell freely down her cheeks. She was almost out of bubbles. Almost out of time. "Gene, don't make me scream."

"No one will hear you. And even if they did, no one would care. You've lost them all, Vanessa. Why not take some comfort where it's offered?"

"If anyone's going to comfort her, it's going to be *me.*"

Vanessa looked past Gene to see Royce standing in the doorway.

The color drained from Gene's face. He rose and faced his son. "Good news. She didn't fall for it. Whatever infidelities she was guilty of in the past, she's over them. She's loyal to you now, boy." He clapped Royce on the shoulder and started to walk around him.

Royce stepped in front of him to block his path. "I trust you and Mother will be leaving first thing in the morning?"

Gene was quiet for a moment, then nodded.

"We won't be there to see you off."

"Goodbye, son. And good luck. If you need anything…."

"I won't be calling you."

Gene nodded and left.

After the bedroom door closed, Vanessa broke down. Royce helped her out of the tub. He wrapped her in a towel and led her to the bedroom, where he scrubbed her dry. The combination of friction of the terrycloth against her skin and his nearness to her body warmed her to her core.

She blinked back more tears and looked up at him. "I'm so sorry."

"For what?"

"I didn't invite him in."

"I know."

"I didn't want you to find out about him like that."

"You've been telling me for years."

"But you didn't want it to be true."

"Neither did you."

She sighed and wrapped her arms around him. He gasped, and she pulled away. "What's the matter?"

"It's nothing."

"It's something. Let me see."

"Really. I'm fine."

"Take your shirt off, or I'm taking it off you."

He looked at her for a moment, then he slowly removed his shirt.

"Oh, Royce. Your ribs! You need a doctor."

"I am a doctor."

"Stop being so proud. Someone needs to look at this."

He narrowed his eyes.

She tipped her head. "Let me call…" She didn't know what to say. Usually she'd suggest Ben. Then Wade. Then Stanford. But Royce wouldn't like any of those suggestions at the moment.

"What?"

She bit her lip.

"You were going to say 'Ben,' weren't you?"

She nodded.

"Ben's the one who did this."

She sighed. "Stanford, then."

"Vanessa. It's fine. They're just bruised. An ice bag, some ibuprofen, I'll be good as new."

"Do you want me to get some tape, or a compression bandage?"

"No. We don't do that anymore. The constriction isn't good for healing. Really, I'm fine. I don't even think the ribs are cracked. It's just a nasty bruise. It doesn't even hurt to breathe. Just when you touch it."

She ran her fingers lightly over every bruise, every cut, on his face, his torso, his knuckles. Each time he tensed, or winced, or pulled back, she breathed a feather light kiss on the area.

She was surprised he allowed her to do it. When she finished, she sat back and looked at him.

"Why'd you do that?" he asked.

"Why'd you let me?"

"I don't know."

"We're a mess," she said. "Physically. Emotionally. Spiritually. We aren't going to heal unless we start treating our wounds." She couldn't help it, but she glanced at the journal lying on the floor where she had thrown it.

He followed her gaze, then got up and walked toward his closet.

"Where are you going?" she asked.

He didn't answer.

She sat on her bed, alone, damp, wrapped in a towel, wondering if she would ever figure out how to get through to him. Just when she felt she made progress, he walked away. Blinking back tears, she clutched her towel to her and started to rise, planning to get dressed for bed.

Royce came out of his closet then, holding a journal identical to the one on the floor. The one in his hands, though, had no shrink wrap on it.

"What's that?" Vanessa asked, sitting back on the bed.

"My journal." He flipped through the pages fast enough that she could see many of them had been written in.

She shook her head. "I… I don't understand. That's your journal." She pointed to the shrink wrapped one on the floor. "I bought it for you the afternoon of our first visit with Dr. Jeffers. I found it in your sock drawer still in the bag. The receipt with my credit card slip was still with it."

"True. You said you went to the lake and then the office supply store that day. I went to the office supply store and then the lake. I'm surprised we didn't see each other."

"Are you saying we went to the same places and bought the same items?"

Royce shrugged.

"And you've been journaling?"

"Every day."

"May I see?"

He shook his head. "No. Tod said these are our private thoughts. I'm not ready to share them. Not yet. But I am doing what he said, Vanessa. I am trying."

Tears welled in her eyes again, but for the first time in a week, it wasn't from pain. She nodded and smiled. "I'm going to get ready to go to sleep. Why don't you take the bed tonight?"

"No. It was me who decided I didn't want to sleep together anymore. I'll take the floor."

"Not with those ribs. Really, I don't mind."

He sighed and held his hand over his ribs. "You know, we're adults. We can sleep on the same surface and it not mean anything more than we're sleeping on the same surface."

She looked at him, hardly daring to hope.

"Don't, Vanessa. Don't look at me like that. I'm still really mad at you. You slept with my best friend."

"I know. And I'm—"

"God, don't. Don't say you're sorry again. I can't hear it. The only reason I'm sleeping in this bed tonight is because I'm sore, I'm tired, and I don't trust my dad."

"Okay." She fought the word past the lump in her throat.

"I said I'm trying, and I mean it. But stop pushing me. Stop reading into things that aren't there. And stop reminding me of things I want to forget." He took his journal and went back into his closet. He stayed in there for a long time, presumably writing his nightly entry.

When he came out, he went straight to the bathroom. Vanessa heard the shower turn on, and stay on for a very long time.

He'd never taken such a long shower in his life. She could only assume he hoped she'd be asleep when he came out.

There was no way she was sleeping that night at all. But the least she could do was give him the satisfaction and pretend.

When he finally went to bed, he balanced on the very edge of the mattress. She feared he would fall off if he fell asleep that way, so she rolled onto her side, perching on her edge of the bed. By her creating that distance, he relaxed enough to move over a bit. Soon he snored softly, and she assumed a more comfortable position as well.

If she wanted, she could reach out and touch his hand, but she refrained. The empty space in the middle of the king size bed was merely feet, but it might as well have been miles.

She'd never felt so far from him. He'd built an eight hundred thread count chasm she didn't know how to breach.

How did things ever get so bad?

As expected, she didn't sleep that night. She went downstairs before dawn to find a note on the kitchen table.

Royce,

Your father had an urgent business matter and we had to leave in the middle of the night so he could make a morning meeting. If you need anything, you know where to reach us.

I'm sending you the names of some good divorce attorneys.

Love,

Mother

She wanted so badly to crumple the note, but decided that would be petty, so she put it in her pocket to deliver to Royce later. No reason why anyone else needed to see it.

The vindictive brat in her reached for the phone to call and tell Liz just what kind of man she was actually married to, but the family girl in her put a stop to it. Of course, Liz wouldn't have believed her anyway, and there was a kind of sweet revenge in letting Liz live with Gene knowing he was a dirty old perv, so maybe the vindictive brat won after all.

She brewed herself a cup of tea and took it outside to watch the sunrise. Soon her father joined her.

"What are you doing up so early?" her father asked.

"Couldn't sleep. You?"

"We're heading out this morning."

"Why?"

"You've got enough going on around here without a bunch of houseguests confusing the matter."

"No, Dad. Royce's parents left. You can stay."

"Honey, you need to get your own house in order," he said.

Her mother stepped out onto the patio. "You've got trouble here, baby girl. Trouble of your own making. You need to get through to your husband. And your kids. Before you lose all of them and not just Hope."

Vanessa looked at her father.

Her mother grabbed her hand. "Honey, I defended you last night to those awful people, but you have to know what you did was wrong. You broke a commandment! Thou shalt not commit adultery! Thou shalt not even covet thy neighbor's spouse. What were you thinking?"

"It was an accident, Mom."

"How do you accidentally fornicate?"

Vanessa sighed. "We were sad, and lonely, and we got drunk—"

"Drunk! Another sin! Nor thieves, nor the greedy, nor drunkards, nor revilers, nor swindlers will inherit the kingdom of God. First Corinthians, chapter six, verse ten."

"Mother, please. It's over. It was a one-time thing."

"That's even worse! You shouldn't be with a man if you have no feelings for him. You should only be with a man you love."

"Well, Ben and I—"

"Ben!" they both said together.

She winced. "Oh, I forgot you didn't know that part."

"Vanessa," her dad said.

"Look, we weren't in love, and it was only one time, but there was affection on both our parts, and—"

"Affection? Affection?" Her mother's voice grew shrill. "So you didn't say, 'I love you.' You said, 'I affect you?'"

"Don't be ridiculous, Mother."

"We raised you better than that, Vanessa."

"I'm sorry."

"Are you? I assume you've confessed your sins."

Vanessa squirmed. Did she lie and compound her sins, or make the lecture worse? Her hesitation decided for her.

"Vanessa. How can you not make this right? Your soul's fate is on the line. Don't you want to spend eternity with your daughter?"

"Dad?" She turned to her father and pleaded with him.

"Mother," he said to Rose. "Back off some, huh? Our little girl's been through enough."

"All the more reason to worry." She turned back to Vanessa. "Honey, we love you, but we're worried. Are you even going to Mass regularly? Are you praying the rosary every day? These things don't happen if you're spiritually healthy."

"Accidents happen to religious people, too, Mom."

"Accidents, yes. Sins, no. Your affair wouldn't have happened. A mismatched blood donation wouldn't have happened."

"Well—"

"Royce's career wouldn't have fallen apart. He wouldn't have lost his friends. He wouldn't have been in that fight. You take responsibility for what you've brought upon your house, and you fix it."

She took a sip of her tea, mumbled, "Yes, ma'am," into her cup, and fidgeted in her seat.

"He who troubles his own house will inherit wind. And the foolish will be servant to the wise-hearted. Proverbs. Chapter eleven, verse twenty-nine."

"And who's the wise-hearted in this scenario? Royce? Because he wasn't exactly innocent in all this."

"God, honey," her mom said. "It's always the Lord."

Vanessa clutched her cup so hard she feared it would break. She put it down and turned away from her mother. "Dad?"

"You need to figure that out on your own. But figure it out." He stood and kissed her on the top of her head. "Before it's too late."

She sighed.

"Gorgeous sunrise," he said.

Vanessa looked out across the yard. The sky overhead was a deep violet, rapidly being chased away by the fiery reds and oranges of the dawn. In just a few minutes, all that would be left of the brilliant display would be a cheerful blue sky and a single luminous orb. The beauty was fleeting, and burned out too quickly. She swiped away a tear.

"The heavens declare the glory of God; and the firmament shows His handiwork. Psalms, chapter nineteen, verse one."

"Really, Mom? Can't you just talk once in a while?"

"I love you, Vanessa."

Vanessa sighed. "Love you, too, Mom." She reached over and squeezed her hand.

"We're all packed, and the car's loaded, so we're going to go."

"Okay. It was good seeing you." She hugged and kissed them both.

"Next time under better circumstances, huh?" he said.

"Now, you make sure you put my quilt back in our room. That's where we want to stay next time."

"Shouldn't be a problem."

Vanessa walked them out and stood in the driveway, watching until she could no longer see their car. The house was just theirs again.

And it never felt more empty.

CHAPTER 17

ROYCE WAS WALKING DOWN THE stairs when Vanessa opened the front door. Aches and pains forgotten, he was instantly on alert.

"Where were you?"

"I'm wearing a robe, Royce. Where do you think I was? An all-night rave?"

He relaxed a bit. "Sorry. I'm just a little on edge."

She shrugged. "I'm a little testy this morning, too. I didn't sleep well."

"Let's start over, then. Good morning."

"Morning."

"Did you bring in the paper?"

She lifted her hands, showing a teacup and no paper. "You stopped the paper, remember? I was actually seeing my parents off. They just left."

He raised a brow. "Really? With everything that's going on? Why?"

"They think I need some space to get my house in order. Speaking of," she reached into her pocket and produced the note. "Your parents are gone, too. I didn't see them leave."

Royce scanned the note. "Hmm. Shame we didn't get to say goodbye. Oh well, I'm sure I'll be hearing from Mother."

"Sounds like," Vanessa said.

"So, I was thinking," he said. When she didn't say anything, he continued. "I was going to go over to the school today and tell Pendleton we'd like Jensen to be valedictorian."

"Are you sure?"

"Why not? The funeral's over, and it would look great on his transcripts."

"The funeral's over, but the scandal hasn't died down. He's already been accepted to Penn. Who cares about his transcripts? If this blows up, it could scar him for life."

"Everyone deserves to walk in commencement. And if you can add speaking as valedictorian, all the better. We shouldn't deprive him of that just because of our mistakes."

"Maybe we should ask him how he feels."

"And what if he chickens out? He could regret that decision later and hate us for it," Royce said. "No. I'm telling the school he'll do it."

"Then why are we even discussing it? Your mind's made up."

"We're discussing it because that's what married couples do."

"But this wasn't a discussion. This was you telling me what you decided."

"What's the difference?"

"Just go, Royce." She waved him off and walked past him up the stairs.

He walked to his car and headed toward town. Vanessa. He just didn't get her. Even when he tried to talk to her, he couldn't talk to her. Or was she right? Was he being controlling again?

So what if he was? He was right about this.

When he passed the accident site, his throat closed to the point that swallowing seemed impossible. He blinked back tears.

Would he ever be able to travel that road without feeling such anguish?

Instead of turning left, he turned right at the T. He wasn't going to the school. Using the onboard phone system, he called Mr. Pendleton. "Jeffrey? Dr. Keller. We've decided Jensen will be able to attend commencement. We haven't told him about being selected valedictorian, just in case it didn't work out, so you can have the honors."

"Well, after your little snafu, we thought maybe we'd go a different—"

"No, that's unacceptable. My 'little snafu' as you call it in no way impacts my son's accomplishments. *Fix it,* Jeffrey. I expect you to call him with the offer today. And I want an email with the details for his address sent to him and copied to me by three this afternoon."

He disconnected the call without waiting for an answer. Pompous prick. How dare he try to remove Jensen's name from the list because of things at the hospital? It was a good thing he didn't talk to Jeffrey face-to-face. He'd have been likely to knock the sniveling prick flat on his ass.

Between the call to the principal and his ranting afterward, the drive went by quickly. Royce drove between two tall iron gates and followed a long, winding drive to a mature oak with a stone bench under it. He parked his car and took a seat on the bench, staring at a mound of freshly dug earth.

He looked around. Despite the fact the other sites seemed well-maintained and often visited, he was alone. Leaning forward, he rested his elbows on his knees and took a deep breath.

"Well. I sure hope this gets easier, because this sucks."

And the tears came. First they fell noiselessly down his face, then he cried softly. Soon he sobbed in earnest. After a few minutes, he left the bench and got on his knees, crawling to the mound of earth. He took fistfuls in his hands and laid his head down, wailing and pounding the ground.

All cried out, he rolled over and gasped for air, holding his ribs to alleviate the pain. He lay there, panting, staring at the sky, physically and emotionally depleted. When he could finally speak, he reached for his phone and dialed.

"Dr. Jeffers? It's Royce Keller. I think I need… Well, hell, I don't know what I need."

"Where are you?"

"Why does that matter?" They were both quiet for a moment. "I'm at Hope's grave."

"So talk to her. That's why you went there, right?"

"Talk to her? That's why I called you!"

"But I'm not the person you have something to say to."

"Fine. But what am I supposed to say?"

"Whatever you need to."

Royce sighed and hung up the phone.

Fat lot of help he was.

Royce realized he was lying where he was likely to be buried someday, and he scrambled to get up. Clenching his side, he managed to sit, grimacing as he did. He twisted himself around to look at where Hope's headstone would be, once it was done.

"Hey," he began. "It's your dad. Well, if you've been paying attention to us down here, I guess you know that's not true. Well, I mean, I'm your dad, just not your biological dad."

He sighed. What the hell was he doing?

He picked at a weed beside the dirt mound and looked toward the as-yet-to-be headstone spot.

"Did you know, Hope? I saw Ben's office. I saw the pictures you drew him, the fun you had with him. On some level, did you know? Is that what you wanted?"

He looked at the sky, as if expecting the answer to appear there.

"I know we drifted apart over the last few years. Was it my fault? Or were you drifting away because you sensed you weren't mine? Because you were mine, Hope. In my heart, you were. I didn't know."

He looked down at the dirt mound.

"Can you ever forgive me? I really thought you were mine. I really thought I could save you. Oh, Hope." He rubbed the dirt again. "I'm so, so sorry."

He didn't think he had any tears left, but a few more fell onto the dirt mound.

"God, please, if you're listening, fix this. I'll do anything…."

Sensing something behind him, he turned around.

Detective Cooper leaned against the tree, chewing on a toothpick. "Sorry to disturb you, Dr. Keller."

"How long were you standing there?" Royce scrambled to his feet, ignoring the pain in his ribs, and brushed his hands off on his pants. Despite his filthy hands, he mopped at his face. "You should announce your presence when you walk up on someone. Clear your throat. Snap a twig. Something. And what are you doing here, anyway?"

"Following up on a lead, and I thought I'd stop by and pay my respects. The funeral was lovely."

"You were there?"

"You don't remember talking with me?"

"I don't know. Maybe vaguely. I don't remember talking with most people."

"Ah, well. It was a stressful time."

Royce studied the dirt under his fingernails for a minute and then his head snapped up. "Wait. A lead. In my case? What happened?"

Detective Cooper laughed. "Your case? Your case is closed."

"Closed? When did that happen? Why didn't anyone tell me?"

"We released the body, I'm sorry—your daughter to you, right?"

"Yes."

"Come on, doc. You know how these things work. We don't release anything until a case is cleared."

Royce sighed. "I haven't been thinking clearly lately. I have a lot going on."

"The death of a child is stressful enough. Add all the other issues, and it's no wonder you're distracted. I do need to ask a favor of you, though."

"What's that?"

"Stay clear of the Andersons. We're looking into it."

"Who are the Andersons? And looking into what?"

He walked to the water pump and wet a handkerchief, which he then brought back to Royce. "For your face," he said. Then he patted him on the shoulder and walked off toward the path.

"But who are the Andersons?" Royce swiped the cloth over his face. It came away brown, so he kept mindlessly scrubbing. "Are they the lead? Are they the witnesses? Come on, Detective. Work with me here."

But Royce just received the same over-the-shoulder two-fingered salute he got the time the detective left his house. Royce followed him, but Cooper got in his car and drove off. Royce looked around, but he didn't see anyone. What lead was Detective Cooper chasing? He got in his car to see if he could follow him, but the cop was long gone. Driving around the cemetery was useless. The place was massive, and he'd get lost if he wasn't careful. There were people visiting random gravesites everywhere, but none that said 'Anderson' and none that he recognized. He'd lost the detective after his second turn. It looked like he would have to get information on his own.

He stopped, took out his phone, and pulled up news reports from the day after Hope's death. Neither Hope's name, nor the name of the motorcycle driver, were released in the article because they were minors. But a quick search of the obituaries showed only two minor deaths that week: Hope's and a boy's named Jimmy Salvo. Not a match, but he was an orphan, survived by his uncle and aunt, Frank and Sally Anderson, and their son. Maybe that was the lead Cooper was chasing?

But Salvo wasn't buried. His death was not under investigation, so his body was released right away. His aunt and uncle had him cremated.

So what was the lead? He read the article again.

Tragic Motorcycle, Car Accident Claims Lives of Three.

A female student at Cathedral Lake Preparatory School and a male student at Cathedral Lake High died Monday when their motorcycle collided with a sedan on Dappled Oak Lane. Police say the riders of the motorcycle were thrown from the vehicle on impact and were not wearing helmets or protective clothing. The couple in the sedan, Mr. and Mrs. Daniel Haggerty of Leedsville, were initially thought to have sustained only minor injuries. Mrs. Haggerty later died in the hospital of cardiac arrest, thought to be stress-induced from the accident.

Investigators' initial report suggest the accident occurred because the motorcycle operator was traveling at a high rate of speed and the road was wet from rain the night before. It is likely the driver hit a slick spot and lost control, causing him to veer into oncoming traffic and crash into the Haggertys.

The motorcycle driver was pronounced dead on scene. His passenger was in critical condition and was rushed to Oakland Regional Hospital, where she later died. The Haggertys were also treated at Oakland Regional. Mr. Haggerty was released that evening.

A witness to the accident said the noise was deafening, like a bomb had exploded. The road was closed for an hour while crews cleared the wreckage.

Police and hospital staff alike warn against the dangers of riding motorcycles without protective gear. One doctor stated, "We're all fallible. Why take unnecessary chances forcing you to leave your life in the hands of a doctor?"

Wade. Jackass. He'd bet his last dollar that quote was from him.

No matter. He was closer to answers. The 'Andersons' in question were obviously that Jimmy Salvo's family. And if the Salvos weren't the family in the cemetery, then it stood to reason the Haggertys were.

But what in the world would he say to them?

Wait. He had no reason to fear them. His daughter had done nothing wrong. She was killed by the same boy that killed Mrs. Haggerty.

Would Mr. Haggerty see it that way?

Probably not. He knew he wouldn't make the distinction if the situation was reversed.

Still, he couldn't help but search out the Haggerty grave. He went to the front office and asked for help. The cemetery sat on forty acres of rolling hills, landscaped plots, architectural features, and manicured tree lines. He almost needed a GPS system to find Hope, and he'd been there before. He wasn't going in search of another dirt mound without guidance.

A glass of water, a round of condolences, a marked park map, and ten minutes later, and he was back on his way. He found the area with little effort. Mrs. Haggerty wasn't in the garden section. She was interred in one of the family mausoleums, and the name 'Haggerty' was already on the structure. No one was in the area when Royce pulled up. If the detective's lead was here, he or she was long gone.

Royce got out of his car and approached the mausoleum. One of the slots had no granite slab on it. It just had the cement cover. He figured that was where Mrs. Haggerty was. They had probably taken the granite slab to engrave her information on it. Looking at the rough gray cement bothered him. The smooth white granite seemed formal, pristine, proper. There was no dignity to the cement.

He wasn't much of a praying man. Rose did enough of that for all of them. But he offered up his version of a prayer for Mrs. Haggerty and her family. They didn't deserve any of this. They were just in the wrong place at the wrong time.

As he walked back to his car, he heard a soft voice. "Excuse me."

He looked around, but didn't see anyone, so he kept walking.

And heard it again, a bit louder. "Excuse me."

Royce stopped and spun back toward the crypt. A tiny woman stood there, holding two roses.

"Are you Mr. Haggerty? Daniel Haggerty?"

"No. No, I'm not."

"Do you know him? I… I have something I'd like to say to him, but I don't know how to reach him."

Royce stepped toward her. She trembled slightly, but lifted her chin. There were circles under her eyes, which were red-rimmed and bloodshot. Her clothes were wrinkled, like she had slept in them, or more likely had sat for many hours in them, and she had tissues tucked into the cuff of her t-shirt.

"I'm sorry. I don't. I don't even know him. I was kind of hoping to meet him myself." He extended his hand. "I'm Royce."

"Royce? Royce Keller?"

"Yes…"

She grabbed his hand and shook it, holding it with both hands. The rose stems scratched his knuckles before she let him go. "I'm so glad to meet you.

I was hoping to find you here, too. I've been coming for days, going back and forth between the two plots."

Royce pulled his hand away and tilted his head. "And you are?"

"Oh, I'm sorry." She took a tissue out of her sleeve and dabbed at her eyes. "My name is Sally."

"Sally Anderson?"

"So you know who I am?"

Royce crossed his arms over his chest. His hand brushed over his ribs, and searing pain ripped through him. He swallowed it down. "I know who your nephew was. Why are you looking for me?"

She sniffled as more tears fell, but she didn't bother to wipe them away. "I just wanted to apologize to you. I know there's nothing I can say or do to repair the damage Jimmy caused. He was troubled. He lost his parents so young. You can't know what it's like to not have your father, your mother... Frank and I raised him as our own, but he struggled with all the loss. Even our son couldn't get through to him."

Royce closed his eyes and tried to tamp his anger down. "Mrs. Anderson. I can only imagine how you must feel. But it's not your place to apologize for your nephew."

"But he isn't here to do it for himself. Someone has to do it. Or the world will only remember him as the bad boy who crashed his motorcycle and took those lives. And he was so much more, Dr. Keller. Or he could have been. If he'd had the chance."

"I don't know what you want from me."

"I want you to know I'm sorry. Jimmy's sorry. I know he is. And while the accident may have been his fault, his life wasn't. I know he didn't set out to hurt anyone."

"Okay, Mrs. Anderson."

"Please, take this." She handed him a yellow rose. "Most people think it means friendship, but it also means new beginnings. It's all I want for those kids. And for all of us." She walked away.

Royce walked back to his car and got in. He sniffed the rose. The scent would forevermore remind him of Hope. He hoped she got a new beginning. He'd never given much thought to an afterlife, but since her death, he fervently believed in one. He couldn't imagine she just *ended*. She had to go on in some sense.

He needed a new beginning, too. A new beginning with Vanessa. And with Jensen and Faith. And obviously with work, assuming he still had a job. Maybe he just needed a new job.

And with Ben and Wade? He didn't think he had friends any longer. He'd need to find new friends. That would be a new beginning, too.

As he drove home, he thought perhaps he could start trying to have new beginnings with the people he loved. Maybe he'd even call Stanford and see how things looked at work. He'd been seeing Dr. Jeffers, he'd been cleared by the police… maybe—

The phone rang, cutting into his thoughts. He looked at the screen. It was Hospital Administration. He listened to what they had to say, hung up, and called Vanessa.

"I need some time to myself tonight. I'm checking in to a hotel. I'll see you tomorrow at our appointment." He heard her yelling about him staying at a hotel, but he hung up without engaging in the debate. It didn't matter that their houseguests were gone and the guestrooms were free. He needed more space than that. And he didn't care what Stanford said about appearances. What he really needed was neutral territory… someplace with no memories, no distractions. Someplace where he could put all the new information into perspective.

CHAPTER 18

VANESSA STORMED INTO DR. JEFFERS'S office ten minutes early. He was walking out of his kitchen with a tray of glasses and a pitcher of water. As she flung the door open, it smacked right into his arms, causing everything on the tray to spill all over him, then fall and shatter on the floor.

He lowered the tray and looked up at her.

Vanessa's chest heaved as she tried to catch her breath. She raised her hand to her mouth, torn between mortification and stifling a laugh. "I'm sorry," she managed. "I should have rung the bell."

"Are you all right?" He started to reach for her. "You're flushed. And out of breath."

His concern for her sent her over the edge of hysteria. She snorted and pointed at his wet crotch. "You have… lemon…" and burst into gales of laughter.

He looked down. "Indeed. That lemon slice did land in an unfortunate place." He plucked it off his pants and looked for a place to put it.

Vanessa leaned on the arm of his chair and continued laughing, deep belly laughs she hadn't experienced in… well, she didn't know how long. Tears streamed down her face and she clutched her stomach. She didn't even know what was funny. She just couldn't stop.

Dr. Jeffers went to the kitchen and came back with a stack of towels. By the time he returned, she'd settled down. Her stomach hurt, and the tears rolling down her face were ones of sadness.

He handed her a towel and watched as she mopped up her face.

"Are you okay?"

She shook her head and studied the wood grain on the floor.

He placed the towels on a table and tipped up her head. "Can you tell me what's wrong?"

She took a deep, shuddering breath. "Let me clean this up. I need a minute before we talk."

"I can clean this. You take some time and compose yourself."

"No. I made the mess. I'll clean it. Besides," she said, taking a clean towel from the table and dropping to her knees, "I could use the distraction."

"I'm not letting a client clean my floor." He joined her in the doorway. "We'll both do it."

They worked in silence, sopping up ice cubes and water, and putting lemon slices and broken glass on the tray. When everything was clean and dry, he helped her to her feet. "Are you ready to talk, or do I have time to go change?" He glanced at his watch. "Royce should be here soon. If you need to tell me something before he gets here, I can wait."

She took another towel off the table. "Let's kill two birds." She dabbed at his pants.

"Vanessa," he grabbed her wrists.

"Are you fucking kidding me?" Royce stood in the doorway.

"This isn't what you think," Dr. Jeffers said.

Royce turned to leave.

"Where are you running to now, Royce? Back to your love shack?" Vanessa called after him.

He turned around and walked deliberately back into the room. "Excuse me?"

"Did you think I wouldn't notice Lydia running out to meet you five minutes after you called me to tell me you were staying at a hotel? I don't know what's worse… Thinking you've been with her in our home when I'm not there or knowing you called her to a hotel right in front of me."

"Called her to—Are you *insane?*"

"I saw her, Royce. She didn't even ask to leave early. I got off the phone with you and she headed for her car. She left dirty dishes in the sink and clothes in the washer. The damn things can mold in there for all I care. It's a load of your scrubs."

"I won't be needing them anytime soon, so it doesn't really matter."

"Well maybe somebody else might need to do laundry. So tell your whore to take care of it!"

"My *whore?* I walk in here and see my wife groping my therapist, and you want to talk to me about what I do behind closed doors? We're only here in the first place because you couldn't keep your legs shut."

She raised her hand to slap him, but he grabbed her wrist.

"Okay, okay," Dr. Jeffers said, stepping between them. "This is good. This is progress. But talk it out. Use your words, not your hands."

Vanessa stepped back and rubbed her wrist. She glared at both men before focusing her attention on her husband. "My mistake was eighteen years ago. Your mistakes are current. We're here because you had to play savior in the ER. Guess what, Royce? You aren't God. Maybe if you spent a little more time working miracles at home and a little less time at work, we'd still have Hope!"

"You're blaming me! That was a pretty fast one-eighty."

"Of course I'm blaming you! You're there for everyone, all the time! Why weren't you there for her?"

"I *was* there for her! That's the damn problem!"

"No, Royce. Not at work. At home. If you'd been more available to her at home, she wouldn't have been such a mess. She felt neglected, ignored. That morning, she told me… Never mind."

"No, let's have it." He stood with his legs together and spread his arms. "You have me on the cross. Might as well hammer the nails in."

She sighed and played with her medal, running it back and forth on the chain. "She said you had plans for Jensen and Faith, but not her. That you'd mapped out their futures, futures neither of them was interested in, by the way. But you didn't ever talk to her about her college, her career path, her life. She was a non-entity to you. The bad stuff she was doing—the clothes, the hair, the motorcycle—that was all to get your attention."

Royce dropped his arms. "She didn't say that."

"She didn't tell me that's why she dyed her hair or dressed that way, but she told me the rest. She needed her dad. Her last words to me were that she didn't have any other choice."

Royce was quiet for a moment. "I think she always had her dad. I saw Ben's office. I saw the pictures, the drawings. She is… she was… close to him."

"And why do you think that was, Royce?" Vanessa walked over to him and took his hands. She pulled him down to sit beside her on the sofa. "He made himself available to her. You were always closed off. That's why Ben and me happened. That's why Hope's accident happened. If you can't make yourself available to your family, you're going to lose it."

"So it's all on me?"

"What'd you do last night, Royce? I was home. I was available. No one wanted my company, my comfort. But I was there for them, if they needed me. Where were you? Off doing what you needed, what made you happy. Or should I say who?"

One mistake eighteen years ago, and she continued to pay for it. The tears fell again, and she grabbed the nearest towel and dabbed at her face. When she realized she'd wiped at Dr. Jeffers's pants with that towel, she threw it aside in disgust and sobbed into her hands.

What was wrong with her? She didn't mean to do the stupid things she did. She just got crazy impulses and acted before she thought them through, trying to cauterize the wounds with instant gratification. Seconds after the impetuous whims passed, though, she suffered through reason and regret. She knew Royce was going to walk in the door when he did. She had seen his car through the window. And part of her wanted him to hurt like he had hurt her the night before. That was why she did what she did. Anger, hurt, and shame, the same feelings that had caused her to crash into the office in the first place, had triggered that response in her. She needed him to feel what she had felt, and damn the consequences. And once he felt it? The consequences mattered. In spades. And she couldn't undo what she'd done.

Her whole life was a series of actions that couldn't be undone.

But they could be atoned for.

"I knew you would be walking in the door," she whispered, not making eye contact.

"What?" Royce asked.

"I came here early because I was upset and wanted time to talk. Alone. I should have rung the bell, but you know me… I just barged in. The water spilling was an accident. When we were cleaning up, I saw you pulling in. I wanted you to hurt the way you hurt me last night, so I reached for Dr. Jeffers's pants, knowing you'd walk in and get the wrong idea."

"Do you realize you could have ruined his career? And given the investigation I'm going through? That you would compromise him like that?"

"I wasn't thinking."

"Not about him, no." Royce got up, ran his fingers through his hair, and started pacing the room. "God, Vanessa."

"Royce, if I could interject a moment," Dr. Jeffers said.

Royce looked at him, but kept pacing.

"No one more than I can appreciate how delicate the situation was that you walked in on. And I certainly don't condone Vanessa's actions. But let's consider the bigger picture here. She's admitting her actions and motivations. She's coming to you openly and honestly. And you learned a lot today about her feelings and about Hope's life. About your whole family. This is a breakthrough moment for you."

Vanessa watched Royce take in Dr. Jeffers's words. She could very well lose her husband because of what she had done. How he reacted to it now meant everything.

Did she even want him anymore? Why did she still fight so hard when he obviously ran the other way? She was no one's sloppy seconds. Especially Lydia's.

She squared her shoulders. Maybe she was done fighting. Maybe it was time to let go.

"I have a proposition for you," Dr. Jeffers said.

"What?" Royce asked.

"I've listened to the two of you recount the days of your early marriage, when the infidelity took place. We're experiencing the present, with all of the problems you're facing. You only ever talk about the bad times. I'd like to hear about a happy time in your past together."

"That's not a proposition," Royce said.

"I'll get to that. Tell me the story first."

"I don't see the point," he said.

"It's always nice to relive a good memory," Vanessa said, still on the sofa. She thought about different times in their life together that made her happy, and she chose one of the best ones. "I remember when I knew I loved him."

"Tell me about it," Dr. Jeffers said.

Vanessa thought back to her freshman year of college. She smiled at the memory, then began to tell her story.

"I'd walked into Intro to Chem and looked around. Like every other class I had, I didn't know a soul. Served me right for going to college so far from home. But not having any friends in that class was a problem, because I was horrible at science and was going to need help. I mean, seriously, why did the freshman core curriculum have to include math and science? I've never used either once since I got my marketing degree."

"Vanessa," Tod said. "Back to your story?"

"Oh. Right." She looked at Royce. He'd stopped pacing and was staring out the window. "Chemistry. So I chose a seat in the first row, hoping I'd learn from the professor by osmosis if not by actual imparting of wisdom. The rest of the room was filling up quickly from the back of the room forward, and I felt like a leper. No one sat by me. No one sat in the first three rows. I was growing increasingly uncomfortable, but then three gorgeous boys walked into the room."

Even from across the room, Vanessa could see Royce's eyes narrow, see his jaw muscle tick. Shrugging, she continued. "Two of them, like everyone else, headed immediately up the stairs, but one of them walked right toward me." She hugged a pillow against her body and again chanced a glance at Royce. He no longer looked out the window. His head was down, his eyes closed. She couldn't read the expression on his face.

"His friends didn't look happy, but they turned around and followed him."

"That was Royce, I take it?" Tod asked.

She nodded. "He slid into the seat beside me and said, 'Hey. Don't you know all the babes sit in the back?' I tried, and failed, not to laugh in his face. I said I didn't know anything about where the 'babes' sat. I was just praying to pass the class."

Royce smirked but didn't look up. "I told you it was easy as basket weaving."

She smiled. "You did. And I told you to consider me a one-armed, thumbless, blind woman."

Royce smiled and Tod laughed. "I'm sorry," Tod said. "Go on, Vanessa."

"He told me his name, and I told him mine. His friends just played it cool and kind of waved, then went back to talking to each other. And instead of Royce making fun of my sad joke, he gave it right back to me. He grinned this devastating grin and said, 'Well, Vanessa. Allow me to be your arms, thumbs, and eyes this semester.' And yes, I knew it was a pickup line, but it was the best one I'd ever heard."

Her cheeks burned, and she knew she must have seventeen different shades of red splotched across her face. Despite her embarrassment, she again peeked at Royce. He had a soft smile on his face. She almost went to him, but couldn't.

"Then what?" Tod prompted.

What the hell. Might as well make her humiliation complete.

"When he said that, I was floored. I needed a big dose of oxygen, but when I took a deep breath, all I inhaled in was his scent. Which was intoxicating. I knew I was blushing, so I looked down at my notebook and hid behind my hair. Not looking at him was just easier. I managed the courage to say, 'I just might take you up on that,' but I couldn't even look at him to see his reaction."

She tossed the pillow aside and poured a glass of water, guzzling it before continuing.

"Class started then, and I had to pay attention. The professor had hardly introduced himself and passed out the syllabus when he started teaching, and he went so fast. I tried to keep up. I furiously took notes, copying everything on the board, but I was lost pretty early. I glanced at Royce, only to discover he hadn't even opened his notebook. He and his friends just sprawled in their seats, legs stretched out or crossed in front of them. I don't know what irritated me more, that Royce wasn't paying attention or that he promised to help me and obviously wouldn't be able to. I wrote him off as a study-buddy and focused on the professor."

"And this is how you fell in love with him?" Tod asked.

"This is the setup. I'm getting to it. Class ended, and I closed my notebook. Before I could put it away, Royce leaned over and wrote his number on it. He said, 'If you get stuck on your homework, give me a call.' I almost laughed in his face. I thanked him, but come on. I wasn't even sure he'd stayed awake the whole hour. I knew he'd be less than useless if I needed help."

Royce smirked, and she looked at him. He had turned from the window and leaned against the bookshelf. When she met his gaze, he turned away. Grabbing the pillow again, she clutched it to her chest, using it as a buffer between the two of them.

"That night, I sat down to do my homework. And two hours later, I was no closer to having it completed than when I'd started. TA hours were long over. Panic consumed me. If I couldn't do the first assignment, what were the odds I could pass the course? I traced my finger over the phone number Royce had scrawled on the cover of my notebook and considered my options. I knew he probably couldn't help me, but he was my only option at that point. Despite the late hour, I grabbed the phone on my desk and dialed."

She poured another glass of water and took a sip. "The guy who answered the phone said, 'Yo.' That didn't add to my comfort any. I apologized for calling so late, and he snorted and told me it was still early. I thought maybe I had misdialed and gotten a frat house, but no. When I asked for Royce, the guy on the phone said, 'Found him.' And my hope plummeted."

Royce laughed, but Vanessa ignored him. She shifted on her seat and readjusted the pillow, gripping and regripping the edges, spinning it and turning it until she had it where she wanted it.

"I sighed, half nervous, half relieved, and told him who I was. I started to remind him where we met, but he cut me off and said. 'Oh, yeah. I was waiting for your call.' You believe that? He was waiting for me to call, like it was preordained or something."

"It was," Royce said. "And I was right. You called."

She glared at him, then continued. "He made me nervous. And angry." She glanced at him again. He still did. And the smirk on his face proved he knew it. "I had been twisting the phone cord around my finger, and I noticed it was purple and numb. I released it and asked, 'How'd you know I'd be calling?' He said it was because I looked lost."

Royce smiled again, and she noticed the familiar crinkles in the corner of his eyes she hadn't seen in a while. She hadn't realized how much she missed them.

"I told him I didn't see him take any notes, and the cocky SOB said, 'I wasn't lost.'"

Royce crossed the room and sat down beside her. Her grip on the pillow tightened, then she started playing with the fringe.

"I thought he was an arrogant ass. But apparently he was an arrogant ass who understood chemistry. So I asked him if he could just get me started. Next thing I know, he's inviting himself to my room. I was in full-on panic mode. I hadn't seen any evidence of my roommate since the first night of orientation. Either she'd hooked up with someone else or she'd quit and gone home. In either event, for all intents and purposes, I lived alone, and inviting a strange boy over terrified me. But he kept at it, asking me where

I was. He even threatened to look me up in the freshman phonebook if I didn't tell him."

She took another sip of water. "I remember cursing the man, woman, or child whose bright idea it was to create that damn phonebook. It was a stalker's wet dream."

"Vanessa?" Tod said.

"So, anyway," she said, back on track, "I finally just told Royce where I lived to avoid a hassle. And it turned out he was in the same dorm, on the same floor. He agreed to meet me in the common area, but only gave me ten seconds to get out there. Just ordered me to be there and hung up. I was certain my hair was a wreck and my makeup had been cried off, but I didn't want him tracking me down in my room, so I gathered my stuff and walked out to the common area. He was already waiting, sprawled in one of the overstuffed loveseats. He held out a bag and offered me popcorn."

Before she had been upset that Royce had been too angry to do anything but pace the room. Now she felt suffocated by his closeness. She'd never told him her perception of how they met. And here she was, sharing the intimate details with not only him, but with a third party, too.

She shook her head, wondering if it was wise to continue.

"How did you feel about seeing him again, Vanessa?" Tod asked.

"I remember feeling panicked. It felt much more like a date than a study session. The only chemistry I was interested in at that moment was what was happening between the two of us. I worried about my breath, my hair, my clothes. I thought about fleeing to my room and bolting my door shut, but at the same time, I didn't want to go." She twisted the fringe around her finger much like she had the phone cord so long ago. When her finger turned red, she released it. "I decided to stay, telling myself it was out of necessity, not desire. But deep down, I knew better. I wanted that time with him and would use any excuse to get it."

Out of the corner of her eye, she saw Royce staring at her. She wondered what he had felt that night, but didn't have the courage to ask him. Instead, she kept telling her story. "I sat down and spread my things out on the table in front of us. Even though he'd said it wasn't late, I knew it was. No one was around, and on a normal night, I'd have been in bed two hours earlier. And thinking about bed didn't help me at all. So I said, 'If you can just get me started, I think I can figure it out from here. It's so late already…' But he turned to face me, and I got lost in his eyes. He has such beautiful eyes."

She turned to look at him, and he didn't look away. She held his gaze, and was transported right back to that common room in her dorm.

"You had on cut-off sweats and a school t-shirt." She spoke softly. "And you looked so good, I almost didn't hear what you said."

"I said since we lived right down the hall from each other, I could teach you anytime."

"But you knew I thought it was late. And you handed me a copy of the homework—completed correctly—and told me to just take it."

"I had made a copy for you that afternoon when I did mine. It surprised you, but I told you Ben, Wade, and I did that kind of stuff for each other all the time. Since grade school."

His expression hardened, and he looked away.

Vanessa bit her lip. She had been so close to chipping through the wall he put up, and just the mention of Ben—his mention of Ben—made the wall that much thicker.

"Then what, Vanessa?" Tod asked.

She sighed. "We talked about his childhood a bit. How the three of them grew up together and always helped each other out. I felt like I was being brought into his inner circle, like I would have people to turn to at that school. A surrogate family, of sorts."

She hugged the pillow closer to her. "I remember sitting there, just staring at him. He thought maybe he'd crossed a line by assuming I'd need his homework. That I was angry with his presumption. But that wasn't it at all. I admitted I wasn't used to people helping me. And then he welcomed me into his group. He said, 'Well, now you have three people who will help you.

Whenever you need it. Well, maybe not Wade. He tends to charge people, even me and Ben, and he's not cheap. But if you need something, just ask. We'll be there.' And just like that, I had family."

She glanced at Royce. His jaw muscle ticked again, and she knew calling Ben 'family' was killing him.

"I said, 'Thanks.' It was all I could manage. I had been taken aback by his generosity as much as I was drawn to his rebellious side. He was a generous bad boy. Dangerous. And irresistible."

The fringe on the pillow became fascinating. She ducked her head to stare at it, then continued. "He dropped his voice to a whisper then, looked into my eyes, and took my hand. He said, 'If I had a choice, though, I'd prefer you called me.'"

She looked up at Tod. "I was exhausted, touched he'd helped me, exhilarated he was flirting. I don't know why I did it, but I threw my arms around him—something I'd never do to a perfect stranger—and thanked him. When he hugged me back, I felt his hands thread through my hair, and it felt so good... so much better than when I'd yanked it in frustration earlier that evening. I could have stayed in his arms forever, but instead, I pulled away and looked into his eyes."

She looked at Royce again. When he turned and looked at her, it was like she was looking at her college sweetheart again. So many memories flooded back, cocooning her in warmth and safety.

"And?" Tod asked.

She couldn't tear her gaze away. Staring at her husband, she said. "And I knew I could look into his eyes every day for the rest of my life and never get tired of it."

Vanessa looked away and dabbed her eyes as tears of realization fell. Remembering that story and sharing it with Royce brought back so many warm and wonderful feelings. And best of all, as she told the story, she'd caught glimpses of the man she fell for. She hadn't seen that young man in a long time. His confidence had grown, stomping out all vestiges of the bad boy who drew her in. But she feared if she looked at him again and didn't see even a hint of her college savior, something inside her would break.

"That's a beautiful story, Vanessa," Dr. Jeffers said. "Royce, you obviously remember that meeting. Would you like to add anything?"

He cleared his throat. "Yeah." His voice was hoarse, and he paused a while. "It was love at first sight for me. I didn't need to see her again that night. I knew when I walked in the door for class and saw her sitting there that she was special. Something just kind of hit me." He patted his chest and he cleared his throat again. "Here."

Vanessa looked at him, willed him to look at her. But he didn't. He seemed to be fascinated with his shoes.

It didn't matter. He'd shared something intimate with her, something she'd never known. It took courage and strength to open himself up like that. That was the man she fell in love with.

"Okay. I want the two of you to think about that this week. Focus on those memories. Channel those feelings. And then go out on a date."

"What?" Vanessa said. She wasn't ready for that.

"Out? No, I don't think—"

"Listen. You are churning through the same toxic environments over and over. You need something fresh and new to try to break out of your rut."

"I don't know…" she said. She didn't even know how to date any longer. How was she supposed to date the man she married? People dated to get to know each other. That ship had sailed years ago. They already knew everything about each other.

Or did they? She bit her lip. Neither of them had known how the other felt about their first meeting.

But still, a date? A romantic evening out together? She wasn't ready for that. It had the potential for disaster.

"We'll let fate decide." He wedged his hand into his damp pocket and fished around, finally able to pull his hand out with a quarter. "Heads a date. Tails you wait."

Royce looked at the door, seeming content to let the coin decide. Vanessa sat on the edge of her seat, watching Dr. Jeffers toss the coin. It landed on tails.

"Heads," he said, and pocketed the coin. "Do you want me to make some suggestions, or do you want to work out the details for yourselves?"

"Dr. Jeffers," Vanessa said. He was lying. Their therapist. Lying! Cheating!

"No arguments. Royce accepts my decision, so will you."

"But—"

"After everything you did today, Vanessa," he said, "are you really going to argue with me now?"

She sat back, properly chastised. She did owe it to Dr. Jeffers to not rat him out about cheating on the coin flip. But a date? With Royce? Which Royce would she be dating? The one who did her homework so she wouldn't fail, or the one who abandoned his family and didn't even realize it?

CHAPTER 19

WHEN ROYCE GOT HOME, HE found Vanessa sitting at the kitchen table. Royce poured them each coffee and joined her there. She smiled and took the cup he offered.

"So, are we really doing this?" she asked.

"That's what the coin said."

She nodded once, but stayed silent.

"Vanessa, I feel like we're all over the place."

"We *are* all over the place."

"I don't like it."

"Me, either."

"Where do you want to be?"

She sipped her coffee and looked up at him.

Lydia came into the room, humming and smiling. "Good afternoon, Dr. Keller. Isn't it a beautiful day?" She glanced at Vanessa. "Oh. Mrs. Keller. I didn't see you there." She kept humming as she started the dishes from the night before.

"*Where* do I want to be?" Vanessa asked Royce quietly, so Lydia couldn't hear her over the din at the sink. "Anywhere but here at the moment." She got up and left the room.

Royce watched her storm off, then he turned to Lydia. She had a smile plastered on her face and was dancing to the tune she was humming.

"Lydia?"

"Yes, Dr. Keller?" She wiped her hands on a dishtowel and turned to face him, leaning against the counter.

"Yesterday, in the afternoon? The way you left had Vanessa very upset."

"Oh, did that cause you problems? I'm sorry about that. Is it a matter of the hours? I can make them up in the evenings, or on the weekend."

"I'm not worried about that." He waved his hand, dismissing her concerns. "It's just the way you disappeared. The conclusions she jumped to…."

"I'm sorry. I didn't mean to make things difficult for you. Is she complaining?" She drew her hand up his arm as she walked past him.

"No. No, it's not that." Well, it was that. He wasn't handling the situation correctly. At. All. "From now on, if you could—"

She smiled. "I'll be more careful from now on." She turned back to the sink and began swaying her hips to the song she hummed.

Royce watched her for a moment, then sighed with relief. Surely he'd handled 'the Lydia issue' to everyone's satisfaction. Convinced the matter was resolved, he put it behind him, already on to other matters. With a last glance at Lydia, he walked to the garage and opened his car door. The intense smell of wilted rose wafted out to him. He took the drooping bloom, just yesterday a fresh yellow in Mrs. Anderson's hand, and walked up to his bedroom.

Going into his closet, he got out his journal and turned to a clean page.

I never realized it before, but I have favorite children. I have a favorite son and a favorite daughter. I have plans for their schooling, plans for their careers. I even have ideal spouses in mind for them and can picture their weddings, their children. I can see working with them, holidays with them. When I picture my golden years, I see them and their progeny with me, and all the professional accomplishments we achieved together.

And I have to admit, long before Hope died, she wasn't there.

How did that happen? How did I construct a future for myself where I carefully built the lives for two of my children—down to the last detail, might I add—and totally missed the third? And is it a coincidence that the child I left out of my life is the child who biologically wasn't mine? Did I know on some level? Is that why there was a disconnect? Or did I cause the disconnect all on my own, and therefore cause her death, just like Vanessa said?

Maybe I am at fault. Not because of not following hospital protocol, but because I pushed Hope away long before she left the house that day.

If I'm going to save my family, I have to embrace what's left of it.

He twirled the limp flower between his fingers and sniffed it. The once fragrant bloom had turned cloyingly pungent, nearly choking him with its scent. He opened the box where he stored his journal. Inside was the bunny he'd taken from Hope's room. Taking it out, he held it to his nose and sniffed it. It still smelled like his daughter, but the scent was fading. He took another deep breath. It was probably the last time he'd smell that apple pie scent. He put the rose in the box and put the bunny back inside with it. Soon the bunny would likely smell like the rose. Then he put the journal in the box and closed it, sliding it back onto the shelf. Finished, he got out his iPad and reclined on the bed. His battery was nearly drained when Jensen knocked on the door. "Can I come in?"

He put the device down and waved him in. "Sure, Jensen. What's up?"

Jensen sat on the edge of the bed, facing his father. "Did you know I was selected valedictorian?"

"I've known for a while now." He leaned forward and clapped him on the shoulder. "Congratulations, son."

"Don't you think that's going to be a little weird? Me standing up and talking about endings and beginnings, given our situation?"

"Jensen, this is an honor. And you earned it. You aren't walking away from it because of me, or Mom, or anyone or anything else. You hold your head high and take that stage with pride."

"I don't think I want to."

"Sometimes we do things we don't want to. It makes us better people."

"And sometimes it takes strength to walk away."

Royce sighed. "Jensen, you'll regret not doing this. This is your chance to let your voice be heard. Say what you want to say and leave your classmates with a lasting impression. Why deprive yourself of that?"

Jensen threw himself back on the bed. "It doesn't feel right. Celebrating. When Hope's…" He paused and swallowed. "And you're under investigation—"

"No. The police cleared me."

"The hospital hasn't. And Mom…"

"What's between me and Mom is between me and Mom. You and Faith need to let it go."

"She lied to you. To all of us."

"She had her reasons for what she did."

"She's a cheater, Dad."

"It's not quite that simple."

"Once a cheater, always a cheater."

"Jensen. Enough. We're working things out. In fact, we're going on a date."

"What? After what she did?" He bounded off the bed and rushed out of the room. "Faith! Faith!"

Royce rubbed his face. His stubble scratched his fingers, reminding him he hadn't been home the night before. He and Vanessa still had a lot to discuss.

Jensen pulled Faith into the room. "Tell her."

"Tell me what?"

Royce sighed.

"What's going on?" Vanessa asked from the doorway.

Jensen spun toward her. "You! You ruined everything and now you talked him into a date?"

"What? You're going on a date?" Faith said, looking at Royce. "You mean, once this investigation is over, you aren't leaving her?"

Royce held up a hand. "Enough. We are a family. You will stop referring to your mother as 'she' and 'her.' That is disrespectful and will not be tolerated. Mom and I are married. We took vows. Sacred vows before God and our family and friends. Do you get that? That's not just something you throw away when things get difficult. We're trying to work things out. What we need is your help and your understanding, not your anger and your derision. There are too many things going against us right now to have you in the opposing corner."

Faith stood there, biting her lip. She reminded Royce so much of Vanessa when they were younger that he would have smiled if the situation wasn't so grim.

Jensen, however, vibrated with anger. His face darkened, and he walked to the door. "I can give you a lot of things, Dad. But I don't know if I have this in me. And it's not fair of you to ask." He left the room and ran down the stairs.

Royce ran after him. "Where are you going?"

But Jensen was already out the door. Royce heard his car peeling out the driveway. He could only pray his son would come home safely.

Faith sobbed and ran out of the room. Royce heard her bedroom door slam a moment later.

Vanessa sat down on the edge of the bed. "Well, that's it, I guess. I lost them, too."

"No." Royce sat on the opposite side of the bed. "It's good he's angry. Anger is passion. That means he's feeling something. It's better than apathy."

She shrugged and looked at her hands, balled uselessly in her lap.

He considered going to her, but he had no comfort to offer. She wasn't ready to accept it, and it wouldn't be genuine, anyway. He felt she deserved some of what she was getting.

"Have you given any thought to our date?"

She snorted. "Are you kidding me? After Lydia practically threw herself on you in the kitchen? No."

"I've been up here doing some research."

"Royce, listen. There's something you should know."

He couldn't take anything else. What? She and Ben were back together? She was pregnant? She filed for divorce? He was afraid to ask. "What, Vanessa? What is it now?"

"You're off the hook. Dr. Jeffers lied."

"What?"

"I watched him flip the coin. It was tails. He's making us go on the date under false pretenses."

Royce didn't realize he was holding his breath until he heard what she said. Then he let it out in one long, slow whoosh. "I don't care. He obviously feels pretty strongly that this is an important next step in our treatment. So I'm on board."

"You want to go out? On a date?"

"Well it seems pretty silly to stay in and call it a date. All we do here is fight."

"We can fight in public, too."

"I'll risk it. We need to get out."

"It doesn't seem right. Your mother would say it isn't proper."

"My mother isn't here."

"Well, you're right about that. But... public?"

"It's kind of hard to face people when we're hiding in here."

He watched her agonize over the decision. He could almost see the synapses firing in her brain as she worked out the pros and cons of their situation.

Finally, a smile crept over her face. "What exactly did you have in mind?"

"Leave all the details to me. Let's go tomorrow."

"Okay. Tomorrow it is."

"Tonight, though, we have some things we should discuss."

The smile instantly faded from her face. "All right. Like what?"

"I went to the cemetery yesterday."

"Without me?"

"No one's stopping you, Ness."

"I know. I just thought the first time we went, we'd go together."

"Can I get on with my story?"

She waved him on.

"I saw Detective Cooper while I was there. I'm no longer under investigation. It's official."

She sighed and pressed her hands to her chest. "That is good news."

"Apparently the case was closed when they released... anyway. Would have been nice if someone had told us, huh?"

She squeezed his hand. "That's one hurdle down. That's great."

"There's more." He told her all about Cooper mentioning a lead, and how that sent him on a quest through the cemetery. She listened with rapt attention while he relayed the details of his finding the article about the accident and his meeting Mrs. Anderson. He didn't tell her about the rose. He decided to keep that to himself.

He ended his retelling of events by mentioning the call he got on the way home.

"I was feeling pretty hopeful, all things considered, after that."

"I would think so, hearing the police cleared you and talking to Mrs. Anderson. So what happened?"

"I was on my way back, planning on telling you everything, when my phone rang. It was Hospital Administration."

"What'd they want?"

"To tell me they anticipate wrapping up their investigation in a few weeks. They want to schedule my hearing in six weeks."

"Six weeks? Why so long? The police only needed a couple of days to know this was a joke."

"Well, HA isn't trying to prove malicious intent. They need to prove incompetence. I guess that takes longer."

"Six more weeks? That will be eight weeks total."

"I know. That's why I freaked yesterday. I just needed some time to wrap my head around everything. They aren't just looking at that one case, Ness. If they need eight weeks...."

"They're building a big case."

"They're building a huge case."

"We'll fight it, Royce. Besides, they don't have anything. Right?"

He shook his head and shrugged. "Not that I can think of. Just…."

She pulled back and looked at him. "Just what?"

"Wade. They have Wade. Who knows what he's giving them?"

"We have six weeks. And we have Stanford. We'll build our own case. We'll call Bradley. And—" Her phone rang. She pulled it out of her pocket and looked at the display.

"Who is it?" he asked.

She bit her lip.

"Ness. Who is it?"

"Ben."

"Put it on speaker."

She answered and put it on speaker like Royce asked. "Hello?"

"What the hell do you think you're doing?" Ben bellowed.

"Um, what?"

"I asked what you were doing. Are you out of your mind?"

"You're on speaker, Ben," Royce said, "and I don't appreciate you calling my wife at all, let alone you screaming at her."

"And I don't appreciate getting visits from your son, all pissed off at me for screwing your wife eighteen years ago. And now you're going out on a date, when Hope's body's not even cold? What the hell kind of message does that send?"

"Mind your own damn business," Royce said.

"I'd love to, if your business didn't keep showing up on my damn doorstep."

"Is Jensen still there?" Vanessa asked.

"No. He ranted and raved, just like his mother, sucker punched me, just like his father, and took off again."

"Then I guess we're doing something right," Royce said, and disconnected the call.

VANESSA SAT AT HER VANITY stroking blush over her cheekbones. She hadn't bothered overly much with her appearance since Hope had died. The days she didn't have to leave the house she merely tied her hair back and dressed comfortably so she could sit in the sunroom and wallow. The days Vanessa had to go out she dressed and styled her hair, but had stopped bothering with makeup. There had been no point… her tears would just wash away any cosmetics she applied.

The fact that she was doing the full treatment felt foreign to her.

And somehow like she was dishonoring her daughter's memory.

She stared at her reflection in the mirror as she raised the black eyeliner to her eye. Pools of tears blurred her vision, and she promptly traded the pencil for a tissue. Good thing she hadn't applied the mascara yet. She gave herself a few minutes to cry before composing herself, then she used some eye drops to eliminate the redness, re-powdered her face, and made-up her eyes. A light slick of mauve lipstick finished her preparations.

The person staring back at her was a stranger. She was thinner than the Vanessa of a few weeks earlier, and the cosmetics couldn't hide the shadows under her eyes or the hollowed look to her already high cheekbones. She was a ghost of her former self, and even the bright makeup, the styled hair, and the cheerful sundress didn't enliven her visage. To her eyes, she looked like a walking corpse.

Just another death.

She blinked rapidly, determined not to shed more tears. If not because of her makeup, then because she didn't want to ruin Royce's evening. Or vice-versa. She wasn't sure which.

Royce stepped into the room. "Are you ready to—You look lovely, Ness."

"Thank you." She looked him over. He was wearing shorts and a button-down shirt. "Am I overdressed? You didn't tell me where we were going."

"You look perfect. Let's go."

Her dress was a little big for her. It swished not just around her legs, but around her stomach, too, making her self-conscious about how she looked. "Maybe I should change into pants…"

"Come on." He held out his hand for hers.

"Just let me grab my sweater."

"It's eighty degrees."

"It might get chilly when the sun goes down." She stepped into her closet, changed into capris and a short-sleeved sweater, and slipped into a pair of sandals. When she walked back into the bedroom, she saw the muscle in his jaw twitch, but he didn't say anything. She followed him down the stairs.

Jensen paced in the foyer. "So you're really going?"

"Yes," Royce said.

Jensen shook his head and headed for the kitchen.

"Jensen, wait." Vanessa started after him, but Royce grabbed her arm.

"He'll have to come to terms with it in his own time. Let's go."

She went with him to the car and sat in silence while they rode through town. After fifteen minutes, and passing Cathedral Lake High School twice, Vanessa finally asked, "Where exactly are we going?"

"Do you remember our first date?"

"The first time we went out, or our first date?"

"Same thing."

"Hardly."

He glanced at her as he took a right past the football field. "What's that supposed to mean?"

"Our first date, we went to the movies and then grabbed a bite to eat after at that little diner two blocks past the campus stadium. The first time we went out, you had your friends with you and acted like I wasn't supposed to be there. After you dumped your friends, you asked me what I wanted to do—when I told you you were supposed to have had the night planned—I said the only thing that mattered to me was that we didn't end up at the Student Union. We drove around for an hour and a half, then ended up grabbing burgers at the Student Union. Honestly, I don't know why I went on that date with you after that horrible first night."

"That first night was our first date, and you went on the second date because you had a great time that first night."

"We fought for ninety minutes over where to go, and then we went the one place I didn't want to be."

"Then why did you go out with me again?"

"I have no idea."

"And why did you kiss me goodnight?"

"Royce, please."

"And invite me in?"

She felt the heat on her cheeks. "So where are we going? The movies and a diner? Are you lost?"

"No. We're reliving our first date. We're driving around, then going to a burger place."

She turned her head slowly and looked at him. "Have you lost your ever-loving mind?"

"What?"

"We're supposed to be getting away from stressful situations, not holding each other captive in the car!"

"I thought you could appreciate the gesture. I'm trying here, Ness."

She sat back and crossed her arms.

"I looked up a lot of different options. Romantic restaurants, concerts, shows at the theater… It all seemed too much pressure. This reminded me of what Jeffers said. About remembering the happier times. This felt right."

"Our first date isn't a lot of pressure?"

"So you admit this was our first date?"

She huffed.

He smiled. "What do you want to talk about?"

"Let me get this straight. You have no destination in mind and no topics of conversation queued up to discuss?"

"You got it."

"Sounds about right," she muttered.

"Come on, Ness. Embrace this. We're supposed to be—"

"I know. I just don't know what got you in the mood all of a sudden."

"Who said I'm in the mood for any of this? I'm just trying."

"If you aren't in the mood and I'm not in the mood, then why bother? Why bother with any of it? In the end, none of it matters anyway." She looked out the window, determined not to let him see the tears fall.

Royce didn't say anything, didn't reach for her. He just continued driving. Soon they came to a stop and she looked out the window. They were sitting at the lake where she had come the day she bought the journal. He had been there, too. She had just missed him.

She seemed to always just miss him.

He got out of the car, leaving her inside, still crying. Soon her door opened and he offered her his hand. "Come here." She allowed him to help her from the car and pull her into a hug.

They stood a moment, embracing. She soaked his shirt as he stroked her hair and rubbed circles on her back. She cried for Hope, for her marriage, for Jensen and Faith. She cried for Royce's job, she cried for the lives lost and changed in the accident. She cried for herself. When she finally pulled away, she saw Royce's shirt was a kaleidoscopic disaster and spun to look at her face in the car window. "God, I'm such a mess." She wiped her eyes, then turned and swiped at his chest. "And look what I did to your shirt. I'm sorry. I don't know what's wrong with me today."

He pulled her down to the ground and cradled her against his chest, rubbing his hand up and down her arm. "Ssh. We're both a mess. And I don't mean physically. Our emotions are all over the place and we can't seem to get through five minutes without losing our tempers or our composure. I'm thinking that's perfectly normal, given the circumstances."

"I don't know if I can take much more of this," she whispered.

"More of which part?"

"More of... of... I don't know. Every time you're nice to me and I think we've turned the corner, something happens and we're back where this started. Flipping back and forth is too much. Just pick one. Are you mad? Sad? Moving past it? What?"

"Yes."

"Yes, what? Which is it?"

"It's all of them, Ness. Sometimes I think about it and I'm so pissed at you. Sometimes I'm devastated. Sometimes I just see how wrecked you are and want to fix it, to hell with how I feel, just as long as I can make it better for you."

"That doesn't make any sense."

"Since when does love make sense?"

"So you still love me?"

"Of course. I'll always love you."

"Is that enough?" She turned and looked at him, barely daring to breathe until she heard his answer.

He met her gaze, and the sadness in his eyes nearly broke her heart.

"I don't know, Ness. I just don't know."

She snuggled tighter against him and allowed the tears to fall silently. She didn't want him to move from the spot she had claimed against him. But he did move. He stood, leaving her alone on the ground. She blinked back the tears and looked up at him.

"Wait here. There's something I want to show you."

She played with a blade of grass and looked across the lake, thinking it would serve her right if he just drove off and left her there. But he didn't. He came back and sat beside her again.

"I can't put my feelings into words right now. It's too immediate with you here. Too raw. But I want you to know what I'm thinking. So I want you to read this passage." He handed her his journal. "Only this one. I'm not ready to share the other thoughts. Not yet."

Her hand trembled as she reached for the journal. "Okay. Just this one."

He met her gaze and held it before finally letting go. "Just this one."

"I promise," she said. She looked down, recognizing his penmanship. A few of the words looked splotchy, like they had had water spilled on them. Or tears. She began reading.

It's one thing to make an error at work. It's another for that error to result in the death of your daughter.

It's one thing to be responsible for your daughter's death. It's another to know she's not your daughter at all.

It's one thing to know someone in your own staff betrayed you to administration. It's another to know it's one of your best friends.

It's one thing to know your wife cheated on you. It's another to know it was with one of your best friends.

How is it that every time I think I can accept whatever horror I'm dealing with, another one pops up to punch me in the gut? I'm surrounded by betrayal.

My wife.

My best friends.

My abilities as a doctor.

My own blood.

Yes, I have to admit some of the fault is mine. If my own hubris had not been so great, I would have waited for Savvi to get the O-neg and treated Hope following the proper protocols. I don't know if she would have made it, but I know she definitely wouldn't have coded from receiving the wrong blood.

Further, if I had been more present eighteen years ago, maybe the affair never would have happened. I thought Vanessa understood what it meant to be married to a doctor, but maybe she didn't. And maybe I could have done more. Could I have explained better? Been home more? Made more of an effort? Even taken that damn call? I don't remember what I was doing that night, who I treated… was I saving a life or just trying to make a good impression? Was it worth it? Did my decision then make a difference in the grand scheme?

Would Ness have cheated on me that night, or another, or never?

Would Hope be mine or never have been born at all?

What would have happened in my ER the morning of Hope's death had I just taken Vanessa's call?

Why wasn't I there for her then?

And all these years later, I still wasn't present. Probably not for any of my family. Not for Vanessa. And not for Hope. If I was, I wouldn't have lost sight of the person she had become. And she might not have been where she was that fateful morning.

So I'll bear some of the guilt, some of the blame.

Which gives me more sadness, more anger.

What am I supposed to do with all of this?

I can't work it off. I can't go to my friends. I can't go to family.

So I keep writing. And writing. And writing.

But it doesn't seem to go away.

I may need to buy a new journal.

She wiped some of her own tears off the page and returned his book to him. "I had no idea you bore some of the responsibility. Not the ER part, or even the family part, but for the night I was with Ben."

"How could I not? Despite what you think, I know my role in all of this. Even eighteen years ago."

"But you never said anything."

He turned away. "I was hurting, Ness. I still am. I don't know how to fix this." He swept his arm in a broad arc in the air. "Any of this. Some of it is broken beyond repair. And I'm not saying I'm even responsible for most of it. I don't know how to break it down. Or if we even should. But I do recognize my part in what is wrong."

"I have to tell you something," she whispered.

He closed his eyes. "Do you? Do you have to? I don't know if I can take any more confessions."

"It goes along with what you just wrote." She handed back the journal.

He sighed. "Fine. Tell me."

"I didn't get it. Not really. Not until Hope died."

"Didn't get what?"

"What you did. I mean, I knew your job was important, but I didn't get it. I always thought you were working long hours and blowing off things I wanted you to do to just try and earn promotions. Or to stay out of the house and away from me. I didn't think bad things, really bad things, happened here. I was too isolated from it. So I blamed you for not being here for me."

"What are you talking about? It's an ER. What did you think I did there?"

"Honestly, now I understand how foolish I was. But then? I thought you were just choosing to treat people who didn't really need you. Treating ear infections and stomach aches. Maybe broken bones and torn ligaments. I never considered the real reason. The accidents. The gunshots and burns and heart attacks and knife wounds. I always thought it was just overreacting mothers and whiny kids."

"Ness, that's such a small part of what I do."

"I know. I get that now. But before? I felt sorry for myself and didn't look at the obvious." Tears welled in her eyes, but she didn't turn away. "You know, Cathedral Lake is such a small, quiet little town. Tragedies don't happen here like they do in movies and on TV." She blinked to clear her vision, and a lone tear rolled down her cheek. "And I've spent so much time in the hospital for different fundraisers. But in all that time, nothing seemed dire. The magnitude of what you do never hit me. Not until Hope." She sniffled and wiped the tear away. "I didn't realize you were needed to save people. If I did, Ben never would have happened."

He stayed quiet for a long time after she spoke. He looked across the lake like he'd find the words there. Finally, although he kept staring at the horizon, he answered her. "Thank you for telling me. But I think maybe on some level, I'm grateful it happened. If it hadn't, we wouldn't have had Hope." Then he looked at her, reached for her hand, and squeezed it.

She squeezed his in return. "So where do we go from here?"

"From here?" He sighed and stood. "From here, we go to dinner."

She got to her feet. "We could go to that nice little Italian place on the river up in—"

"Not a chance. We're reliving our first date, remember?" He got her settled in the car, then he joined her. "Ninety minutes of fruitless arguing, then ending up at a crappy burger place." He pulled out and headed toward town.

"But that was on campus."

"We're nowhere near college. You'll have to make due."

"What if I order a burger at the Italian place?"

"Nope. Not close enough to the same experience."

"Times are different now."

"All the more reason to recapture the spirit of that first night." He pulled into the parking lot of Patty's Melt, the local greasy spoon, and cut the engine.

"You don't really plan on eating here, do you?"

"Why not? They have the best burgers in town."

"Look at all the cars, Royce. They look pretty busy." She sunk down in her seat.

"We have to go out eventually. It's probably mostly just kids. You aren't going to run into anyone you know. And so what if you do? We're allowed to eat."

"You're right. It's just… weird."

"Let's go. Before I change my mind."

She never stopped to consider that he might feel uncomfortable going out in public, especially given it was his career hanging in the balance. She squared her shoulders and stepped out of the car.

They walked to the counter and placed their orders. She kept her head down and didn't talk to Royce until they had their tray of food. He chose a table in the corner, far from the door, and she slouched in her seat, nibbling at her fries.

"See?" he said after a bite of his burger. "This isn't so bad."

"You're right. We have nothing to hide." Sitting up, she took a bite of her sandwich. She'd barely managed to chew it when a voice behind her sent chills through her body. She forced the food past the lump in her throat and turned around.

Savvi and a few of the other ER staff stood there, to-go bags in hand. "Dr. Keller. Mrs. Keller. I wouldn't have expected to see you out."

"People have to eat, Savvi."

"But so soon after… I just thought you'd be home. Usually people eat the food sent to them. Unless, of course, no one—"

"We have plenty of food at home, thank you," Royce answered in a clipped tone.

"You would know that if you had come to the funeral," Vanessa said.

Savvi's eyes opened wide for a moment, then narrowed. She turned away from Royce and focused all her attention on Vanessa. "I wasn't sure it was appropriate to express my condolences, given I wasn't sure he was grieving. There was talk it was intentional, you know."

"If the police thought it was intentional," she said, "we wouldn't have been allowed to bury our daughter."

"We? Our? That's not quite accurate, though, is it, Mrs. Keller?"

"Savvi, I don't know what you're trying to prove, exactly, but—"

"I'm not the one who has to prove anything," Savvi said. "I didn't do anything wrong."

Royce wiped his mouth and put his napkin down. He looked at Vanessa.

"I didn't realize the clientele in here had gone so far downhill since we'd last been here," Vanessa said. "Let's go."

Royce took their tray to the trash and Vanessa followed him toward the door.

"You can't run from your problems forever, Dr. Keller," Savvi said.

"Oh, we aren't running from anything," Vanessa said. "We're just looking for some better company."

CHAPTER 21

"I JUST DON'T GET IT," Royce said in the car. "I always liked Savvi. And I always thought she liked me. What could possibly have happened to have changed things so drastically?"

"Not what, Royce. *Who.*"

"What?"

"Never mind. This is turning into an Abbott and Costello skit."

He raised an eyebrow.

"It's Wade. He's the common link. Obviously he's said or done something to poison the well. If you were counting on any of your staff to be character witnesses on your behalf, you better rethink your strategy."

He pounded his fist on the dash. "I don't need this right now."

She lifted her hand and ran her fingers through the hair at the nape of his neck. "What do you need?"

He looked at her. "Do you know what I really want?"

"Anything. How can I help?"

"I want to see Hope."

He could tell she expected a different answer. Her fingers stilled and she dropped her arm. "Whatever you need," she finally whispered.

She didn't sound too convinced, but he needed to go there. He'd coddled Vanessa all evening. She could suck it up and help him out for a few minutes.

He'd only been to the cemetery a couple of times, but he drove there almost like the car ran on auto-pilot. When he stopped in front of Hope's plot, the sun began to dip in the horizon, its rays slanting through the trees at a low angle, acting like a spotlight on the mound where she was laid to rest.

He got out of the car and sat on the bench. Vanessa sat beside him.

"We really picked a beautiful spot," she said, looking at the sunlit earth.

"It's peaceful."

"She'll have a nice view of the sunset every day."

He turned and looked at her. "There you go again. You understand she's not really here, right?"

She sighed. "I meant, we will, from here. I just said it wrong."

He studied her face. He couldn't tell if she was telling the truth. He didn't care at the moment, either. That was something he'd rather deal with at another time. Guilt had been eating away at him like vultures at carrion, and he needed another opinion before everything inside him rotted into something unrecognizable.

"Do you think she's forgiven me?" Royce asked Vanessa.

"What? You didn't kill her, Royce. No matter what anyone tries to make you think."

"You blame me."

She sighed and looked out over the dirt. "Part of me blames you for her feeling so abandoned. I tried to make up for that, to be there in your place. But I wasn't enough for her. And I carry the blame for that. And for not telling you the truth about her parentage. But for her medical care? I don't blame you for that. I know you did what you thought was best. You're Royce-freakin'-Keller." She smiled and took his hand. "If anyone could have saved her, it was you."

"That's just it, though, Ness. What if I could have saved her? What if she really is dead because of me?" He pulled away and leaned forward, putting his head in his hands.

"Don't make me call my mother, Royce."

He looked at her.

"She'll tell you it was Hope's time, and there was nothing you could have done about it."

"But what if I could have?"

"And what if all this happened for a reason? What if this is one big cosmic test? What are we going to do about everything that's left to us to deal with?"

"If it is a test, I think I'm failing."

"Well then, you better cram, mister, because you're the one who helped me with the hard subjects, not the other way around. Remember?"

He tried to smile, but fell short.

"We've got some tough times ahead. Most days I feel like crawling right down beside her." She pointed to the dirt mound. "If we're going to get through this, I need you on your A game."

He shook his head. "It can't all be on me, Ness. Not this time."

"It won't all be on you this time. But you can't give up. Not now."

He looked out over the spot where Hope's headstone would someday be. The sky had turned deep indigo in the east, and the first stars were starting to show. The sun had almost set. The pinks and oranges on the western horizon had given way to reds and violets, and soon the whole sky would be black. If the stone had been there, it would be reflecting the last colors of the day. He could almost see Hope standing there, the light a halo behind her. He started to reach for her, then dropped his hand. She wasn't there. That was exactly the kind of thing he cautioned Vanessa against. He closed his eyes and rubbed them while the sun disappeared. When he opened them, a man approached them from the shadows in the gloaming.

"Hey, folks. Park's closing. You can't be here."

"We were just leaving," Royce said.

The man glanced at the ground then swept his hat off his head. "I'm sorry. You must be the Kellers. My condolences."

Vanessa nodded.

Royce said, "Thank you."

"Don't think I'll ever get that out of my mind. I can't imagine what you folks have been through."

"I'm sorry," Royce said. "Out of your mind?"

"I was on Sycamore waiting to pull out on Dappled Oak. Saw the whole damn thing. Just knew it was going to happen, but there was nothing I could do. Like I said, I'll hold on to this one."

The witness!

"Mr. Uh—"

"Poleski. Stan Poleski. But just call me Stush. Most everybody does."

"Okay. Stush. Can you tell us what really happened? The police won't give us any details."

"What'd the doctors say? Isn't that what really matters?"

"We know what happened at the hospital. We want to know what happened at the accident. The truth."

Stush rubbed his balding pate, shiny in the fading light. He sighed and finally said, "Maybe if the police didn't say, it's better if you don't know."

Vanessa put her hand on his arm. "If it was your daughter, wouldn't you want to know?"

"Aw," Stush shuffled his feet and patted her hand. "You might want to sit. You aren't going to like it." When they both stood there, Stush turned his back to them. "I was sitting on Sycamore, waiting to pull out. I had enough time. The bike was pretty far down the road. But it was going fast. And weaving. First way too close to the berm, then well into the oncoming lane. I was going to pull out, thinking I wanted to be in front of them, but then I thought he might try to catch up to me, so I decided behind would be best. I waited for them to pass. I was sick when I saw a car coming around the bend." He paused and took a deep breath. "I looked back at the bikers and could see the driver was cranking the brakes."

"How could you tell?" Vanessa asked.

"Do you know anything about bikes?" he asked.

They both shook their heads.

"There are two brakes. One on the right handlebars and one on the right pedal. The kid was working his hand and foot like crazy, and nothing was happening. In fact, they were headed downhill, so they were picking up speed. The one on the back—your girl—was trying to reach the handlebars, but couldn't quite. I think she was going for the kill switch."

"The kill switch?" Royce asked.

"It's a switch on a bike that will shut off the engine. There was something wrong with the brakes, and the boy panicked. Your girl kept her head, and she was trying to save them. He just didn't let her. She was a hero."

Vanessa plopped down on the bench and cried.

Royce stood there, holding back the tears in front of 'the witness.' Where'd Hope learn about kill switches? And why was she in a position to have to know?

"Again, folks. I'm really sorry. You take a few minutes to compose yourselves, but then you have to go. We're closing the park, and the gates will be locked."

Royce stuck out his hand. In a gravelly voice, he managed, "Thanks, Stush."

The groundskeeper walked down toward a cart Royce hadn't noticed before, then he turned around. "Hey. When my wife died, I couldn't get a straight answer from the doctors about how she passed. How do you know the hospital was honest with you about what happened to your girl?"

Royce swallowed. "Because I was the doctor who worked on her in the ER."

Stush whistled low and turned around. "Damn hard on you." He got in his cart and drove off.

"Are you okay?" Vanessa asked.

He shook his head to clear his vision. "I don't know what I am. But Stush is right. It's dark, and they'll be locking up soon. Are you ready to go?"

She nodded, and they headed for the car.

"You know, I was thinking," he said while they strapped in, "as much as I didn't want to see Dr. Jeffers, it's been beneficial in some ways."

"I think so, too."

"Maybe we should bring the kids with us next time."

She looked at him through the darkness. "I think that's a great idea. I'll call him and set it up."

While Vanessa talked on the phone, Royce drove and thought about the absurdity of it all. He'd never believed in therapy, but there he was not only going, but requesting it for his kids, too. If he'd gone earlier, maybe Hope would still be with them.

How long would he be playing the 'what if' game? Would he second guess every decision he made for the rest of his life? That was no way to practice medicine.

Of course, he probably wouldn't be doing that any longer, so the point was likely moot.

They drove the rest of the way home in silence. The headlights shone on the shadowy landscape, cutting a path through the darkness. He was in the driveway before he realized he'd driven right past the scene of Hope's accident and not even realized it. Distracted by his churning thoughts and focused on just the path his lights illuminated, he'd missed that sickening spot on the road.

He wasn't sure if that was progress or a setback.

The house was dark, but all the cars were there. Jensen and Faith were probably both in bed, despite the early hour, angry at him for taking Vanessa out.

"Do you want me to tell them about tomorrow myself, or should we tell them together?" he asked.

"I don't know. What do you think?"

Again. Up to him. Always up to him. "It looks like they're both in bed. Why don't I talk to Jensen. You can tell Faith."

"And if they happen to be together?"

"Then I'll do it myself. I don't think Jensen needs to hear it from you right now."

She shrugged her shoulders. "Whatever you think is best."

They got out of the car and he guided her into the house by placing his hand on the small of her back. It was a simple gesture, one he had done thousands of times before, but one he must not have done in a while. He felt her spine stiffen the second he did it and nearly pulled his hand away. But she relaxed just as quickly, and he left his hand there until they walked inside.

A nightlight burned in the kitchen, but the rest of the rooms were dark. Royce led Vanessa upstairs, but the kids' bedrooms were empty.

"Where could they be?" she asked. "Jensen's car is in the driveway."

"I'll check downstairs. They're probably in the game room or home theater."

"I'll check out back."

"Don't worry about it. Go ahead and get ready for bed. If they aren't downstairs, I'll check outside. If I can't find them—and I'm sure I will, but if I can't—I'll call them."

She grasped his hand. "Why wait? Why run all over the house? Just call them now. I need to know where they are."

It was irrational, but he understood her panic. She'd already lost one child. The thought of losing the others had to be unbearable, and she was already on that path because of her actions. If they had run away, or God forbid, if something had happened to them.... The prospect frightened her. It disturbed him more than he wanted to admit.

He patted her hand then took out his phone. Jensen answered on the third ring. "Jensen? Where are you? Is Faith with you?"

When Jensen told him they were both in the media room in the basement, he let out a sigh of relief. He hadn't even realized he'd been holding his breath.

Vanessa, wringing her hands, almost ripped the phone away from him. He waved her off and said to his son, "Stay there. I want to talk to you. I'll be right down." He disconnected the call and looked at his wife. "They're fine. They're watching a movie downstairs. I'll go talk to them. Why don't you just get ready for bed?"

Her body sagged to the bed as a calm radiance flooded her face. She probably looked as relieved as he felt. He couldn't say the words aloud, but it just kind of hit him—hit both of them, he supposed—how precious those kids were and how fleeting life was.

CHAPTER 22

EVEN THE SHORT AMOUNT OF time Vanessa hadn't known where the kids were had wreaked havoc on her emotions. The whole night had been a series of ups and downs, highs and lows, and she couldn't take much more. Confusion seemed to be the only constant in her life, but as she undressed, she tried to focus on the kids… Safe. Secure. At home. She couldn't ask for anything more at the moment, and exhaled a slow sigh of relief.

That relief was short-lived.

Post-date jitters had kicked in. She hadn't felt those since college and almost didn't recognize them. Once she did, she entered full-on panic mode. The goodnight-kiss-at-the-door part of their relationship ended more than twenty years ago. They shared a bed—hell, they'd shared a life—for more than two decades. What did he expect when he made his way back to the bedroom? And what was she willing to give him? They may have shared a bed for all those years, but they hadn't shared their bodies in… well, she didn't know how long. Had it been four months? Five? Their sex life had dwindled into nearly non-existent, the few times a year more an obligation than a need. How had that happened? And should that change?

Biting her lip, she looked in the mirror. Wow. She looked positively ghastly. Her cheeks had no color except for the dark circles under her eyes, and that wasn't a color she was shooting for. Maybe she didn't have a decision to make. Maybe she'd read the signals wrong.

But maybe he expected to end their date in a more intimate manner. Their first date certainly had ended at more than a handshake and a 'good-night.'

If he was, she was going to look a damn sight better than she did at the moment. A plan formed in her mind, and she quickly got to work, knowing she had only minutes to spare.

She finished lighting the candles on her nightstand and dashed over to the door, flipping the light switch off just before Royce entered. She glanced down and realized that could work in her favor. The dim, flickering light showcased her breasts—heaving as she tried to catch her breath—nearly spilling out of the barely-there concoction of frothy lace she'd squeezed them into. She'd bought the lace-up teddy at a Naughty Nights party, but had never found the nerve or the occasion to wear it for him. She'd chosen the perfect time to unveil it...old/new lingerie for an old/new romance.

Royce said, "Why didn't you leave the light on?" His hand groped for the switch on the wall.

Vanessa seized her opportunity. His momentary confusion, his unawareness of the mood lighting, his not seeing her standing by the door... It all worked to her favor. She stopped his hand with her own, and with her other hand she pulled his head toward hers, locking them in an embrace as she claimed his mouth in a searing kiss.

For a moment, he didn't respond, and she almost pulled away. Then his fingers dug into her hip, pulling her to him as his other hand plunged into her hair, fisting in her tresses, tugging her head to the side so he could take the kiss deeper. He ravished her mouth in a way he hadn't in years, and it was everything she remembered his kisses could be—hot, mind-melting kisses that made her forget everything but his name, and she'd pant it, scream it, if her mouth wasn't so otherwise gloriously occupied.

More. She needed more. Her fingers skimmed over his jaw, danced across his shoulders and down the firm planes of his torso. Skin. She needed flesh. Heat. As she lifted the hem of his shirt, his hands clamped down on her wrists and he broke off the kiss, stepping back from her. His eyes were dark, and she read incalculable pain in their depths.

"What the fuck are you playing at?" His voice was low, gritty. His breathing, ragged.

Her breathing labored as much as his, and this time, instead of appreciating the effect of her breasts heaving over the top of her teddy, it humiliated her. Not bothering to blink back the tears, she grabbed the throw off the foot of the bed and wrapped it around herself. "Playing? I'm not playing at anything. I thought this was what you wanted."

"Why in God's name would you think that?"

"Because you knew the coin flip was fixed, but you went anyway. And you tried so hard to make the night just like our first date. You didn't just walk me to my door that night."

"I see."

She sniffled and sat on the edge of the bed. "Besides, you kissed me back."

"Well, what the hell do you expect? It's been a long time. And then a gorgeous woman dressed in a get up like that throws herself at me? Who wouldn't react?"

"I don't know if I should be flattered you still think I'm gorgeous or scared you'd kiss any woman who threw herself at you."

He sighed and sat beside her. "Be flattered. Forget about the other part. I'm not thinking clearly. There's not much blood in my brain at the moment."

She glanced at his lap and saw he was telling the truth. "Well, what am I supposed to make of that?"

"You're a beautiful woman, Vanessa. Always have been. You know I've always thought so."

"So why have things been so... perfunctory... between us for the past several years? This kiss tonight has been the first of its kind in, well, I don't know how long."

"Perfunctory. That's a good way of putting it." He thought for a minute. "I don't know. We let life get in the way, I guess."

"That's not much of an answer."

He reclined back on the bed and put his arm over his eyes. "I don't have much of an excuse. But it goes both ways. When was the last time you wore lingerie to bed? When was the last time you initiated sex? It's not always up to the man, you know. Besides, I get tired of being shot down."

"Shot down?" She spun toward him and moved his arm so he'd look at her, the blanket falling away in the process. "When did I ever say no to you?"

"You said no before I had a chance to ask. Announcing you had a headache or saying you were tired as you got ready for bed were clear 'hands-off' signals. And you did it with more and more frequency. Why would I try? And you never tried. So don't tell me I lost interest. You lost it long before I did."

"Did you ever think maybe you could have offered to rub my head or give me a massage? Maybe bring wine to the bedroom? How about expressing some interest before going to bed so I knew the offer was on the table?"

"What are you talking about?"

"Foreplay's not just a few strokes in bed before the deed, Royce."

"I'm aware of what foreplay is, thank you."

"That's not what I mean. It's hand-holding while watching a movie. Caressing my arm as you walk past me. Rubbing your foot up my leg during dinner. Calling while you're at work just to say you're thinking about me. Sending a naughty text telling me what you can't wait to do later. It's all build-up to the main event. That's foreplay. That's how you get a woman in the mood."

He propped himself up on one elbow and turned toward her. After a long moment of staring at her, he reached over and adjusted her blanket so she was covered again. When he spoke, his voice was low. "So what put you in the mood tonight?"

She knew her face flamed and was grateful for what little cover the candlelight provided. "I told you already. All the work you put into recreating our first date. Effort is sexy. And I miss you, Royce. I miss us."

He leaned toward her and kissed her on the forehead. "Then I'll put more effort into this. Into us. But I'm not there yet. I'm sorry." He rested his fore-head against hers, then got up.

"Does that mean maybe you will be someday?"

"You're definitely worth the effort, Ness. If this is salvageable, we'll get there." He walked into the bathroom.

It was the best she'd gotten from him yet. She'd take it.

After he was done in the bathroom, he went into his closet, probably to get ready for bed and to write in his journal. Vanessa went into the bathroom to shower and brush her teeth.

When she came out, dressed in conservative pajamas, Royce was asleep in the bed.

In *their* bed.

He was definitely making an effort.

She crawled into her side of the bed, resisted the urge to cuddle against him, rolled away from him, and closed her eyes.

In the morning, things were back to normal in the Keller household. If normal was Vanessa waking to an empty bed, going downstairs to a breakfast she didn't like made by a woman who hated her, and sitting at a table with two hostile teens and an awkwardly silent husband.

Normal sucked.

She glanced at her watch. "We need to leave in fifteen minutes if we don't want to be late. Go brush your teeth and get ready."

The kids just looked at her and didn't budge.

Royce put his coffee cup down. "You heard your mother. Go."

Faith pushed back from the table and left the room, munching on an apple.

Jensen said, "I don't want to go."

"It's not up for debate. You're going."

"I'm eighteen. I'm legally an adult."

"My house. My rules," Royce said. "If you want to move out in the next ten minutes, tell me now."

Jensen clenched his jaw.

"No?" Royce asked. "Very well, then. Go get ready."

Jensen threw his napkin on the table and stormed out of the room.

"He's never going to get past this," Vanessa said, rubbing her finger around the rim of her coffee cup.

Royce took her free hand. "I think he will. And if not? He's an adult. He won't be here much longer, so you won't have to worry about it."

"I don't want him leaving angry with me," she whispered. She was glad she hadn't eaten, because her stomach swirled. Even the coffee threatened to not stay down.

"Vanessa. Vanessa, look at me."

She forced herself to meet his gaze.

"You can't control how he feels. Stop worrying about him. About Faith. About me."

She knew her eyes widened, but she couldn't hide her reaction. It felt like another goodbye. And so soon after they'd made progress.

"For now, just focus on you. Let the rest of us deal with our own issues on our own. We'll all get there."

She nodded, but didn't feel any confidence in her reaction.

"Let's get ready. We need to go." Royce got up and headed for the stairs.

She followed him, intending to look put together, even if she felt like she was falling apart.

Neither of them spoke a word on the way to therapy. Vanessa had plenty she wanted to say. She even opened her mouth once or twice. But the words never actually formed on her lips. The kids didn't want to hear from her, anyway. She'd have to leave it all in the doctor's capable hands.

Once inside, she noticed there were subtle changes to the room compared to when she and Royce had gone by themselves. The refreshment tray was already set up, but it was on a cart by the window instead of on the coffee table, and it held far more selections than water and iced tea. There were sodas and juice, as well as fruit, cheese, and crackers. The tray wasn't on the table because the table was gone. Instead, large pillows littered the floor, making for a comfortable sitting area should someone want to lounge there instead of sitting in the furniture. Two additional chairs had been brought in to form a circle around the pillows, completing the gathering space. It was a far more casual space than the one she and Royce usually met in. She wanted to nestle into the pillows, but the kids settled into them right away. She and Royce took their usual places on the couch and waited for Dr. Jeffers to lead the discussion.

"Jensen, Faith. I'm Tod. Thanks for coming today."

"I didn't have a choice," Jensen said.

Royce nudged him in the back with his toe.

"Oh?" Tod said. "Do you have somewhere else to be?"

"I should be writing my commencement speech. It's tomorrow and I haven't finished it yet."

"You didn't write it yet?" Royce exploded. "What've you been waiting for?"

"Well, I've been a little busy, haven't I? And it's not like I wanted to be valedictorian, anyway. I told you I didn't want to do it, but you made me. So I've been putting off finishing the speech, hoping you'd change your mind. It's started. It's just not done, so relax."

"Jensen," Royce said, "you earned the right to deliver that speech. Why shouldn't you?"

"I don't want to. Having the right and having the desire are two different things, Dad. I don't even want to go to graduation, let alone want to give the valedictory address. It's ridiculous."

"Why?" Tod asked.

"Why what?" Jensen asked.

"Why is it ridiculous? It's more than a matter of you having the honor of delivering the speech. You are more qualified than anyone in your class to send those students off with the right message. It's an obligation. Why should you shirk it? What has changed that makes you feel unworthy of the responsibility?"

Jensen blinked a few times before he answered. "Obligation? Responsibility? No. It's just a title they give to the kid with the best grades."

"No. I'm afraid it's much more than that. If they wanted to honor the student with the best academic record, they'd just call you up, hand you a certificate, and send you back to your seat. They're asking you to speak because they know it took something special for you to earn your place among your peers, and they want you to impart some of your wisdom before everyone moves on. They want everyone to benefit from your experience before they enter the next phase of their lives."

Jensen stared at his hands, crossed in his lap.

"You've been looking at it from a pretty selfish angle."

"I guess."

"Do you do that a lot?"

"What do you mean?"

Vanessa recognized this tactic. She'd fallen for it enough in her own sessions to appreciate it when it was used on someone else. She sat back and watched, playing with her St. Luke medal as Jensen got sucked in to the discussion. A quick glance at the clock on the wall told her they'd have plenty of time to cover this topic. In depth.

"It's okay. Most teens do. Most people do. We get so caught up with how things affect us, we don't look at the bigger picture. We don't realize there are other pieces at play on the board, and sometimes we're just a pawn or a knight, not a king or a queen."

"That's bullshit."

"Jensen!" Vanessa said.

Tod waved her off.

Faith got up and grabbed a water and some grapes.

"I'm sorry, but it is. In my life, I'm always the king. It's my life. My board. My game. That makes me the king."

"Really?" Tod asked. "Does that hold true for everyone?"

"You bet."

"So, by your way of thinking, in my life, I'm always the king."

"Yep." Jensen sat back, pride on his face for outwitting his therapist.

"So as I'm here trying to counsel your family through this difficult time, who's the king? Me, you, or your dad?"

The grin faded from Jensen's face, light dimmed from his eyes. "Well…"

"One game, one board, Jensen. You can't have three kings."

"Umm…."

"I think you've been trying so hard to protect the king that your knight has been taking a beating. Which is unfortunate, because in this case, you're the knight. It's time to reassess."

Vanessa didn't approach him yet, didn't interrupt. She knew she wasn't welcome yet. But her heart ached for him as she saw tears welled in his eyes.

"No more analogies, Jensen," Tod said. "I get that you're hurt. But you do understand that what happened all those years ago was between your mother and your father? It had nothing to do with you."

He whispered past the tears threatening to fall. "It feels like she cheated on me, too. I was alive then. If she cheated on Dad, maybe it wasn't that she was unhappy with her marriage. Maybe it was that she was unhappy because of me."

Now she was needed. Vanessa scrambled down onto the pillows beside him and took his face in her hands. "Jensen. You listen to me. You've never given me the chance to explain, so please hear me now. What happened between me and Ben was a onetime thing that had absolutely nothing to do with you. I was over the moon with joy when I found out I was expecting you, and I grew happier every day since. I couldn't be more proud of you, and I couldn't love you more. Nothing that happened was your fault. Do you understand me?"

"So you don't blame me?"

"No, baby. Never."

"And it was just the one time?"

"Yes, honey. I love your father. I've always loved him."

"Then I don't understand how it could have happened."

"That's between me and Dad."

He shook his head. "It feels like a secret between us."

"Kings and queens, Jensen," Vanessa said. "Knights are on a need-to-know basis."

Faith put her bottle aside and sighed. "Well, this has been a real eye-opener."

"What's wrong, moppet?" Royce asked.

He hadn't called her moppet since she was little. It seemed everyone was reaching deep into their bags of tricks. Vanessa wished she had something—anything—to dig out, but her bag was woefully empty. She glanced at the clock again. At least they had some time to spare before their hour was up.

"Kings. Queens. Knights. Apparently Hope and I were expendable pawns, because as usual, we've been left out of this whole thing. Or at least I have."

"Expendable?" Tod asked. "Hardly. We're all here because of you. Because of Hope. And pawns. Not by a long shot. Rooks, perhaps." He tapped his lip as he studied her.

"Rooks? Those are the castles, right?" Faith asked. "They're hardly bigger than the pawns. No one notices them, either."

"You don't play, do you?" Tod asked.

She shook her head.

"In chess, there are major pieces and minor pieces. The knights and the bishops are the minor pieces. But the queen and the rooks? They're the major pieces. Don't let size deceive you."

"So you're saying I'm relevant?" she asked.

Tod leaned forward. "Faith. You're not only relevant. You're necessary. Why don't you think so?"

She looked at the floor. "Because Mom always liked Hope best."

Did all the oxygen just get sucked out of the room? Vanessa had trouble taking in air. She was vaguely aware of shaking her head even as Jensen was nodding his in agreement. They couldn't possibly mean that.

But they did.

She looked to Royce for help, but his face was emotionless. He refused to turn to look at her. Instead, he rubbed Faith's back and put his hand on Jensen's shoulder.

When she looked to Tod for help, he met her gaze with a question. "What do you think about that, Vanessa? How does it make you feel when your children tell you they know you had a favorite… and neither of them was it?"

Her pulse reverberated in her ears, competing with the ticking of the wall clock, each one echoing in her head, a cacophony of noise in her already over-crowded brain. Memories bounced off each other, speeding faster and faster like a movie reel on overdrive…family dinners, vacations, excursions, social outings. Each one a reminder of ways Royce, Jensen, and Faith were a unit she and Hope didn't fit into, each one a recollection of how it was always an unbalanced three-against-two in favor of 'them.'

She turned toward her kids. "As far back as I can remember, any time there was a family event, a decision to be made, a game to be played, the two of you always chose your dad. If he and I disagreed on a restaurant, you sided with him. If we picked teams for touch football, you wanted to be on his team. If he wanted to go camping and I wanted to go to the beach, you were in the garage looking for tents and fishing poles. I don't know if Hope took my side to be difficult, if I took her side just so someone would… maybe we just had the same interests and that's how it worked out. But it always felt to me like it was you guys against us. Always you two and Dad against me and Hope. I felt ex-cluded from you. And now, with Hope gone, it's an even more lopsided fight."

"It always felt like you loved her more," Jensen said. "Like you were siding with her because you liked her better."

"Even if the three of us were fighting," Faith said, "you always gave her the benefit of the doubt."

Vanessa stopped and stared at them. "I did?"

They nodded.

"Was it because you loved her more?" Faith asked. "Because she was Ben's?"

"No, baby," Vanessa said.

"But did you? Love her more?" Faith asked. "Because of Ben? Do you wish I was his, too?"

For the first time, Royce turned his head and looked at her.

Vanessa grabbed Faith's hands, then dropped one of them and took one of Jensen's. "I want you both to listen to me very carefully. Look at me when I tell you this, so you know I'm telling you the complete truth. I love you both, wholly and completely, exactly as you are. And I wouldn't change a thing about either of you. And, yes, I loved Hope, too. I always wished she was biologically your father's, but I never said anything in all these years because in my mind, in my heart, she was his. I never had a favorite child. I'm sorry if you felt that way. I'm sorry if my actions somehow led you to believe I did. From here forward, I'll do everything in my power to prove to you that I love you both fully and equally and beyond measure. But never think I want anything from you other than what you are. Okay?"

Tears were in Jensen's eyes again. They fell freely down Faith's cheeks. Vanessa squeezed their hands, unsure if her speech meant anything at all to them. Then Faith launched herself into her mother's arms. Jensen wrapped his arms around them, too. And Vanessa relaxed for the first time in days. She took a deep breath as she held her two babies on the floor. Babies she'd raised from tiny bundles of joy to young adulthood. They didn't fit in her lap any longer. They barely fit in her arms. But she had no interest in ever letting go of them again.

CHAPTER 23

ROYCE WAS RELIEVED THEY HAD decided to take the kids to therapy with them. Sure, they still had a long way to go, but they had made a huge breakthrough that morning, and for the first time in, well, he didn't know how long, everyone had spent the day together without any awkwardness or hostility. They spent the day like a family.

If only his family was whole.

The sound of Vanessa singing drifted out of the bathroom. She hadn't sung in the shower in, well, he didn't know how long that had been, either. It seemed a lot of things were changing. While she was scrubbing to the tune of 'Don't Stop Believing,' he sat on the bed with his journal.

This must be how washcloths feel. Wrung out. Set aside.

A second thought.

He thought for a moment.

Am I jealous?

He looked back at the bathroom door and listened to his wife belt out Journey lyrics. She obviously wanted to hold on to the feelings she had experienced that day. He wasn't sure he did. He didn't like where his thoughts were. Gripping his pen tighter, he looked back down at the page.

I thought getting the kids to talk out their feelings would be good for all of us. As it turns out, it was good for everyone but me.

Jensen came to terms with the fact that the infidelity was not because of him. Directed at him.

Faith learned she's just as important to Ness as Hope.

There are no favorites.

Vanessa got her family back.

What did I get?

Replaced.

In all the hostility, all the animosity, all the drama, I never realized I was thriving by being the one the kids turned to. Without them needing me, without them wanting me more than their mom, what do I have?

He thought back over how they spent their day. Vanessa had sent Lydia home again so they'd have privacy. That was her call, and probably a good one. But they hadn't gone straight home. First was the picnic by the lake—that Vanessa suggested and bought the food for. Then the movie in the basement—that the kids let Ness choose, and then sat on either side of her during. And then dinner around the pool—pasta salad and chicken cutlets, Vanessa's one and only specialty. And the kids helped her make it. Well, Faith wouldn't go near the chicken. But she helped with the salad.

Everyone had retired to their rooms early. It had been a long and emotional day. But there were smiles on faces and hugs all around. And 'I love you, Mom' was said to Vanessa from both kids for the first time in—well, Royce wasn't sure how long that was, either, but he knew it had been a long time.

I have a family who is piecing itself back together. And it doesn't seem to need me to do it. Me, the doctor who is used to patching people up. And I'm not needed at work or at home.

I thought therapy would be good for the kids, and it was. I'm glad I did it for them.

I just didn't realize the toll it would take on me.

How could fixing everybody else leave me so broken?

And how do I put me back together?

The water had stopped running in the bathroom. Royce returned his journal to his closet and dressed for bed. By the time Vanessa stepped into the bedroom, he was under the covers and faking sleep. She turned out the light and crawled in after him, still humming softly to herself. She was obviously too delighted to stop singing, but she was trying not to wake him. Soon the tune faded away and her breathing regulated.

His thoughts churned as he slipped into a restless sleep. In his dreams, shadows searched for something hiding in the dark, reaching out to him, their gloomy claws scratching at him but passing straight through. Was it he who was ephemeral or the phantoms? Or were they one and the same? He didn't know any longer. He felt nothing at all. So he searched for the light, for any emotion, any feeling at all until dawn broke. Then he finally managed to fall asleep.

Later that morning, Royce woke completely on edge. Exhausted from lack of sleep and still touchy from his revelations the day before, he had only one thing on his mind: coffee.

Not bothering to shower or dress, he made his way to the kitchen clad only in his pajama bottoms and an old college t-shirt. When he got there, he was surprised to see his whole family dressed and nearly through with breakfast.

Who's the outcast, now?

"Why's everyone up and about so early today?" he asked on the way to the coffee maker. Empty. Of course.

"It's not that early. And commencement's this morning, Dad," Jensen said. "You didn't forget, did you?"

Shit. He'd forgotten. "Of course not. It just seems a little early to be ready to walk out the door."

"Mom wanted to go early so she got a close seat. For my speech. We made plans for this yesterday before I went to my room to finish it. Remember?"

Vaguely. It came up somewhere between 'we like Mom better now' and 'who cares what Dad wants.' He put his cup back in the cabinet. No caffeine jolt to make things better. Maybe a cold shower. "Let me go freshen up. I need about ten minutes."

"I'll take some pictures while you get ready," Vanessa said. "I can't believe you stayed in bed this long."

"You could have gotten me up." So it was all on him again.

She looked at him and raised her eyebrows. "I did. An hour ago, on my way downstairs. You said you were getting right up."

Huh. Was she covering her tracks, or did he really sleep talk? He hadn't done that since med school. Why would she lie, though? Of course, she didn't have a record of honesty. He sighed. "I'll be right back. Don't leave without me."

"Why would we leave without you?" Jensen asked.

Royce looked at his son for a second, then left the room, not bothering to answer.

He got ready in record time, easy enough since he speed-showered and skipped shaving, opting for the rugged look. He was far more presentable when he went downstairs again. At least outwardly. On the inside, he was still a mess. And when no one was in the house, anger and insecurities flooded his system, fighting for a foothold against his sanity.

Rushing to the garage, he hopped in his car and barely contained himself while the door opened. He backed out and saw his kids posing for pictures by the tree in the front yard.

And exhaled a breath he didn't know he held.

Who were those people?

For the first time, he looked at his kids. Really looked at them.

Jensen looked like a younger version of Royce. He had the same athletic build, the same blue eyes that crinkled in the corners when he laughed, the same light brown hair. Royce kept his cut short for convenience. Jensen wore his longer, the waves falling over his forehead in a careless manner. If he looked closer, he'd see the same hands. Doctor's hands. Healing hands.

Change the clothes, and that was me going to college.

When did that happen?

People had told him, but he never looked. Not that closely.

Faith stood beside her brother, light brown hair falling softly past her shoulders. She had the same blue eyes as her brother, but that's where their similarity ended. People said she looked like him, but in his mind, she looked exactly like her mother. Slim build from hours of dance and sports. Wavy hair with natural blonde highlights from the sun. High cheekbones, pert little nose....

But she wasn't a little girl any longer. She was a young lady and Jensen was a young man. They had grown into young adults. Young adults who reminded him so much of when he and Vanessa were young and had bright futures before them. Futures they made, not ones forced on them by their parents, or anyone else.

How had he messed everything up so badly?

Faith stepped away from Jensen and he stood alone, tall, mortarboard tipped at a jaunty angle. He was ready to take on the world. He'd suffered a great loss and come out the other side stronger for it.

Who would have thought the father would learn from the son?

Vanessa snapped the photo. That was one he knew he'd want to remember.

They came to the car then, and he drove them to the school. He was silent as he listened to their banter, glad they were in a good mood. It should be a happy occasion. Even if he wasn't quite able to muster up the joy they felt, they deserved the festive atmosphere. At least for one day.

Family and friends were just starting to fill the gym when they arrived at the school. A quick, "Good luck!" to Jensen and he darted off, leaving them in the first row reserved for guests. Royce could only be grateful his parents and Vanessa's parents had gone home. It was sort of sad for Jensen that he didn't have extended family there, but frankly, they didn't need the drama.

"I can't believe you're going through with this," a voice said from behind him.

Ah. Drama.

Mrs. Prindle walked down the aisle and turned to face them.

"Going through with *what*, exactly?"

"Showing up here at commencement, of course. And having your son deliver the valediction."

"He earned it. He has every right."

"It's a violation of the morality clause."

"You're a violation of the morality clause." He hadn't realized how good it felt to just let loose and say what he really felt, immature or not. When he heard his daughter snicker, it finally registered. Sometimes taking the high road wasn't worth it. There was no winning against folks like that. With them, it wasn't a matter of descending to their level. It was a matter of getting underneath them so you could toss them away.

"Well!" Her eyes widened and she took a step back. "You won't think you're so witty when your daughter isn't welcomed here next year."

"Why in God's name would you think I'd want to send her back here?"

"Why wouldn't you? We're the most prestigious school in the area. And as such, we have the right to refuse anyone."

"It's kind of hard to refuse someone who isn't applying."

"Yes, well...."

"Let me explain a few things to you, Charlotte. First, you're a receptionist. That means your job is to *receive*. Unless you've been put on the board or your job title has changed, you don't have the right to deny anyone anything."

Her face turned red.

"Second, I have no interest in sending my daughter back to Cathedral Lake Prep. If you're any indication of the type of person working here, it's full of pretentious snobs whose only concerns are about the reputation of the school and not the welfare of its students. I think more highly of my kids than to continue to subject any one of them to a culture like that."

"That's—"

"And finally," he said, cutting her off. "I simply don't like you. I never did. So to give you any authority over even one of my offspring for another minute is simply an anathema to me. I won't tolerate it."

A smile played on her lips. "One of your offspring? Really? Aren't you being a little… generous?"

"Say anything to the contrary and I swear to God, I'll sue you for slander. And please, Charlotte, I'm begging you, do it. I'd love to take you and this godforsaken school for every last penny."

Her face darkened further, but she spun on her bargain store pumps and stormed away.

Vanessa and Faith burst into laughter.

Royce looked around. Mrs. Prindle wasn't the only one who had a problem with them being there. The gym was filling up, and a lot of people gave them dirty looks. No one sat by them, though. It was like they had a protective bubble of two seats around them in all directions. He hoped his family didn't notice. They seemed to be enjoying themselves too much to have their spirits dampened by such a grim observation.

When their mirth subsided, Faith said, "I've never seen anyone talk to Mrs. Prim-and-Dull like that."

"It's high time somebody does, don't you think? She needed to be put in her place."

"Her place shouldn't be at this school."

"Well, I don't really have the clout to influence that. Not anymore."

"About not going here next year," Faith said.

"Yeah, sorry about that." Royce rubbed his chin. Maybe he should have taken the time to shave. Stubble from the day before scratched under his hand. "I probably should have talked to you before. But after everything that's happened, there was no way—"

"It's okay, Dad. There was something I wanted to talk to you about, anyway."

"Oh?" He raised an eyebrow.

"Mom and I discussed it this morning, and she's on board. If you are."

She talked to Vanessa first. So the tide had already changed, and he was on the other side. It felt like the undertow.

Vanessa leaned over. "Here and now probably isn't the best place and time."

"You're right." Faith squeezed Royce's hand. "Hey. Has Jensen read any of his speech to you?"

Royce shook his head. "When exactly would he have done that?"

"Oh, wait till you hear it," Vanessa said. "It's lovely."

Of course they'd both heard it. Everyone was in the loop but him.

He leaned over and whispered to Faith. "If you want to tell me what you're thinking about next year, you can whisper it." He pointed to his ear.

She shook her head. "It'll keep. Besides, Jensen's class is marching in."

Sure enough, the band had begun playing "Pomp and Circumstance" and the graduates entered the gym. The talk with Faith would have to wait. Royce had a speech he was dying to hear.

He sat through insufferably long speeches made by the principal and the guidance counselor before they finally got to the part he was waiting for.

"And now," Principal Pendleton said, "a brief word from your valedictorian, Jensen Keller."

Talk about an unenthusiastic introduction. And an equally unenthusiastic reception. There was nothing more than a polite smattering of applause from the adults in the room. The students started clapping but, confused by the lackluster response, quickly stopped.

Royce wondered if he had been wrong to force Jensen into making the speech. Facing a hostile crowd was difficult for anyone. Doing it at eighteen when the hostility was misplaced had to be a nightmare.

Jensen adjusted his cap, straightened his note cards, and cleared his throat. Then he looked out over the audience. Royce didn't know if he could see them in the crowd, but his eyes paused briefly in their general direction as he scanned the room. Then he began.

"Principal Pendleton. Counselor Davis. Faculty, classmates, and honored guests. Welcome.

"I stand before you today not because I am your valedictorian, but because I was forced to be here. It's a funny story, really. Given current circumstances, most people would prefer I wasn't in attendance at today's event at all."

Royce squirmed in his seat. But he wasn't the only one. Much of the audience did as well, and Jeffrey Pendleton had leaned forward, looking as though he was ready to stand and cut Jensen's speech short.

Jensen looked in Royce's direction and continued. "But then I realized something. Something important. Something, to my young and inexperienced mind, that seemed profound. I had the opportunity to be here. That was something my sister would never have.

"For those of you who are unaware, my sister recently passed away. She was in a motorcycle accident and died in the ER. I can't imagine the pain she experienced when she wrecked or the fear she felt in the last moments of her life. And frankly, I probably wouldn't want to if I could."

He paused, closed his eyes, and took a deep breath.

"But she's gone. She'll never have the chance to stand in front of her class and remind them of all their shared memories. She'll never get to congratulate them on all their accomplishments. She'll never get to thank the people responsible for their collective successes. She'll never inspire her classmates on to prosperous futures. And she'll never get to tell any of them goodbye.

"I didn't want her legacy to be mine. And I know she'd want more for me than that."

He took another breath and wiped a single, silent tear off his cheek. Royce looked around the gym. Girls in Jensen's class wiped their eyes. A few of the boys rubbed their noses with the backs of their hands. He heard sniffles from behind and beside him. His own face was chilled, and when he touched it, it was wet with tears. Wiping them off, he turned his attention back to his son.

"I remember our first day at CLP, how we were all intimidated by the introductory assembly and all the rules in the handbook. Then Timmy Gardner got yelled at for talking and threw up on Counselor Whitmore—"

"And we still call him Chunks Gardner!" someone yelled from the seats.

Everybody laughed.

Timmy Gardner stood up and bowed.

Principal Pendleton glared into the audience.

Jensen smiled and continued. "That was certainly an explosive way to start our era here." He got a few more laughs.

"There was Missy Tambor's science experiment. I think they're still cleaning lava off the ceiling. And the burnt spaghetti sauce in Ms. Cellini's third period Home Ec class that set off the fire alarm and the sprinkler system. Her room still kind of smells like a dirty ashtray."

The students started shouting out memories of their own.

"Dissecting frogs in Kauffman's class… except for the ones we put down the girls' shirts!"

"Hiding in Mr. Jenkins' closet and jumping out at him on Halloween!"

"Eating all of Ms. Harp's reward candy!"

"Lame."

"Switching the salt and sugar in the cafeteria!"

"Extracurriculars under the bleachers!" That one got a lot of cat calls and more than one name shouted out. Jensen's name wasn't one of them, but Royce noticed his cheeks redden and he smiled at Simone, who sat in the front row.

"Spiking the punch at the prom!"

"Pendleton doesn't know about that!"

Counselor Davis cleared his throat and pointed into the crowd.

Jensen held up his hands. "Okay, okay." The students cheered and laughed while Jensen tried to settle them down. "It's pretty clear we have a lot of good memories here. Or, at least, memorable memories here." He glanced at the administration and offered a sheepish grin. When the room quieted, he continued.

"But we're so much more than a collection of events, memorable as they are. Through hard work and dedication, many of us are going on to good schools, studying medicine, law, engineering, business… not just with the desire to make a decent living, but with the intent to change the world for the better.

"I'm lucky to be standing here today, going forth with you in a few months to make my mark in the world. But I realize it's not a few months or a few years that make all the difference. It's a few minutes, a few seconds.

"A few weeks ago, if I had left the house a few minutes later, maybe I wouldn't be here.

"We need to recognize every second is precious. We need to make every moment count.

"We don't know what's going to happen in our lives. We can plan, we can prepare. We can study and hope and dream. But life is fleeting, unpredictable, and far from fair. One wrong turn, one zig when we should zag, and it's gone.

"I wasn't going to come here today because I was angry and sad and embarrassed. I was hurt. But I came. I came because my sister never can.

"As you go out into the world, hold your heads high, regardless of what's behind you. Hold your heads high, because you can. Because you're here. Because there are so many people who are gone and chances that are passed, if you don't seize the opportunity while you have it, you'll never get it again.

"We all have goals and dreams. We all have things we're embarrassed of that we'd like to put behind us. Graduation is a time to reflect on where we've been, but also to look forward to where we can go. No more hiding. It's time to get out there and take the world by storm.

"I'm proud to be graduating with you. Congratulations, one and all. Now friends, I leave you with this final thought, an ancient Chinese proverb. 'The gem cannot be polished without friction, nor man perfected without trials.' We may be diamonds in the rough, but that just means we're diamonds in the making. We're brilliant, we're beautiful, and we're strong. Let's all go forth and shine."

He made the sign of the cross, kissed his fingers, and pointed up, a final nod to his departed sister. Meanwhile, everyone in the gym jumped to their feet. Thunderous applause bounced off the walls and reverberated from the rafters in the ceiling to the scuffmarks on the floors. Jensen's face was red as he acknowledged the crowd with a wave, then took his seat.

Royce wiped more tears from his eyes. That was his boy on that stage. No, not a boy. A man—strong, articulate, intelligent. Wise beyond his years.

Jensen had been angry since he learned about Ben, but he'd really pulled it together.

Royce wished he could do the same.

The rest of the ceremony flew by. When Jensen crossed the stage to accept his diploma, a loud burst of applause echoed through the room. Clearly any animosity directed at the Keller family would no longer be directed at Jensen. Hopefully not at Faith, either.

Royce could accept that.

He just didn't know if he could accept everything else.

CHAPTER 24

VANESSA RAN UP TO JENSEN while he was surrounded by his friends and threw her arms around him. "Congratulations, honey!"

He squeezed her back and didn't pull away, which was all the affirmation she needed that things were better between them. She kissed his cheek, then wiped the lipstick print off. Ignoring the snickers from a few of his buddies, she said, "Your speech was wonderful."

"You heard most of it this morning."

"Keller, catch up with you later?"

"Sure, Austin."

"See ya, Mrs. K."

"Bye, boys."

Jensen's friends walked off, and Vanessa slipped her arm through her son's. "Honey, I have to admit, with everything that's been going on, I haven't even given thought to your graduation party yet."

"That's okay."

"No, it's not." He was such a good son. "Why don't you let us take you out to lunch, and we can discuss what kind of party you want, and when you'd like to have it?"

"Honestly, Mom? If it's okay with you guys, I'd just kind of like to hang out with my friends for a while. Miles is having a pool party this afternoon, and Brett's party is tonight."

The initial sting of rejection was immediately replaced with relief that he still had friends who accepted him and gratitude that he once again respected her enough to talk to her, discuss his plans with her, even call her 'Mom' again instead of 'her.' She squeezed him against her side. "Of course, honey. It's your day. Whatever you want. But no drinking."

"You got it." He kissed her cheek. "A lot of juniors will be at the parties. Do you care if I bring Faith along?"

Such a good son. "No, I don't care. But keep an eye on her. I don't want her drinking, either. And I definitely don't want anyone taking advantage of her."

"Like I want that?" He snorted.

"Be careful. And have fun!"

He waved and walked off to find his sister.

"I love you," she said to his retreating back.

Royce walked up to her. "Have you seen Jensen and Faith? I brought the car around. I thought we could go out to eat."

"Yeah, I thought so too. But apparently they had other plans. They're going to a party."

He scowled. "Don't you think we should be celebrating Jensen's graduation as a family?"

"I do," she said. "And we will." His expression stayed dark. "But we didn't have any firm plans, and his friends did. They deserve some fun. We'll do our celebration another time."

His face smoothed out a little. "I guess you're right. But Faith, too? I wanted to talk with her about school."

"I guess it will have to wait."

"You could tell me."

"It's her plan to tell. Not mine."

"But you know."

"Yes. Well, I know what she told me. I'm sure there are many more details to work out." She got in the car and strapped in.

Royce crossed to the driver's side, got in, and slammed the door. "So we're back to keeping secrets."

"What?"

"It's like Ben all over again. You have your secrets and your private clique who's in the know, and I'm on the outside of it all."

"Royce." She looked at him as he drove. His knuckles were white as he gripped and re-gripped the wheel. "What's gotten in to you?"

"Are you going to tell me or not?"

She dug out her phone and called Faith. Their relationship was tenuous, and she didn't want to do anything to damage it. Especially something like breaking a confidence. "Faith? Hey. You didn't talk to Dad about school yet. Is it okay if I fill him in?... Oh. Okay. Are you sure?... All right. Well, have a nice time tonight, sweetie. And be careful... Okay. Goodnight." She sighed and put away her phone.

"Well?" he exploded.

"She wants to talk to you herself."

Royce pounded on the steering wheel several times.

"Royce. Royce! Stop! Stop it!" She reached for his hand, but he was too strong, the anger driving his fist no match for her fear and desperation to stop him. She gripped the dash and prepared for the worst.

Finally he pulled to the side of the road and rested his head on the wheel.

She didn't know if she should offer comfort or censure. So she sat there, staring at him, waiting for his breathing to return to normal and him to sit up. It was fifteen long minutes before either happened.

And then he merely put the car in gear and got back on the road.

"Are we going to talk about what just happened?" she asked.

"No."

"Don't you think we should?"

"No."

They drove in silence for a while longer, but she couldn't take it any longer. "Royce—"

"Leave it alone, Vanessa. You have your little secrets. The least you can do is let me have mine."

It wouldn't have stung more if he'd slapped her across the face. She wasn't keeping secrets. Not hers, anyway. She'd told him about everything, every clandestine act she'd ever committed, every skeleton in her closet. He knew it all. But the thing about Faith? That wasn't hers to tell.

He wasn't being fair.

She thought of suggesting the two of them go somewhere for lunch, but she wasn't about to make that mistake. She knew what the answer would be. Besides, she'd lost her appetite. Instead, she looked forward to going home, putting on a swimsuit, and lounging by her own pool. It wouldn't be a party, but it sounded relaxing.

As they pulled into their driveway, they passed Jensen's car. Faith rode in the backseat, Simone in the passenger seat. It seemed Jensen was really going to celebrate his graduation. Royce tried to flag them down, but the kids just waved and kept going. Vanessa noted the huge grin on her son's face.

"Damn it," Royce muttered.

Obviously he hadn't noticed.

"It's no big deal," Vanessa said. "Don't get so upset."

"Easy for you to say. You weren't the one left out of the discussion. Again."

She sighed and got out of the car, but Royce sat in the driveway with it idling. "Aren't you going to park and come in?"

He thought for a few seconds, then shook his head. "No. I don't think so. I need to clear my head."

Vanessa bit her lip. "Royce, I don't know if you should be driving while you're this upset."

"Don't worry about me, Ness. I'm fine."

"I *do* worry about you. I love you." Oops. She'd dropped the L-bomb on him when he was already on fire. Not the smartest thing she'd ever done.

He avoided looking at her and instead put the car in gear. "You've got a funny way of showing it." And he peeled out of the driveway.

It could have been worse. He could have flat out told her he didn't love her anymore.

It didn't take the sting away from the fact that he didn't say it back, though.

When she went inside, Lydia was walking through the foyer carrying a basket of laundry. "Where is everyone? I thought you were spending the day together. You know, as a family."

Lydia's simpering smile, her saccharine tone… they grated on Vanessa's already fraying nerves, more than they should. She took a deep breath and said, "I'm sure you already saw the kids leave with their suits. You know where they went." She tried to brush past her and walk up the stairs, but Lydia followed her.

"And Dr. Keller? Isn't he spending the day with you?"

Vanessa stopped and spun around on the stairs. Lydia was trailing so closely on her heels, she nearly knocked her over. "Is there something I can do for you?"

"No. I was merely trying to find out where everyone was."

"Why? How do our whereabouts affect you?" Vanessa enjoyed the two step height advantage, towering above her. Lydia didn't exactly cower under her, but at least she got to loom over her, lording her physical advantage for the moment, and even her professional station, if not her status with Royce. It was high time she became the intimidating force in her relationship with Lydia, at least while she still had dominion in her home. If Royce kicked her out, she'd leave knowing she had dominated that conniving bitch at least once. She leaned a little farther, causing Lydia to take another step back or risk falling.

"I needed to know how many of you would be home for dinner. I have to plan."

"I know all about your plans. You wanted to know if Dr. Keller was around." She leaned a little further, just to make sure her meaning was clear. "Let me make it easy for you. He's not here, but he's not available to you, regardless of where he is. And don't worry about cooking tonight. I have dinner covered. You can leave when your housework is done."

She pushed her face toward Lydia's, causing her to jolt backward, then she turned and went to her room, leaving her on the stairs. Based on the clothes she saw in the basket, Lydia should have followed her straight into her closet. She took perverse pleasure in the fact that her intimidation strategy worked. She was alone in her room, and Lydia had apparently not even followed her up the stairs. Nice.

Vanessa changed into a modest red tankini and headed for the pool with her Kindle and a towel. She relaxed all afternoon, reading and lounging poolside. She didn't see Lydia for the rest of the day.

She didn't see Royce, for that matter, either.

That got her thinking. Maybe she'd overplayed her hand. Maybe she didn't scare Lydia away. Maybe she'd sent her running right off into Royce's waiting arms.

She had too much nervous energy to keep reading. She got up and went for a swim.

The water was cool, almost cold, and as it sluiced over her body, it rinsed the tension from her muscles. Each stroke invigorated her tired limbs, reminding her that she'd been dormant for too long.

She was still young. *Stroke.*

Vibrant, vital. *Stroke.*

Royce didn't know. *Stroke.*

What he was missing. *Stroke.*

Why choose Lydia? *Stroke.*

When he could have her? *Stroke.*

She swam until her muscles screamed from the exertion, but she hadn't felt that good in weeks. When she got out of the pool, she lay on the lounge chair and napped in the sun, exhausted but content. When she woke, she picked up her Kindle and contented herself to read some more, her mind finally stilled. But by dusk, she'd had enough swimming, reading, and sunbathing for the day. Her stomach rumbled, her earlier aversion to eating long gone. Thinking about dinner, her mouth watered and the gurgling in her belly grew louder.

She wrapped her towel around her, headed inside, and called out. Complete silence greeted her.

Not only wasn't Royce home, a quick check of her phone showed he hadn't checked in, either.

Jensen had called, though. She quickly typed in the code for her voicemail and listened to his voice, straining to be heard over the din of a party.

"Hey, Mom. Hope you're somewhere having as much fun as we are. My phone's about to die, but I wanted to tell you we aren't coming home tonight. Brett's having a bonfire, and his parents said everyone could just stay. No, we aren't drinking, and yes, I'm keeping an eye on Faith. We're just hanging out with our friends. We'll see you in the morning."

Faith yelled from the background, *"Thanks! Love you!"*

"See, she's fine. Gotta go, or I'll miss my turn at the skewers for marshmallows. Love ya."

Brett's family lived on several acres of farmland out past the old mill. If anything came up, she knew where to find her kids. But they needed some time away from the death pall and the tension of the investigation... and the mood swings of their parents. It was graduation, for Pete's sake. They deserved a little fun.

She scrolled through her messages again. Nope. No missed messages from Royce. Not wanting to be too needy, she sent him a text.

Hope UR OK. Remember—Tod @ 10:30 am.

She waited for a few minutes. No reply.

There went her appetite. The rumbling in her stomach only made her feel queasy, sick. She gathered her things and went upstairs to shower and get ready for bed.

An hour later, she was in her pajamas, under the covers, alone.

So much for progress with Royce. She took one step forward with the kids and how many back with her husband? What was she supposed to make of that? And just where had Lydia gone for the day?

Vanessa knew it wasn't the nap that kept her from sleeping that night. The unknown, the uncertainty, tormented her. She didn't know where Royce was, what he was doing, or most importantly, who he was doing it with. She counted the seconds until their session with Tod, assuming Royce even bothered to show. Her anticipation was every bit as elevated as a kid's on Christmas Eve, but nowhere near as joyous. It killed her, moment by moment.

The first bird's chirp announcing the breaking of dawn offended her. She crawled out of bed and headed back to the shower. Maybe a cold splash of water before a hot cup of coffee would help perk her up.

A few hours later, she sat alone in Tod's office, so angry she wished she had forgone the caffeine jolt.

"First he leaves the house. Then he doesn't come home. Now he doesn't show for our appointment!"

"Vanessa," Tod said, "you need to calm down."

"We're in therapy because his boss mandated it, and he's the one who blows it off. Why do *I* have to calm down?"

"Because this level of aggravation isn't good for you at all. I understand you're upset—"

"Upset? Upset?" Her voice grew more shrill with each syllable. "You have no idea. I've gone along with all of this. I've told him every secret. I've bared my soul, not only to him, but to you, a complete stranger, in order to make this work. I've embarrassed myself in front of my kids. I went on that sham of a date and then embarrassed myself again. And worst of all, I've tolerated that horrible shrew of a woman. And for what? To get stood up? At therapy? Are you kidding me?"

"Maybe we should have had a one-on-one session by now, anyway. Let's talk about what you said. How did you embarrass yourself on your date?"

Vanessa shook her head. "No. Oh, no. I'm not revisiting that."

"Vanessa. Come on. This is a safe space. This is where you're supposed to talk about these things."

"Why did you make us do that? You lied about the coin toss. Fate wasn't ready for us to go."

"Do you believe in fate?"

She thought for a minute. Was there a right answer to that question? Probably not. But did Tod think so? Glancing at his bookshelves, she took in all the psychiatric books as well as many philosophy and religion books. Descartes, Socrates, Plato, Hume, Kierkegaard, Nietzsche… many others. She couldn't remember. Did they believe in fate or free will?

The hell with it. Royce was paying for this. She'd get her money's worth.

"Well, you have an answer planned for me no matter how I answer you that's going to take me to where you want me to be, so either way, the result is preordained, isn't it?"

He sat back in his chair. "Vanessa. I'm not trying to manipulate you here. I'm curious about how you operate."

She sighed. "Fine. You want me to be honest? I don't know. I feel like you manipulated us into that date. I feel like Royce manipulated me into feelings I wasn't ready to experience. And then, when I acted on them, he shut me down."

"Tell me about what happened."

She got up and went to the bookshelves, tracing her fingers over the spines of the books. She smiled when she saw *Men are from Mars, Women are from Venus*. He really had a book to cover everything. Too bad she hadn't read any of them. Surely one of them would have been of help to her.

"He tried to recreate our first date." When Tod didn't reply, she continued. "It's funny, because I don't even consider it our first date, it was so awful. But he's right. It was the first time we went out. He hadn't made any plans, so when he picked me up, he didn't have a destination in mind. Instead of standing in the lobby or even sitting in the parking lot and discussing it, we drove around for the longest time. I told him I'd go anywhere, as long as it wasn't the Student Union, because I didn't want to be under all that pressure from everybody staring at us."

"Let me guess. That's where you ended up."

She smiled and turned to face him, leaning against the bookcase. "Yep. We drove aimlessly for about an hour, and when the car was on fumes, that's where we went. It was awful. Everyone stared at us, and then the gossip started."

"Are you sure, or are you projecting?"

"Does it matter?"

He shrugged.

"I actually ate in front of him. I ordered a burger, fries, and a shake. And I finished all of it."

"That was unusual?"

"Oh, my God, yes. I'd never eaten in front of a date before that. In my day, girls didn't eat in front of boys. We didn't want them to think we were fat."

"That's ridiculous. People eat."

"We were hyper-critical then. What if someone saw us eating and then called us Thunder Thighs or something? How would we ever live that down?"

"And you wonder why girls have stigmas about their body images?"

"Do you want to hear this story, or not?"

He gestured for her to continue.

"So I ordered and ate an entire meal. I knew right then and there I was completely comfortable with him."

"Because you could eat in front of him?"

"Yes. Especially because I was furious at the time."

"I don't follow."

"I should have just made him take me home, but I stayed. I stayed and I ate."

"I see."

"So anyway, Royce tried to recreate all of that. We drove around for the longest time. We had a nice chat. Then we went to a burger place. I thought he was going for the full first date experience."

"So what happened?"

She felt the heat in her cheeks, but she continued with the story. "When he took me home, I tried to finish the date." Finishing the story was more diffi-cult than she thought. She turned back to the bookcase and trailed her fingers over the spines of more books, this time not even noticing the titles.

"Vanessa? What happened on the night of your real first date?"

"You remember we told you we lived on the same floor? And I lived alone?" She barely spoke above a whisper. "I was just going to kiss him at the door. I don't even know why. The date was so bad. But there was just something about him… And his eyes were so blue… Anyway, I kissed him goodnight. At the door. Like I planned."

She got lost in her memories for a moment.

"And then what?" Tod prompted.

"I opened the door." Even retelling the story left her a bit breathless. "And pulled him inside with me." Her face burned with humiliation, but she couldn't take the words back and felt she had to explain. She spun around. "You have to understand. I'd never done anything like that before, but I knew, I just knew, I was going to marry him."

"There's no judgment here, Vanessa. It's okay."

"He was my first." The words kept tumbling out.

"It's all right."

"So that's what I thought he wanted again. He was recreating our first date. But he turned me down. He didn't even want to kiss me! Can you imagine what it's like to be denied like that?"

"Shh, Vanessa. It's okay." He offered her a tissue, and she crossed the room to take it.

"I keep saying, 'It's only sex.' But it feels like so much more."

"Vanessa, he made a lot of effort with you that night. I don't think he was saying no to you. I think he was just saying no to the sex. Sometimes sex and love don't go together."

"So it's okay for me to get past it by telling myself it was no big deal, it was just sex?"

"Well, I'm delighted to hear we're giving free passes now," Royce said from the doorway.

CHAPTER 25

JUST WHAT EVERY MAN WANTS in on… his wife fondling his therapist while she explains it's just sex and nothing more. They'd gone there for help, but she totally missed the path to redemption. Making him nothing more than a pathetic cuckold.

So much for progress.

"You know, I was going to apologize for being late, but instead, I'm just going to go."

"Royce, wait!" Vanessa ran to him and grabbed his arm.

He looked down at her hands and then up at her tear-streaked face. "I'm done, Vanessa. It's over."

"You don't mean that! You don't understand!" She looked at Tod. "Tell him. Explain!"

"Royce, I'm afraid you've misconstrued what you walked in on."

"Is that so?"

"Please?" Vanessa tugged on him.

"Let go of my arm." His voice was soft. His words clipped, measured.

More tears fell as she released him. She stepped back and raised her hands as if showing she was no threat.

"Royce," Tod said, "you know you have to be here as a condition of your possible return to work. Why don't you have a seat and let us explain what you overheard?"

He ground his teeth, enjoying the feeling of his jaw muscles clenching and releasing. That was the only concession he allowed himself as he walked to the sofa and sat across from his doctor. "Please. Enlighten me."

"Vanessa was describing your first date to me, and your attempt at reenacting it the other evening. Because you declined her advances at the end of the night, we discussed the possibility of separating sex and love. She wondered if the two necessarily went hand in hand."

"Is that so?" It sounded like an excuse, but he remembered the details of their dates, and it was plausible. "And just what is the good doctor's advice?"

"It certainly depends on the situation. And in marriages, I hate to say the two aren't intertwined—" Vanessa stifled a sob. "—but in your case, I think the two are completely unrelated. You went to a lot of trouble arranging your date. That's a love issue. The physical intimacy that may or may not follow at the end? That's a sex issue. The two are separate. It seems like you made progress in one area. It doesn't matter that you didn't in the other. It will happen when the time is right."

Royce continued clenching his jaw. He didn't know what he wanted. All the talk about sex and love, all the secrets Vanessa kept… it all circled back to her affair. She wouldn't like it if she was the one in his shoes.

"Speaking of time," Vanessa said, "where were you last night?"

"Out."

"I know that. Where?"

"Around."

"Royce," Tod said. "That's not very productive. We need to open the lines of communication if we want to make any progress here today. And we don't have much time left in our session. We're past being evasive."

Oh, are we? Seemed okay when Vanessa kept secrets. She got away with stalling before she finally revealed the whole Ben story.

Instead of answering, Royce sighed.

"Were you with Lydia?" Vanessa asked. "She rushed right out after you left again yesterday. Tell me. I have a right to know."

And it came out of his mouth before he could stop himself.

"And what if I was? You had your little tryst. Don't you think I'm entitled to a little something on the side, too? Just to even things up?"

Vanessa recoiled like she'd been slapped. "Is that what this is to you? A contest? Our situations aren't even close to the same, but if you're comparing, believe me, you won."

"I won?" He stood and leaned over her. "How do you figure?"

She jumped up and pushed him back. "I made a mistake! I slept with Ben *once!* Do you get that? *One. Time.* I didn't love him. It was a stupid, drunken mistake when I was sad and vulnerable. And it was eighteen years ago! You're having an ongoing affair with someone I hate! Someone who has actively been plotting to take over my life since the day she met me! How do you not get I'm the bigger loser in this?"

"How? Because your dalliance cost me my job, probably my career, my reputation, my best friend, and oh, let's not forget, my daughter! It's not a matter of frequency or recently, it's a matter of loss. And I lost everything! Jensen and Faith don't even come to me anymore. You've taken it all!" His tirade had him panting for breath.

"Excuse me," Tod said. "What do Jensen and Faith have to do with this?"

Royce slumped back in his seat. "Ever since we brought them here, they've been talking to Vanessa more and more."

"That's what you wanted, right?"

"I thought so," he said. "I just didn't realize they'd be excluding me in the process. Now Faith and Vanessa are keeping secrets. Once again, I'm left out. The only one who doesn't know something important."

"Vanessa?" Tod prompted.

"We aren't keeping secrets. She wants to tell him. There just hasn't been time yet."

"And why haven't you, his wife, told him?"

"She asked me not to. It's her story to tell, and I'm on such shaky ground with her, I don't want to ruin the foundation we're building."

"I can respect that. But you're on shaky ground with your husband, too."

Vanessa sighed and rubbed her head. "I don't understand why you can't just wait."

"I don't understand why you can't just tell me."

"I don't want to betray her trust in me."

"And I can't have any trust in you when you don't talk to me."

"You're one to talk about trust." She grabbed her purse and walked out.

Every cell in Royce's body screamed at him to get up and stop her. Every cell but the ones controlling his feet. Those stayed quiet, still. He watched her leave and never said a word.

When she was gone, Tod said, "Well, that didn't exactly go according to plan, did it?"

"No? And what was on the agenda for today?"

"It doesn't matter. We're a little off course, but we'll get back on track."

"Another secret?"

"Royce, just because someone doesn't tell you something doesn't mean it's a secret. Sometimes it's a matter of timing. Sometimes it's a surprise. Sometimes it's just none of your business. Now, For your homework—"

"Ness left. Why do I have to have homework if she's gone already?"

"Because you're the one whose attendance is mandated. For your homework, I want you to do one nice thing for each family member. You can't tell them you're doing it for homework. Just do something kind for them. And nothing they ask for or nothing they need. It has to be from your heart."

"Why?"

"Who's in charge here, anyway?"

Royce made a noise somewhere between a groan and a growl, but he knew he'd do what was asked of him. He got up to leave.

"Are you still writing in your journal?"

"Yes."

"Why don't you bring it with you next time?"

"I thought you said we didn't have to share."

"I might have changed my mind."

Another noise, definitely closer to a growl, escaped his lips. He left without even a goodbye.

On his way home, Royce passed Cathedral Lake Nursery. He'd passed it hundreds of times, probably thousands, as he navigated his way around town, and he'd never given it much thought. Of all the times he'd been by it, he'd only stopped in once. Years ago, when they were picking out the stone for around the pool and the rest of the backyard, he'd been there. He didn't even remember the proprietor's name. Olney or something.

Something about it beckoned him, though, and he turned around.

When he went inside, he recognized the owner behind the counter. He wore the same uniform of jeans, chambray shirt, and work boots from twenty years earlier, only the size had increased a bit. His hair had grayed, but Royce knew his weathered face. It held pride and joy in it. He could recognize those qualities on his features as much as the features themselves.

Royce approached him and held out his hand. "Good morning, sir."

The man enveloped Royce's hand in a warm, firm grip. "Afternoon, now, son. And a pretty one at that. What can I do for you today?"

"Mr. Olney, right?"

"Ah. Close. Olnick. Charley Olnick."

"Sorry. It's been about twenty years since I've been in."

"Well, what's been keeping you, son? Is your yard so perfect that it don't need maintaining?"

Royce had the good graces to display a rueful grin before continuing. "Been busy with work, sir. I'm a doctor. ER. Dr. Royce Keller."

"Keller. Ah. I read about your little girl in the paper. Tragedy. You have my sympathies."

"Thank you."

"I remember you. Slate and bluestone. Special order on the Mountain Mist and Laurel Gold for the fountain."

"Good memory."

Olnick pointed to his temple. "Like a steel trap."

Royce smiled. "I have a service that tends the lawn, but I—"

"Bah. A service. A man's got to work his own land with his own hands."

"Well, that's kind of why I'm here, Mr. Olnick."

"Better late than never. What can I do ya for?"

Royce spoke with him for a long time, asking questions and listening to answers. Then he walked the property with him, taking in even more detailed information. He left two hours later with an order in the process of being filled.

His next stop was a car dealership, where he didn't even bother with negotiating. He took the first deal offered to him and traded in his Infiniti Q70 Hybrid for a fully-loaded GMC Sierra 1500. An hour later, papers signed and insurance company notified, he headed back to Cathedral Lake Nursery.

Yes, he'd spent a ton of money in a short time—money he didn't really have—but he hadn't felt this lighthearted since Hope entered his ER.

An hour later, he was on his way home with a head full of knowledge and a truck full of soil, tools, and plants.

He didn't go in the house when he got home. Facing Vanessa wasn't something he was ready to do. Besides, he had work to do.

Instead of driving into the garage, he drove straight around to the back of the house.

Vanessa lounged by the pool in a sexy black two-piece. He had to admit, even after two pregnancies and twenty-three years of marriage, she still looked incredible. When she saw a vehicle enter her private domain, she hurried to cover herself with a towel and started yelling at him to stop.

Maybe he should have given her a heads up.

When he got to the back corner of the property, he stopped the truck and cut the engine. Then he waited for her to catch up to him. Only then did he get out of the truck.

"Royce? What… Where did… What?"

"Ness." He walked to the bed of the truck and opened it. He had a lot to do, and it would be dark in a few hours.

"Where's the Q70?"

"I traded it. I needed a truck."

"But…."

"But what?" He stopped and looked at her, pots of lilies in each hand.

"But we each had an Infiniti."

"So?" He shrugged.

She blinked a few times, then whispered, "Never mind."

He went back to unloading his truck.

"What are you doing?"

"What's it look like I'm doing? Baking a cake?"

She turned and walked away.

"Ness," he called.

But she kept going.

"It was a stupid question, anyway," he muttered and finished unloading the car. He took some time to arrange the pots in a way he thought would be most pleasing to the eye, then he stood back. Yeah. That would work. He took his phone out and snapped a picture, then he moved everything out of his way and started the backbreaking chore of clearing all the grass. It was getting dark by the time he was done, and he hadn't dug his first hole. He'd also likely ruined his clothes. So he got the hose out and watered the plants, planning on getting an early start in the morning.

He was exhausted when he came in, but he heard the kids in the family room and wanted to check in. "Hey. How was yesterday?"

Faith came over, but stopped short of hugging him. "Ugh. You're filthy."

"Hard work will do that to a person. You should try it sometime."

She laughed. "I wanted to talk to you, but I guess you're going to get a shower. And by the sounds of it, you're tired."

"I always have time for you, moppet. What's up?"

"Go get cleaned up, Dad. You stink." She waved her hand in front of her face. "We'll talk later. Or tomorrow. Whenever." She turned to go back into the family room, but he grabbed her hand.

"We can talk now, Faith. My shower can wait."

"No. It really can't." She walked away, leaving him alone in the kitchen.

Tired as he was, he dashed up the stairs. He wasn't going to let another opportunity pass him by.

When he got to his room, he heard the shower water running.

Damn it all to hell!

As gross as he was, he didn't really want to take a bath, but he would if it got him downstairs quicker. He went to open the bathroom door, and—

Locked.

Damn it all to hell, twice.

He took a deep breath, calmed himself, and knocked. Banged, actually. "Ness, you almost done?" he yelled through the door.

"Can't hear you! Just got in the shower! Give me fifteen minutes or so!"

That probably meant twenty.

He sighed and ran his hand through his hair. Ugh. He got a whiff from under his arm. He did smell rank.

That was it. He grabbed boxers, shorts, and a t-shirt and walked down the hall and showered in the kids' bathroom.

Ten minutes later he smelled like Jensen and perched on the edge of the ottoman in the family room. He faced his kids, who all but clung to each other on the couch. They looked like they were facing a firing squad, not their father. Horrible scenarios flitted through his mind, each worse than the last, but no one spoke. He couldn't take it any longer.

"Somebody say something. I'm going crazy here."

Faith reached out and grabbed his hand. "It's not that bad, Daddy. Really. Don't worry."

"Don't worry? You should see your faces. You haven't looked this serious since—" He didn't finish the thought. Surely the situation wasn't that dire.

She squeezed his hand. "No. No! Nothing like that. This is a good thing. I think it's a good thing. It's good, right, J?"

He swallowed and nodded.

"Just get on with it, Faith," Royce said. "You wanted to talk to me about school next year." She probably needed an opening. He'd give her a place to start.

"What do you know about dual enrollment plans?" she asked.

"Dual enrollment in what?"

"College and high school."

He sat back and studied her for a moment. She was thinking about college already. That was good. Still, doubling up could be difficult. "Maybe a community college class or two might do you some good while you're finishing up your senior year. If you're in public school, I'm sure you'll have free time you wouldn't have otherwise, and—"

"No. That's not exactly what I had in mind."

"Oh?" He grew a little more cautious.

"I applied to a college program where I could study as a freshman—an actual freshman—right away."

"But you aren't a freshman yet."

"I only have to take two courses to graduate. Two. I want to home school and take them online. That way I can go to college early."

"I see."

"And you'll love this."

He raised his eyebrows.

"There's a chance I can home school through CLP so my transcripts will look like I graduated from there without me actually ever setting foot there again. So it's the best of both worlds. I get their credentials without the politics. If it doesn't work out, I can home school through the public school system for free. Or another private one, depending on the tuition."

He smiled. "I see you thought this through."

"I did."

"So this school? Does it have a good business program? Or is it a community college and you'll just transfer to a four year college after your first year?"

"About that...."

"Yes." When she didn't answer, he said, "I'm waiting."

"Dad, I don't want to go into business."

"So what do you want to do?"

She paused, took a deep breath, and said, "Veterinary Medicine."

He blinked. And blinked again. "You want to be a vet."

"Yeah. I want to help animals. That's what I really want to do."

"I see." He sat there a moment, processing all the information that had just been thrown at him.

Faith leaned toward Jensen. "While he's in shock, you should just tell him."

Royce looked at his son. "Tell me what?"

Jensen cracked his knuckles.

"Jensen...."

"I don't want to be a doctor." He said it so fast, it sounded like one long word all strung together. "I want to be an engineer."

Royce's dreams of 'the family business' shattered as he looked at the two of them sitting there before him. No father-son ER team. No daughter in Hospital Administration.

Who was he kidding? He wasn't even going to be working at the hospital officially much longer.

And he'd learned his lesson. It really wasn't up to him to dictate what path his kids chose. It was for them to decide. Not him.

"I'm starting to realize my dreams for your future are just that—my dreams. You have your own dreams to work toward, regardless of what I've been planning. As long as you're happy. I'm behind you, one hundred percent," he said. "Let me know if I need to sign papers, or anything." He leaned forward and kissed them each on the forehead. Then he got up and headed to bed, leaving them staring at him with wide eyes and open mouths.

He wondered if that counted as his something nice for Jensen and Faith.

CHAPTER 26

VANESSA'S BODY ACHED FROM SLEEPING on the floor. Well, 'slept' was a generous word. While Royce seemed to have no problems sprawling in their bed and sleeping all night long, she couldn't make herself do it. In fact, she couldn't even sit on the bed. Looking at it made her sick. She spent the night wondering how many times Lydia had lain in it, rolled around in it, thrashed and writhed while sweating and moaning....

She had to swallow to keep the bile down.

Was it any wonder she'd spent the night on the floor?

She turned her back to the bed. Sleeping beside it was one thing. Staring at it was quite another.

Deciding some yoga was what she needed to work out the kinks and rid herself of at least a fraction of the stress she was feeling, she took a few deep breaths to center herself. Then she got on her knees and folded her upper body over her thighs so her forehead touched the floor in child's pose. She immediately felt her hips and thighs stretch and she began to sink into the pose, trying to relax. After holding the pose for about a minute, she rolled up to a seated position, then got on her hands and knees, in a tabletop position. Then she alternated between sagging her back in cow pose and arching up into cat pose, stretching her sore back and neck. Only once her spine and neck were feeling better did she get to her hands and feet like an inverted V and stretch in the downward facing dog position, stretching the backs of her legs as well as her upper back. She felt her stress flowing through her body, toward her extremities, and out through her fingers and toes.

"That's a great view to wake up to."

She jumped up and spun to face Royce. Seeing him in the rumpled sheets, hair tousled and eyes heavy-lidded, was more than she was ready for. He looked that way so many mornings after they'd had wonderful nights together. She thought she was the only one who'd ever seen him that way. Knowing Lydia had too made her sick. All the tension she'd stretched away reappeared, constricting her muscles into rigid cords. Reaching for the throw at the foot of the bed, she covered herself. "Stop staring at me."

"You're the one doing yoga in your PJs. And you don't need to cover yourself. I was admiring the view for the past five minutes. Besides, I've seen you in a lot less."

She clutched the blanket closer to her body. "Well, it's a view you aren't privy to anymore."

He snorted. "You're wearing cotton shorts and a tank top. You wear less at the pool."

She walked into the bathroom and closed the door, locking him out. How did their situations reverse so quickly?

Lydia.

Getting in the shower, she allowed the sound of the water to drown out the sound of her tears. How could she have been so stupid? She'd seen the signs. And she probably deserved it on some level. But she'd cheated once, years ago. He cheated who knew how many times and was still doing it. And out of revenge! With Lydia!

It was more than degrading. It was painful.

And she was the one who moved mountains to get the kids to forgive her. Meanwhile they had been worshipping at the altar of St. Royce.

But she loved them too much to hurt them by telling them he'd betrayed them all.

So did that mean walking away from her marriage? After she'd fought so hard to save it?

She didn't know if the shower ran loud enough to cover her sobs, but she didn't care.

When she had finally composed herself and had finished in the bathroom, Royce had left the bedroom. She was relieved. It made getting ready for the day so much easier. She dressed, for the first time not wearing her engagement ring or St. Luke medal, and went downstairs.

Jensen and Faith were at the kitchen table, and she put on a bright smile for them. "Good morning."

"Hi, Mom," Faith said between spoons of yogurt.

"Hey," Jensen said. He munched on an apple. "Do you know what's gotten into Dad?"

She poured herself a cup of coffee and took a sip. It was delicious. Damn. Lydia's here. "What do you mean?"

"We talked to him last night about school, and he was fine with it. And he's planting stuff all over the yard."

Vanessa looked out the window. Royce was already outside, working where he had left off the day before. "Well, it's good he's supportive of your choices, right?"

"Yeah, but... it's weird."

"Yeah, Mom," Faith said. "He should have lectured, and yelled, and, I don't know. Forbidded it."

"Forbade," Vanessa said.

"Whatever. The point is, he was fine with it."

"Good. You should be happy."

"Mom," Jensen said. "First he washed the car. Now he's digging holes. In the dirt. And he asked us if we wanted to help."

Vanessa took another sip. Damn it. It tasted really good. "Look. We've all changed over the last few weeks. If Dad has learned to be less rigid when it comes to the two of you making decisions about your futures, just be grateful. Sign the papers and send in the checks before he changes his mind."

"But the planting...." Jensen said.

She looked out the window. "I always thought our yard was a little austere. I think it's going to look nice when he's done."

The kids left the kitchen, and Vanessa kept looking out the window. The backyard wouldn't just look nice when Royce finished. It would look stunning. From what she could see, he had pots of roses, lilies, alstroemeria, carnations, chrysanthemums, gladioli, freesia, and assorted perennials and shrubs. He worked like a machine: dig, potting soil/fertilizer, plant, backfill, water, repeat. Each plant took him roughly three minutes to put in. The barren yard was quickly becoming an oasis. She wondered if she'd live there long enough to enjoy it.

Hearing whistling coming from the laundry room, her stomach flopped. The coffee, as much as she'd enjoyed it, almost reappeared. There was no way she could stand to see Lydia's face. She left her cup on the counter, grabbed her purse and keys out of the hall closet, and hurried into the garage.

The sight of the GMC next to her Infiniti made her sad. Another set of twins broken up. She sighed and got in her SUV. She needed to leave everything that reminded her of Royce and Lydia behind for a while.

It wasn't like she actually had a plan when she left. She was lucky she got out of there without running into her husband and his mistress. But once behind the wheel, the route mapped itself out.

She went to visit Hope.

Looking back, she'd say the car made all the turns on its own. Before she knew it, she was sitting on the bench under the tree looking at Hope's tombstone, surprised it had been installed without anyone notifying them. Maybe it was better to just discover it.

A sob escaped from deep within her.

Maybe preparation would have made it easier.

She had to admit, the monument itself was lovely. They'd chosen a color called sunrise, a rusty shade that coordinated with the copper color of her coffin. Sid had pointed out that the two would never be seen together, and therefore didn't need to match, but Vanessa knew it would be important to Hope that everything was in the same color palate. Besides, her daughter loved warm colors.

But it was the craftsmanship that stole her breath. They'd had Hope's picture laser etched on the right side of the headstone, and on the left they had a poem engraved into the granite—the first one Hope had written, at least to Vanessa's knowledge. She had written it when she was fourteen years old, on the anniversary of Cornelius' death, and had read it at his grave while Faith played 'Amazing Grace' on the flute. Then the two of them made flower chains and left them on his stone.

Vanessa had saved the poem, never thinking she'd have occasion to use it again.

We do not bury our treasured memories.
Fun-filled days, comforting caresses,
Joyous laughter and whispered dreams...
Those we carry in our soul.
For our sorrow there are no remedies,
Just time until our grief subsides.
We put ourselves back together,
And pray we end up whole.

Under Hope's picture were her name and epitaph:

Hope Mercedes Keller
Beloved Daughter ~ Sister ~ Friend
Taken From Us Too Soon

There were dates under it, but try as she might, she couldn't bear to read them. The poem, the name and the epitaph... they were painful enough.

Looking at the dates made Hope's passing too final, too permanent. Reminded her Hope's death was far too soon—a death that was ultimately Vanessa's fault.

She stood to the side of the mounded earth dotted with new grass shoots and rubbed her hand over the stone. Despite the sun being out, the granite was still cool to touch. Her tears fell onto the marker, creating brown wet spots on the headstone.

"Oh, baby. I'm so, so sorry."

She cried quietly for a moment, getting lost in thoughts of self-loathing and regret. The sound of a clearing throat jolted her back to reality. Spinning, she saw a middle-aged couple approaching her.

"Excuse me," the woman said. "We don't mean to interrupt."

And yet you are. "May I help you?" Vanessa said.

"You're Vanessa Keller, right?" the woman asked.

Vanessa tipped her head. "I'm sorry. Do I know you?"

The couple stepped closer, and the woman extended her hand. "I'm Sally Anderson. This is my husband Frank. I'm sure your husband mentioned meeting me over by Mrs. Haggerty's grave."

"He did." Vanessa had forgotten all about that. It hardly seemed relevant in the grand scheme of things. She shook their hands and offered them the best smile she could muster.

Both Frank and Sally seemed to relax. Frank shuffled his feet and couldn't meet her gaze, but he managed to ask her, "So, we hate to be forward, but we were wondering… Did anyone contact you about a lawsuit?"

"A lawsuit?" More legal trouble? "About what?"

"Mr. Haggerty is suing us for the wrongful death of his wife."

"But you didn't cause his wife's death."

"I'm sorry. He's suing Jimmy's estate. Our lawyer hasn't received any information other than that yet. We were wondering if your daughter was named in the suit, too."

Vanessa's legs gave out and she plopped down on the grass. "I'm sorry, Mr. Anderson. Mrs. Anderson."

"Frank and Sally," Sally said. "Are you all right?" She walked over toward her.

Vanessa waved her off. "I'm fine. I'll be fine. Just a little overwhelmed with everything. Um… Ah, no. I mean, I don't know. I haven't heard anything."

Frank reached into his pocket and produced a card. "If you do, would you mind calling us? We're kind of like fish out of water here."

Vanessa took his card. "Sure. I'll do that."

He nodded. "Much obliged."

"You sure you're okay?" Sally asked.

Vanessa nodded and waved. "Yes, thanks. I'm just going to sit here for a while."

"If you're sure…" Sally said.

"I'm sure."

"Come on, Mother," Frank said. "We left our boy waiting by the car. He wouldn't come up. We should be going."

Vanessa glanced down at their vehicle. A sullen-looking boy stood, leaning against the passenger door. Too wrung out to even answer them, she nodded, and they turned and left. The boy slid into the backseat and slammed the door. Frank and Sally looked at each other and shook their heads as they approached their car.

Vanessa put them out of her mind. For the love of all that was holy… another investigation? She didn't think she could stand it.

"Oh, Hope, honey. If you've got any pull up there, you might want to start using it. We need some help down here."

She spent a few more minutes with her daughter before leaving.

Hungry, having skipped breakfast, she decided to pop into her favorite deli before going home. After ordering a Reuben sandwich, side of slaw and an extra pickle, she slid into a booth in the back and hoped to pass the time unnoticed behind a free "homes for sale" booklet. There weren't many people there, and Vanessa hid in the dark corner, away from the windows and the order counter, invisible to the world.

She stayed tucked behind her book, listening to the 70s music being piped through the restaurant, waiting for her food. There were a few three bedroom bungalows that actually looked appealing.

"Nessa?"

Only one person called her that. She put the booklet down. "Mia. What the heck are you doing here?" Vanessa stood, and the two women embraced. "Sit down. Seriously, what are you doing here? I thought you were in Italy. Or Spain. Or somewhere wonderful."

"I was, darling. Then I heard there was a bit of drama back here and I thought my best friend might want some support. As soon as the yacht docked, I booked a flight."

"Well…." Vanessa let her words trail off and took a sip of water.

"Nessa. You didn't even contact me. That hurt."

"Mia. I didn't call my parents for two days. It's been rough." Mia sat back and studied her. Vanessa tried not to squirm. "How'd you hear, anyway? Really?"

"Ben told me."

"I wasn't aware you and Ben still spoke."

"We're divorced. Not dead."

Vanessa blanched.

"Sorry, hon. I wasn't thinking."

Vanessa waved it off.

"We are, hmm… what's the term? Divorced with benefits."

Vanessa almost dropped her water.

"Oh, don't be so prudish. Ben and I were always good in bed. That wasn't the problem. We just had different goals in life. As the years went on, we realized we could take the parts of our marriage that worked for us and use them to our advantage and I wasn't obligated to provide him with the other parts he wanted that I disagreed with. No strings."

"Are you kidding me? All this time? And you never said?"

"I can't believe you never figured it out."

"Contrary to popular belief, Mia, most women don't spend every waking minute obsessing about sex. Especially other people's sex lives."

Mia raised an eyebrow and shrugged. "Whatever you say."

"What's that supposed to mean?"

"Nothing."

Vanessa chose to ignore the comment and pressed on. "So if you and Ben have been hooking up for all these years, why not just get back together?"

"It's like I told you, we want different things. When we got together in college, it was all about the sex. But when you and Royce started getting serious, the dynamics changed. Ben was talking marriage and kids, and I was talking jet-setting and diamonds. I think we both thought the other would change when you and Royce had kids. So we got married, too. And you had Jensen."

"So what was the problem?"

"Obviously Ben loves kids. He's a pediatrician, for God's sake. I should have realized… Anyway. He saw you two with Jensen and saw baby booties and teddy bears and soft blankies. I saw three a.m. feedings and dirty diapers and stretch marks."

"I don't have stretch marks."

Mia raised her eyebrows again.

Vanessa just sighed and said, "Go on."

"So we reached an impasse. We loved each other—and that never changed—but neither of us was ever going to change our minds."

"But what about now? You're both older. That doesn't have to be an issue anymore, does it?"

"Are you really worried about me and Ben? Or just Ben?"

"What do you mean?"

Mia sighed. "Okay, we'll take the long way around."

"What?" Vanessa had no idea what Mia was talking about.

The waiter brought Vanessa's meal and looked at Mia. "Could I get you something, ma'am?"

She shook her head, and he walked away. "I hate it when they call me ma'am. I look better than that."

"We've been ma'ams since we were in our twenties."

"I can still pass for in my twenties, thank you very much."

She wasn't wrong. Vanessa didn't know if Mia lived the world's cleanest life or if she had the best plastic surgeons on the planet, but she looked great. The bitch.

"So, Nessa. Now that I cut my holiday short—"

"Cut your holiday short? Your whole life is one big holiday."

"Semantics." Mia waved off her comment like she was shooing a fly. "Anyway, darling, how are you? Really."

Vanessa grabbed her fork and moved the coleslaw around in her plate. The lump in her throat made it impossible to even consider eating, but she needed something to do with her hands while she talked. "Royce is cheating on me."

"Well, tit-for-tat, I suppose. What are you going to do about it?"

"Excuse me?"

"I know about your dalliance. I know about Royce's mistake in the ER. I know everything."

"Everything, huh?" Vanessa couldn't imagine Ben had been one hundred percent forthcoming. There was no way Mia would be there to support her if he had.

Mia sighed and sat back. "Okay. I'm tired of the long way. I'm just going to get right to it. I know everything, Nessa. I've known for years."

Icy fingers of dread and shame skittered down Vanessa's spine. "Excuse me?"

"That's right. I know about you and Ben. What do you plan on doing about him now that the cat's finally out of the bag?"

CHAPTER 27

ROYCE WALKED THE PATHS OF Cathedral Lake Nursery with Charley Olnick. The guy knew his stuff. He was able to easily pick out plants that went with what Royce had already purchased without ever referring to his old order sheet or asking for a refresher.

"How do you remember all this?" Royce asked.

"I love it. It's like seeing a work of art. Once you've seen the *Mona Lisa* or *David*, you know what they look like. You don't forget."

"Yeah, I guess you're right." He analyzed a burgundy plant. "So, your kids… Do they help you out? Mine aren't interested in following in my footsteps."

Charlie laughed and grabbed the plant… a barberry. "I wish my kids had the passion for this that I did. Nope. My kids don't even live here."

Royce stopped on the peat moss path and scraped his toe across the loamy surface, making patterns in the sphagnum. "It doesn't bother you that they're gone?"

"They moved away from town, not me. Besides, they knew what was best for them. They wouldn't have done well here. One's an editor in New York and one is a marine biologist in Hawaii. They followed their passions. They're happy, and they're good at what they do. I can't help but be proud."

"Didn't you worry you wouldn't be able to help them? With them being so far away?"

"Who says I can't help them if they need it?"

Royce smoothed out the pattern on the ground. "Yeah, I guess you're right."

"You don't stop being a father just because your kid left the house." He led Royce down another path.

"I guess we have more in common than I thought," Royce said.

Charlie clapped him on the back. They both reached for a burning bush and smiled at each other. "How do you feel about weigela?"

After another hour, Royce drove home with another truckload of supplies and a new appreciation for his decision to let his kids go their own way. He felt pretty good about himself, the best he'd felt since Hope's death.

As he pulled up to the house, he saw a middle-aged man in a rumpled suit leaning against a faded blue sedan parked in the middle of the driveway. He pushed to his feet when Royce pulled in.

Royce hopped out of the cab of his truck to greet him. "Hi there. What can I do for you?"

"Are you Royce Keller?"

"I am."

"You can take this." He handed Royce an envelope. "Consider yourself served." The man got back in his car and drove off.

So much for his good day. Royce tore open the envelope. The estate of Hope Keller was being sued in the wrongful death of Paula Haggerty.

Unbelievable.

Spencer Bradley was going to be able to retire off the business he got from Royce alone.

Maybe he needed to get a job. They were going through their savings faster than he anticipated, and they'd had quite a generous portfolio. He knew it was his fault, but he had to get the flowers, had to make a tribute to Hope. If worse came to worse, the landscaping would add value to their property and he'd make it back in the sale.

God forbid he have to sell.

Royce called his lawyer and filled him in on the latest development. After a quick discussion, he went inside and faxed him a copy of the papers.

Spencer assured him he'd take care of it. Nothing more to do but work. He went out back and started digging.

There was something cathartic about working in the yard. He didn't know why he'd paid for landscaping for all those years. Well, he did know. He hadn't had the time for it, and his hands had been too valuable to risk damaging.

Now he had the time, and his hands weren't really worth anything.

The sun beat down on his already warming muscles, and he stripped off his shirt. A light sheen of sweat already covered his body, and the gentle breeze cooled him. He resumed his task, the shovel biting into his blistered hands, stinging with each thrust of the blade into the virgin earth. The shock of the tool digging into the ground reverberated up his arms, his biceps and triceps screaming with each impact.

He craved it.

Every aching muscle, every searing torn blister, every slip that caused a cut or a bruise… those pains were his punishments. He didn't know how else to atone. He couldn't go back in time to be a better husband, a better father… hell, a better doctor. His hubris had destroyed their family. But maybe, just maybe, he could create a little bit of beauty and start to set things right.

He grabbed a pot holding clusters of tiny blue flowers. "I have a special spot for you." He bent down and grabbed another pot when Vanessa came out of the house.

"We have a guest," she said.

She looked like she'd been crying, so he guessed whoever the guest was, he wasn't going to like it. But when he saw who followed her out of the house, he put the forget-me-nots down on the ground and ran toward the patio. "Mia! How are you?"

"Come here, you big stud!" She held out her arms.

He lifted his arms to accept her embrace, but stopped. "Wait. I'm sweaty."

"Just the way I like my men."

She wrapped him in a massive hug he couldn't help but return. "Don't blame me when you're dress is stained." He noticed Vanessa standing back and biting her lip.

"This old thing?" Mia looked down at her dress. "Who cares? It's so last season. I need to go shopping, anyway."

Royce didn't know if it was old or not. He suspected Mia wouldn't wear anything other than the latest fashion, and even then not more than once. But he had no doubt she'd be shopping soon to replace what he'd just sweated on. "So, what brings you by?"

"A little birdie told me there was trouble in paradise. And neither of you thought to call." She affected a pout.

He led them over to the patio table, and they took a seat.

"I'll go get us iced tea," Vanessa said.

"Don't go to any trouble," Mia said. "Stay."

"I wouldn't mind a drink, actually," Royce said.

Vanessa bolted into the house.

"What's going on, Mia?"

"Nessa's just a little out of sorts because I told her I know she slept with Ben."

Royce sat back and laughed to hide his shock. "Is there anyone in this town who doesn't know?"

"Who cares?" Mia said. "We're adults. Ben's a great lay. I'm surprised it was just the one time. I just wondered if it was going to happen again. Apparently it's not."

"Mia." The smile fled from Royce's face. "Ness and I are married. Were married when it happened. You and Ben were married at the time. How can you be so blasé about it?"

"It's just sex, Royce. It's not love."

"It's intimate. Personal. And it's a huge betrayal."

"This, coming from the man who's screwing his maid."

"Excuse me?"

"Come on, Royce. Just because I spend more time in Europe now than here doesn't mean the grapevine doesn't grow that far. I have a source in town. Quite a reliable source. So I'm always aware of all the juicy morsels. And *you*," she trailed her finger across his chest and down his abs to linger at his waistband, "are one juicy morsel."

He grabbed her hand and pushed it away. "Mia, stop."

Vanessa walked out with a tray of refreshments. "Are you kidding me?"

"Ness, it's not what you think," he said.

She turned and walked back into the house.

"Damn it," he said.

"Look, Royce," Mia said. "I really did come here to clear the air with Nessa. I was tired of all the secrets, and I wanted to know if she was going after Ben. She and I have cleared the air. I thought you and I should, too. You're the cherry on top of my sundae. Ben and I have an open relationship. I didn't know you would ever look at anyone other than Nessa. But now that I do, I want you to know, I'm here."

He shook his head. "You're out of your mind."

"What?"

"Regardless of my relationship with Vanessa, I could never be with you. You're gorgeous, but come on, Mia. You're Ben's. The baggage there... the triangle, or rectangle if we include Ness... it would be a nightmare of mammoth proportions. I'd never consider it."

"Too bad, stud." She stood up and walked toward the house. "You don't know what you're missing."

"I've heard the stories. I know."

She smiled and opened the door. "I'll try to fix things for you with Nessa."

"Just leave it alone. If it's fixable, I need to do it myself."

"You two are fixable. You should see the way you look at each other."

"Sex was never our problem." He thought about it for a second. At least it hadn't been when they were having it. It wasn't a total lie. "And it's not enough to save a marriage."

"Maybe not. God knows, Ben and I tried. But if you're doing it right, it's a hell of a start." She walked inside and closed the door.

Royce blew out a pent up breath. What a vixen. It was a good thing she wasn't around more often.

His phone rang, and he answered it without looking at caller ID. "Keller."

"Royce? Glad I caught you."

Disbelief and rage vied for dominance, roiling in the very blood surging through his veins. "Wade?"

"Yeah. To be honest, I didn't think you'd take my call."

"To be honest, if I'd looked at caller ID, I wouldn't have." He was about to disconnect.

"Don't hang up!"

Royce paused, finger poised over the *END* button.

"Look, I know there have been a lot of rumors flying around. I just heard a few disturbing ones myself. Ones pointing to me as being behind all of this."

"Rumors? I heard it straight from the source."

"No. No. You have it all wrong. You have to let me explain."

"I don't have to do anything."

"Five minutes. Please? Let me come to the house. Or we can meet in the most public spot you can think of. Tons of witnesses."

Publicity is the last thing Royce wanted. If he decked Wade, he didn't need fifty phones capturing it and putting the video on YouTube.

"Come to the house. When can you get here?"

"I'm actually on the way. Consider me optimistic."

Royce sighed. "I'm in the backyard. Just come around when you get here."

"I'll be there in five." He hung up.

Royce walked back toward his latest landscaping project and grabbed his shirt. After donning it, he looked at the holes in the ground, the plants waiting to be installed, the forget-me-nots he had been moving to another section of the yard. His property was a work-in-progress, one that was coming along quite nicely.

Even as all his relationships fell apart.

He couldn't fathom what Wade had to say. Already he regretted agreeing to the meeting.

But what if he was telling the truth? What if Wade was a patsy in the whole thing, too?

Then that was one relationship he could salvage.

He grabbed one of the pots and walked back to the patio just as Wade rounded the corner, striding right toward him, arms out in greeting.

Royce held his hand up, signaling him to stop. He needed the distance. He wasn't ready for a reunion yet.

Wade dropped his arms and nodded. "I get it. I need to work for it. Can we sit?"

Royce gestured to the patio, where the untouched refreshments were from Mia's visit.

"Rolling out the red carpet, huh?" Wade said, a nervous chuckle behind his words.

"No. Company just left, actually. I'm surprised you didn't pass in the driveway." He took a seat and put the pot down on the ground beside him.

"Really? Who was here?"

"What do you want, Wade?"

He looked around. "I know you heard it was me who informed on you to HA. It wasn't. It was Ellie."

Royce clenched his jaw and took a deep breath before speaking. "And now I know you're lying. I heard straight from Administration that it was you. Get out." He stood.

"That's what I'm trying to tell you. They're framing me to protect her. Plus, they know if they separate you from your friends, you'll have less help. Someone wants you gone."

"Who? Someone in Administration? Who in HA benefits from me leaving?"

"You aren't going to like it."

"Because I liked everything else that's happened so far."

"Stanford."

"Get the hell out of here." Royce stood up again. He wasn't going to stand there listening to Wade accuse his mentor of that kind of duplicity, no matter how many secrets he'd kept.

"Wait, Royce," Wade said. "Think about it. The old man trained you. You're his golden boy. You were poised to take his job."

"That's what he wanted. He was grooming me for it."

"Yeah. To take over for him when he moved up. But they aren't moving him up. The dean has been interviewing everyone personally. Stanford isn't getting a spot on the HA Board. That means he either stays where he is, or he goes. And they're worried about his age, man. He's not young anymore. It's a concern for HA, and Stanford knows it. If you move up to Chief of Staff, then he's out of a job."

Royce dropped back down in his seat. The chair was the only thing keeping him upright. "Stanford wouldn't do that to me."

Wade leaned across the table. "No? How much help has he really been to you since all this happened?"

"He... he saved my job."

"Did he? How?"

"He got me put on leave instead of fired."

"That's just HA standard practice, man. One week and you should have been back."

"No. The investigation... he said you got the investigation extended."

Wade shook his head. "Not me. What else did he say?"

"My return, assuming I'm accepted back, is conditional on me completing a counseling program. One with a therapist he chose."

"Let me guess. Tod Jeffers?"

Royce snapped his up and looked at him.

"That's his go-to guy. Interesting, don't you think? And any therapy is bullshit, and you know it. Other doctors don't go through any at all. And you're not only in mandated counseling, you're going to someone Stanford handpicked."

Royce stood and paced. "How could he do this to me? I'm like a son to him."

Wade crossed to him. "Don't beat yourself up over it. You were so easily taken in because you only ever saw the good in people. That's not a character flaw. It's a strength. We could all learn to be more like you in that regard."

Royce glanced at him, then looked away. "It's a flaw when it keeps burning me."

Wade clapped him on the shoulder. "The hearing will be over soon. We'll go in, tell them what we know. It'll all work out the way it's supposed to."

"Thanks, Wade."

After Wade left, Royce sat down and looked over his yard. The holes, the empty pots, the piles of dirt. Sometimes things had to be completely destroyed before they could be built back up again. And in the best of cases, even though the work was difficult, the result was spectacular. He could only hope he was so lucky.

He stood up and brought the potted plant into the house.

CHAPTER 28

VENESSA SAT IN HER THERAPIST'S office, legs crossed, right foot bouncing in staccato rhythm. She was desperate for some advice, bursting to blurt out a number of problems she wanted to discuss. The day before she'd done everything she could to avoid Royce, which meant she hid from Mia when she left, and she hid when Wade showed up. That didn't stop her from eavesdropping, though. She'd heard it all. Or enough, anyway.

And she was finally ready to talk about it.

There was also the 'little' matter of Lydia that needed to be addressed.

But it wasn't her turn to speak.

She'd tried three times to say something, but Tod silenced her with a raised hand each time. He clearly had something else on his agenda.

"Vanessa, please. We'll get to it. All of it, I promise. Right now, though, I want to discuss how we ended our last session. You had gone, and I gave Royce an assignment."

She looked over at her husband. He stared at Tod, seemingly engaged in the discussion.

"Royce, do you want to talk about it, or should I explain it?"

He just shrugged.

Tod sighed, but continued, turning to Vanessa. "I asked Royce to do something nice for you, Jensen, and Faith. Something he gave freely, without telling you it was his assignment." He turned to Royce. "So, how did it go?"

"I did it. I don't know how it went."

"What did you do?"

"Jensen and Faith wanted to talk to me about school next year. I listened to them and agreed to their requests without yelling or lecturing."

"And you think that's doing something nice for your children?" Tod asked.

"Look, my kids don't need anything. They have every material convenience money can buy, and since their session with you, they aren't really interested in even talking to me much. So I figured this was the best thing I could do for them."

"Hmm," Tod said. "Maybe we'll come back to that. What about Vanessa?"

No kidding. What about Vanessa?

She thought what he'd done for the kids was ridiculous. A parent should never yell at a child about pursuing a dream. Of course, they were talking about Royce. That was probably a huge breakthrough for him. It was enough of a change that the kids were worried about him. He probably did consider it a kindness. But for her? She hadn't noticed him do anything at all.

"I've always given Ness anything she wanted. I didn't know what else to do for her."

Just as she thought. He did nothing.

"So I washed her car."

Jensen did say he had washed a car yesterday. She'd taken it out. Hell, she'd even stared at the two, comparing the Infiniti and the GMC, and she hadn't noticed.

"That's a nice gesture," Tod said. "But why did you decide to do that?"

"I got rid of my car and bought a truck. It bothered her for some reason. She seemed pretty attached to her car after that. So I thought I'd do something to care for her car."

"I see."

"I wasn't sure the car would be enough of a statement, though. Especially because I don't understand why it suddenly matters to her. So I brought a pot of forget-me-nots into our bedroom. I even tied one of Hope's hair ribbons around it."

Really? She'd spent the night on the floor again and hadn't even noticed. It had been so important to her to enter the bedroom when the lights were already off and get up in the morning before dawn, getting ready in her bathroom and closet and creeping downstairs before anyone was up—who was she kidding? Before Royce was up—that she hadn't looked around her room.

"And why forget-me-nots?" Tod asked.

"It had been important to Ness to have them in the arrangement when we buried Hope. She said she didn't want Hope to forget us, or to think we forgot her. I thought I'd let her know I remembered."

Vanessa tried to swallow, but that darn lump was back in her throat again. She didn't want Royce to see her cry, so she turned her head and wiped them away as they fell. Sometimes he made it so hard to be angry.

"Vanessa, do you have anything to say to that?"

She took a deep breath and focused on the kernels of hurt still popping around inside her. "Do you know why the car mattered to me?"

"No, I told you I didn't get it."

"Because we got them at the same time. They were the only twins we had left. And you destroyed that set, too. Without any compunction whatsoever."

He angled himself to face her. "Are you kidding me? They're just cars."

"*Our* cars. Yours and mine. And now one is gone." This time she let the tears fall freely. When Royce reached for her, she pulled away. "Don't touch me!"

"Ness...."

"I don't know where those hands have been. Or I guess I do. God!" She got up and paced.

"But you expect me to move past you and Ben?"

"I told you. It's not the same thing!"

"And I told you, I don't see how it's different."

Ooooh. He was so frustrating.

"Royce, did you bring your journal with you, like I asked?"

"Yeah."

"Maybe you'd like to read your entry from the night of our last meeting."

"Why?"

"I think it's time you let Vanessa into some of your more personal thoughts."

"You said we didn't have to share our journal entries if we didn't want to."

"And I told you last time, I might change my mind."

Royce just sat there.

Vanessa watched the exchange with curiosity. Tod obviously thought Royce had written something that was going to help them.

"Let me see your journal, Royce," Tod said. "Maybe I'm wrong, and we can avoid this part of the session."

Still Royce didn't budge.

"For God's sake, Royce. We're paying by the hour. Let's at least get our money's worth."

Royce glared at her, then threw the book at Tod.

"Code?" he asked.

Royce leaned over and opened the book.

Tod flipped through the journal until he got to the pages he was looking for. After a few seconds of skimming, he looked up. "I'd like you to share this with Vanessa."

"No."

"Fine. Then I will." He handed her the journal.

"I'm not reading this if he doesn't want me to." She stood there, book out in front of her, away from her line of vision.

"Vanessa, you need to see what's on those pages," Tod said.

"You obviously knew what was in them," Vanessa said. "I probably have a clue."

"Trust me," he said. "You don't."

"Then how did you?"

"I'm trained to see things you don't."

"Yeah, but we don't even know if we can trust you," Royce said.

"What?" Tod asked.

Vanessa knew he was talking about Stanford referring them to him. That was one of the things she was so eager to talk about. The sooner this mess with the journal was resolved, the sooner they could move on to pertinent issues.

"I don't know if you're really trying to help us," Royce said. "We didn't hire you. Stanford did. You could have ulterior motives."

Tod made a note in their file. "Such as?"

"You're the expert at reading subtext. You figure it out."

Vanessa looked at Royce. "Do you want this back?" She held out the journal.

He shrugged. "Read it. I don't care. I'm tired of this, anyway."

So she opened to the entry Tod wanted her to read.

I don't know what I was thinking.

The only words that come to me now are Asshole. Bastard. Fuck-up.

If I knew worse ones, I'd use them.

Sure, I can say technically I didn't lie. Ness jumped to conclusions and filled in blanks. She filled them in wrong, and I didn't bother to correct her.

Doesn't that make me Husband-of-the-Year? What kind of jackass am I, anyway? She's hurting, and I pile it on?

I'm hurting, too. That doesn't make it right. An-eye-for-an-eye went out of vogue with the Old Testament. Rose could probably site me chapter and verse proving we've moved past that.

I need to make this right, before it gets out of hand. Well, further out of hand.

Look at her, curled up on the floor. She thinks I can't hear her sobs.

I wonder if she heard my tears when I slept on the floor. Tried to sleep on the floor. Doesn't she know every tear she sheds rips a hole in my heart? She's crying because she thinks I destroyed something she's been trying so hard to repair.

And I didn't. I couldn't. I'd never.

The one thing I'd never do is intentionally throw our marriage away.

But by letting this deception occur, I'm afraid that's exactly what I did.

All because I wanted her to know how I felt.

Maybe I should have just told her. She's always understood.

I can only hope she'll understand this time.

If I ever get the courage to come clean.

I'm such a schmuck.

Her body flushed with cold tingling prickles of shock. He couldn't possibly have meant what she thought. Knees buckling, she dropped onto the sofa beside him.

"Say something," Royce said.

She shook her head and read the passage again.

"Ness."

He didn't. He couldn't. He'd never.

An-eye-for-an-eye?

Was he serious? Did that mean what she thought?

"Are you saying you lied to me about you and Lydia?"

Royce didn't say anything.

"I think, technically, what he's saying is he never actually lied," Tod said. "You inferred, and he let you believe it."

"Royce?" she whispered.

"I'm sorry, Ness," he said. "I was just so mad. I saw a chance to make you understand where I was coming from, and before I knew it, I took it. If I could go back—"

"Oh. My. God. If I hear that from you one more time, I'm going to tear your tongue out. That's all we do. We hurt each other and then say we wish we could go back. Where does it end?"

"Let's let it end here."

"You can't just decide that, Royce. It doesn't work that way."

"Why not?"

"Because there's always something else."

"Only if we let there be something else."

"You don't get it. You lied to me. You talk about trust and keeping secrets, but then you lied."

"Well, technically, I—"

"So help me, if you say you didn't actually tell any untruths, I will slap you."

"Violence," Tod warned.

"And you," she turned on him. If Royce wasn't required to be there for his job, she'd be out of there. His methods made no sense to her. All she did was write and cry, trying to tell lies from truths and intentional hurts from accidental ones. The last thing she needed was a manipulative therapist, too. "You knew he hadn't cheated and you let this go for days?"

"No. I suspected. And I wanted to see how you worked it out on your own. When you didn't, I stepped in."

"That's pretty crappy, any way you look at it." She'd ranted so long and hard, she nearly panted for breath. "How'd you know, anyway?"

"He seemed to be pretty careful about his words. He never actually admitted to the affair when you were arguing. He kept turning it back on you, saying it would only be fair if he had. Classic case of deflection."

"Well, I think it stinks. It's worse than if he had actually cheated."

"What?" Royce asked.

"You don't mean that," Tod said.

"Yes, I do. The cheating would have been because I had cheated, to get even. I got that. I hated it, but I got it. The lying? That's just to hurt me."

"No, Ness. That was to make you understand. To put you in my shoes for a day or two. I fully intended to tell you after you knew how I felt."

"Okay. If that's how you want to play it. What can I do to you so you can see how I felt?"

His jaw dropped. "I never thought of it like that."

"We can't keep doing things to each other, Royce. No one wins."

"I know, babe. I get it. I'm so, so sorry."

Babe. He hadn't called her that in years.

She walked to the window and looked out at the street. Her Infiniti gleamed in the sunlight, parked one spot away from his brand new GMC, already dusty from use.

Did she judge him on his efforts or his errors?

"I have a new homework assignment for you," Tod said.

God. Not another one. Every time he assigned something, the shit hit the fan. Of course, then it got better. She and Royce had made strides. Well, before this setback. And he'd even helped the kids. That alone was worth all the diamonds in South Africa.

Maybe he deserved another chance. More often than not, he knew what he was doing.

After Tod gave them their next assignment, she wanted to take that thought back.

CHAPTER 29

ROYCE SAT ON THE BED looking over the top of his iPad at Vanessa. She sat at her vanity putting lotion on, staring out the window. Her expression hadn't changed much all day. It was a mix of shock and incredulity.

If he wasn't mistaken, it mirrored his own.

Tod had upped the stakes. He not only wanted them to go on another date, he wanted them to try incorporating some intimacy in their evening. He thought they were ready.

Royce thought he was bat-shit crazy.

But he wasn't a quitter.

So he tore his eyes away from Vanessa and continued to scroll through local events, looking for something the two of them could do. Something that wouldn't put pressure on them, but would set a romantic, intimate mood.

Like such an affair existed.

He leaned back against the pillows and stretched out his legs, crossing one foot over the other. "Ness, the symphony is playing a benefit concert at the Kilpatrick Center tomorrow night. We may still be able to get tickets."

"There won't be any good seats left. Besides, I don't think I want to go anywhere that dressy."

Good call on that one. He wasn't looking forward to donning formal wear if he could avoid it. He kept going through screens, but nothing jumped out at him.

"Baseball game?"

She wrinkled her nose.

"Dinner and a movie?"

"That's what our first real date was," she said.

"Our first real date was our first date," he said. "Driving around and ending up at the burger place. Why won't you just admit it?"

"Because riding in a car for an hour and a half is not a date. It's a drive."

"We ate."

"At the Student Union. I ate there with my friends all the time And I wasn't dating them."

"So you'd rather have had sex with me before we had our first date?" He uncrossed his legs and sat up, staring at her.

She put her lotion down and picked up her brush. Bending over so her hair flipped toward the floor and covered her face, she said, "Fine. That was our first date. Happy?" She stroked the brush roughly through the underside of her hair, the light brown waves straightening under the strain, then bouncing back up.

He crossed to her and took the brush out of her hands. "You're going to hurt yourself." Pulling her to an upright position, he began running the brush through the back of her hair. Her rigid muscles slowly relaxed with each stroke he made. After about twenty passes, she sighed, but he kept going. The strands were glossy, smooth… a silken cascade through his fingers.

She allowed him to continue for a few more minutes, then she reached for his hand. "Thank you."

He hated to stop, but he sensed he'd worn out his welcome. Handing her the brush, he stepped away. "Anytime." His voice sounded husky to him, so he cleared his throat and turned his back to her. Going back to the bed where he'd left his iPad, he sat down. When he looked up, she was right beside him, surprising him.

"So," she said, and sat beside him, squeezing next to him on his side of the bed. "Any other suggestions?"

He put the iPad down on his lap. His body seemed to be betraying him. Without proper blood flow to his brain, he didn't have any suggestions at all.

It was the hair. He should never have touched her hair.

There she was, plastered against him. Hair falling around her shoulders in flowing caramel waves. Skimpy tank and tiny pajama shorts revealing smooth, creamy skin sun-kissed from recent tanning. As her arm brushed his, he got a whiff of her lotion—night blooming jasmine. He'd just learned the name of it, but the scent was synonymous with her since the day they'd met. A forbidden nectar, sensual and erotic, it captivated him. Enraptured with the sight of her, the feel of her, the very essence of her, common sense and reason betrayed him.

He reached for her hand, rubbing his thumb across her knuckles.

And he couldn't have stopped shorter if he'd run into an invisible wall.

Her hand stiffened and she pulled it away, and just as quickly she stood and walked into her closet. Soon she returned wearing an oversized t-shirt and pajama pants. "It's a little chilly in here, don't you think?"

She hadn't been cold. Her skin had been rosy, flushed under his touch. If she was cold now, it was because of the mood in the room—the mood he'd caused. Not because of the temperature.

"Do you want me to adjust the AC?"

"No. I'm better now that I changed."

Polite conversation. Wonderful. How would they get through a date when they couldn't even get through planning one?

"So, what do you think? Did you find anything?"

"The old standby? Dinner and a movie?" he suggested.

"Our first-date date?" Her eyes were wide, her voice high.

"You'll love it. I promise."

"Whatever you want. I'm tired. I'll leave the planning up to you."

Of course she would. It was always all up to him.

She walked to her side of the bed and looked at him. Then she looked at the floor. Finally she grabbed her pillow and started to walk away.

"Ness, stop."

She turned and looked at him.

"We're going on a date tomorrow. One where we're supposed to try and, well, you know. Don't you think sleeping on the floor is kind of ridiculous at this point? Especially since we were sharing the bed a few days ago."

"That was before you lied to me."

He was going to point out that technically he hadn't lied, but figured that wasn't the time. "We can dwell on the past, or we can move forward. Which do you choose?"

"Are you ready to move past my sleeping with Ben?"

Was he? He wasn't sure. But he wasn't letting her sleep on the floor again, and he sure as hell didn't want to. "Yes. I've come to terms with that. It's new to me, but it was almost twenty years ago. I'm moving past it."

She wavered. "I don't think you can just declare that and it happens. We still have a lot of work to do."

He agreed. Just saying the words didn't make it so, but saying the words was a step in the right direction. "We're not going to solve anything with one of us on the floor. Come to bed. We'll work on us more tomorrow."

She stood there for a few more seconds, then finally put the pillow down on the bed and crawled under the covers.

Royce powered down his iPad and turned out the light. They each stayed on the edges of their sides, giving each other a wide berth in the middle of the bed.

It had been a long day, and he was mentally exhausted. They hadn't solved any of their problems, although some truths had come to light. And he'd had a nice moment with Ness.

Nice? Who was he kidding? She took his breath away.

He hadn't stopped out of anger or revulsion. He'd stopped because feeling that way again shocked him. It felt good. It felt right.

He'd been working the program Tod gave them. At first, he just went through the motions, but at some point, he really began trying. There were setbacks, sure, but now he knew something he hadn't when this all started. One very important thing.

He was willing to fight for his marriage.

The next morning, sunlight streamed in through the window and slanted across Royce's face. When he worked at the hospital, he never slept late enough for the light to land on him in the mornings. Stretching, he squinted at the clock. Eight-thirty. Time to get up. Lots to do.

He didn't bother with showering, because landscaping was a dirty job. But he did have one item of business to attend to before heading to the nursery.

When he got downstairs, he saw his family seated at the kitchen table. The sight of Hope's vacant seat still tore a hole in his heart, but he was coming to terms with it. They were still intentionally leaving space in front of her chair, so Royce picked up the juice carafe, poured himself a glass, and put the pitcher down where Hope's plate would be. They needed to stop saving her spot. He winced on the inside as hard as everyone at the table did on the outside, but no one questioned him on it.

He smiled. "Good morning, everyone."

"Hey, Dad," Jensen said.

"Morning."

"How'd you sleep?" Vanessa asked.

He grabbed an apple and shrugged. "I had trouble falling asleep, but once I did, I was out. You?"

"Just the opposite. I passed out, but woke up in the middle of the night. I finally came down around four."

"Did you make the coffee?"

"No." She sighed. "Your precious Lydia did. It tastes fine."

"Speaking of Lydia, where is she?"

Vanessa glared at him, but didn't answer.

Jensen looked back and forth between the two of them, then finally said, "She's cleaning my bathroom, I think. Do you want her for something?"

Vanessa mumbled something Royce couldn't make out.

"I'll go upstairs and talk to her."

"I don't think that's necessary," Vanessa said.

Royce went to the bottom of the stairs and called up, "Lydia! Could I please see you for a minute?"

"Coming!" she yelled back.

He expected her to run down to him. She always did everything she could to please him. Well, usually did all she could. Sometimes she did little things to push his buttons. This time, she didn't hurry. It must have been one of those button-pushing times. Royce sighed. No matter.

He glanced down the hall toward the kitchen, where he could see the table. His kids were staring at him, concern on their faces. Vanessa looked at her plate, pretty much stabbing each bite of her food. He couldn't see her face, but he knew she was seething.

A *pat-thump, pat-thump* turned his attention from the kitchen. Lydia was making her way down the stairs, her leg in a large immobilizing brace.

"My goodness, Lydia. What happened?"

"Just a little accident, Dr. Keller."

"Are you all right?"

"Fine, fine."

"Did you go to the ER? Do you need to see a specialist? What's the prognosis? I can refer you to—" She gazed at him, a small smile on her face. He backtracked. "You know what? I'm sure you have it under control."

"You can check it, if it will make you feel better." She sat on the step and lifted her leg out in front of her.

Royce stooped and removed the brace. He gently probed her knee, moving his fingers softly around her kneecap. She closed her eyes and moaned.

"Did that hurt?"

"Hmm? No. Not too much."

"Are you doing what the doctor said? What exactly did the doctor say? Who'd you see, anyway?"

"Like I said, it's no big deal. I was even cleared to work."

He refastened her brace and stood up. The subject was clearly closed. "About that." Now he really felt like a jerk. "Why don't you come into my office?"

"I don't want to walk more than I have to." She patted the spot beside her. "Whatever you need to say, you can say right here."

"Are you sure you wouldn't like more privacy?"

"We're like family, Dr. Keller." She beamed up at him.

He took a deep breath. "Lydia." She looked at him, brown eyes wide. "Lydia." He couldn't face her, so he spun away and faced the door. "Lydia."

"Okay. You've said my name three times now. What is it? Come on. You can tell me anything."

He breathed out slowly. It was easier when he didn't look at her, when she said things like that, things he knew were intended to hurt Vanessa and entice him. "Lydia, I'm afraid I have to let you go."

"Excuse me?"

"You were a loyal employee for several years, and we'll give you exceptional references. But a lot has changed over the last several weeks, and we aren't the same family anymore. We have different needs, different expectations. This isn't going to work any longer. Of course I'll give you two weeks' severance, but I'm afraid you're terminated. Effective immediately."

"Look at me."

He didn't want to, but he figured he owed her that. He spun around.

She'd pulled herself to her feet, and because she was still on the steps, she towered over him. Using the height differential to her advantage, she loomed over him, jabbing her finger into his chest and sticking her face into his. "You're firing me. You? *Firing me?* Just who do you think you are? Stringing me along? Letting your wife mentally torture me? Physically assault me?"

He backed away. "I don't know what you're talking about."

She pointed at her leg brace. "This. This is a souvenir from the esteemed Mrs. Keller. Don't act like you didn't know. She threw me down the stairs! I'll take my two weeks' severance. Then I'll take you for everything you've got. You haven't heard the last of me. I know every dirty secret you have, and I'm going to expose every last one of them."

She hobbled out the door, slamming it behind her.

Royce was so ready to start some yard work. He already felt dirty, he might as well look the part.

He turned to walk to the garage and saw Vanessa had crept up the hall. She stood there, staring at him.

"The kids and I heard the whole thing."

"Then I suppose you heard her blame you for her injury."

"You know I'd never do that, don't you?"

"I wasn't even going to ask. Besides, she's not really injured."

"What?"

"She let me check her knee. There's no swelling, no heat, no bruising. There's nothing wrong with her. She wouldn't tell me what facility she went to, what doctor she saw, what protocol she was following. It's a ploy for attention. Don't worry about it."

"She's threatening to sue. We don't need more legal troubles."

"She'll need medical bills to sue. I'm not worried."

"Speaking of bills, I was thinking…"

He looked at her and waited for her to continue.

"You know I don't do charity work in the summer. Since I have so much free time and we don't know what the future holds, I was thinking I'd start looking for a job. If I find something before fall, I'll just turn the fundraisers over to the other committee members. There were a few promising leads online."

"But you love your charity work."

"No. I love having something to do. And I can't think of anything more important than doing something for my family."

He smiled. "You'd go back to work? For me?"

Vanessa looked at him and smiled. "You fired her. For me."

He smiled back. "I fired her for us."

"And I'll work. For us."

He pulled her to him and wrapped his arms around her. "I have a few ideas, too. It'll be okay."

She wrapped her arms around him. "I know."

He embraced her, a hint of jasmine just drifting to him. He kissed the top of her head. "You won't be so grateful when you're scrubbing toilets next week."

"I'm placing an ad for a new housekeeper today."

He chuckled and pulled away. "Get a cheap one. We aren't earning money yet, and our savings will only hold for another six to nine months. A year if we're careful." He pulled out his wallet and leafed through the cash. "I'm on my way to the nursery."

"You just said we had to be careful. And now you're going back to Charlie's? Why?"

"I just need one more plant for the back yard. It won't be a lot of money."

"It's already gorgeous. What more could you possibly add?"

He grinned and waved as he walked out. Hopefully Charlie sold jasmine.

MUCH TO ROYCE'S SURPRISE, JENSEN and Faith helped in the yard for a few hours that afternoon. Because of their assistance, he not only finished the plant beds he'd started, he managed to get all the forget-me-nots planted around the fountain and the jasmine planted around the hot tub. Vanessa came out when they were done with drinks for everyone. The delight on her face would have been enough, but the fact that she said the yard took her breath away made it all worth it. His next project was a pergola with a swing—he thought Ness would love that—but it was definitely a two-person job. If Jensen wasn't interested, he would have to contract that one out to someone.

It was getting late. He needed to shower the filth off his body and the soreness off his muscles. Tod gave him an assignment, and it was time to do his homework.

Again, when he went to his room, Vanessa was in their bathroom getting ready. He didn't even knock. He just grabbed his things and went to the kids' bathroom. Ten minutes later he emerged—clean, dressed, and smelling like his son again.

He waited for Vanessa on the patio with a glass of water. He'd sat there for years, enjoying sunrises, watching the kids in the pool, entertaining friends at barbecues. But never did he get so much pleasure from sitting there than at that moment, looking out over what the yard had become. Just days earlier, there had been nothing much more than grass and hardscape. Now, everywhere he looked, he saw Hope. Every flower from her funeral was there.

He'd planted a rose garden of peach, white, and yellow roses. Peach for sympathy and pride, white for purity and innocence, and yellow, because Sally Anderson told him they were for new beginnings. In front of claret barberry, he'd planted white lilies, symbolizing virtue, and by dark boxwood, the burgundy alstroemeria, to signify devotion. Behind the wine-and-roses weigela he planted apricot, pink, and white gladioli, tall floral stalks suggesting strength. And in the corners, in front of the burning bushes, he planted white chrysanthemums. In a few months, when everything else began fading, their broad faces would bring a cheerfulness to the beds.

That's what his garden was. A cheerful tribute to his departed daughter. Just two months earlier, his yard was clinical, cold. Like him. Now it was a riotous mass of colorful blooms and perennial plants he could cultivate and tend. Like he should have done for the daughter it represented. He'd learned the names of the plants and what they represented. Which ones liked a lot of water and which ones preferred a lot of sun. He took the time to ask questions and get the answers. He listened. And he learned.

He should have done that with Hope.

The garden was a poor substitute, but it was the only homage he could offer her.

"Are you ready?"

He'd been so lost in thought, he hadn't noticed Vanessa step out onto the patio.

How it escaped his attention, he didn't know.

CHAPTER 30

VANESSA SQUARED HER SHOULDERS, SIGHED, and stepped onto the patio. "Royce, are you ready?"

God, she hated feeling like the marionette at the end of Tod's strings, but as long as she was forced to assume the role of powerless puppet, she was going to look the part.

Royce hadn't told her where they were going, but Tod had said they were supposed to try to be intimate with each other that night. That didn't necessarily mean sex, he said. But he did say they were married and it was time they started acting like it. Physical contact—and not accidentally rubbing elbows in an elevator—was necessary.

She didn't know how she felt about this stage of the plan, so she had taken a page from Mia's book.

When they were young, they often double-dated. Vanessa always felt insecure next to Mia's blatant confidence and overt sexuality. One day, while lingerie shopping, Mia noticed Vanessa's reticence about, well, everything, and let her in on the secret. "Honey, all this," she gestured to her body, clad in a hot pink chiffon baby doll well outside the confines of the dressing room, "isn't natural to anyone. Fake it till you make it." When Vanessa asked her what she meant, she explained. "If you want to get in the mood for your man, dress the part."

While getting ready for her intimate evening with Royce, Vanessa didn't feel in the mood. She didn't even know if she wanted to be in the mood. Or if she wanted Royce to be in it. But Tod told them to try, and Royce certainly had been trying. So she 'faked it.'

She dug in the back of her lingerie drawer for the scarlet push-up bra and matching thong set she'd purchased on a whim two years before. They still had the tags on them. She'd never worn panties like that out of the house and wasn't certain she could tolerate such a foreign feeling for several hours. But she thought about Mia's fake it till you make it mantra and decided, if nothing else, it would give her something to think about during their date. She removed the tags, slipped the garments on, and looked at herself in the mirror.

Her skin had the faintest beginnings of a tan, but next to the deep red of the lingerie, it looked creamy. She slid her fingers under the waistband, smoothing the lace to sit over her hipbones. Her legs seemed to extend much longer than usual. She didn't look short. And the bra? It worked so much more than a miracle. She actually had cleavage. Cleavage! She could see where Royce would like this set. She should have worn it years ago. Maybe it would have piqued his interest when he had started to operate on autopilot.

She put on a short black skirt and a black, sleeveless blouse. She started to tuck the blouse in, but thought about Mia's advice again, and instead tied it so just a promise of skin showed above her waistband. Looking in the mirror, she decided to unbutton another button. And another. She pulled the collar wide, exposing enough of her throat and never-before-seen cleavage that she got a much needed confidence boost. She walked into her closet and skipped her everyday shoe selection. Bending down, she chose a pair of three-inch heel sling backs from the boxes on the floor.

Note to self. No bending in a thong.

Going back to her vanity, she took out her cosmetics bag. She pulled out all the stops, using every dramatic tip she'd ever learned. Hope would have said she was "vamping it up." She would have loved it. Vanessa needed a minute to compose herself. The last thing she needed was to start crying. It would take at least half an hour to remove all that makeup and start all over again.

When she was done, she pulled her hair up off her neck in a loose twist, letting loose tendrils fall by her ears and at the nape of her neck. If she was going to all the trouble of dressing for the night, she was going to draw attention to herself, not hide behind her hair.

A few spritzes of her signature scent… earrings and engagement ring… final check in the mirror… one last underwear adjustment… She was ready for her date, letting her appearance set the mood.

She must have done something right, judging by Royce's reaction. When she had finally walked onto the patio, she left him speechless.

"Royce?" she asked again.

He cleared his throat and blinked a few times. Scrambling to his feet, he stepped to her. Close to her. Looking down into her eyes, he said, "You look… incredible."

His voice was husky. It was his bedroom voice. Mission accomplished. At least, part one of it. She smiled. "Thank you."

It felt strange standing that close to him and not wrapping her arms around him, but she wasn't ready for that. Apparently he wasn't either, because he didn't reach for her. But neither did he step away. They stood there, breathing each other in, staring into each other's eyes. In the quiet warmth of the evening, the gentle breeze wafted the sweet perfume of the new garden to them, and the only sounds she heard were her labored breathing and her racing pulse pounding in her ears. She grew dizzy, swimming in the sensations but having no anchor to ground her.

She stepped back.

"So, are you ready?"

"If you are," he said, voice soft. He opened the door for her and she led the way to the garage.

He seemed to know without even asking that she didn't want to take his truck. He opened the passenger door of her vehicle for her, and she got in. "Thank you."

He smiled and closed her in.

So formal. So stilted.

So awkward.

When he got in and they started driving, she asked, "So you never told me, where are we going?"

"Well, you seem to think our second date was worth remembering, so I thought we'd try to recapture that."

Their second date, the one Vanessa called their first real date, had been a movie and dinner. The theater closest to campus had "Throwback Thursdays" where, with college IDs, students could get in for fifty cents and watch an old film. They'd watched *Casablanca* before going to a cute little diner down the road. It was known for having amazing pie, and she hadn't been disappointed. They both got the meatloaf special and split a piece of chocolate crème pie.

"Are we renting *Casablanca?* I didn't need to get dressed up for that."

"Personally, I wouldn't mind if you looked like this every day, and no, we aren't renting a movie. However, there is a theater about forty minutes away that only shows old films. Right now, their selections include *A Streetcar Named Desire, The Godfather, Guys and Dolls, On the Waterfront, Apocalypse Now,* and *The Wild One.*"

"Do I sense a theme?"

"Marlon Brando died on July first. They're running a sort of retrospective in his honor."

"What? Are you channeling Siskel and Ebert?"

"One, I'm not a medium. If I was, I could think of better people to channel." He was silent for a moment, then shook his head slightly before continuing. "And two, no. I looked it up when I saw their focus on Brando."

That was the Royce she knew. Always researching, always prepared.

"So, does any of that appeal to you?"

She looked at him and caught him sneaking a peek at her cleavage. He quickly averted his eyes and turned his attention back on the road.

Fake it till you make it. "Not showing *Last Tango in Paris*, huh?"

His breath left him in a whoosh that he tried to cover with a cough. He finally answered, "Uh, no. Not that I recall. Are you in the mood for something a little more… provocative tonight? The Starlight opened Memorial Day weekend." He shot her a sideways glance and smiled.

She giggled. The Starlight was a drive-in off River Road that only showed pornography. Its clientele consisted almost exclusively of vagrants, college kids, and high schoolers who slipped the bored ticket-taker an extra five bucks instead of their IDs. Every now and then they heard rumors of people they knew having been seen there. The question was, who saw them to spread the rumor? No, if they thought the town was talking about them now, the last thing they needed to do was be seen entering or leaving The Starlight. Besides, that was way too much pressure for her.

"Can you imagine? Us? At The Starlight?"

"The way you look tonight? I'm imagining all sorts of things."

She felt her cheeks flush and turned to look out the window. What were they doing? She flirted, she pulled back. He was obviously interested, but hadn't made a move. Being with a spouse should be the most comfortable thing in the world, and here she was, totally out of her element. It felt so wrong.

And the thong was not comfortable.

"Why don't we get to the theater and just see what movie is about to start?"

"Sounds good."

"But not *Apocalypse Now.*"

He laughed and speeded up.

When they got to the theater, they were selling tickets for *Apocalypse Now,* starting in ten minutes. The next movie, *Guys and Dolls,* didn't start for twenty minutes after that. And while that was one of Vanessa's favorites, she knew Royce wasn't fond of musicals. While they stood there and deliberated, the boy taking tickets stared at her chest. She looked around. He wasn't the only one.

Several of the men standing around looked at her with slight smiles on their faces. Most of the women didn't look nearly as happy.

She took a deep breath and turned to Royce. "Do you want to skip the movie? At least for now? Why don't we go grab something to eat and then come back?"

"Are you sure? On our date, we did the movie first."

"Yeah. I'm sure. Let's go."

She was glad to be out of the theater, away from eyes other than Royce's. He let her lead the way, and as he followed her to the car, she got the feeling he chose to lag behind so he could admire the view. If that was the case, she decided to put some effort into placing her legs slowly on the ground, stretching on top of already high heels, swaying her hips under the soft, clinging material of her skirt. Well, she did that for about five steps. Then she realized Mia was a sociopath. She felt ridiculous. It was highly likely she was going to break an ankle in those heels. And even though she had no panty lines, her clothes were completely inappropriate. She began untying her blouse so she could tuck it in.

Royce put his hand over hers and stopped her. "What are you doing?"

"I'm going to tuck my shirt in. Button a few buttons up. Maybe see if I can tug my skirt down a little. Or convince you to stop at Nordstrom before dinner."

He moved her hands off her shirt and gently retied the knot. "Ness. You look beautiful. Breathtaking. Leave your clothes alone and let's go get something to eat."

She took a shaky breath, but decided to leave her outfit alone. She'd liked it enough in her bedroom, although she'd been thinking like Mia then. Royce seemed to love it. Of course, so did all the other men she'd seen that night. What the hell. She didn't know anyone for miles. She'd go with it.

Royce once again opened her door for her and helped her in. Stepping up into the SUV in three inch heels wouldn't be easy on a good day. Doing it in a short skirt, keenly aware of her undergarments and her husband made the whole thing feel like it took forever. Royce rushed to his side and, before she could react, leaned over her and grabbed her seatbelt, slowly pulling it across her body and fastening it at her hip. Then he took his time adjusting the shoulder strap, making sure it was snug.

"Comfortable?" he whispered in her ear, his breath warm and moist against her skin.

She'd been holding her breath as he strapped her in, and she let it out slowly, unable to speak. Instead, she just nodded.

He breathed in deeply before pulling away. "Mmmm. Jasmine."

"How do you know that's what I'm wearing?"

"I planted some in the yard. You smell divine." He situated himself behind the wheel, strapped himself in, and started the car. As they pulled out, he said, "There's a little diner not far from here. It got pretty decent reviews. You game? They probably have a meatloaf special and chocolate crème pie."

"You remembered."

"Of course I remember." He glanced at her, then turned his attention back on the road.

"Sounds good." She put music on as they drove toward the diner. It took the pressure off her having to make small talk. And she was too nervous and befuddled to bother trying.

He pulled into a parking lot of a diner called The Mustard Seed. It looked like many other diners she'd seen before—glass windows in front showing booths and a counter inside; a giant florescent sign on the top proclaiming its name in gold letters; economy sedans in the parking lot, their owners likely there for the blue plate special. Royce parked and they got out, skirting the dusty vehicles on their way to the entrance.

He opened the door for her and she stepped inside. The general din typical of a diner—flatware clattering on plates, people talking, servers scrambling back and forth—all came to a screeching halt. Vanessa stood, frozen at the door, while everyone in the restaurant turned to face them.

Royce cleared his throat. "Hi. Uh, table or booth for two, please."

A waitress wearing a gold polyester uniform and crepe-soled shoes strolled over toward them. She cracked her gum and tucked her pen behind her ear before she answered. "See that?" She pointed to a weathered, yellowed sign that had obviously been hung when the diner opened, probably back in the forties.

WE RESERVE THE RIGHT TO REFUSE SERVICE TO ANYONE

That couldn't be right, could it? That wasn't even legal. Was it? And, more to the point, were they referring to her and Royce? What had they done to warrant exclusion? She glanced behind her to her husband, who looked just as confused as she did.

"Well, come on. Can't you read?" the waitress asked.

"Yes," Royce said. He tucked his arm around Vanessa's waist and pulled her toward him. "What about it?"

The cook, a burly man with a ruddy complexion and a scar over one eye, came out from the kitchen and wiped his hands on a grease-stained apron. "Trouble out here, Lena?"

"I don't know, Fred. These folks say they can read the sign, but they ain't makin' no move to leave."

Fred looked them over and took a toothpick from the counter. He made a show of cleaning his teeth and examining the pick before flicking it away, Vanessa hoped to a trashcan behind the bar. "This here's a family diner," he said, and ran his tongue along the outside of his teeth, making loud sucking noises as he did. "A Christian diner." He finally looked at them again. "We don't hold no truck with your kind."

Vanessa backed up, taking comfort from feeling Royce standing with her.

"I'm sorry," he said. *"Our* kind? And what kind are we, exactly?"

Fred looked at his nails, then cracked his knuckles. Vanessa heard, actually felt, Royce breathe in. She knew how much he hated it when Jensen did that. Seeing this man do it in an obvious attempt to intimidate them had to be grating on his nerves. It certainly didn't do much for hers.

"What kind?" Lena asked, looking them over the way Fred had. "Looks to me like the kind from that *Pretty Woman* movie."

Vanessa gasped. "Excuse me?"

Whether she heard Vanessa or not, whether she cared that she offender her or not, Lena continued. "Rich man paying a trampy lady—"

"She was no lady," one of the patrons interjected.

"Ain't that the God's honest truth," Lena said.

"You're talking about my wife," Royce said.

Vanessa could feel the blood draining from her face. The rest of the arguments they had were just noise to her, a distant roaring in her ears. She swayed on her feet and leaned into Royce for support. It was all wrong.

The movie? A bad idea.

The diner? A nightmare.

The clothes? Obviously disastrous.

She spun to face him and, clinging to his arm, looked up into his face. "Please. Let's just go." Pushing him, she forced him against the door until he turned and opened it, taking them both into the parking lot and to their car. When they left, they could hear the patrons cheering and whooping behind the closed door.

As they drove away, Royce turned to her. "I'm so sorry. I can't imagine what that was all about."

"We probably should have expected something like that. The place is called The Mustard Seed. It's like we stepped into a scene from a movie. A bad scary movie."

"More like they thought we were the characters in a movie," he said.

"I can't believe that. From religious people! Even my mother wouldn't have behaved that way."

"So they're zealots. And they misread the situation." He patted her hand. "It's okay. We got out of there. Safely. We'll laugh about this someday."

"Laugh? I hardly think so. Royce, they thought I was your whore. A bought and paid for whore."

This time when she reached for the knot in her shirttails, he didn't stop her.

"I thought you looked gorgeous tonight."

She looked at him. "Maybe I did. But obviously I didn't look appropriate for public." She reached for the buttons at the top of her blouse, but he grabbed her hand.

"Stop, Ness. Who cares what a bunch of religious fanatics stuck in the forties think?"

She could feel her hands tremble as she fought back tears, so she let her hands fall to her lap, not wanting him to know how close she was to losing it. Instead of letting her hands go, he kept hold, holding her hand in her lap. They drove in silence for a long while, and Vanessa had nothing but time to think. Time to realize she was a mess, and her marriage was in serious trouble.

Then Royce spoke up. "This was all my fault. I shouldn't have tried to recreate that date. I should have come up with something pressure-free. And I should have researched where we went to eat, so we didn't end up at Café Puritan for dinner."

"No. I'm the one who tried too hard. I dressed like Mia and wore all this damn makeup—"

"Okay. Stop. I love how you look, but if you're uncomfortable, then you shouldn't dress that way. At least, not in public. And I should have been more careful with our plans. We both made tactical errors. It's done. Let's put it behind us and move on."

"Royce, I know Tod wanted us to do this, but maybe this was a sign. Maybe we aren't ready."

He squeezed her hand then dropped it to pull into their garage.

When he turned off the engine, he took her hand again. "I don't know when we'll get back to where we were before. Actually, where we were before wasn't that good. I want to get somewhere better." He stroked his thumb over her knuckles. "We have to start somewhere. And if that means twenty or thirty awkward starts, then that's what we'll do." He brought her hand up to his lips and kissed it. "Let's go in and put this first one behind us."

She was all too happy to do that. She scrambled out of the car and walked around it, meeting him at the door. In her haste to go inside, she stumbled in her high heels, and he caught her. She looked up into his eyes, eyes that held so much history and understanding. Eyes that, no matter what they were going through, she loved.

It happened effortlessly. His head bent down, hers tipped up. Her lips brushed softly against his for just a moment, a whispered promise of all that had been right between them, then they both moved to deepen the kiss.

His mouth crushed against hers. She turned her head the same way he did, their noses smashing against each other's before he turned his head the other way. She leaned into him, and her teeth scraped off his. Finally she put her hands on his shoulders and pushed away.

They were both a bit winded, and she was unsteady on her heels. Mostly, she was frustrated and humiliated.

"Not quite the choreographed ballet it used to be, huh?" he asked, and he wiped his mouth. He looked at his fingers and rubbed them to try to get rid of the lipstick he'd just wiped off.

She couldn't let him see her cry. That would be the final indignity she couldn't suffer. She ran in the house and up the stairs as fast as she dared on those dangerous heels. And so he didn't see her, she ran right into her closet and shut the door.

The first thing she did was kick off those ridiculous shoes. They immediately got shoved to the back corner. She'd never wear them again. She'd only bought them on a whim, anyway. Maybe Faith would want them.

She wiped away the tears as she took off her skirt and top. No point in hanging them. To her mind, they should be burned, but at the very least, they needed a good washing. Or seven. She left them in a heap on the floor. Looking down, she saw the scarlet underclothes she wore and choked back another sob. Obviously those weren't going to be put to good use.

Ever.

Her pajamas weren't in her closet, they were in her dresser in the bedroom.

No matter. She needed to shower, anyway. Just as she was putting on her robe, Royce opened her closet door.

His wide eyes and open mouth told her all she needed to know. She didn't get her robe on and closed in time.

"I thought I heard you crying. Are you okay?"

Let's see… she was crying in a closet while wearing her 'fuck me now' underwear. After the night they'd just had? Yeah. She was peachy.

CHAPTER 31

OKAY, SO THE EVENING DIDN'T go as planned. So the kiss wasn't quite a success. Who was he kidding? Both were unmitigated disasters. But he couldn't stand to hear her cry. Never could. That was the only reason he opened her door. He wanted to comfort her.

What he saw before she belted the robe? Breathtaking.

He didn't know when she started wearing bras and panties like those. He didn't care. If she told him she bought them with Ben in mind, he'd be jealous as hell, but he'd deal with it. Because that night, she'd worn them for him.

And she looked exquisite.

The deep red was dark against her pale skin, an enticing contrast that made him itch to explore every piece of fabric, elastic strap, lace edge… every tiny triangle covering parts he hadn't seen in so long. He wanted to trace his fingers along the garments, feel the softness of the satin, the roughness of the lace. He wanted to follow that same trail with his tongue and explore the taste and scent of her skin, feel it heat under his touch.

My God. Was she talking? His mind was a mile away.

He held out his hand to her. "Come here." He pulled her into his arms, careful to keep his groin turned away from her. She didn't need to know his body and his mind weren't on the same page. What he really wanted to do was comfort her. She didn't need to feel threatened by him.

"Why don't I draw you a nice hot bath? I can go get you some wine and just let you soak for a while."

She sighed, her breath still quivering with suppressed sobs. "That sounds really nice. Thanks."

He stepped away from her and went to the bathroom. There was a bottle of verbena on the tub, but he never knew her to use that. He reached instead for the jasmine. After he got the water to the right temperature, he added the soap to it. Once he was satisfied the bath was filling properly, he called to her. "Do you want to keep an eye on this while I go to the kitchen?"

She agreed, so he headed for the door. He hated himself, but he couldn't help it. He turned for one last look. She was dropping the robe as he closed the door, and—sweet mother! She had on a thong.

He shook his head, trying to clear it of the image as he went downstairs. It was all he could do to not picture her in that skimpy underwear, or naked and bubbly in the tub. Going to the kitchen for the wine should give him time to get the blood flowing back where it belonged. While he was down there, he cut some fruit and cheese and put it all on a tray with crackers, olives, two bottles of her favorite Gewürztraminer (which didn't seem to pair with anything on the tray, but she loved it with everything), and two glasses. It wasn't a meal, but it was better than nothing.

When he returned to their room, she was out of the tub and back in their room, wrapped in her robe, towel-drying her damp hair. She'd scrubbed all the makeup off her face, and her cheeks were rosy. Despite how stunning she'd looked earlier, she looked even more beautiful to him then, fresh faced and dewy, right out of her bath. Like the college girl he'd fallen in love with. The sight of her stopped him mid-stride just inside their door.

"What's wrong?" she asked.

He shook his head. "Nothing. It's just...."

"What?"

"You're beautiful."

She blushed and turned away.

He put the tray down on the bed and crossed to her. Taking the towel from her, he threw it on her vanity bench then grabbed her hands in his own. Looking down at her, he waited until she met his gaze. "Why do you do that? Listen to me. When I saw you tonight, I thought you were stunning. And you were. You know you were. You saw all those men ogling you at the theater. All those women jealous of you because their men couldn't keep their eyes off of you. I didn't think I'd ever seen you look better. Until right now." She looked away, but he squeezed her hands and pulled on her until she faced him again. "You look just like you did when we met. Better. Ness, you get more beautiful every day. I don't know why I didn't notice for so long. Or why I never told you. I won't make that mistake again."

He saw the tears in her eyes, but hoped they were there for different reasons this time. He pulled her into an embrace and breathed in her scent. Remarkable that just a few weeks ago, he didn't know what scent she wore, and now he not only knew it was jasmine, but had forever linked the scent with her, exotic and rich.

"Come on," he said. "You missed dinner. I made a snack. Or we could order pizza."

"I'm not really hungry." She let him lead her to the bed.

"You have to at least eat this. The pizza is negotiable." He got her situated against the headboard and joined her. Putting the tray across both their laps, he opened the first bottle of wine then began to feed her.

"I can feed myself."

"If I feed you, I'll know how much you ate."

"You'll know how much I ate by subtracting how much you ate and what's left." But she didn't protest.

He held an olive up to her lips. When she opened her mouth for it, he let his thumb linger.

"You forgot napkins," she said.

"We'll think of something."

He continued feeding her the choicest selections of olives, cheese and crackers, grapes, and slices of pineapple and mango while he took the less desirable pieces for himself. As they drank, she held her own glass, but he kept offering it to her, and it wasn't long before the first bottle was finished and he'd opened the second.

"What are you doing?" she asked. "I think I've already passed my limit."

"You only had two glasses."

"I had at least three."

"Besides," he continued like she hadn't spoken, "it's not like we're going anywhere." He put the tray aside and refilled her glass. After putting the bottle back on the tray, he readjusted how they were sitting so he reclined against the headboard and she nestled in the crook of his arm, leaning against him. "Comfy?"

"Isn't this a little weird?"

"Why?"

"We haven't been together in bed like this in, well, in years."

"Tod said to try to be intimate. This feels pretty intimate to me."

"I'm not sure this is what he meant."

"I don't care what he meant. This feels right. I miss this, Ness. I miss holding you, cuddling with you. Eating a damn snack together and sharing a bottle of wine."

She turned her head at an odd angle and looked up at him. "This is more than a bottle, and I think I'm a bit tipsy. How do you feel about getting drunk with me?"

"I miss that, too." He leaned down and kissed the tip of her nose. "Maybe that's just what we need."

"You won't be saying that when you're holding my hair back."

"I've done worse."

"You don't drink much." Her words were beginning to slur.

"I'm drinking tonight."

"How much?"

"Don't worry about it. Just enjoy the wine."

She held out her empty glass. "Hit me."

He poured her another glass and held her tight as she snuggled against him.

She raised her glass. "To im-tan-macy."

He chuckled. "To intimacy." He lifted his glass and sipped.

"Thass wha I said." She drained her glass and held it out for a refill. "It-miss-ant-cy." She fell asleep before he could pour her another. She'd been through almost a bottle and a half on her own. He hoped she'd eaten enough crackers to absorb it all.

Finishing his glass, he set both of them on the tray. Then he lay her down beside him and snuggled her against him, in the crook of his arm, for the night. He hadn't slept that close to her in years. And it felt good. Even if he had to trick her into it.

He woke the next morning to a painful arm and the sounds of moaning. Looking around to get his bearings, he realized Vanessa had slept on him all night and his arm had fallen asleep. As he wiggled his fingers, they tingled, the 'pins and needles' sensation jarring his hand awake as the blood flow returned. Vanessa sat beside him, her head cradled in her hands.

"Morning," he said.

She slowly turned and peeked at him through her hair. "You did this to me."

She hadn't said that since she was in labor. Uh-oh.

"I guess I shouldn't ask how you're feeling."

All she managed was another moan.

"How about you take a shower—"

"Are you saying I stink?" she whispered.

"Not at all." He lied effortlessly about the post-binge odor. "I just think some cool water might refresh you a bit. In the meantime, I'll go make some coffee. And I'll get rid of this tray."

She groaned again at the mention of the tray of food and wine.

"And I'll bring you some ibuprofen. And water. You need to rehydrate."

He helped her off the bed and she started toward the bathroom. When he was sure she could make it on her own, he headed toward the bedroom door. Turning back to check on her before he left, he saw she'd dropped the robe. She hadn't worn anything under it all night. Had he known that, he probably wouldn't have slept as soundly as he did. When she closed the bathroom door behind her, he left the bedroom and went to the kitchen.

He put the tray on the counter and got started on the coffee. Once it was brewing, still with no chicory because he couldn't find where Lydia had hidden it, he disposed of the garbage from the tray and rinsed the dishes. By the time he had tidied up, the coffee was ready. He poured two mugs, grabbed a bottle of ibuprofen, and was about to go upstairs with them when he noticed a note on the kitchen table.

Mom and Dad,

Thought you might want some time to yourselves after your big night. We went out for breakfast. And probably lunch. No, dinner. Actually, we'll watch a movie or something tonight, so don't expect us until curfew. Enjoy your day. You have the house to yourselves.

Love,

Jensen and Faith

It was written in Jensen's handwriting, but he could hear Faith telling him what to write. That's why they went through three meals and an after dinner activity before finally settling on curfew as the deadline. Great kids. It wasn't necessary, but they were trying, too.

He carried the coffee and medicine upstairs. "Who wants caffeine?"

Vanessa perched on the edge of the bed, a towel wrapped around her, hair hanging in her face and dripping down her back.

"Oh, babe." He chuckled and crossed to her. "You look...."

"How?" She looked up at him and took one of the mugs of coffee. "How do I look?"

He bit his lip and thought a moment before answering. "You look like you feel awful. Here." He put his coffee down and opened the bottle of ibuprofen, shaking two out into his hand. "This should help you feel better. And once you drink some coffee, we'll get you some water."

She glared at him, but took the pills and drank the coffee.

"Why don't you let me comb the tangles out, and you can just sip that?" She didn't answer, so he took that as a yes. He grabbed a wide-toothed comb and began working it through her hair while she sat there, sipping her coffee and moaning into her mug.

After a few minutes, she said, "Why did you let me drink that much? Or maybe I should ask why you *made* me drink that much?"

"You had a rough night, Ness. You've had a rough couple of months. You needed to just relax and let go for a night."

"Yeah?" She took another sip and sighed. "And what about you? Like your life's been a cakewalk."

"You know? I'm okay."

"Really? After Hope? And Ben?"

He kept pulling through the tangles while he thought about it. "Yeah. Really. I'm okay."

"And after what Wade said about Stanford?"

"That one kind of blindsided me. But yeah. I'm good."

She sighed. "I'm not. I'm not good with any of it."

He ran his fingers through her hair. "Tangle free. And almost dry."

"Thanks."

"Also, I should tell you the kids gave us the house to ourselves for the day." He showed her the note.

She blushed and put the note in her robe pocket. "I'm sorry, Royce. I don't think I'm in any condition to make use of their gift at the moment."

He smiled. "I'm not asking you to. I just thought you'd want to know what they did for us. Besides, we're supposed to go back to Tod's today and tell him how it went."

She sighed and dropped her head. "That won't be at all embarrassing."

He put his hand under her chin and tipped her face up so he could look at her. "I'm not embarrassed about trying to reconnect last night. And you shouldn't be either. Besides, I think we made progress."

She covered her nose and mouth, and he knew she remembered the world's worst kiss in the garage.

"That's not what I'm talking about. I'm talking about sleeping in each other's arms."

"I was drunk."

"I don't care. It counts."

"You got me drunk on purpose."

"Still counts. Now get dressed."

She shrugged and headed toward the closet. "I want to talk to him about Stanford, anyway."

"Me, too. I want to know where we stand with him. In fact, I think I'll call Stanford and ask him to meet us there. That way, we can avoid the whole discussion about last night."

"Good call," she said.

"Hey, Ness?" he called to her while she was in her closet.

She poked her head back out. "What?"

"Don't suppose you could wear another thong-and-bra set like yesterday's?"

Her face turned a bright red before she ducked back into her closet and she slammed the door closed.

He knew the noise had to hurt her head, but she didn't make a sound. Smiling, he grabbed the phone and texted Stanford. Calling and talking to him would give him a chance to decline. Texting him was a safer bet that he'd show. A few seconds after he sent the text, he got a reply.

I'll be there.

Maybe things were finally going his way after all.

Two hours later, he and Vanessa sat in Tod's office trying to avoid discussing their date night.

"Listen," Royce said. "I know you think this is important, but we need to discuss something else with you."

Tod sat back in his chair. "Seems like you're deflecting again, but go ahead."

"I've asked Stanford to join us today, so I have to make this quick." Tod raised his eyebrows, but stayed silent. "The other day, I had a visit from my old friend Wade, who told me he's being set up to take the blame for ratting me out to HA. He said really it's Stanford behind it all."

"I see."

"Now, if Wade is telling the truth, then Stanford sent us here to benefit him, and whether you're in cahoots or you're an innocent pawn, these visits are going to come back to bite me in the ass."

Tod just blinked and stared at him, revealing nothing.

Royce continued. "Wade and I have been friends for pretty much all our lives. I couldn't get over him throwing me under the bus just because of some petty jealousy."

"And Stanford?" Tod asked.

"Stanford was my mentor." When Tod didn't speak, Royce went on. "I mean, I haven't known him as long as I've known Wade, but I was never in competition with him. He's only ever had my best interests at heart."

"So why would that change now?"

"Wade said I was in competition with him now."

"And why would you believe Wade?"

"Yes, Royce," Stanford said from the doorway. "Tell us all why would you believe Wade?"

Tod got up and hugged Stanford, who returned the embrace. After Tod pulled a chair over so Stanford could join them, he and Stanford sat, both seemingly relaxed. Royce looked at Vanessa. The tide had turned. They were the ones who felt on edge.

"Wade told me you didn't get your promotion, and if I got mine, you'd be out of a job."

"And just like that, you believed him," Stanford said.

"Why would he lie to me?"

"To cover his ass and see what information he could get from you before the hearing."

"I don't get it," Vanessa said. "The hearing doesn't impact him any. Why would he care?"

"He cares because if Royce doesn't keep his job, Wade will become Chief of Emergency Medicine, possibly even get the promotion that Royce was due."

"But, if you don't get your promotion...," Royce said.

"Son, I got my promotion two weeks before you left."

Royce fell back in his seat. "Why didn't you say anything?"

"Because the hospital didn't want people vying for my replacement. They wanted me to get to name my successor without a bunch of doctors clamoring for the job. And I was ready to. If it wasn't for that damn missing medicine, there wouldn't have been any delay at all."

"But if you already got your promotion, then that means everything Wade told me was...."

"A lie," Stanford said.

"Why?" Vanessa asked. "Why risk it? He has us where he wants us."

"No. There's still a chance the board will vote with me. He wants all the dirt he can get so he can come in fully armed and loaded."

"And we probably gave it to him," Royce said. "I probably gave it to him."

"What'd you tell him?"

"I have no idea. But I know I agreed with him that you were no friend to me. I can just imagine what I let slip."

"I know," Vanessa said.

"What?" Royce asked.

"I know what you told him. You confirmed you were seeing Tod. I was listening at the door."

Royce grabbed her hand and kissed it. "I should be angry that you didn't trust me, but I'm not. I'm glad you were listening. I wish you had come out and shoved a sock in my mouth."

"Royce didn't tell him Tod's name," she said. "Wade came up with it on his own. How would he know that?"

Stanford looked at Tod, who shrugged. "We don't like to advertise it," Stanford said. "Tod doesn't want to trade on my name. And he hasn't. He's earned everything on his own merit. But he's my nephew. More than, really. He's like a son to me. Joan and I raised him."

"My parents died in a car wreck when I was just a baby. I don't even remember them. Uncle Stan and Aunt Joanie took me in."

"How did we not know that?" Royce asked.

"Like I said," Stanford said, "we don't talk about it."

"But we're not just anybody," Royce said. "We're...." His voice trailed off.

"Family? Yes, you are. And I should have told you. I'm sorry."

Royce shook his head. "But shouldn't we at least have met before?"

"I've seen you at Aunt Joanie's parties," Tod said, "but with the other hundred people there, it's hardly surprising we didn't officially meet."

"Well, Stanford," Royce said, "all I can say is I'm sorry."

"And it's no wonder you recommended Tod so highly," Vanessa said.

"No," Stanford said. "I recommended him because I believe in the quality of his work. I wouldn't have sent you here if I didn't think he could help you."

Royce leaned forward and put his hand on his old friend's arm. "Stanford, I'm so sorry I doubted your intentions. Or your friendship. I've known Wade since we were kids and I just didn't want to think he'd betray me like that. But deep down, I know, I've always known, that he's always been jealous and manipulative. I should have trusted you."

"You've always looked for the good in the people you love, Royce. That's not a bad thing. It's only a problem when it pits two people you love against each other. I came out on the wrong side."

"Yes, but I was wrong."

"And you learned your lesson. Now what are we going to do about it? It would seem Wade has been busy building quite a case for the hearing. And there's more bad news."

"I'm afraid to ask," Royce said, "but what?"

"There haven't been any more drug thefts since you left the hospital."

"None?" Vanessa asked.

Stanford shook his head. "Not one."

"Well, it looks like we've got a lot of prep work to do," Vanessa said.

"Actually, I think we need to talk," Royce said. "I want you to be prepared for what's going to happen in there."

CHAPTER 32

VANESSA WAS STILL TRYING TO process everything Royce said when her cell phone rang.

"I thought we agreed no phones during session?" Tod said.

"After Hope's accident, I never turn mine off. The kids might need me." She scrambled in her purse and got to her phone on the last ring. It was Faith. "Hello?"

"Mom?" She sniffled.

"What is it, honey?"

"I'm so sorry to bother you, but we need you and Dad. Something's happened."

Vanessa was glad she was sitting, because the room dipped. She gripped the phone tighter and reached for Royce's hand. "Are you at the hospital? We'll be right there. Is it Jensen? What's wrong?" Royce pulled her to her feet and they started walking to the door.

"No, no. We're fine. We're at the animal shelter."

She stopped cold, pulling Royce to a halt with her. "I'm sorry, what?"

"It's not us. Just, please. Get here as fast as you can." She disconnected the call.

Vanessa looked up at Royce. "The kids are okay. But they seem to need us for something."

He shrugged. "Okay. Let's go then." He turned to Stanford. "Again, I'm sorry. I'll talk to you later. But I have to go."

Stanford and Tod were also on their feet. "No, don't think of it. Go take care of your family."

"We're good?" Royce asked, inching toward the door.

"Always. Now go."

Vanessa tugged on him, and they ran out to the car.

"Where are we headed?" he asked.

"The animal shelter."

"The pound? What do you think they're doing there?" he asked, accelerating through town.

"I don't know, but she sounded really upset."

"Call her back."

Vanessa tried both Faith and Jensen, but didn't get through to either of them. "We'll be there soon. I guess we'll find out then."

She slid her St. Luke medal back and forth on her necklace, listening to the soft zip as the bail slid over the links of the chain. She couldn't fathom why her children were at an animal shelter or what had them so upset. But if recent events taught her anything, she knew if it was important to them, it was important.

When they pulled into the parking lot at the shelter, she noted there were three police vehicles as well as four news vans there. She jumped out of the car before Royce had fully rolled to a stop. Running inside, she looked for someone to help her, but no one manned the front desk. So she followed the commotion to the back of the building.

Cages lined one wall, most of which held rambunctious dogs and cats pawing at their doors, howling at the commotion, and generally adding to the cacophony in the room. But the majority of the drama came from the end of the hall, where Jensen and Faith were standing—no, apparently where they had zip-tied themselves to a cage. They were arguing with a veterinarian while news crews wedged themselves in an adjoining hallway, trying to report on the whole thing. Two police officers stood at the end of the hall. They hadn't engaged in the situation. Yet. Vanessa imagined it was only a matter of time until their involvement was required, and she would prefer to avoid that. She rushed down the hall to her kids, Royce tight on her heels.

"What's going on here?" Royce demanded.

"Faith. Jensen. Are you all right?"

"Mom! Dad!" Both kids called. Faith started sobbing. Jensen began yelling.

"Are these your children?" the veterinarian asked.

"Obviously," Vanessa said.

The reporters rushed forward, firing questions at them. Vanessa couldn't make anything out over the commotion in the hallway. One of the officers stepped forward.

Royce held up his hand. "Quiet!" Jensen immediately stopped talking. The reporters didn't, of course, but they did talk softer as they asked their questions in rapid succession, never stopping for answers before shooting off the next. The officer stepped back again. Royce turned his back on everyone and faced the vet. "Is there somewhere we can talk? Privately?"

"This way." He gestured to a closed door beside the cage their kids were tied to.

"Mom!" Faith said, her eyes wide and teary.

"Let us get some information, then we'll be back." She wiped Faith's tears with her thumbs as she walked past her, squeezed Jensen's shoulder, then followed Royce and the vet into a private room.

It wasn't very big. It had a fold-up exam table against the wall, a few stools in the corners that the vet started pulling out, one counter with a sink under which were closed cabinets, and glass-fronted cabinets above that appeared to have different bottles of medicines in it. Gloves and soap sat on top of the counter. Vanessa was grateful the table wasn't down. She didn't think there would be room for all three of them if it was.

"Please. Sit," the vet said.

They perched on the tiny stools while the vet lowered himself comfortably onto his own, secure in his own element. "I'm Dr. Zeke Jones. I'm the on-call veterinarian here today."

"Dr. Royce Keller. My wife, Vanessa. What's the problem?"

The vet sighed. "Your kids were here visiting and playing with the animals. Happens a lot. We don't mind. It frees our workers and it's good for the cats and dogs to socialize a bit. But the timing was bad." He ran his hand through his already mussed hair. "Normally I wouldn't say anything, but you're going to read about it anyway." He took a roll of mints out of his pocket and offered it. "Mint?"

They shook their heads.

"No?" He popped one in his mouth, then continued. "You've seen the news, I reckon? You know about the dog fights?"

They nodded.

"What you don't know is they've been going on for a lot longer than the media knows. About a year. I know, 'cause they've been bringing me the dogs they find that they have to destroy. Managed to keep it under wraps for a while, but the story finally broke a couple months ago. The cops have been trying to track down the fights, the dog owners... any leads at all. They never had any luck. I guess the mastermind behind it all died several weeks back and the kid who took over is more sloppy. They found the last fight and busted it up. They arrested a bunch of kids, called PETA in to help with the dogs. But today they brought me one while your kids were here...."

Vanessa knew where he was going. She didn't want him to continue.

"This one's just too far gone. Your kids saw him, and they know what I have to do, but they don't want me to. They want to take him home, nurse him back to health." He stood and tried to pace in the little room, but there was nowhere for him to go. He looked at them, agony plain on his face. "Do you have any idea what that poor dog has gone through? They're just delaying the inevitable. They can't help him."

Vanessa couldn't help the tears that fell. He couldn't possibly know, couldn't possibly understand how they all felt right now. She glanced at

Royce, who stared at the floor. She stood. "Dr. Jones. Do you have any idea who those children are?"

He shook his head.

"I'm sure you've seen the news. My children lost their sister recently. The motorcycle accident on Dappled Oak Lane."

"I'm so sorry. I didn't know."

She waved him off, brushed away her own tears, and continued with resolve. "My husband had the misfortune of having to work on her in his ER." She saw the look of horror cross the vet's face, but continued. "You are looking at this from a humane perspective, thinking of what that dog has endured. You just want to end his suffering. But my children are seeing their sister, and they're seeing all these people just wanting to throw away a life so callously when it should be fought for and preserved."

"I understand now, Mrs. Keller. I really do. But there's really nothing I can do. I could treat all his injuries, and he'll still die. Just a lot slower, and more painfully. The humane thing is to help him pass. With dignity."

She sighed and plopped back down, exhausted, defeated.

"I can give you a few more minutes to explain things to your kids, but for the good of the dog, I really must insist you hurry. He's suffering."

She stood, and Royce with her. "What's the dog's name, Doctor?"

"No one knows."

Shaking her head, she turned to the door. Turning back around, she said, "Can we stay with him?"

He raised a brow. "Of course. I think he'd like that."

"Doctor," Royce said. "Get rid of the press."

"Certainly."

When they went out into the hall, the vet, with the help of the officers who had been looming in the background, managed to wrangle the press down the hall and out the door. Vanessa turned her attention to her kids, hoping desperately Royce would be able to help.

"Okay, guys, we talked to the doctor." She wasn't quite ready to meet their gazes. Instead, she rooted around in her purse for her manicure set, and find-ing it, set about the task of cutting through their bindings.

"So you fixed it?" Faith asked. "He's going to work on the dog? We can take him home when he's all better?" She rubbed her wrist while Vanessa cut Jensen free.

Vanessa didn't answer right away. Instead, she looked past her kids to the dog in the kennel. She had no idea what breed—or breeds—he was. He was a bigger dog, with a square-shaped head and shorter fur. What fur there was. He was probably mostly black with rust patches, like a Rottweiler, but there were definitely other breeds mixed in there. She'd know more if large patches of his coat weren't missing. She didn't know if he had mange or if hunks had been bitten off and scarred over. He lay on his side, panting for breath despite the cool air and his sedate posture. She wondered if something was wrong with his lungs. His eyes were barely open, yet he blinked rapidly, tears leaking out of the corners of them. And he held one of his front paws at an odd angle, seemingly because of the way his knee bent.

"He has a corneal ulcer in his right eye and a severe globe rupture in his left," Dr. Jones said over her shoulder.

Vanessa saw Faith stiffen. "So what? So what if he goes blind? Like a blind dog has no worth? Like he can't be loved?"

"He also has a ruptured cruciate ligament in his right front leg. He'll never walk correctly. Possibly never at all."

"There are dogs with three legs. We can make him a little cart. Tell him, Mom. Tell him!"

Vanessa's heart broke with each plea Faith made. She knew the next one would be her last.

"His ribs are broken. His breathing is labored."

"So? Ingrid Newkirk says—"

"And he has damage to his abdominal organs."

"How do you know? You've barely had time to diagnose him."

"His stomach is grossly distended! I did a peritoneal lavage and it was almost all blood. At the very least, he'd need exploratory surgery, and he's not strong enough to survive it. I'm really sorry, but there's nothing I can do."

"Mom. Dad. Please!"

Vanessa looked at Royce, but he was pale, his jaw clenched. She could only imagine the number of times he'd been through scenarios like this one, telling patients they needed to say their goodbyes. In the past, she hadn't given his job much thought, but he'd probably had to deliver bad news hundreds, maybe thousands of times over the years. It wasn't long ago when he'd had to deliver it to their kids. And she'd made him do it. She was too weak to do it herself.

This was one time when she could ease his burden.

"Faith. Jensen. Listen to me." She took their hands and finally mustered the strength to look at them. "This poor, sweet dog has been through hell. And no one has ever been his advocate. No one has ever loved him. You've given him more in the last few hours than anyone's given him in his whole life. You did that for him. But he's suffering. And he's ready to let it all go. Instead of pulling him back into a life that makes him miserable, let's stand beside him as he moves on to a better one."

"But we can love him, care for him." Faith sniffled and clutched her mother's hand tighter.

"I have no doubt you would love and care for him. But you can do both now. Show him your love and your care. Let's go with him while the doctor helps him rest."

Jensen cried silent tears, but he nodded.

"Jensen, not you too?" Faith said.

"Mom's right," he said, voice breaking. "We're not doing this for him. Not really. We're doing this for us. If we're really concerned about him, we'll let him go. It's the humane choice, Faith."

Faith threw herself into Jensen's arms and sobbed. The doctor opened the kennel door and walked over to the dog. When he petted his head, he bent down and said, "It's almost over, fella."

Faith looked up and said, "Fella? Can't you at least address him by name?"

He shook his head. "I don't know his name."

"We have to at least give him a name!"

The doctor unlocked the wheels on the cart the dog was on and started pushing him out the door and down the hall. "Whatever you suggest is fine by me."

Vanessa watched Faith trail along beside the ailing dog, her hand stroking the patches of fur that she could reach. "I don't know. It's such a tough decision. I mean, that's the name he'll have for the rest of..."

Jensen looked at her, then at the dog. "What about Duke? It's kind of regal, but still approachable and friendly. Just like I think he would have been, if he'd been ours."

"Duke?" Faith tried it out. "Duke. Yeah." She leaned down and whispered it close to the dog's face. "Duke? Do you like that? Is that your new name? Duke?"

The dog rolled his watery eyes toward the sound of her voice, and his tail twitched.

"Duke it is then," she whispered. She kept her hand on him when the vet got to a wide room in the back of the building. He stopped the cart and put on the brakes, then walked away. Jensen, Vanessa, and Royce gathered around the table and placed their hands on the dog, too.

"Take care around his stomach," Royce said, uttering his first words since they left the private meeting with the vet. "It's probably pretty tender."

Dr. Jones came back into the room with a needle full of pink liquid. "Is everyone ready?"

Faith broke down again. "I just need one more minute."

"I'm sorry, big guy," Royce said, petting his back. "Duke."

Vanessa stroked him under the chin. "Say hi to my little girl for me, okay?" she whispered.

"We tried, Duke," Jensen said, rubbing his flank. "We really tried."

Faith composed herself. "Oh, Duke. What happened to you is so not fair." She bent down and kissed him on the nose. "I'm sorry I couldn't make it right. Safe travels."

Royce nodded at the doctor, and he administered the shot.

Duke's watery eyes blinked, drooped, and then closed. He was gone.

Faith threw herself into Vanessa's arms. "Why do these bad things keep happening to us?"

Vanessa had no words for her. She just held her until she was all cried out. "Come on, honey," Vanessa said. "Let's get you home."

"What about Duke?" she asked.

Vanessa looked at Royce.

"We'll take him. We can put him next to Cornelius in the backyard."

"Thanks, Daddy." She sniffled.

"Doc, what arrangements do I need to make?"

Vanessa left Royce talking to the veterinarian while she walked her kids outside. When she opened the door, they were met with the same reporters from the hallway.

"That's the family who lost their daughter in the motorcycle accident!"

"Is it true your daughter was dating the boy who orchestrated the dog fighting operation?"

"Is that why you're here?"

"Was your daughter involved in the dog fights?"

"Is it true your husband lost his job because of your daughter?"

Vanessa pulled Faith and Jensen back inside the animal shelter and closed the door on the reporters. Grabbing their hands, she pulled them back toward the room they had just left, looking for Royce and Dr. Jones. She found them exiting the euthanasia room.

"Ness? I thought I was meeting you in the parking lot."

"The reporters, Royce. They're right outside the door. And they're hungry."

Royce sighed. He turned to the veterinarian. "Can't you have them escorted off the property?"

"I got them out of the building. And if the police didn't leave, I can have them moved away from the door. But I can't stop them from standing on the street and yelling at you or filming you."

"We just want to get to our cars," Vanessa said.

"Let me see what I can do." He walked away.

"Why are they doing this?" Faith asked.

"Must be a slow news day," Royce said.

"Seriously, Dad. All that stuff they were saying."

Royce looked at Vanessa.

"What's really going on, Dad?" Jensen asked. "What was Hope into? And are you losing your job? What will we do about money?"

"Don't worry about the money. We have ample savings. We'll be fine. As for the animal fighting? We just heard about it today. And I have a hard time believing Hope knew anything about it. I don't know what all that boy was involved in, but Hope wouldn't have stood for animal fights. If we have to get her phone records to prove she barely knew this kid, then we will. I think she just met him and went for a ride. Wrong place, wrong time kind of thing. That's all."

"Don't be so naïve, Dad," Jensen said. "He came to our house. She had to have known him."

"You two went to school with her. Did she ever mention him? Where would she even have met him?"

"I never saw her with him," Jensen said. "Never heard her talk about him."

"Me, either," Faith said.

"Ness?"

"No. She never mentioned him to me."

"Well, she had to have met him somewhere," Royce said. "We need to clear her name and move past this."

Dr. Jones came back down the hall. "They're off the property. Just off. They didn't leave, though. I'd expect a lot of attention for the next few days."

"Thanks, Doc." Royce shook his hand. Then he gathered a large bundle and led his family down the hall.

Out in the parking lot, the media continued yelling questions from the edge of the parking lot. Vanessa ignored them, and instructed the kids to do the same.

Once Royce had the bundle in the car, he said, "Follow us home. Stay close. Don't stop for anything. Got it?"

"Yes, sir," Jensen said.

"Anyone approaches your car, keep the windows up and stare straight ahead."

"Okay."

"You have enough gas?"

"Yeah. We're fine."

"All right. Do you want to ride with us?"

"No. I'll follow you. I don't want to leave my car."

"Okay." Royce thought for a moment. "You know what? Faith, you ride with me. Ness, ride with Jensen. That way one parent will be with each kid."

Vanessa noticed the relief on Jensen's face, but she didn't comment. She just walked to Jensen's car and got in. The whole process was filmed by four different news stations, who managed to get in their vans faster than her family settled into their vehicles. She just prayed the ride home would be uneventful.

CHAPTER 33

FOUR NEWS VANS AND AT least seven cars followed them the whole way home and parked at the edge of their driveway. Royce ignored them and drove straight to the backyard, where the cameras couldn't see them. Once there, he took Duke's body out of the car and laid it on the ground near Cornelius's grave. He'd begin digging Duke's final resting place as soon as he changed his clothes.

Jensen tossed a couple of shovels down on the ground.

Royce jumped. He hadn't heard anyone approach.

"I'll park the car and meet you back here."

Royce clapped his son on the shoulder and headed inside to change his clothes. By the time he got to the backyard, Jensen had already begun digging. He joined him, and the two of them worked in silence while Vanessa and Faith kept a silent vigil. It wasn't long before they had a deep hole dug and he was ready to lay Duke to rest.

"Dad?" Faith said. "Aren't you going to say something?"

"Maybe you should."

"I want you to."

What could he say? This was the part he tried to avoid at the hospital. "Let me finish here, moppet. Then I'll say something." But he couldn't let Faith down, either.

As quickly as the hole emptied, it filled up even faster. And Duke was laid to rest beside Cornelius in the yard. Royce was out of time. He looked at Faith. "Are you sure you don't want to say anything?"

She shook her head and whispered, "I can't do it."

He took a deep breath, linked his fingers together, and looked at the ground.

"Today we lay to rest Duke, a noble animal, next to Cornelius, a loyal friend. These two animals couldn't have led more different lives. One had several pampered years, each day was marked and remembered. He had a name, celebrated birthdays, went on vacations, played fetch, enjoyed belly rubs and car rides. The other? We don't know how old he was, what he was called when he was born. He probably never had any joyful moments with his owners. He spent his days fighting, but he didn't know why. His successes weren't celebrated and his failures were met with more torment and abuse. It's a travesty that can't be expressed in words."

Vanessa widened her eyes and shook her head as Faith choked back sobs. Jensen had tears in his eyes.

"But the one thing these dogs shared that no one can ever take from them is the compassion and love of these two fine people here."

Jensen looked at his feet, and Faith blinked and looked at her father.

"When it mattered most, they gave Duke an identity, and they gave him love. He was allowed to leave this world happier than he had lived any day on it. And he will rest here, welcomed into the home of the family who comforted him when he most needed it. Godspeed, Duke."

Royce used his shovel to pat the fresh earth into place. Jensen did the same. Vanessa bent and patted the ground. Faith touched a kiss to her fingertips, then touched the earth.

She threw her arms around Royce. "Thank you, Daddy."

He hugged her back. At least he was able to ease someone's pain. Jensen and Vanessa stepped into the hug, too. He felt like his family was finally mending, finally almost whole. Even if it took a slew of tragedies to bring them together, they were getting there.

Contrary to how Royce saw things, the news that evening made them out to be the world's most dysfunctional family, second only perhaps to the Kardashians. Royce had no intention of granting them an interview, but they were not to be deterred. They camped out at the edge of the driveway. He had only a few days before his hearing. Hopefully they'd tire of the inactivity and leave before he had to.

For someone with so little to do, he was incredibly busy. Not only did he spend an inordinate amount of time in the garden—weeding, pruning, watering—he spent a sizeable chunk of his time on the phone. Some of the time was tracking down items he was looking for, but most of it was with his attorney. He was certain he was paying for Spencer's summer home, or a new boat. Maybe another car, or a gift for his wife. Definitely some unnecessary extravagance to pad his portfolio of assets.

The remaining time left in his days was spent in Hope's room with Vanessa. She determined everything would be boxed up and cleaned before the new housekeeper started. He didn't think it was all for their new employee. She had admitted to an ulterior motive.

"If we're careful, if we look at everything, we might find a clue to where Hope met Jimmy. Some indication of how long she'd known him and how well."

"Like what?" Royce asked as he tossed a bunch of makeup in the trashcan.

"I don't know. A diary. A box of mementos. Something." She carefully folded a CLP sweatshirt and set it aside.

Royce put his hands on her shoulders and pulled her against him so her back nestled against his chest. "It'll be okay, Ness."

She sniffled and turned into his hug. "What if we never find anything? Or what if we do? What if there's something here that proves she knew about the dog fights? We'll have to tell the police, and then…"

He rubbed her back. "We know our girl better than that. Let's just see what we have here and go from there."

She straightened and pushed away from him, turning back to her packing.

Royce knew the family needed a break, so he once again called on his mentor for help, and Stanford once again came through. He braved the throng of reporters, using boxes and tape as a ruse for showing up there. He backed into the garage and unloaded the car so the reporters could see what he was doing before closing the door on them. Then Jensen and Faith hid in his car and Stanford left, taking them to his home for privacy. They deserved some free time away from the fishbowl.

On the third day of packing, Royce turned to Vanessa. "I miss the kids."

"Me, too."

"And I miss Hope."

She sighed and whispered, "Me, too."

"Come here," he said, sitting on the edge of Hope's bed. She put down the books she'd been boxing and joined him. He put his arm around her and pulled her into an embrace.

"I knew it would be hard, but I didn't think it would be this hard."

"I know." He kissed her forehead.

"I just can't believe she's gone. She's never going to read that book again." She started pointing around the room. "Wear that sweater. Write in that notebook." She picked up Hope's phone. "Make another call."

"Hey, let me see that," Royce said, and took it from her. "Do you know her password?"

"No, but one of the kids might. Besides, it's not charged."

He turned it around in his hands, the dark purple metal reflecting the light coming in the window. Something white caught his eye, and he spun it in his hand again.

"What are you doing?"

"There's something behind this case," he said. He fiddled with it until he managed to pull it apart. A piece of paper fell onto the floor. He bent to pick it up. What he saw there made him sick.

It was a flyer, showing a picture of what looked like a rabid dog. It read:

BEAST BATTLE—PLACE YOUR BETS
Friday, 9:00
Druitt Barn on Old Mill Road
Password at the Gate: Cujo

His hand shook as he read it.

"Royce, what is it?"

He shook his head and crumpled the paper, but she took it from him.

"No." She too shook her head. "No. No. She couldn't have known. She wouldn't have… No."

Royce pulled her against his chest and let her cry. Apparently they didn't know their little girl at all.

An hour later, Royce was on the phone again, doing what he did best: making plans. He'd always been methodical. A planner, a thinker, a doer. It was time he stopped being reactive and started being proactive.

It wasn't long before he was scanning his computer for a list of all the phone numbers Hope had dialed the month before she had died. He chastised himself for not thinking to do this sooner. He should have logged into the account and looked at her call history immediately. Scanning the file, he saw two kept popping up. One he didn't recognize, so he called it. He got Jimmy Salvo's voicemail. Not surprising.

There was one he knew too damn well. He called it next, and was surprised when it was answered on the first ring.

"I thought we agreed we were done with each other."

"That was before I found out my daughter was calling you every two damn minutes the month before she died."

"Oh, so now she's your daughter again. I'm never sure if she's going to be yours or mine when we talk."

"Damn it, Ben. I don't have time for this." Royce picked up Hope's picture from his desk and almost threw it across the room. Then he thought better of it and put it back down. "Why was she calling you? What was going on?"

"Maybe she just wanted to chat."

"Ben, for the love of God—"

"What? You're not the only one whose life is crumbling, Royce."

"I need to know what was going on. Ness needs to know."

"She needed to talk. She needed advice."

"So she went to you?"

"Is it so inconceivable that she came to me?"

"She could have come to me. Or Ness."

"She came to her father."

"Is that…" Royce stumbled over the words, icy fingers of fear and pain squeezing his heart. "Is that what she wanted to talk about? Did she know?" he whispered.

"No, damn it. She never knew."

"Then what?"

"Fuck." He sighed. *"She got mixed up with the wrong kid and needed help getting out. She was scared."*

"Jimmy Salvo."

"Yeah. The little prick who killed her."

"Did he… did he hurt her?"

He sighed again. Royce heard him swallow and imagined he'd gotten a beer. They could both use something stiffer after this conversation. *"I don't know, man. I never did get details. And for the record, I did tell her to talk to you and Ness. She didn't want to. So we went with plan B."*

"Which was?"

"I talked to the cops. Detective Cooper. This kid was bad news. He was into all sorts of shit. Alcohol. Drugs. Dog fights. Hope said she saw him with a gun more than once. She was scared out of her wits. She tried to break it off with him, but he said no. You get that? He said no. So she came to me, and I went to the cops. Cooper was supposed to bust him the night of the accident. He said he was going to talk to you. We were one day too late. One fucking day. It was eating at me. I talked to Wade about it, and he agreed I did the right thing. He said if I went to you, you'd

be pissed Hope came to me, so I should let the cops handle it. So I waited. And it's been eating at me ever since."

The irony of the whole thing hit Royce like a punch in the gut. Hope went to her biological father for help instead of him, and she didn't even know it. Detective Cooper was the one assigned to both cases. Twelve hours would have made all the difference in his daughter living or dying. And Ben thought he had it rough? He dropped the phone and ran to the bathroom, getting there just in time to lose his lunch in the toilet.

When he got back to his office, Ben had hung up the phone. He didn't call him back. There was really nothing more to say.

Then he picked up the phone again. He had a lot more to say. He stabbed at the numbers on his phone. It was answered on the second ring.

"Cooper."

"This is Royce Keller. Do you know why I'm calling?"

"Actually, Dr. Lyndon just gave me a courtesy call. He thought you might be getting in touch with me."

"We need to have a conversation. And I'd prefer it be man-to-man, not man-to-cop."

"I agree, we should talk. I'm coming over, Doc, but don't get excited. I'm wearing my shield."

"Scared to face me without hiding behind your badge?"

"No. I'm protecting you by keeping my badge on. See you in ten." He hung up the phone.

Royce seethed while he waited. More secrets he wasn't privy to. He'd spent weeks alternating between blaming himself and his wife for Hope's death, but it turned out there were other people just as culpable. He heard the detective's car in the driveway and strode to the door, flinging it open before the car had rolled to a complete stop. He was out the door and hauling Cooper out of the car before the ignition was off.

"Do you really want to do this here?" Cooper asked. "With the media on your front lawn?"

Royce flung the detective back into his car and marched back into his house. He heard the engine cut, and Cooper followed him inside, where Royce rounded on him, grabbing him by the shirt and shoving him against the closed door.

"Dr. Keller, I get that you're upset, but I told you on the phone, I was coming here as a cop. Don't do something you're going to regret. I don't want to have to take you in."

Royce readjusted his grip on his shirt and pushed him again against the door. "She was my daughter. My *daughter!* What gave you the right?"

Vanessa called from upstairs, "Royce? What's going on?"

"What am I supposed to tell my wife?"

Cooper held his hands out to his sides, like a man approaching a scared animal. "Let's not do anything rash. I came here to talk."

Vanessa appeared at the top of the stairs. "Oh my God! Royce!" She ran down the stairs. "Let him go!"

"Do you know what he did? What he and Ben did?"

She tugged at his arms. "Royce. Let go. We'll talk it out."

"It's his fault, Ness. All of it. We've been blaming ourselves, but it was him and Ben all along."

She dropped her hands, and he finally did, too. "What?" she asked.

"Come on, folks" Cooper said. "Let's sit down and discuss this."

Vanessa stumbled into the kitchen and dropped into a chair. Royce directed Cooper to follow, and they sat around the table. "Talk."

"Dr. Lyndon brought Hope to see me. She was in a relationship she wanted out of. Seemed simple enough. I told her to break it off. But she said she did, and the guy said no. And she was scared. She said he packed. Carried a gun, knives. That got my attention."

"But you didn't call us?" Royce asked. "We're her parents! You shouldn't have even said 'boo' to her without one of us there."

"Do you want the story or not?"

"Go on," Vanessa said.

"I ran a background check, but nothing major popped. He'd had some minor drug trouble, but nothing I could bring him in for. She said he wasn't just using anymore, he was dealing. I asked if she knew who his connection was, but she didn't know anything. So I said I'd keep an eye on him, but that was all I could do, unless she got a judge to issue a restraining order and he violated it. Lyndon wanted me to bring him in for the concealed weapons, but I couldn't do that without seeing them myself, and I couldn't pull him over without probable cause. She gave it to me."

"The place he dealt from?" Royce asked.

"No. He didn't have a set place, or set customers. She said she couldn't figure out how he made the deals. There was only one place she knew for sure deals went down."

"No," Vanessa whispered.

"You let her go to the dog fights?" Royce asked.

"No, I didn't let her do anything. For the record, she told me where the next one was going to be, and we intended to be there to stop it. And I was on my way to your house the morning of her accident to talk to you. I didn't think it was an appropriate conversation for the phone, and I wanted to be sure Hope was out of the house when I approached you."

"When did you talk to her?" Royce asked.

"Just the night before."

"That's what she meant when she said she had no choice," Vanessa said and reached for Royce's hand. "She didn't mean with you. She meant about Jimmy."

Royce squeezed her hand. It was all making sense. "Did she tell you how she met him?" he managed past the lump in his throat.

"She said it was at the hospital. She was headed into the ER to talk to you about something. He was headed out and wasn't watching where he was going. They ran right into each other."

"When was this? Hope never came to the ER."

"About a month before the accident. She never did make it inside. She ended up spending the evening with Jimmy instead."

"Did she say what she wanted?"

"No."

"Why was Jimmy there?" Vanessa asked.

"We checked the hospital records. He wasn't treated. He could have been visiting someone. Or…."

"Or he's the one who's been taking our meds."

"That means he had inside help," Cooper said.

Royce sat back in his seat. Someone from his hospital, from his staff, was giving that little punk the missing pain meds.

"Detective," Royce said. "We ran into Stush Poleski at the cemetery. He said it looked like Jimmy was having trouble with the brakes on the bike."

Cooper sighed and shook his head. "I'm really sorry… If it's any consolation, I think Salvo was supposed to lose control of his bike before he got to your house. When CSI looked over the bike, they found the brake line had been cut. I don't think your daughter was supposed to be involved. The brake line just bled too slowly, and Salvo had already picked her up when the brakes gave."

Vanessa sobbed into her hands, and Royce rubbed her back.

"So now what?" Royce asked.

"We busted the dog ring. Hopefully one of those guys knows the drug supplier and will roll on him. Maybe we'll even find out who cut the brake line. It's a waiting game now."

"Why didn't you say anything?"

"It's an ongoing investigation. I shouldn't have said this much. But you deserved to know. And for the record, when Lyndon called me, he told me he was bringing his daughter in to talk to me. So I didn't know I was doing anything wrong until after I had her statement. When I found out Lyndon wasn't her father, I looked you two up."

Royce held his head in his hands, too numb to speak.

"Thank you, Detective," Vanessa said.

Royce looked up and nodded. That was all he could muster.

"Now, I have to go. I have some reporters making a disturbance that I have to disperse." He offered a two fingered salute and let himself out.

Vanessa stood and walked into Royce's arms. He held her while she cried, breathing in her scent and clinging to her warmth. He needed the comfort as much as he gave it. When they finally stepped apart, she looked up at him with tear-reddened eyes and placed her hands on his cheeks. "Thank you."

"For what?"

"For answers. For support. For… just thank you. I'm going to go wash up. Maybe lie down. I just need…" She kissed him softly on the lips. "Thank you," she whispered, and headed upstairs.

He understood. He needed space, too.

After pulling himself together, he made a few more calls. One was to Charlie Olnick. He asked a ton of questions and negotiated a good deal for himself. Another was to the car dealership, where he made a not-so-wonderful arrangement. But he didn't care. When he was done, he got everything ready for the evening. He was taking his life back.

Royce spent time relaxing in the shower for the first time in days. He felt bad that he'd ever doubted his daughter, sad that her last days were filled with stress and fear, especially since she hadn't turned to him. But he was relieved to know she was clear of any wrong doing. He could profess her innocence with pride and certainty. And he intended to do so.

After drying off and dressing, he called a cab and went in search of Vanessa. He found her in Hope's room, not packing, not moving. Just sitting, looking lost and forlorn.

"Ness?"

She looked up, eyes dry but bloodshot.

"Go get ready. We have a big night tonight. We're going out."

"Out? But… no, I don't think—"

"Don't worry about it. Any of it. It's fine. It's all fine. Just go get ready. I've taken care of everything." He stepped into Hope's room and pulled her to her feet. "Come on."

"Where are we going? What should I wear?"

"Just something comfortable." He kissed her on her nose and pushed her gently toward their room. "I'll be back soon. Be ready."

He bounded down the stairs and out the door, where a cab waited. The reporters, who had left for a few hours after Cooper had sent them away, were back at the front of his property, filming, snapping pictures, and shouting questions. He got in the taxi and said to the driver, "Stop by the road. I want to make a statement."

They rode down the driveway, and the cab stopped by the media. Royce rolled down his window and listened to the questions for a moment. More of the same that he'd heard at the animal shelter. He held up his hand for silence. When it was quiet, he spoke. "You've been out here for days, and I'm sorry to disappoint you, but there is no story. My daughter is dead because she was a victim of Jimmy Salvo, not an accomplice. If you have any questions or assertions to the contrary, you can talk to Detective Cooper. I'm sure he'll be able to clarify the situation for you."

He patted the back of the seat, and the driver hit the gas. The news vans were right behind them. They followed along for about ten minutes, but finally turned left toward the town center and the police station when the cab turned right toward the commerce district. Royce breathed a sigh of relief.

Two minutes later, the driver pulled in to Royce's first destination. He paid the driver, thanked him, and got out. He hoped his whole round trip would be an hour at the most.

He was close. An hour and a half after he left the house, he returned. Excited. Nervous. Anxious.

"Where have you been?" Vanessa sat on the patio, drinking a glass of iced tea. Her legs were crossed and she was bouncing her top leg viciously, her sandal slapping rapidly against her foot. Thwap, thwap, thwap.

"Sorry." He bent down to kiss her, but she turned her cheek. "It took a little longer than I thought. But I got rid of the reporters." He smiled and raised his eyebrows in a gesture of good will.

She sighed and stopped bouncing her foot. "I thought Cooper did that."

"They came back."

"Well, that's something. You said we had to talk."

"And we will. It's good news. Great news. But not here. Let's go." He extended his hand.

She looked at it, and finally accepted it, letting him pull her to her feet.

He escorted her to the front door, then said, "Close your eyes."

"What?"

"Humor me. Close your eyes. I'll help you."

She shook her head, but closed them. He took her hand and opened the door, then said, "Step down," helping her navigate the step to the front of their house. He then guided her down the sidewalk and across the driveway. "Okay. You can open them."

"This had better be—" She interrupted herself when she saw their old Infiniti in the driveway. Tears welled in her eyes. "What did you do?" she whispered.

"When you explained how important it was to you, I contacted the dealership. They hadn't sold it yet, but they had slated it for auction. It took some finagling, but I managed to convince them to sell it back to me, instead."

She threw her arms around him. "Oh, Royce. Thank you. I know it's a stupid, foolish thing, but it just mattered to me."

"If it's important to you, it's important to me. I shouldn't have traded it in without talking to you first, anyway."

She leaned up and kissed him on the cheek. Not quite the response he was going for, but he'd take it. "Now let's go."

"Go? We're really going somewhere?"

"Yep. Get in." He walked her to the passenger side and opened the door for her. After making sure she was tucked safely inside, he walked to the driver's side and got in. "Ready?"

"Where are we going?"

"We're having a date."

"We're oh-for-two. Maybe you should stop while you're ahead."

"Nope. My mistake was trying to recapture the past. We aren't those kids anymore. I'm doing something different tonight."

She shrugged and leaned back in her seat. "Okay. I'm game if you are."

He drove them to the lake and got out of the car.

"Are you sure about this? The last time…"

He opened her door and took her hand, pulling her out. "Positive." Then he popped the trunk and grabbed a picnic basket and blanket. "Come on." He took them toward the shore where he spread the blanket out, and he put the basket down.

"So, what did you bring?"

"Fried chicken, macaroni salad, watermelon, and chocolate cake. Oh, and lemonade to drink."

"Actual picnic food?"

"Actual picnic food."

"That's a change for us."

"We needed a change." He got out the containers, paper plates, disposable napkins and cutlery, and started dishing out the food.

"We haven't eaten like this in… I don't know how long," she said.

"It's good, isn't it?"

"Feels right." She licked her fingers and giggled.

"What do you think of everything we learned today?" he asked.

"I can't believe what she went through without us."

"She must have been terrified. But at least she had Ben."

"And that doesn't bother you?" she asked.

"It did at first. But I'm glad she had someone to go to. I'm not happy we were out of the loop. They should have come to us immediately, not waited for the morning. But we probably wouldn't have done anything differently. I just hate how it all ended up."

"It's not fair."

He ran his hands through her hair. "No. It's not fair. But at least we know for certain now. She was a good girl."

"She was a terrorized girl. And we weren't there for her." She sniffled as tears ran down her cheeks.

"We were there for her. She just didn't come to us."

"Same difference."

"So let's learn from it and not make the same mistakes again." He lay beside her and propped himself up on his elbow. "Let's make it a point to be there for Jensen and Faith. And each other."

She blinked and nodded her head. "I can do that."

He wiped the tears off her face. "Glad to hear it. Let's start with this." He lowered his head and brushed his lips softly against hers. She opened her mouth on a surprised gasp, and he seized his opportunity to deepen the kiss, teasing her mouth open with his tongue. This time they moved in perfect synchronicity, their heads tilting at the same time, at the perfect angles. Their breaths merging, him swallowing her soft moans, her expressing her ardent desires. She trailed her nails down his back and chills raced down his forearms to the tips of his fingers, chased up his spine to the nape of his neck. He twined his fingers in her hair and held her close to him, his muscles quivering with restraint.

He pulled back from her and looked into her eyes. They held promises he hadn't seen in years, secrets he couldn't wait to discover. "Let's go home."

"You get the basket," she said, "I'll get the blanket."

She scrambled to her feet and wrapped the blanket in a ball, all their trash inside it. He was fine with that. They could deal with it later. They darted to the car and threw everything in the trunk, then got in and headed for home.

"You know what, Royce?" she said.

"What?" he asked, trying to focus on the road.

"Scarlet wasn't the only color I bought that underwear set in."

He glanced at her. "I don't suppose you have another color on now?"

"Guess you'll have to check and see when we get home."

He pressed down on the accelerator.

CHAPTER 34

VANESSA WOKE UP WITH A smile on her face, well-rested and relaxed. All the stress she'd been carrying in her shoulders and neck seemed to have melted away overnight. Well, the massage Royce had given her probably helped. Among other things.

She reached her arms over her head and stretched. Then she turned to face Royce for a little good morning repeat performance.

Except he wasn't there.

She got up and went to the bathroom, showered, and wrapped her robe around her. Skipping the slippers, she padded downstairs in her bare feet. The smell of coffee greeted her before she reached the kitchen.

"Mmm. Something smells good."

Royce stood at the stove, stirring something in a pan. "It's the coffee. I found the chicory."

She poured herself a mug and took a sip. Despite it scalding her tongue, she couldn't help but moan. "Oh, yes. That's good stuff."

He turned and offered her a plate with an omelet, or his best effort at an omelet. It was definitely eggs, cheese, spinach, and mushrooms. The shape? She'd call it omelet-esque. At best.

But she wasn't complaining. She didn't have to cook it. And it smelled divine. "Thanks. What's the occasion?"

"You." He kissed her neck and made her shiver. "What'd I tell you yesterday? I promised I was going to be here for you."

"I thought you meant for the important things."

"Everything is an important thing. I don't want to miss another moment." She smiled up at him.

"Eat your breakfast before it gets cold. We have to leave in an hour."

Back to Tod's. He had been good for them, but she wasn't sure what more he could do for them. He'd helped her come clean about Ben. Helped them deal with the aftermath of those consequences. Helped them manage all their feelings regarding Hope's death. Helped them put their family back together. Even helped them discover Wade's real role in Royce's dismissal as well as Stanford's role in helping Royce keep his job. For the time being.

She could think of half a dozen things she'd rather be doing, but she'd go again. She owed him a lot. She owed him her life.

After finishing breakfast, she hurried upstairs to get ready. For a change, she wasn't worried about sharing the room or taking turns getting dressed. It was their room once more. Their sanctuary. She was again comfortable in her house, in her bedroom, in her own skin. Things finally felt right.

As she was getting dressed, Royce walked in and smiled. She didn't scramble or try to cover up. He didn't ignore her or avert his eyes. Instead, he walked over to her and took the sweater out of her hands. He kissed her neck, her collarbone, her shoulder. "You smell incredible."

"I don't even have anything on."

"Must be your natural scent." He nuzzled her neck and breathed in deeply.

She tipped her neck back. "Or my soap. I did shower this morning."

He trailed kisses down her back. "Your back smells good. How'd you wash that without me?"

She closed her eyes and suppressed a shudder. "I've managed on my own for quite a while now."

"I'll help you with it later." He pressed his lips to the center of her spine. "Right now, though, we need to go." He stepped away. "You better get dressed, or we'll definitely be late."

"Whose fault is that?"

"Mine, babe." He kissed her hand as he walked toward his closet. "Definitely mine. With you, I have almost no willpower."

She finished getting ready with a smile on her face. Her makeup looked more radiant. Her jewelry looked more vibrant. Her clothes more fashionable, her hair more stylish. When she took a final look in the mirror, she looked like a different woman. Not the shell of Vanessa Keller that had been walking around for two months, but the old Vanessa Keller she remembered from a long time ago. Or maybe a new and improved Vanessa Keller. In any event, she liked what she saw.

Royce stepped up behind her and wrapped his arms around her. "You look gorgeous." He kissed her neck.

"Thank you." She flushed at the compliment like a school girl. He made her feel like they were in college again. "You," she turned to him, trailed her hands up his arms, across his shoulders, and down his chest, "look positively edible." She couldn't believe she said that aloud. It made her blush even more.

"Keep talking like that, and we won't make it."

She rose to her toes and kissed him.

He groaned and stepped back. "Seriously. We won't make it to the bed. Are you ready?"

She nodded.

He offered her his arm, and he escorted her to the car.

She found their conversation to be easy, unforced, and they chatted effortlessly on the way to Tod's. The time flew by, and they were there before she knew it. They walked inside, hand-in-hand, and greeted their therapist with smiles.

"So, it would seem the two of you have settled your differences."

Vanessa sat next to Royce on the sofa. He put his arm around her shoulders and she reached for his other hand. "I don't know that we've weathered all our storms, but we've certainly built the storm cellar."

Royce squeezed her hand.

"I'm so glad you two have worked on all your issues. You really feel like you've rebuilt your foundations, then?"

"You don't?" Royce asked.

"Actually, I think you've come further in these last couple of months than I expected you to. And to that end," he closed his folder, "I have something I'd like to discuss with you."

Vanessa glanced at Royce, then looked back at Tod.

"My treatment plan for you has never been conventional," Tod said. "I've been seeing you more often than usual as a favor to my uncle, and because of that, I've tried to do things a bit differently."

"Are you telling me we were guinea pigs?" Royce said.

"No. I wouldn't look at it like that. You still went through the five stages of grief, and at your own pace. I couldn't change that."

"Five stages?" Vanessa asked.

"Denial. Anger. Bargaining. Depression. Acceptance."

"Oh. We did?"

"You did. And I counseled you through them. My methods had to work through them. And no matter what I did, you wouldn't be rushed through the stages. But I did have to make sure that as you moved through the stages, you were still moving forward in your marriage, working on your family, coming to terms with your professional life."

"I see," Royce said.

"Don't say it like that. You know my methods worked. You're in a better place now than you were before Hope died."

Vanessa squeezed Royce's hand. "I won't argue with you. I'm happy with the results."

"Well, that's what I wanted to talk to you about. This isn't conventional, but your treatment hasn't been, so why should this be?"

"What are you getting at?" Royce asked.

"Usually when therapists terminate, they give advance warning. But I think you're ready now."

"Terminate?" Vanessa asked.

"Sorry. Industry term," Tod said. "Bring an end to therapy sessions. I think I've done all I can for you. I think we're done."

"You mean," she looked at Royce and back to Tod, "you mean we don't have to come back?"

"That's right. I'm ready to sign off for the hospital. And of course I'm here if you ever want to talk. But regular visits? Not necessary. You don't need them anymore."

She turned to her husband. "Did you hear that, honey? We're fixed."

He kissed her. "It feels good to know the professionals can tell we aren't broken. It feels official."

Tod opened his folder and removed a piece of paper. "Here's my report." He handed it to Royce. "If you have no objection, I'll send a copy to Hospital Administration this afternoon."

Royce held it so Vanessa could see it, too, and she scanned it quickly. He managed to address all the hot button issues the hospital would question without revealing any of their personal business.

-Bursts of anger a result of the sudden and tragic loss of his daughter, compounded by the fact that he was forced to treat her in the ER. Anger issues situational and under control.

-Family issues all culminating from the loss of his daughter. Resolved.

-Work competency not an issue. Decision to break protocol a one-time special circumstance and will not be a factor again.

It is the opinion of this therapist that the doctor in question is no risk to his patients, his coworkers, himself, or the hospital, and can be cleared for immediate reinstatement.

That was why he was such a great psychiatrist. He could manipulate matters of the mind like nobody's business. She stood and went over to Tod, who rose from his chair. He started to extend his hand, but she threw her arms around him. "Thank you, Tod. For everything."

He put his arms around her and patted her back. "It was my pleasure, Vanessa. Truly."

Royce got up and extended his hand. After they shook hands, Vanessa hooked her arm through Royce's. "We'll be seeing you around, Doc."

"I'm here if you need me. But let's shoot for more informal settings, shall we?"

"You got it." She turned toward the door and led Royce out.

At the car, she said, "Can you believe it?"

"Feels like it's all coming together, doesn't it?" He leaned against the door and pulled her into his arms.

"Royce. We're in public."

"Didn't stop you at the lake yesterday."

"That was a picnic. This is a street."

He laughed and kissed her on the nose. "I love you."

Her heart fluttered. Actually skipped a beat. "I love you, too."

He stepped away from the car and opened her door. "Let's go. One more stop to make before I can take you home and show you how much."

Again she didn't notice the length of the drive. She just enjoyed the company. All too soon they were pulling into the parking lot of Cathedral Lake Nursery. "I don't remember it being this big."

"I don't know if it was this big when we bought the stone," he said. "Charlie might have expanded since then. Come on. I want you to meet him."

They went inside and Vanessa followed Royce up to the counter where a young girl was working.

"Hi, Micayla."

"Hey, Royce. Back again? Need more mulch?"

"No, not today. I wanted my wife to look around."

"Oh, hi, Mrs. Keller. Pleasure meeting you."

"Hello." Vanessa took in her chambray shirt, her khaki shorts, her tidy ponytail, and her cheerful disposition. She could understand why Royce enjoyed shopping here rather than at discount garden stores. They'd only been there thirty seconds and they'd already been greeted by name and smiled at three times. She couldn't buy that kind of service anywhere else.

"Well, is there anything special you want to see, or are you just browsing?"

"We're just going to mosey around. Is Charlie busy?"

"He's on the phone, but when he's done, I'll tell him you're here."

"Okay, thanks. We'll be out in the yard."

"If you need something, just holler. I can send someone out to you."

Royce gave her a wave and led the way toward the gardens.

"It was nice meeting you, Mrs. Keller!" Micayla called after them.

"You, too," Vanessa yelled back over her shoulder.

"So we talked a little about what I was thinking. Now I'm curious to know what you're thinking."

"Give me the tour, and we'll go from there."

Royce took her out into an Eden of sorts. He took her through an oasis of ferns and hostas near a koi pond with a natural-looking waterfall. She toured a greenhouse filled with orchids. He walked them past a small forest of trees—evergreens, fruit, ornamental, deciduous. She saw all the flowers he purchased for their yard—roses, lilies, gladioli, chrysanthemums, alstroemeria, forget-me-nots, carnations, orange blossoms, jasmine. She saw all the perennials, too. He took her past ivies, ground covers, pansies, tulips, daffodils, crocuses, and violets. She saw the rocks, the tiles, the mulch and the soil. They even spent some time in the statuary and lawn ornament section, and finished by walking through the store and looking at the tools and supplies.

It was everything he'd promised. And in some respects more. But the business-mogul in her was itching to dig in and make a few changes. There were areas that could be beefed up, others that could be cut back. And the nursery didn't advertise at all. That had to change. She started thinking through plans and making mental lists.

They ended their tour, walking back toward Micayla at the counter. Just then Charlie exited the office and approached them with a huge smile on his face. "Royce. Glad you made it."

"Charlie. How are you today?"

"Good. Good. So, this is Vanessa?"

Vanessa extended her hand. "Royce has told me so much about you."

"So glad to meet you, darling. Sorry I wasn't free to give you the tour. I was tying up some loose ends."

"I wish you could have joined us," she said. "Your nursery is wonderful. I don't remember it being so big."

"When Royce first stopped in, I told him he shouldn't have stayed away so long. A lot has changed since you were last here. I'm glad you like what I've done with the place."

"It's quite impressive."

"Why don't you come up to the office? We can talk more."

She followed them to Charlie's office, excited at the prospect Royce had arranged. After a thirty-minute conversation, things were resolved better than she could have hoped. She shook hands with Charlie and left Royce to say his goodbyes. She wanted another look at the place.

"Take your time, Royce. I'll be over by the pond."

"You sure?" he asked.

She nodded. "I'm sure."

He gave her a kiss and squeezed her shoulders. "I shouldn't be long."

"Take all the time you need." She waved at Micayla then headed out into the gardens again.

Finding the oasis, she sat at the edge and watched the fish. They swam in random patterns, coming to the surface to snatch at water drops they thought were food. She listened to the water splashing into the pond, looked at the leaves blowing in the breeze, tipped her head up to the warmth of the sun. Hope would have loved sitting there with her. She probably could have written a poem capturing the beauty of the area, the serenity of the moment. Possibly she would have found the experience uplifting and transcendent. Or maybe she would have found something haunting in the solace.

Vanessa trailed her finger through the water and watched the fish scurry from the invasion of their sanctuary. Just a few days earlier, moments like these would have had her inconsolable. The grief would have washed over her, consumed her, sent her running for her place of comfort as fast as the koi took off for theirs. But now she knew her marriage was in a better place. She was a better wife, a better mother. It took a terrible loss to get her there, but there she was. She couldn't bring herself to thank Hope. She'd never be grateful for her daughter's death. But she was grateful for what she learned because of it.

Royce walked up to her. "We're all set. You ready to go?"

"I'm ready."

"You okay?"

She sighed. "Better than I have been in a long time. You?"

He took a deep breath. "Me, too. And as soon as this hearing's over, I'll be fan-freaking-tastic."

"Well, at this time tomorrow, we'll celebrate," she said.

"Let's go home and start the celebration early."

CHAPTER 35

DESPITE HIS BRAVADO FOR VANESSA'S benefit, Royce really didn't sleep well the night before. It meant the world to him that his family was put back together. And terminating therapy and working things out with Charlie were two huge feathers in his cap. But if he was completely honest, he needed the hospital to side with him. He needed that vindication. Not for the money and employment. Not for bragging rights over Wade. He needed it for Hope. He needed it so he knew, on some visceral level, on some cosmic scale, he wasn't going to be forever accountable for her death. It was like HA was her proxy. If they acquitted him, she forgave him. If they rejected him, then so did she. And he wasn't ready to face her condemnation.

He straightened his tie and looked at Vanessa. "How do I look?"

"You look great, honey. Are you ready?"

"As I'll ever be. Have you seen Spencer yet?"

"He's already inside."

"All right, then. Let's go."

They walked in to the conference room. It was set up to look like a Congressional Hearing room, with a row of tables in front facing two separate tables. There were individual seats behind the individual tables. Spencer sat at one of the individual tables, and Royce joined him. Vanessa sat behind them, right beside Stanford, who was already in there. Across from them, Wade lounged in one of the empty seats, and behind him was a lot of the ER staff. In front of him at the table was the hospital's legal counsel.

"Spencer," Royce said.

"Royce. Glad to see you."

They shook hands. "Are you clear about the plan?"

"I am. Are you ready for what's going to happen here today? Worst case scenario?"

"Yes. Not that it really matters at this point."

"No. I don't suppose it does."

The hospital administration filed in and took their seats at the front table, the dean sitting in the very center.

"I see you brought legal counsel, Royce," Dean Vermeel said. "I was hoping to keep this matter informal."

"You have counsel representing your interests," Royce said. "Are you willing to waive them? I'll have mine leave right now."

"Royce," Spencer said under his breath.

"Ours has to be here."

"Then mine stays."

"Very well. I'd still like to waive formalities, if you don't mind. Stanford assures me we can keep this brief."

"Fine by me," Royce said.

"Oscar, for the record, will you state the complaint?" Dean Vermeel looked at the hospital's counsel.

Oscar opened a folder and looked through some papers. Then he stood and straightened his tie. "Dr. Keller performed a blood transfusion directly from his arm to a patient in the ER. A patient the staff knew to be his own daughter. That was a breech in three hospital policies: not conducting a type and cross, transfusing directly from his body to a patient, and working on a family member."

"Can we address these allegations as they are made, or do we need to wait until the argument is done?" Spencer asked.

"Please wait," the dean said.

"After the patient coded and died, we learned she was not his biological daughter. Based on his outburst of temper, witnessed by nurses in the ER and to such capacity that Security later had to be called in his office, it was suggested he didn't make a mistake in the ER and he intentionally chose to give her the wrong blood. The police even investigated the allegation, so it was deemed to have been credible. The investigator in Trauma Bay One intimated there may have been alcohol involved."

"Is there anything else?"

"We also have a witness who has intimate knowledge of the family workings who can testify to the discord of the family unit."

"I see. I don't know that we'll be needing any witnesses today. Like I said, we want this to be informal."

"Dean Vermeel," Wade interrupted, "if you just give our witness a few minutes, you'll see Dr. Keller's behavior is not a matter of a single incident, but is actually symptomatic of chronic behavior of both him and his wife, if in fact they are still together."

The dean sighed. "Wade, I understand you have a pretty large stake in this matter, but comport yourself with some dignity, would you? If I want your opinion, I'll ask for it. Now," he turned to Royce and Spencer, "how do you answer these allegations?"

Spencer stood and glanced at his notes. "My client didn't choose to work on a relative. There was an accident, and the ER was busy. Everyone was busy with patients. It was just happenstance that the patient in his bay was a relative. Dr. Unger should have forced him out, but he didn't. Because Dr. Keller wasn't removed, he took it as an opportunity to save his daughter's life, not end it. While one of the nurses ran to get blood, he began a direct transfusion. He knew he was a match due to the fact that he knew he had dual A antigens in his blood. Any child of his had to have at least one A antigen, and therefore would be a safe recipient of a donation from him. He did not know she wasn't biologically his, and the police ruled out that allegation quickly as nonsense."

"Thank you. That addresses almost all of our concerns. What about the possible alcohol issue?"

"Did anyone report the possibility of alcohol abuse while he was on duty? Did anyone test him while he was on duty?"

The dean looked up and down his panel. "Well?"

Oscar said, "No. It seems the investigator mentioned smelling alcohol when Dr. and Mrs. Keller entered the trauma bay after Dr. Keller was already off duty. He doesn't know which of them smelled like alcohol, nor did anyone take a blood test to monitor Dr. Keller's alcohol level at that time."

"Which would be irrelevant, as he was off duty then," Spencer said.

"Agreed," the dean said. "And what about the issue of his temper and anger outbursts?"

"You should have received a report from a licensed therapist Dr. Keller has seen at the suggestion of Dr. Hammond," Spencer said. "He's already been released from his care and has been deemed no threat to himself, his coworkers, his patients, or this facility."

The dean looked through a file and perused a paper, then nodded, satisfied. "Stanford, it would appear you were correct. Given Dr. Keller has already served a suspension for conduct unbefitting a doctor, I see no reason why he can't be reinstated immediately. Or is there something else?"

"There is the matter of his decision to call TOD," Oscar said.

"What are the details?" Dean Vermeel asked.

Oscar looked through the file. "Statements taken from everyone in the ER corroborate with each other. After the transfusion, Dr. Keller stopped working. Dr. Unger took over. The patient—Dr. Keller's daughter Hope—"

"We all know who the patient is, Oscar," the dean said. "Get on with it."

"Yes. The patient coded on the table. Dr. Unger began CPR, to no avail. He then used the paddles, but after administering only two charges, Dr. Keller called TOD and stopped all life-saving efforts. This, combined with the facts that Dr. Keller didn't get along with his daughter and initially didn't even recognize her, were the factors that led the staff to believe perhaps his motives were… selfish. Particularly once her paternity came to light."

The dean looked over at Royce. "Dr. Keller. Would you like to address these issues?"

Spencer started to stand, but Royce touched his arm and stood. "The police cleared me of any wrong doing, so my innocence is without question. But I will answer you. I didn't know I wasn't Hope's biological father. When she was born, I thought she was mine. I raised her as my own, and until the day I die, I will think of her as my daughter. If I had known she wasn't mine biologically, I certainly wouldn't have done the transfusion. But make no mistake. She is my daughter. And always will be.

"Over the last few years, Hope and I grew apart. I didn't share her interests, and I didn't understand her. But I loved her. And no, I didn't recognize her when she came in. First, because I wasn't looking at her face. I was assessing her injuries, as any doctor should. And second, because she'd changed her appearance so drastically that with a quick glance, she didn't resemble anyone I knew. So I'm sorry I didn't recognize her. Had I immediately realized who she was, perhaps I would have chosen a different patient, and we wouldn't be in this situation.

"But I stand by my actions. If my daughter Faith came into my ER today with life threatening injuries, I wouldn't hesitate to give her my blood if she needed it. Because I am a doctor, and I took an oath to preserve life at all costs. I would never do anything to intentionally harm someone. That includes calling TOD. I couldn't stand to see Wade beating on her chest, shocking her heart… Hope's body had been through enough. It was mercy that had me calling it. Not jealousy or vindication."

"Wait," the dean said. "I'm sorry. Did you say you'd treat Faith the same way? Isn't she Hope's twin sister?"

"She's Hope's twin, but half-sister. They are heteropaternal superfecundation births."

"Fascinating," Dean Vermeel said. "Okay, anything else?"

Wade cleared his throat. "I hate to bring it up, but…."

"I'm sure you do." The dean's voice was dry. "What is it?"

"There's the matter of the missing pharmaceuticals."

"That has nothing to do with this," Stanford said.

"It might not have anything to do with Dr. Keller's behavior in the ER," Oscar said, "but it may have some bearing on his status as a doctor in this hospital. The administration may find it interesting to note the drugs only ever went missing during Dr. Keller's shifts, and once he was on suspension and had no access to the meds, the thefts stopped."

"Point of order," Spencer said. "Not only does this have nothing to do with Dr. Keller's behavior during Hope Keller's treatment, it is just as likely that whoever is stealing the drugs has taken this opportunity to frame Dr. Keller by halting their activities during his forced absence."

"Come on," Wade said. "Do you expect us to believe that—"

"As I was saying," Dean Vermeel said, "I've heard enough. The pharmaceutical theft is not up for discussion during these proceedings. I'm prepared to offer reinstatement, effective immediately, probation served." He looked up and down the panel, but his assessment was met with nods from everyone on the board. "Anyone opposed?" No one spoke. "Very well."

"You've got to be kidding me!" Lydia stormed in to the room, clip-clopping on crutches, her leg in a brace. "I was promised I'd get to testify! I was supposed to get to tell you what a no-good, lying bastard he is. And what his bitch of a wife did to me!"

"Security." Dean Vermeel gestured to the guards at the door, and they approached Lydia as she hobbled toward the panel. The two guards each grabbed her by an arm and carried her out as she screamed threats at Vanessa and Royce.

"You know, Wade," the dean said, "you have a promising future here. You're a talented doctor. But this isn't the way to go about securing your place. I suggest you go deal with that. Because any further interruptions like this won't look favorable on your record."

"Yes, sir," Wade said, and hurried from the room.

"Well, that's it, then. Take the weekend, and we'll see you Monday," the dean said and stood.

Everyone started heading out, but Royce said, "Vanessa, I'm going to need a minute with Vermeel. I'll meet you outside."

She kissed him. "Good luck, honey." And she walked outside with Spencer.

Royce approached the dean and cleared his throat, but he was saved from starting the discussion.

"As I'm sure you probably know, Stanford has taken a promotion, so his position as Chief of Staff is vacant. Given your record and his recommendation, you will still be considered for the post, if you're interested. Of course, there's still the matter of the missing pharmaceuticals."

"Actually, sir," Royce said, "I'm not interested in the job."

"Excuse me?"

"This little forced sabbatical has given me some time to consider my options. And after a long talk with my wife and an even longer period of soul-searching, I know I can't do this anymore."

"Do what, exactly? Be a doctor? That's what you were trained for."

"No. I can't answer to someone else. I need to be my own boss. Run my own business. Make my own decisions."

"It's a fad, Royce. A mid-life crisis. A kneejerk reaction to a tragedy. You'll get over it."

"I don't think so. Besides, it's done. Vanessa and I bought a place."

The dean just stared at him for a moment, not saying anything.

"It's the right decision."

"So let Vanessa run it, and come back to the hospital."

"No. This is our thing. We're doing it together."

"You're going to regret it."

"And what's my other option? Working here? With Wade? I don't think so."

"It doesn't have to be awkward, Royce. This will blow over. You'll see."

Royce scoffed. "It's too late."

"Tell you what. Don't let your license expire. Consult for us. Maybe teach. We don't want to lose you. You saw what Wade was like in here. That's not exactly the attitude we want to build our future on."

"Yes, I saw. But you didn't do anything about it. He's still here. He manipulated this whole thing. And that's why I have to go."

"Will you keep your license? Consider my offer?"

"Write something up and send it to my attorney."

Dean Vermeel stuck out his hand. "We'll be in touch. In the meantime, good luck, Royce."

"Thanks, sir."

Royce walked out into the hallway, where Vanessa waited for him. "Where's Spencer?"

"He's gone."

"I wanted to thank him."

"He said he'll send us a bill. That'll be thanks enough for him."

Royce laughed.

"So, you told them you aren't coming back?"

"Yep. I'm free."

She threw her arms around him. "And the paperwork's all filed?"

"That's what Spencer said. We're the official owners of Cathedral Lake Nursery. Charlie's going to stick around for a while and show us the ropes, just to make sure we know what we're doing. Then it's all ours."

"I can't believe we're really doing this."

"Vermeel wants me to keep my license active. He said he wants me to consult. Maybe teach."

"You'll probably miss it. It's not a bad idea to keep your options open."

"Right now, I just want to be with you. Put this place far behind me."

"Not yet."

"Why not?"

"Cooper's here. He says he has something you won't want to miss."

Royce sighed. "Where is he?"

"Stanford's office."

"Let's go." They took the elevator to the tenth floor, and walked down the hall. Stanford stood outside his door, waiting for them.

"I didn't think you'd ever get here. The dean will be up here shortly, so get inside, quick."

"What for?"

"Just go!" Stanford pushed him inside.

Cooper had Wade in handcuffs and was leaning against Stanford's desk. "Here's your chance, Royce. If you have anything you want to say to this SOB, say it now."

"What's going on? Why's he in cuffs? And what would I possibly have to say to him? I just want to put this all behind me."

"You didn't put it together yet?" Cooper asked. "One of the kids we arrested from the dog fighting ring finally gave us a name. It was Dr. Unger here."

"What? *Wade?*" Vanessa said.

"It was Wade behind it all. He was the one supplying the drugs to Salvo. When he found out Jimmy was sniffing around your girl, he put a hole in his brake line. He thought the kid was trouble and wanted to get rid of him. It all comes back to him. So if you have something you want to say before I take him in—"

Rage and disbelief warred inside Royce, with fury ultimately winning. All instinct, no rational thought, Royce's hand balled into a fist. He punched Wade in the nose, taking small satisfaction at the sound of cracking bone.

Wade's head snapped back and he wailed. "Royce! Royce! I'm sorry!"

"Shit. I didn't see that coming," Cooper said. He made no move to clean up the blood pouring down Wade's face, though.

"Let's go, Ness."

"It wasn't supposed to happen like that! *Royce!*" Wade wailed.

Royce turned around. "And just how was it supposed to have happened?"

"I just needed some extra money. You and Ben, you've always had more than me. Since we were kids, through school, even in our jobs. You got Chief of Emergency Med and you were going to get Stanford's job. I was just trying to level the field a little."

"By *killing* my *daughter?*" Royce bellowed.

"No. No!" Wade said. "Hope was never supposed to be involved. I was selling on the side, trying to make a few extra bucks. But that bastard Salvo got greedy, and you were snooping around. I had a plan to get rid of him, and I was trying to make you look suspicious in the process, just so I'd get the promotion instead of you. It was never supposed to go this far. I didn't want you to lose your job, I just wanted your position. And I had no idea Hope was involved. When Ben told me, I tried to scare Jimmy straight. Hope wasn't supposed to be with him."

"You killed them both!" Vanessa said. "And an innocent woman in another car."

"They shouldn't have died. None of them." Wade looked back and forth between the two of them. "There's a kill switch on the handlebar. He was just supposed to be scared. It was just a warning. So he knew I could get to him. So he knew I was in charge. All he had to do was flip the switch. How was I to know he'd panic? How was I supposed to know Hope would be with him? I was trying to scare him away from her."

"You're pathetic." Royce took Vanessa's hand and turned to leave.

"Royce? Royce," Wade continued calling after him as he walked down the hall. "I'm sorry! You have to believe me! *Royce!*"

"See ya, Stanford," Royce said.

"I'll be in touch," he said. "You know, with Wade out of the picture, there's no reason you can't come back now."

Royce looked at Vanessa. She shrugged. "Maybe," he said. "We'll talk."

"You know you'll miss it, Royce." Then he looked past Royce to Wade's bloody visage. "Holy Mother of—" He ran into his office.

"So now what?" Royce asked Vanessa.

"You know what I want to do?"

He waggled his eyebrows.

"Not that." She smacked his arm.

"What?"

"I want to go to our nursery and get some forget-me-nots. I want to plant them at Hope's grave. Maybe Cornelius's and Duke's, too."

He offered his arm. "Your wish. My command."

"And afterward, we can do what you wanted."

He smiled. "I thought you'd never ask."

"Technically, I didn't ask. I'm just giving you the go-ahead."

"Babe, with you, I'll take it any way I can get it."

She slid her sweater to the side and showed him the color of her bra strap. It was the scarlet one he loved. He groaned. "But I really love it that way."

"Let's go get those flowers planted."

"Maybe we can do the planting tomorrow," he said. "After all, we do own the nursery now." He picked her up into his arms and carried her, giggling, down the hospital hallway.

A NOTE FROM STACI

HI! THANKS FOR READING *Type and Cross.* I loved writing it and bringing these characters to life. I hope you enjoyed it as well. If you wouldn't mind investing a few more minutes in this work, I'd really appreciate it. Please let me know what you thought of this story by leaving a review online (Amazon, Barnes & Noble, Goodreads—wherever you share your opinions with other readers). It doesn't take long, but it really helps me craft stories you enjoy, as well as reach other readers. I value your comments and am grateful for whatever your share.

The other way we can connect is through social media. Stay up to date with both my Cathedral Lake and Medici Protectorate series by visiting these links:

Facebook: Author Staci Troilo • Twitter: @stacitroilo
www/stacitroilo.com

I'm really looking forward to hearing from you. Until next time....

STACI TROILO GREW UP KNOWING family is paramount. She spent time with extended family daily, not just on holidays or weekends. Because of those close knit familial bonds, every day was full of love and laughter, food and fun. Life has taken her a thousand miles away from that extended family, but those ties remain. And so do the traditions, which she now shares with her husband, son, and daughter... even her two dogs. And through her fiction, she shares the importance of relationships with you. Mystery or suspense, romance or mainstream—in her stories, family is paramount.

Facebook: Author Staci Troilo
Twitter: @stacitroilo
Amazon: http://amazon.com/author/stacitroilo

WWW.STACITROILO.COM

www.ingramcontent.com/pod-product-compliance
Lightning Source LLC
Chambersburg PA
CBHW022204030726
47494CB00019B/314